THE COMPLETE
BRIGADIER GERARD

He handed our letters to us.

• THE BARNES & NOBLE LIBRARY OF ESSENTIAL READING •

THE COMPLETE BRIGADIER GERARD

Sir Arthur Conan Doyle

Introduction by Clifford S. Goldfarb

BARNES & NOBLE BOOKS

NEW YORK

THE BARNES & NOBLE
LIBRARY OF ESSENTIAL READING

CONTENTS

INTRODUCTION

THE Emperor Napoleon fondly said of Etienne Gerard "that if he has the thickest head he has also the stoutest heart in my army." This description accurately captures the self-described hero of eighteen gem-like short stories produced by Arthur Conan Doyle for the delight of readers of *The Strand Magazine.* Brigadier Gerard, a bombastic, heroic gascon hussar, doer of many improbable deeds, was an unimaginative man of small intellect, but brave and resourceful in a crisis. Among all of Conan Doyle's creations, he is a character second only to Sherlock Holmes. As Napoleon was the "great shadow" looming over England in the first decades of the eighteenth century, so the shadow of Sherlock Holmes has for too long deprived the Gerard tales of their rightful place among the finest short historical fiction of their time.

Arthur Conan Doyle (1859–1930) was born in Edinburgh into a family of well-known Anglo-Irish artists. At the peak of his career, between 1891 and 1905, he had established himself as Britain's most popular and best-paid writer, perhaps the best-known Britishman of his day.

He was educated in Jesuit schools and at the University of Edinburgh Medical School, taught by Joseph Bell, whose amazing deductions about patients were the model for Sherlock Holmes. One summer vacation was spent as the medical officer of a Greenland whaler, another on a freighter to the west coast of Africa.

He renounced his Catholic faith in his youth, cutting himself off from his aunts and uncles, who would have assisted him in the establishment of his career. He simply could not pretend to be something he was not. After a spectacular false start in practice with a classmate in Bristol, which formed the basis for his semi-autobiographical novel, *The Stark-Munro Letters,* he settled in Southsea in 1882, where he ultimately developed a successful practice and became a pillar in the town's literary and sporting life.

He had already begun to establish himself as a writer when the first Holmes story, *A Study in Scarlet,* appeared in 1888. The second Holmes story, written on commission following a dinner at which the other main guest was Oscar Wilde, was *The Sign of the Four* (1890). It isn't difficult to find Conan Doyle's impressions of Wilde in the settings and characters of *The Sign of the Four.*

In 1891, he spent several months in Vienna studying eye surgery. But, after he recovered from a life threatening bout with influenza, he realized that he could make a better living from his writing and gave up medical practice. During the Boer War in 1900, he went to South Africa as a doctor with a mobile field hospital. On his return he wrote a pamphlet defending British military actions, for which he was knighted in 1902.

Conan Doyle was an active sportsman, playing rugby and cricket at the highest level. He tried many other sports, including fox hunting, billiards, golf and motor racing, and helped to introduce cross-country skiing to Switzerland. Twice he stood unsuccessfully for Parliament in hostile Scottish ridings. He wrote hundreds of letters to the press, on almost every conceivable topic, including divorce reform, safety measures for the military, free trade, and spiritualist topics. When his highly developed sense of justice was aroused, he was quick to take up causes.

His nonfiction included *The Great Boer War* (1900), *The Story of Mr. George Edalji* (1907), *The Crime of the Congo* (1909), *The Case of Oscar Slater* (1912), and literally dozens of works on spiritualistic topics. He wrote a six-volume military history of the Great War. In 1917 he decided to devote the rest of his life to the cause of Spiritualism, in which he had been interested for decades.

Although he is mainly known today for his Sherlock Holmes tales, his favorite writings were his historical fiction, including *The White Company* (1891) and *Sir Nigel* (1906); novels about the Middle Ages and the romance of knighthood, like *Micah Clark* (1889) and *The Refugees* (1893); novels about the English Revolution and the persecution of the Huguenots; and short stories about Roman centurions and the Spanish Main.

Conan Doyle was fascinated by the Napoleonic Wars, particularly the Battle of Waterloo, in which several of his ancestors fought. While the Sherlock Holmes stories were written with little preparation, he took great pains with his Napoleonic works, striving for atmosphere and accuracy. He read more than twenty books of English and French military memoirs and histories and filled several notebooks with facts and quotes that he intended to use later. He was also familiar with the literary genre, which included such well-known characters as William Thackeray's Colonel Gahagan and Alexandre Dumas père's heroes in *The Three Musketeers* and *The Count of Monte Cristo*.

His interest in Napoleon Bonaparte was almost an obsession. He chose to portray him as an irascible, socially inept, but benevolent paterfamilias. He expressed a more negative view of him in his nonfiction writing, suggesting that he was evil, but concluding doubtfully: "[A]fter studying all the evidence which was available I was still unable to determine whether I was dealing with a great hero or with a great scoundrel. Of the adjective only could I be sure." This fascination was reflected in the Brigadier Gerard tales, as well as the novels *The Great Shadow* (1892), *Rodney Stone* (1896), and *Uncle Bernac* (1897), the short story "A Straggler of '15" (1891), converted into the play *Waterloo* (1894), and the short story "A Foreign Office Romance" (1894). The play *Adventures of Gerard* was produced in the United States, London, and Australia between 1903 and 1906. Three films, two of them silent, and one television production have been made from the Gerard stories.

The first group of Brigadier Gerard stories was published in *The Strand Magazine* between December 1894 and December 1895, with illustrations by W. B. Wollen. They then appeared in book form as *The Exploits of Brigadier Gerard* in 1896. The Brigadier made a "guest appearance" in the serialized novel *Uncle Bernac* in 1896. "The Crime of the Brigadier" appeared in January 1900 (the only one of the Gerard stories to be illustrated by Sidney Paget, the pre-eminent illustrator of Conan Doyle's Holmes stories). The second group of stories, *The Adventures of Brigadier Gerard,* was published in *The Strand Magazine* between August 1902 and May 1903. This group of stories, including "The Crime of the Brigadier," was published in book form in 1903. "The Marriage of the Brigadier," illustrated by Gilbert Holiday, appeared in *The Strand Magazine* in September 1910. All of the Brigadier Gerard stories were also published in the American edition of *The Strand Magazine,* which appeared one month after the British edition ("The Crime of the Brigadier," published in *Cosmopolitan* in December 1899, was the sole exception).

The Gerard stories were immediately popular with the British public and well received by critics when they first appeared. They have always been considered among Conan Doyle's best work. Many of his contemporaries, as well as writers from Winston Churchill to Graham Greene and George Macdonald Fraser, are on record as preferring Gerard to Holmes. Unfortunately, although the stories have been reprinted on many occasions, they have always been overshadowed by the Holmes tales.

Gerard was a hussar—an officer of the elite light cavalry. The rank of brigadier was an error by Conan Doyle. In the French army, this would have been equivalent to a corporal, but Conan Doyle intended him to be a colonel. The primary source for Gerard was Baron Jean-Baptiste Antoine Marcelin de Marbot (1782–1854), a Lieutenant-General in the French hussars. *The Memoirs of Baron de Marbot* (Paris, 1844) was published in English translation in 1892. The work was instantly popular in Great Britain, helping to revive interest in the Napoleonic era. Conan Doyle already had a considerable interest in the Napoleonic era before he came across Marbot. The short story "A Straggler of '15" and the novel *The Great Shadow* were both written before he had read Marbot. He borrowed aspects of Marbot's character and some of Marbot's adventures for his Gerard plots. Some of the plots and Gerard's simplicity also clearly came from the *Notebooks of Captain Coignet* (Jean Roch Coignet, 1776–1865). The tone of Coignet's memoirs is much closer to Gerard than Marbot's memoirs.

The coming of the railroads and a significant increase in literacy in the late nineteenth century created a demand for magazines that could be read in the course of a journey. *The Strand* was one of the most successful of these magazines, because it had the Sherlock Holmes stories. Novelists such as Charles Dickens had been serialized with great success — readers eagerly anticipating each new instalment. But with Sherlock Holmes, Conan Doyle invented an even better marketing attraction — a series of short stories, each one complete in itself, but with recognizable characters who would continue from month to month.

By 1893, Conan Doyle was finding Holmes a burden — he regarded the stories as trivial, dashed off to earn money, but distracting him from his more important historical fiction. So when he made Sherlock Holmes disappear in a confrontation with the arch-criminal Professor Moriarty at the Reichenbach Falls in the December issue of the *Strand,* Conan Doyle needed a replacement, and Brigadier Gerard was an excellent solution. With the exception of the "The Hound of the Baskervilles" (1901), set prior to the Reichenbach incident, no further Holmes story was to appear until "The Adventure of the Empty House" in October 1903. The stories of the *Exploits* and *Adventures* all appeared during this eleven-year hiatus.

Even so, by 1903 Conan Doyle was as anxious to "kill off" Gerard as he had been to get rid of Holmes a decade earlier, as he made clear in a letter to his editor. To all intents and purposes, he did dispose of the Brigadier with "How Etienne Gerard Said Good-Bye to His Master," in which Gerard undertakes a clandestine mission to rescue Napoleon from St. Helena, only to find him on his deathbed. Gerard was brought back for one more round in 1910, but that story is anomalous—it marries off the lifelong bachelor—and has only recently been collected with the other Gerard stories.

Conan Doyle was not a great novelist, and even some of his best long works can be a bit clumsy in construction. But he was a master storyteller, especially in his short stories. The Gerard plots are generally straightforward, and the stories are told in a simple narrative fashion from beginning to end, with an average length of 9,300 words for *Exploits* and 7,400 words for *Adventures*. Except in "The Crime of the Brigadier," he never tells us anything about the plot that is not available to Gerard. This simplicity, characteristic of all his short stories, is part of what makes the Gerard stories so readable and entertaining. Most of the plots have him being sent on a dangerous mission for Napoleon or one of his generals. Although there are numerous references to the battles and generals of the era, most of the stories take place away from the battlefield, where it is not necessary for Conan Doyle to awkwardly fit Gerard into well-documented events.

As in his Holmes stories, Conan Doyle sometimes recycled plots —for example, having Gerard stuck behind enemy lines and avoiding capture by hiding in a loft, where he can overhear the enemy officers discussing important military matters ("The Crime of the Brigadier" and "The Adventure of the Nine Prussian Horsemen"). The murderous guerrilla leaders who capture Gerard, in "How the Brigadier Saved an Army" and "How the Brigadier Held the King," are interchangeable. Both appear rather mild-mannered and civilized, but end by demonstrating their bloodthirsty character. In these tales, as in several others, Gerard is rescued from a hopeless situation by the fortunate intervention of an outside force—we come to expect the unexpected to rescue Gerard, just when everything seems darkest.

With the exception of the very first story, all of the Gerard stories are told in flashback by an old soldier to his cronies in a Parisian café. The stories are written as if meant to be read aloud, in a French stage accent. This verbal quality gives them a great deal of their flair and charm. Conan Doyle uses these introductions to give us some of the flavor of the elderly Gerard's life. In "How the Brigadier Came to the Castle of Gloom," Gerard tells us that he had been dozing that day in his armchair and had awakened with a shout, which had given his landlady a good laugh. In "How the Brigadier Was Tempted by the Devil," we learn that Gerard is now a half-pay officer, earning one hundred francs per month. In other tales, he tells us that he has had to turn to planting cabbages to supplement his pay. In the last of the tales, "The Marriage of the Brigadier," he invites his friends to accompany him back to his little white-washed cottage beside the Garonne, so he can show them the medal he received from the Emperor.

In contrast to the Holmes tales, most of the introductions are short; a paragraph or two and we are right into the adventure. One exception is "How the Brigadier Rode to Minsk," which has a fairly lengthy description of a parade of soldiers about to go off to the Crimean War. Conan Doyle contrasts the pomp and spectacle of a parade through peaceful Paris with a description of the horrors of a retreat by the beaten and ragged French army, slogging half-starved and beaten through the snows of a Russian winter. In the two-part Waterloo story, "Brigadier Gerard at Waterloo," at the start of the second story Gerard briefly recaps the events of the first story. However, even in this case, each story stands on its own.

Having Gerard tell his own stories is a major reason for their success. His absolute lack of self-awareness gives the tales their tone and charm. Unlike the Holmes tales, where the use of Dr. Watson as narrator is essential—because it allows us to see a genius through the eyes of an ordinary person—the exact opposite thing would happen here. This is graphically demonstrated in *Uncle Bernac*, where Gerard is seen through another's eyes and the result is totally unmemorable.

The only exception is "The Crime of the Brigadier," which is introduced by a third-person narrator after Gerard's death. We learn that Gerard went to his grave never realizing how much the

British hated him for his unsportsmanlike conduct in severing the fox's head with his sword. The story itself is then told in the traditional manner by Gerard, in "that humble café where, between his dinner and his dominoes, he would tell, amid tears and laughter, of that inconceivable Napoleonic past when France, like an angel of wrath, rose up, splendid and terrible, before a cowering continent." It is a bit jarring to find this introductory device used, when Conan Doyle could easily have worked Gerard's ignorance of the rules of the foxhunt into the fabric of the story. However, in "How the Brigadier Saved an Army" and "The Brigadier in England," Gerard boasts of his fame among the English for his success with the fox. Since Gerard must never realize the faux pas he has committed, the third-person narrator is a necessity.

Gerard often succeeds on a mission in spite of his lack of understanding of the situation. His superb riding skills, pluck, and swordsmanship pull him through where a lesser man would surely fail. Few of the other characters in the stories have any depth to them — Gerard sees only their surface, and that's how he describes them. A few of the lesser characters are at least a bit memorable. In his preface to *Man and Superman*, George Bernard Shaw admits that he has borrowed the character of El Cuchillo, in "How the Brigadier Held the King," for his character, Mendoza: "The theft of the brigand-poetaster from Sir Arthur Conan Doyle is deliberate." Shaw has created a kinder, gentler Mendoza in his play; Conan Doyle's El Cuchillo is a Jekyll and Hyde character, quoting poetry and torturing prisoners to death.

Although the first impression many people have of the Gerard stories is of the arrogance and buffoonery of their principal character, the moods and emotions evoked by the stories vary widely. In "How the Brigadier Rode to Minsk," the mood is somber from beginning to end, with very little humor. The story conveys a strong image of the retreat from Moscow. Conan Doyle briefly breaks the mood, sending Gerard on a mission to take corn from

Minsk back to the starving army. He intercepts a Russian aide-de-camp bearing a message in Russian. Gerard relies on a beautiful Russian woman to translate it for him. As is usually the case when Gerard relies on a beautiful woman, she cleverly tricks him. Gerard rides into a trap and loses half his men.

"How the Brigadier Came to the Castle of Gloom" is a combination of a gothic horror novel and fast-paced adventure story. The horror story comes first, when Gerard and his companion, Duroc, arrive at the door of the evil castle inhabited by a monster, Baron Straubenthal. A sinister-looking servant warns them to beware of the Baron. The atmosphere is further heightened by the silent appearance of the beautiful stepdaughter from behind the curtains of the Baron's study, to tell them how happy she is that they will try to kill her wicked stepfather. However, the horror story turns into a fast-paced adventure when Gerard and Duroc are locked in the storeroom and the stepdaughter smuggles in the key to the powder magazine. The fight to the death with the villain, followed by the narrow escape from the castle, just in time to avoid being blown to bits, is pure Ian Fleming. The only difference is that here Gerard does not get the girl—he seldom does!

The stories evoke other emotions as well, including revulsion when Gerard comes across a dying Frenchman who has been tortured by the enemy ("How the Brigadier Joined the Hussars of Conflans," "How the Brigadier Saved an Army").

As the series continued, Gerard became a far more complex character than his original stereotype. At times he is thick-headed and unsophisticated, usually when it comes to dealing with beautiful women. At other times, especially when he is placed in a crisis situation, he becomes quick-witted, decisive, and masterful. His sensitivity to the mood of the retreat in "How the Brigadier Rode to Minsk" does not seem uncharacteristic, yet is totally unlike the Gascon braggart of "The Medal of Brigadier Gerard." The Gerard who nearly persuades a vacillating prince to support Napoleon in the face of overwhelming opposition from his wife and members of the court and then reports on the power of poetry to evoke irrepressible nationalist emotions ("How the Brigadier Played for a Kingdom") is not the philistine dim-wit who fails to understand the civic outrage of the Venetians at the removal of four ugly (to Gerard) bronze horses from St. Mark's Square ("How the Brigadier Lost His Ear").

It almost appears that Conan Doyle had an internal conflict over what to do with Gerard. The character grows in humanity as he is given flesh and blood, but then swings back to buffoonery when Doyle feels him growing too sophisticated. Gerard's character reaches its ultimate sophistication in "How the Brigadier Was Tempted by the Devil," where Doyle gives a fairly realistic portrait of Napoleon and Gerard only has one or two lapses into swagger. Gerard reaches his nadir in "How the Brigadier Lost an Ear," the first instalment of *Adventures*. Seven years had passed since publication of *Exploits* and Doyle must have felt the need to re-establish him. Here Gerard is almost a comic-book French chevalier — ignorant of art, a womanizer, sentimental, super-patriotic, and egoistic.

Gerard refers to his poor widowed mother in almost every story, echoing, perhaps consciously, Conan Doyle's deep affection and attachment for his own mother. The real soldier, Marbot, also refers many times to his widowed mother, sometimes in terms that are clearly echoed by Gerard. In his moment of truth, whenever triumph or death appear imminent, Gerard inevitably thinks of his mother and the Emperor (always the "Emperor," never "Napoleon," as if the institution were more important than the man), and then of the many women who will weep over his loss. And always his mother comes before the Emperor — her pride in his achievements, her small income, and his joy at being able to visit her (echoing Marbot's repeated joy when he was able to return to Paris after a long campaign).

Gerard also tells us that he is a great lover. Obviously, Gerard has fooled himself into believing that a beautiful woman had reciprocated his feelings. It is clear that the woman is hardly aware of him, or is simply using him. Gerard, of course, is convinced she loves him deeply, but is holding in her feelings out of a sense of propriety. The woman, of course, has pretended to be helpless so she can delay Gerard in carrying out his mission or steal the important papers he is carrying.

Gerard, of peasant stock, is less sophisticated in court manners than Marbot, whose own father was a general. However, in "How the Brigadier Played for a Kingdom," Gerard manages to put up quite a sophisticated front while, at the same time, allowing himself to be hoodwinked yet again by a beautiful woman. Gerard must complete the mission of a dying French diplomat to the mythical German principality of Saxe-Felstein. He is to deliver a letter from Napoleon to convince the Prince to throw his support behind the French, rather than the British and Austrians. On the way, Gerard meets a beautiful woman in distress and, of course, she manages to purloin the letter. He presses on and makes his way into the presence of the Prince and a very hostile court, where he discovers that the Princess, who leads the opposition to Napoleon, is his beautiful trickster. Nevertheless, Gerard delivers Napoleon's message verbally, and almost succeeds in swaying the Prince until a young soldier-poet, Körner, makes a stirring speech and carries the day. Gerard acquits himself with great delicacy and almost succeeds in an impossible mission. The facts of this story are quite similar to and were likely inspired by Marbot's 1806 mission to the King of Prussia, with the addition of Gerard's romantic interlude with the Princess and the Körner element. The portrait of the German romantic nationalistic poet, Karl Theodor Körner, is quite accurate, but Conan Doyle clearly invented Körner's mesmerizing song, for it contains non-Germanic elements and does not match any of Körner's published poetry.

Unlike the Holmes stories, in which any humor is incidental, there is deliberate humor in almost every Gerard story. Usually, but not always, the humor is in the introduction. Humor is rare in the denouement, one exception being the Brigadier's marriage in

"The Marriage of the Brigadier." The humor is always based on Gerard's popinjay, vainglorious swagger, abysmal cultural ignorance, and incredible bravado. The most humorous of the Gerard stories are those that poke fun at the British, and especially their love of sports. In "The Brigadier in England," Doyle uses Gerard's ignorance of the British to make fun of their love of cricket, boxing, pheasant shooting, and even their attitude to the law. It seems strange to hear Doyle making fun of sports he loved passionately—cricket and boxing. In "How the Brigadier Held the King," he devoted several paragraphs to the British moneyed class' great love of gambling on just about anything—something that Gerard was willing to get caught up in himself. Perhaps one of the funniest scenes in all of the Gerard stories is the foxhunt in "The Crime of the Brigadier."

These stories are about more than humor, however. In "How the Brigadier Rode to Minsk," set amid the snow and despair of the retreat from Moscow, there is precious little humor and instead there is sardonicism and bitterness. In addition, in many of the stories—"How the Brigadier Joined the Hussars of Conflans," "How the Brigadier Held the King," and "How the Brigadier Saved an Army," for instance—the humor is mixed with realistic scenes of pain and horror.

Conan Doyle's best short stories, well crafted and superbly written, the Brigadier Gerard tales, are almost wholly unknown to the public. They have been obscured by another shadow—the shadow of Sherlock Holmes—for too long.

A Note on the Text

Each story in *The Complete Brigadier Gerard* was first published in the monthly *Strand Magazine* in London by George Newnes, Ltd. The U.S. edition of *The Strand* was published one month later than the British edition. All of the stories appeared in the British edition. With the exception of "The Crime of the Brigadier," they also appeared in the U.S. *Strand.*

Notes:
- numbering system is that used by the *Strand*
- all illustrations are by W. B. Wollen, R.I., unless otherwise noted
- the second title is that used in subsequent book publications
- the first dates given are for publication in the British edition of the *Strand*
- the date and journal of U.S. first non-*Strand* serial publication is given if available

The Exploits of Gerard

"The Medal of Brigadier Gerard." *Strand Magazine* v. VIII, No. 48, Dec. 1894, p. 563; ["How the Brigadier Won His Medal"]; American copyright 1894, Bacheller, Johnson & Bacheller: *Leslie's Weekly,* Feb. 6, 13, 1896, pp. 89, 105 [illus. Clinedinst].

I – "How the Brigadier Held the King." *Strand Magazine* v. IX, No. 52, Apr. 1895, p. 363; American copyright 1895, Bacheller, Johnson & Bacheller.

II – "How the King Held the Brigadier." *Strand Magazine* v. IX, No. 53, May 1895, p. 501; American copyright 1895, Bacheller, Johnson & Bacheller.

III – "How the Brigadier Slew the Brothers of Ajaccio." *Strand Magazine* v. IX, No. 54, June 1895, p. 631; American copyright 1895, Irving Bacheller.

IV – "How the Brigadier Came to the Castle of Gloom." *Strand Magazine* v. IX, No. 55, July 1895, p. 3; American copyright 1895, Irving Bacheller: *Pocket Magazine,* Nov. 1895, p. 1, Vol. 1, no. 1.

V – "How the Brigadier Took the Field Against the Marshal Millefleurs." *Strand Magazine* v. IX, No. 56, Aug. 1895, p. 201; American copyright 1895, The Standard Press Company in *The Standard.*

VI – "How the Brigadier Was Tempted by the Devil." *Strand Magazine* v. IX, No. 57, Sept. 1895, p. 335; American copyright Sept. 1895, John Brisben Walker in *Cosmopolitan Magazine* [illus. T. de Thulstrup].

VII – "How the Brigadier Played for a Kingdom." *Strand Magazine* v. IX, No. 60, Dec. 1895, p. 603; American copyright 1895, Bacheller, Johnson & Bacheller: *Chicago Tribune*, Dec. 29, 1895; *Pocket Magazine*, Feb. 1896, p. 1.

The Adventures of Brigadier Gerard

"The Crime of the Brigadier." *Strand Magazine* v. XIX, No. 109, Jan. 1900, p. 41 [illus. Sidney Paget]; ["How the Brigadier slew the Fox"]; *Cosmopolitan Magazine*, Dec. 1899, p. 171 [illus. F. Klepper] [included as part of *Adventures* despite publishing date].

I – "How Brigadier Gerard Lost His Ear." *Strand Magazine* v. XXIV, No. 140, Aug. 1902, p. 123; ["How the Brigadier Lost His Ear"]; American *Strand*, Oct. 1902, p. 123.

II – "How the Brigadier Saved the Army." *Strand Magazine* v. XXIV, No. 143, Nov.1902, p. 483; ["How the Brigadier Saved an Army"]; American *Strand*, Dec. 1902, p. 483.

III – "How the Brigadier Rode to Minsk." *Strand Magazine* v. XXIV, No. 144, Dec. 1902, p. 604; American *Strand*, Jan. 1903, p. 603.

IV – "Brigadier Gerard at Waterloo: [I] The Adventure of the Forest Inn." *Strand Magazine* v. XXV, No. 145, Jan. 1903, p. 1; ["How the Brigadier Bore Himself at Waterloo - I - The Story of the Forest Inn"]; American *Strand*, Feb. 1903, p. 3.

V – "Brigadier Gerard at Waterloo: [II] The Adventure of the Nine Prussian Horsemen." *Strand Magazine* v. XXV, No. 146, Feb.

1903, p. 123; ["How the Brigadier Bore Himself at Waterloo - II - The Story of the Nine Prussian Horsemen"]; American *Strand,* Mar. 1903, p. 123.

VI – "The Brigadier in England." *Strand Magazine* v. XXV, No. 147, Mar. 1903, p. 244; ["How the Brigadier Triumphed in England"]; American *Strand,* Apr. 1903, p. 243.

VII – "How the Brigadier Joined the Hussars of Conflans." *Strand Magazine* v. XXV, No. 148, Apr. 1903, p. 363; ["How the Brigadier Captured Saragossa"]; American *Strand,* May 1903, p. 363.

VIII – "How Etienne Gerard Said Good-Bye to His Master." *Strand Magazine* v. XXV, No. 149, May 1903, p. 483; ["The Last Adventure of the Brigadier"]; American *Strand,* June 1903, p. 483.

"The Marriage of the Brigadier." *Strand Magazine* v. XI, No. 237, Sept. 1910, p. 259 [illus. Gilbert Holiday].

Clifford S. Goldfarb is a Toronto lawyer who specializes in charities and business law. He regularly writes and lectures on Arthur Conan Doyle and has written *The Great Shadow* (1997), a study of Conan Doyle's Napoleonic war stories.

THE EXPLOITS OF BRIGADIER GERARD

THE MEDAL OF BRIGADIER GERARD

The Duke of Tarentum, or Macdonald, as his old comrades prefer to call him, was, as I could perceive, in the vilest of tempers. His grim Scotch face was like one of those grotesque door-knockers which one sees in the Faubourg St Germain. We heard afterwards that the Emperor had said in jest that he would have sent him against Wellington in the South, but that he was afraid to trust him within the sound of the pipes. Major Charpentier and I could plainly see that he was smouldering with anger.

"Brigadier Gerard of the Hussars," said he, with the air of the corporal with the recruit.

I saluted.

"Major Charpentier of the Horse Grenadiers."

My companion answered to his name.

"The Emperor has a mission for you."

Without more ado he flung open the door and announced us.

I have seen Napoleon ten times on horseback to once on foot, and I think that he does wisely to show himself to the troops in this fashion, for he cuts a very good figure in the saddle. As we saw him now he was the shortest man out of six by a good hand's breadth, and yet I am no very big man myself, though I ride quite heavy enough for a hussar. It is evident, too, that his body is too long for his legs. With his big round head, his curved shoulders, and his clean-shaven face, he is more like a Professor at the Sorbonne than the first soldier in France. Every man to his taste, but it seems to me that, if I could clap a pair of fine light cavalry whiskers, like my own, on to him, it would do him no harm. He has a firm mouth, however, and his eyes are remarkable. I have seen them once turned on me in anger, and I had rather ride at a square on a spent horse than face them again. I am not a man who is easily daunted, either.

He was standing at the side of the room, away from the window, looking up at a great map of the country which was hung upon the wall. Berthier stood beside him, trying to look wise, and just as we entered, Napoleon snatched his sword impatiently from him and pointed with it on the map. He was talking fast and low, but I heard him say, "The valley of the Meuse," and twice he repeated "Berlin." As we entered, his aide-de-camp advanced to us, but the Emperor stopped him and beckoned us to his side.

"You have not yet received the cross of honour, Brigadier Gerard?" he asked.

I replied that I had not, and was about to add that it was not for want of having deserved it, when he cut me short in his decided fashion.

"And you, Major?" he asked.

"No, sire."

"Then you shall both have your opportunity now."

He led us to the great map upon the wall and placed the tip of Berthier's sword on Rheims.

"I will be frank with you, gentlemen, as with two comrades. You have both been with me since Marengo, I believe?" He had a strangely pleasant smile, which used to light up his pale face with a kind of cold sunshine. "Here at Rheims are our present headquarters on this the 14th of March. Very good. Here is Paris, distant by road a good twenty-five leagues. Blucher lies to the north, Schwarzenberg to the south." He prodded at the map with the sword as he spoke.

"Now," said he, "the further into the country these people march, the more completely I shall crush them. They are about to advance upon Paris. Very good. Let them do so. My brother, the

King of Spain, will be there with a hundred thousand men. It is to him that I send you. You will hand him this letter, a copy of which I confide to each of you. It is to tell him that I am coming at once, in two days' time, with every man and horse and gun to his relief. I must give them forty-eight hours to recover. Then straight to Paris! You understand me, gentlemen?"

Ah, if I could tell you the glow of pride which it gave me to be taken into the great man's confidence in this way. As he handed our letters to us I clicked my spurs and threw out my chest, smiling and nodding to let him know that I saw what he would be after. He smiled also, and rested his hand for a moment upon the cape of my dolman. I would have given half my arrears of pay if my mother could have seen me at that instant.

"I will show you your route," said he, turning back to the map. "Your orders are to ride together as far as Bazoches. You will then separate, the one making for Paris by Oulchy and Neuilly, and the other to the north by Braine, Soissons, and Senlis. Have you anything to say, Brigadier Gerard?"

I am a rough soldier, but I have words and ideas. I had begun to speak about glory and the peril of France when he cut me short.

"And you, Major Charpentier?"

"If we find our route unsafe, are we at liberty to choose another?" said he.

"Soldiers do not choose, they obey." He inclined his head to show that we were dismissed, and turned round to Berthier. I do not know what he said, but I heard them both laughing.

Well, as you may think, we lost little time in getting upon our way. In half an hour we were riding down the High Street of Rheims, and it struck twelve o'clock as we passed the cathedral. I had my little grey mare, Violette, the one which Sebastiani had wished to buy after Dresden. It is the fastest horse in the six brigades of light cavalry, and was only beaten by the Duke of Rovigo's racer from England. As to Charpentier, he had the kind of horse which a horse grenadier or a cuirassier would be likely to ride: a back like a bedstead, you understand, and legs like the posts. He is a hulking fellow himself, so that they looked a singular pair. And yet in his insane conceit he ogled the girls as they waved their handkerchiefs to me from the windows, and he twirled his ugly red moustache up into his eyes, just as if it were to him that their attention was addressed.

When we came out of the town we passed through the French camp, and then across the battle-field of yesterday, which was still covered both by our own poor fellows and by the Russians. But of the two the camp was the sadder sight. Our army was thawing away. The Guards were all right, though the young guard was full of conscripts. The artillery and the heavy cavalry were also good if there were more of them, but the infantry privates with their under-officers looked like school-boys with their masters. And we had no reserves. When one considered that there were 80,000 Russians to the north and 150,000 Russians and Austrians to the south, it might make even the bravest man grave.

For my own part, I confess that I shed a tear until the thought came that the Emperor was still with us, and that on that very morning he had placed his hand upon my dolman and had promised me a medal of honour. This set me singing, and I spurred Violette on, until Charpentier had to beg me to have mercy on his great, snorting, panting camel. The road was beaten into paste and rutted 2ft deep by the artillery, so that he was right in saying that it was not the place for a gallop.

I have never been very friendly with this Charpentier; and now for twenty miles of the way I could not draw a word from him. He rode with his brows puckered and his chin upon his breast, like a man who is heavy with thought. More than once I asked him what was on his mind, thinking that, perhaps, with my quicker intelligence I might set the matter straight. His answer always was that it was his mission of which he was thinking, which surprised me, because, although I had never thought much of his intelligence, still it seemed to me to be impossible that anyone could be puzzled by so simple and soldierly a task.

Well, we came at last to Bazoches, where he was to take the southern road and I the northern. He half turned in his saddle before he left me, and he looked at me with a singular expression of inquiry in his face.

"What do you make of it, Brigadier?" he asked.

"Of what?"

"Of our mission."

"Surely it is plain enough."

"You think so? Why should the Emperor tell us his plans?"

"Because he recognised our intelligence."

My companion laughed in a manner which I found annoying.

"May I ask what you intend to do if you find these villages full of Prussians?" he asked.

"I shall obey my orders."

"But you will be killed."

"Very possibly."

He laughed again, and so offensively that I clapped my hand to my sword. But before I could tell him what I thought of his stupidity and rudeness he had wheeled his horse, and was lumbering away down the other road. I saw his big fur cap vanish over the brow of the hill, and then I rode upon my way, wondering at his conduct. From time to time I put my hand to the breast of my tunic and felt the paper crackle beneath my fingers. Ah, my precious paper, which should be turned into the little silver medal for which I had yearned so long. All the way from Braine to Sermoise I was thinking of what my mother would say when she saw it.

I stopped to give Violette a meal at a wayside auberge on the side of a hill not far from Soissons—a place surrounded by old oaks, and with so many crows that one could scarce hear one's own voice. It was from the innkeeper that I learned that Marmont had fallen back two days before, and that the Prussians were over the Aisne. An hour later, in the fading light, I saw two of their vedettes upon the hill to the right, and then, as darkness gathered, the heavens to the north were all glimmering from the lights of a bivouac.

When I heard that Blucher had been there for two days, I was much surprised that the Emperor should not have known that the country through which he had ordered me to carry my precious letter was already occupied by the enemy. Still, I thought of the tone of his voice when he said to Charpentier that a soldier must not choose, but must obey. I should follow the route he had laid down for me as long as Violette could move a hoof or I a finger upon her bridle. All the way from Sermoise to Soissons, where the road dips up and down, curving among fir-woods, I kept my pistol ready and my sword-belt braced, pushing on swiftly where the path was straight, and then coming slowly round the corners in the way we learned in Spain.

When I came to the farmhouse which lies to the right of the road just after you cross the wooden bridge over the Crise, near where the great statue of the Virgin stands, a woman cried to me from the field saying that the Prussians were in Soissons. A small party of their lancers, she said, had come in that very afternoon, and a whole division was expected before midnight. I did not wait to hear the end of her tale, but clapped spurs into Violette, and in five minutes was galloping her into the town.

Three Uhlans were at the mouth of the main street, their horses tethered, and they gossiping together, each with a pipe as long as my sabre. I saw them well in the light of an open door, but of me they could have seen only the flash of Violette's grey side and the black flutter of my cloak. A moment later I flew through a stream of them rushing from an open gateway. Violette's shoulder sent one of them reeling, and I stabbed at another but missed him. Pang, pang, went two carbines, but I had flown round the curve of the street and never so much as heard the hiss of the balls. Ah, we were great, both Violette and I. She lay down to it like a coursed hare, the fire flying from her hoofs. I stood in my stirrups and brandished my sword. Someone sprang for my bridle. I sliced him through the arm, and I heard him howling behind me. Two horsemen closed upon me, I cut one down and outpaced the other. A minute later I was clear of the town and flying down a broad white road with the black poplars on either side. For a time I heard the rattle of hoofs behind me, but they died and died until I could not tell them from the throbbing of my own heart. Soon I pulled up and listened, but all was silent. They had given up the chase.

Well, the first thing that I did was to dismount and to lead my mare into a small wood through which a stream ran. There I watered her and rubbed her down, giving her two pieces of sugar soaked in cognac from my flask. She was spent from the sharp chase, but it was wonderful to see how she came round with a half-hour's rest. When my thighs closed upon her again, I could tell by the spring and the swing of her that it would not be her fault if I did not win my way safe to Paris.

I must have been well within the enemy's lines now, for I heard a number of them shouting one of their rough drinking songs out of a house by the roadside, and I went round by the fields to avoid it. At another time two men came out into the moonlight (for by this time it was a cloudless night) and shouted something in German; but I galloped on without heeding them, and they were afraid to fire, for their own hussars are dressed exactly as I was. It is best to take no notice at these times, and then they put you down as a deaf man.

It was a lovely moon, and every tree threw a black bar across the road. I could see the country side just as if it were daytime, and very peaceful it looked, save that there was a great fire raging somewhere in the north. In the silence of the night-time, and with the knowledge that danger was in front and behind me, the sight of that great distant fire was very striking and awesome. But I am not easily clouded, for I have seen too many singular things, so I hummed a tune between my teeth and thought of little Lisette, whom I might see in Paris. My mind was full of her when, trotting round a corner, I came straight upon half-a-dozen German dragoons, who were sitting round a brushwood fire by the roadside.

I am an excellent soldier. I do not say this because I am prejudiced in my own favour, but because I really am so. I can weigh every chance in a moment, and decide with as much certainty as though I had brooded for a week. Now I saw like a flash that, come what might, I should be chased, and on a horse which had already done a long twelve leagues. But it was better to be chased onwards than to be chased back. On this moonlit night, with fresh horses behind me, I must take my risk in either case; but if I were to shake them off, I preferred that it should be near Senlis than near Soissons. All this flashed on me as if by instinct, you understand. My eyes had hardly rested on the bearded faces under the brass helmets before my rowels were up to the bosses in Violette's side, and she off with a rattle like a *pas-de-charge*. Oh, the shouting and rushing and stamping from behind us! Three of them fired and three swung themselves on to their horses. A bullet rapped on the crupper of my saddle with a noise like a stick on a door. Violette sprang madly forward, and I thought she had been wounded, but it was only a graze above the near-fetlock. Ah, the dear little mare, how I loved her when I felt her settle down into that long, easy gallop of hers, her hoofs going like a Spanish girl's castanets. I could not hold myself. I turned on my saddle and shouted and raved, "Vive l'Empereur!" I screamed and laughed at the gust of oaths that came back to me.

But it was not over yet. If she had been fresh she might have gained a mile in five. Now she could only hold her own with a very little over. There was one of them, a young boy of an officer, who was better mounted than the others. He drew ahead with every stride. Two hundred yards behind him were two troopers, but I saw every time that I glanced round, that the distance between them was increasing. The other three who had waited to shoot were a long way in the rear. The officer's mount was a bay, a fine horse, though not to be spoken of with Violette. Yet it was a powerful brute, and it seemed to me that in a few miles its freshness might tell. I waited until the lad was a long way in front of his comrades, and then I eased my mare down a little—a very, very little, so that he might think he was really catching me. When he came within pistol shot of me I drew and cocked my own pistol, and laid my chin upon my shoulder to see what he would do. He did not offer to fire, and I soon discerned the cause. The silly boy had taken his pistols from his holsters when he had camped for the night. He wagged his sword at me now and roared some of his gibberish. He did not seem to understand that he was at my mercy. I eased Violette down until there was not the length of a long lance between the grey tail and the bay muzzle.

"Rendez-vous!" he yelled.

"I must compliment monsieur upon his French," said I, resting the barrel of my pistol upon my bridle arm, which I have always found best when shooting from the saddle. I aimed at his face, and could see, even in the moonlight, how white he grew when he understood that it was all up with him. But even as my finger pressed the trigger I thought of his mother, and I put my ball through his horse's shoulder. I fear he hurt himself in the fall, for it was a fearful crash, but I had my letter to think of, so I stretched the mare into a gallop once more.

But they were not so easily shaken off, these brigands. The two troopers thought no more of their young officer than if he had been a recruit thrown in the riding-school. They left him to the others and thundered on after me. I had pulled up on the brow of a hill, thinking that I had heard the last of them; but, my faith, I soon saw there was no time for loitering, so away we went, the mare tossing her head and I my busby, to show what we thought of two dragoons who tried to catch a hussar. But at this moment, even while I laughed at the thought, my heart stood still within me, for there at the end of the long white road was a black patch of cavalry waiting to receive me. To a young soldier it might have seemed the shadow of the trees, but to me it was a troop of hussars, and, turn where I could, death seemed to be waiting for me.

Well, I had the dragoons behind me and the hussars in front. Never since Moscow have I seemed to be in such peril. But for the honour of the brigade I had rather be cut down by a light cavalryman than by a heavy. I never drew bridle, therefore, or hesitated for an instant, but I let Violette have her head. I remember that I tried to pray as I rode, but I am a little out of practice at such things, and the only words I could remember were the prayer for fine weather which we used at the school on the evening before holidays. Even this seemed better than nothing, and I was pattering it out, when suddenly I heard French voices in front of me. Ah, mon Dieu, but the joy went through my heart like a musket-ball. They were ours—our own dear little rascals from the corps of Marmont. Round whisked my two dragoons and galloped for their lives, with the moon gleaming on their brass helmets, while I trotted up to my friends with no undue haste, for I would have them understand that though a hussar may fly, it is not in his nature to fly very fast. Yet I fear that Violette's heaving flanks and foam-spattered muzzle gave the lie to my careless bearing.

Who should be at the head of the troop but old Bouvet, whom I saved at Leipzig! When he saw me his little pink eyes filled with tears, and, indeed, I could not but shed a few myself at the sight of his joy. I told him of my mission, but he laughed when I said that I must pass through Senlis.

"The enemy is there," said he. "You cannot go."

"I prefer to go where the enemy is," I answered. "I would ride through Berlin if I had the Emperor's orders."

"But why not go straight to Paris with your despatch? Why should you choose to pass through the one place where you are almost sure to be taken or killed?"

"A soldier does not choose—he obeys," said I, just as I had heard Napoleon say it.

Old Bouvet laughed in his wheezy way, until I had to give my moustachios a twirl and look him up and down in a manner which brought him to reason.

"Well," said he, "you had best come along with us, for we are all bound for Senlis. Our orders are to reconnoitre the place. A squadron of Poniatowski's Polish lancers are in front of us. If you must ride through it, it is possible that we may be able to go with you."

So away we went, jingling and clanking through the quiet night until we came up with the Poles—fine old soldiers all of them, though a trifle heavy for their horses. It was a treat to see them, for they could not have carried themselves better if they had belonged to my own brigade. We rode together, until in the early morning we saw the lights of Senlis. A peasant was coming along with a cart, and from him we learned how things were going there.

His information was certain, for his brother was the Mayor's coachman, and he had spoken with him late the night before. There was a single squadron of Cossacks—or a polk, as they call it in their frightful language—quartered upon the Mayor's house which stands at the corner of the marketplace, and is the largest building in the town. A whole division of Prussian infantry was encamped in the woods to the north, but only the Cossacks were in Senlis. Ah, what a chance to avenge ourselves upon these barbarians, whose cruelty to our poor country-folk was the talk at every camp fire.

We were into the town like a torrent, hacked down the vedettes, rode over the guard, and were smashing in the doors of the Mayor's house before they understood that there was a Frenchman within twenty miles of them. We saw horrid heads at the windows, heads bearded to the temples, with tangled hair and sheepskin caps, and silly, gaping mouths. "Hourra! Hourra!" they shrieked, and fired with their carbines, but our fellows were into the house and at their throats before they had wiped the sleep out of their eyes. It was dreadful to see how the Poles flung themselves upon them, like starving wolves upon a herd of fat bucks—for, as you know, the Poles have a blood feud against the Cossacks. The most were killed in the upper rooms, whither they had fled for shelter, and the blood was pouring down into the hall like rain from a roof. They are terrible soldiers, these Poles, though I think they are a trifle heavy for their horses. Man for man, they are as big as Kellermann's cuirassiers. Their equipment is, of course, much lighter, since they are without the cuirass, back-plate, and helmet.

Well, it was at this point that I made an error—a very serious error it must be admitted. Up to this moment I had carried out my mission in a manner which only my modesty prevents me from describing as remarkable. But now I did that which an official would condemn and a soldier excuse.

There is no doubt that the mare was spent, but still it is true that I might have galloped on through Senlis and reached the country, where I should have had no enemy between me and Paris. But what hussar can ride past a fight and never draw rein? It is to ask too much of him. Besides, I thought that if Violette had an hour of rest I might have three hours the better at the other end. Then on the top of it came those heads at the windows, with their sheepskin hats and their barbarous cries. I sprang from my saddle, threw Violette's bridle over a rail-post, and ran into the house with the rest. It is true that I was too late to be of service, and that I was nearly wounded by a lance-thrust from one of these dying savages. Still, it is a pity to miss even the smallest affair, for one never knows what opportunity for advancement may present itself. I have seen more soldierly work in out-post skirmishes and little gallop-and-hack affairs of the kind than in any of the Emperor's big battles.

When the house was cleared I took a bucket of water out for Violette, and our peasant guide showed me where the good Mayor kept his fodder. My faith, but the little sweetheart was ready for it. Then I sponged down her legs, and leaving her still tethered I went back into the house to find a mouthful for myself, so that I should not need to halt again until I was in Paris.

And now I come to the part of my story which may seem singular to you although I could tell you at least ten things every bit as queer which have happened to me in my lifetime. You can understand that, to a man who spends his lifetime in scouting and vedette duties on the bloody ground which lies between two great armies, there are many chances of strange experiences. I'll tell you, however, exactly what occurred.

Old Bouvet was waiting in the passage when I entered, and he asked me whether we might not crack a bottle of wine together. "My faith, we must not be long," said he. "There are ten thousand of Theilmann's Prussians in the woods up yonder."

"Where is the wine?" I asked.

"Ah, you may trust two hussars to find where the wine is," said he, and taking a candle in his hand, he led the way down the stone stairs into the kitchen.

When we got there we found another door, which opened on to a winding stair with the cellar at the bottom. The Cossacks had been there before us, as was easily seen by the broken bottles littered all over it. However, the Mayor was a *bon-vivant*, and I do not wish to have a better set of bins to pick from. Chambertin, Graves, Alicant, white wine and red, sparkling and still, they lay in pyramids peeping coyly out of the sawdust. Old Bouvet stood with his candle, looking here and peeping there, purring in his throat like a cat before a milk-pail. He had picked upon a Burgundy at last, and had his hand outstretched to the bottle, when there came a roar of musketry from above us, a rush of feet, and such a yelping and screaming as I have never listened to. The Prussians were upon us.

Bouvet is a brave man: I will say that for him. He flashed out his sword and away he clattered up the stone steps, his spurs clinking as he ran. I followed him, but just as we came out into the kitchen passage a tremendous shout told us that the house had been recaptured.

"It is all over," I cried, grasping at Bouvet's sleeve.

"There is one more to die," he shouted, and away he went like a madman up the second stair. In effect, I should have gone to my death also had I been in his place, for he had done very wrong in not throwing out his scouts to warn him if the Germans advanced upon him. For an instant I was about to rush up with him, and then I bethought myself that, after all, I had my own mission to think of, and that if I were taken the important letter of the Emperor would be sacrificed. I let Bouvet die alone, therefore, and I went down into the cellar again, closing the door behind me.

Well, it was not a very rosy prospect down there either. Bouvet had dropped the candle when the alarm came, and I, pawing about in the darkness, could find nothing but broken bottles. At last I came upon the candle, which had rolled under the curve of a cask, but, try as I would with my tinderbox, I could not light it.

The reason was that the wick had been wet in a puddle of wine, so suspecting that this might be the case, I cut the end off with my sword. Then I found that it lighted easily enough. But what to do I could not imagine. The scoundrels upstairs were shouting themselves hoarse, several hundred of them from the sound, and it was clear that some of them would soon want to moisten their throats. There would be an end to a dashing soldier, and of the mission and of the medal. I thought of my mother and I thought of the Emperor. It made me weep to think that the one would lose so excellent a son and the other the best light cavalry officer he ever had since Lasalle's time. But presently I dashed the tears from my eyes. "Courage!" I cried, striking myself upon the chest. "Courage, my brave boy! Is it possible that one who has come safely from Moscow without so much as a frost-bite will die in a French wine-cellar?" At the thought I was up on my feet and clutching at the letter in my tunic, for the crackle of it gave me courage.

My first plan was to set fire to the house, in the hope of escaping in the confusion. My second, to get into an empty wine-cask. I was looking round to see if I could find one, when suddenly, in the corner, I espied a little low door, painted of the same grey colour as the wall, so that it was only a man with quick sight who would have noticed it. I pushed against it, and at first I imagined that it was locked. Presently, however it gave a little, and then I understood that it was held by the pressure of something on the other side. I put my feet against a hogshead of wine, and I gave such a push that the door flew open and I came down with a crash upon my back, the candle flying out of my hands, so that I found myself in darkness once more. I picked myself up and stared through the black archway into the gloom beyond.

There was a slight ray of light coming from some slit or grating. The dawn had broken outside, and I could dimly see the long curving sides of several huge casks, which made me think that perhaps this was where the Mayor kept his reserves of wine while they were maturing. At any rate, it seemed to be a safer hiding-place than the outer cellar, so gathering up my candle, I was just closing the door behind me, when I suddenly saw something which filled me with amazement, and even, I confess, with the smallest little touch of fear.

I have said that at the further end of the cellar there was a dim grey fan of light striking downwards from somewhere near the roof. Well, as I peered through the darkness, I suddenly saw a great, tall man skip into this belt of daylight, and then out again into the darkness at the further end. My word, I gave such a start that my busby nearly broke its chin-strap! It was only a glance, but, none the less, I had time to see that the fellow had a hairy Cossack cap on his head, and that he was a great, long-legged, broad-shouldered brigand, with a sabre at his waist. My faith, even Etienne Gerard was a little staggered at being left alone with such a creature in the dark.

But only for a moment. "Courage!" I thought. "Am I not a hussar, a brigadier, too, at the age of thirty-one, and the chosen messenger of the Emperor?" After all, this skulker had more cause to be afraid of me than I of him. And then suddenly I understood that he was afraid—horribly afraid. I could read it from his quick step and his bent shoulders as he ran among the barrels, like a rat making for its hole. And, of course, it must have been he who had held the door against me, and not some packing-case or wine-cask as I had imagined. He was the pursued then, and I the pursuer. Aha, I felt my whiskers bristle as I advanced upon him through the darkness! He would find that he had no chicken to deal with, this robber from the North. For the moment I was magnificent.

At first I had feared to light my candle lest I should make a mark of myself, but now, after cracking my shin over a box, and catching my spurs in some canvas, I thought the bolder course the wiser. I lit it therefore, and then I advanced with long strides, my sword in my hand. "Come out, you rascal!" I cried. "Nothing can save you. You will at last meet with your deserts."

I held my candle high, and presently I caught a glimpse of the man's head staring at me over a barrel. He had a gold chevron on his black cap, and the expression of his face told me in an instant that he was an officer and a man of refinement.

"Monsieur," he cried in excellent French, "I surrender myself on a promise of quarter. But if I do not have your promise, I will then sell my life as dearly as I can."

"Sir," said I, "a Frenchman knows how to treat an unfortunate enemy. Your life is safe." With that he handed his sword over the top of the barrel, and I bowed with the candle on my heart. "Whom have I the honour of capturing?" I asked.

"I am the Count Boutkine, of the Emperor's own Don Cossacks," said he. "I came out with my troop to reconnoitre Senlis, and as we found no sign of your people we determined to spend the night here."

"And would it be an indiscretion," I asked, "if I were to inquire how you came into the back cellar?"

"Nothing more simple," said he. "It was our intention to start at early dawn. Feeling chilled after dressing, I thought that a cup of wine would do me no harm, so I came down to see what I could find. As I was rummaging about, the house was suddenly carried by assault so rapidly that by the time I had climbed the stairs it was all over. It only remained for me to save myself, so I came down here and hid myself in the back cellar, where you have found me."

I thought of how old Bouvet had behaved under the same conditions, and the tears sprang to my eyes as I contemplated the glory of France. Then I had to consider what I should do next. It was clear that this Russian Count, being in the back cellar while we were in the front one, had not heard the sounds which would have told him that the house was once again in the hands of his own allies. If he should once understand this the tables would be turned, and I should be his prisoner instead of he being mine. What was I to do? I was at my wits' end, when suddenly there came to me an idea so brilliant that I could not but be amazed at my own invention.

"Count Boutkine," said I, "I find myself in a most difficult position."

"And why?" he asked.

"Because I have promised you your life." His jaw dropped a little.

"You would not withdraw your promise?" he cried.

"If the worst comes to the worst I can die in your defence," said I; "but the difficulties are great."

"What is it, then?" he asked.

"I will be frank with you," said I. "You must know that our fellows, and especially the Poles, are so incensed against the Cossacks that the mere sight of the uniform drives them mad. They precipitate themselves instantly upon the wearer and tear him limb from limb. Even their officers cannot restrain them."

The Russian grew pale at my words and the way in which I said them.

"But this is terrible," said he.

"Horrible!" said I. "If we were to go up together at this moment I cannot promise how far I could protect you."

"I am in your hands," he cried. "what would you suggest that we should do? Would it not be best that I should remain here?"

"That worst of all."

"And why?"

"Because our fellows will ransack the house presently, and then you would be cut to pieces. No, no, I must go up and break it to them. But even then, when once they see that accursed uniform, I do not know what may happen."

"Should I then take the uniform off?"

"Excellent!" I cried. "Hold, we have it! You will take your uniform off and put on mine. That will make you sacred to every French soldier."

"It is not the French I fear so much as the Poles."

"But my uniform will be a safeguard against either."

"How can I thank you?" he cried. "But you—what are you to wear?"

"I will wear yours."

"And perhaps fall a victim to your generosity?"

"It is my duty to take the risk," I answered, "but I have no fears. I will ascend in your uniform. A hundred swords will be turned upon me. 'Hold!' I will shout, 'I am the Brigadier Gerard!' Then they will see my face. They will know me. And I will tell them about you. Under the shield of these clothes you will be sacred."

His fingers trembled with eagerness as he tore off his tunic. His boots and breeches were much like my own, so there was no need to change them, but I gave him my hussar jacket, my dolman, my busby, my sword-belt, and my sabretasche, while I took in exchange his high sheepskin cap with the gold chevron, his fur-trimmed coat, and his crooked sword. Be it well understood that in changing the tunics I did not forget to change my thrice-precious letter also from my old one to my new.

"With your leave," said I, "I shall now bind you to a barrel."

He made a great fuss over this, but I have learned in my soldiering never to throw away chances, and how could I tell that he might not, when my back was turned, see how the matter really stood and break in upon my plans? He was leaning against a barrel at the time, so I ran six times round it with a rope, and then tied it with a big knot behind. If he wished to come upstairs he would, at least, have to carry a thousand litres of good French wine for a knapsack. I then shut the door of the back cellar behind me, so that he might not hear what was going forward, and tossing the candle away I ascended the kitchen stair.

There were only about twenty steps, and yet, while I came up them, I seemed to have time to think of everything that I had ever hoped to do. It was the same feeling that I had at Eylau when I lay with my broken leg and saw the horse artillery galloping down upon me. Of course, I knew that if I were taken I should be shot instantly as being disguised within the enemy's lines. Still, it was a glorious death — in the direct service of the Emperor — and I reflected that there could not be less than five lines, and perhaps seven, in the *Moniteur* about me. Palaret had eight lines, and I am sure that he had not so fine a career.

When I made my way out into the hall, with all the nonchalance in my face and manner that I could assume, the very first thing that I saw was Bouvet's dead body, with his legs drawn up and a broken sword in his hand. I could see by the black smudge that he had been shot at close quarters. I should have wished to salute as I went by, for he was a gallant man, but I feared lest I should be seen, and so I passed on.

The front of the hall was full of Prussian infantry, who were knocking loopholes in the wall, as though they expected that there might be yet another attack. Their officer, a little rat of a man, was running about giving directions. They were all too busy to take much notice of me, but another officer, who was standing by the door with a long pipe in his mouth, strode across and clapped me on the shoulder, pointing to the dead bodies of our poor hussars, and saying something which was meant for a jest, for his long beard opened and showed every fang in his head. I laughed heartily also, and said the only Russian words that I knew. I learned them from little Sophia, at Wilna, and they meant: "If the night is fine we shall meet under the oak tree, and if it rains we shall meet in the byre." It was all the same to this German, however, and I have no doubt that he gave me credit for saying something very witty indeed, for he roared laughing, and slapped me on my shoulder again. I nodded to him and marched out of the hall-door as coolly as if I were the commandant of the garrison.

There were a hundred horses tethered about outside, most of them belonging to the Poles and hussars. Good little Violette was waiting with the others, and she whinnied when she saw me coming towards her. But I would not mount her. No. I was much too cunning for that. On the contrary, I chose the most shaggy little Cossack horse that I could see, and I sprang upon it with as much assurance as though it had belonged to my father before me. It had a great bag of plunder slung over its neck, and this I laid upon Violette's back, and led her along beside me. Never have you seen such a picture of the Cossack returning from the foray. It was superb.

Well, the town was full of Prussians by this time. They lined the side-walks and pointed me out to each other, saying, as I could judge from their gestures, "There goes one of those devils of Cossacks. They are the boys for foraging and plunder."

One or two officers spoke to me with an air of authority, but I shook my head and smiled, and said, "If the night is fine we shall meet under the oak tree, but if it rains we shall meet in the byre," at which they shrugged their shoulders and gave the matter up. In this way I worked along until I was beyond the northern outskirts of the town. I could see in the roadway two lancer vedettes with their black and white pennons, and I knew that when I was once past these I should be a free man once more. I made my pony trot, therefore, Violette rubbing her nose against my knee all the time, and looking up at me to ask how she had deserved that this hairy doormat of a creature should be preferred to her. I was not more than a hundred yards from the Uhlans, when suddenly, you can imagine my feelings when I saw a real Cossack coming galloping along the roadway towards me.

Ah, my friend, you who read this, if you have any heart, you will feel for a man like me, who had gone through so many dangers and trials, only at this very last moment to be confronted with one which appeared to put an end to everything. I will confess that for a moment I lost heart, and was inclined to throw myself down in my despair, and to cry out that I had been betrayed. But, no; I was not beaten even now. I opened two buttons of my tunic so that I might get easily at the Emperor's message, for it was my fixed determination when all hope was gone to swallow the letter and then die sword in hand. Then I felt that my little crooked sword was loose in its sheath, and I trotted on to where the vedettes were waiting. They seemed inclined to stop me, but I pointed to the other Cossack, who was still a couple of hundred yards off, and they, understanding that I merely wished to meet him, let me pass with a salute.

I dug my spurs into my pony then, for if I were only far enough from the lancers I thought I might manage the Cossack without much difficulty. He was an officer, a large, bearded man, with a gold chevron in his cap, just the same as mine. As I advanced he unconsciously aided me by pulling up his horse, so that I had a fine start of the vedettes. On I came for him, and I could see wonder changing to suspicion in his brown eyes as he looked at me and at my pony, and at my equipment. I do not know what it was that was wrong, but he saw something which was as it should not be. He shouted out a question, and then when I gave no answer he pulled out his sword. I was glad in my heart to see him do so, for I had always rather fight than cut down an unsuspecting enemy. Now I made at him full tilt, and, parrying his cut, I got my point in just under the fourth button of his tunic. Down he went, and the weight of him nearly took me off my horse before I could disengage. I never glanced at him to see if he were living or dead, for I sprang off my pony and onto Violette, with a shake of my bridle and a kiss of my hand to the two Uhlans behind me. They galloped after me, shouting, but Violette had had her rest and was just as fresh as when she started. I took the first side road to the west and then the first to the south, which would take me away from the enemy's country. On we went and on, every stride taking me further from my foes and nearer to my friends. At last, when I reached the end of a long stretch of road, and looking back from it could see no sign of any pursuers, I understood that my troubles were over.

And it gave me a glow of happiness, as I rode, to think that I had done to the letter what the Emperor had ordered. What would he say when he saw me? What could he say which would do justice to the incredible way in which I had risen above every danger? He had ordered me to go through Sermoise, Soissons, and Senlis, little dreaming that they were all three occupied by the enemy. And yet I had done it. I had borne his letter in safety through each of these towns. Hussars, dragoons, lancers, Cossacks, and infantry—I had run the gauntlet of all of them, and had come out unharmed.

When I had got as far as Dammartin I caught a first glimpse of our own outposts. There was a troop of dragoons in a field, and of course I could see from the horsehair crests that they were French. I galloped towards them in order to ask them if all was safe between there and Paris, and as I rode I felt such a pride at having won my way back to my friends again, that I could not refrain from waving my sword in the air.

At this a young officer galloped out from among the dragoons, also brandishing his sword, and it warmed my heart to think that he should come riding with such ardour and enthusiasm to greet me. I made Violette caracole, and as we came together I brandished my sword more gallantly than ever, but you can imagine my feelings when he suddenly made a cut at me which would certainly have taken my head off if I had not fallen forward with my nose in Violette's mane. My faith, it whistled just over my cap like an east wind. Of course, it came from this accursed Cossack uniform which, in my excitement, I had forgotten all about, and this young dragoon had imagined that I was some Russian champion who was challenging the French cavalry. My word, he was a frightened man when he understood how near he had been to killing the celebrated Brigadier Gerard.

Well, the road was clear, and about three o'clock in the afternoon I was at St Denis, though it took me a long two hours to get from there to Paris, for the road was blocked with commissariat waggons and guns of the artillery reserve, which was going north to Marmont and Mortier. You cannot conceive the excitement which my appearance in such costume made in Paris, and when I came to the Rue de Rivoli I should think I had a quarter of a mile of folk riding or running behind me. Word had got about from the dragoons (two of whom had come with me), and everybody knew about my adventures and how I had come by my uniform. It was a triumph — men shouting and women waving their handkerchiefs and blowing kisses from the windows.

Although I am a man singularly free from conceit, still I must confess that, on this one occasion, I could not restrain myself from showing that this reception gratified me. The Russian's coat had hung very loose upon me, but now I threw out my chest until it was as tight as a sausage-skin. And my little sweetheart of a mare tossed her mane and pawed with her front hoofs, frisking her tail as though she said, "We've done it together this time. It is to us that commissions should be intrusted." When I kissed her between the nostrils as I dismounted at the gate of the Tuileries there was as much shouting as if a bulletin had been read from the Grand Army.

I was hardly in costume to visit a king; but, after all, if one has a soldierly figure one can do without that. I was shown up straight away to Joseph, whom I had often seen in Spain. He seemed as stout, as quiet, and as amiable as ever. Talleyrand was in the room with him, or I suppose I should call him the Duke of Benevento, but I confess that I like old names best. He read my letter when Joseph Buonaparte handed it to him, and then he looked at me with the strangest expression in those funny little, twinkling eyes of his.

"Were you the only messenger?" he asked.

"There was one other, sire," said I. "Major Charpentier, of the Horse Grenadiers."

"He has not yet arrived," said the King of Spain.

"If you had seen the legs of his horse, sire, you would not wonder at it," I remarked.

"There may be other reasons," said Talleyrand, and he gave that singular smile of his.

Well, they paid me a compliment or two, though they might have said a good deal more and yet have said too little. I bowed myself out, and very glad I was to get away, for I hate a court as much as I love a camp. Away I went to my old friend Chaubert, in the Rue Miromesnil, and there I got his hussar uniform, which fitted me very well. He and Lisette and I supped together in his rooms, and all my dangers were forgotten. In the morning I found Violette ready for another twenty-league stretch. It was my intention to return instantly to the Emperor's headquarters, for I was, as you may well imagine, impatient to hear his words of praise, and to receive my reward.

I need not say that I rode back by a safe route, for I had seen quite enough of Uhlans and Cossacks. I passed through Meaux and Château Thierry, and so in the evening I arrived at Rheims, where Napoleon was still lying. The bodies of our fellows and of St Prest's Russians had all been buried, and I could see changes in the camp also. The soldiers looked better cared for; some of the cavalry had received remounts, and everything was in excellent order. It is wonderful what a good general can effect in a couple of days.

When I came to the headquarters I was shown straight into the Emperor's room. He was drinking coffee at a writing-table, with a big plan drawn out on paper in front of him. Berthier and Macdonald were leaning, one over each shoulder, and he was talking so quickly that I don't believe that either of them could catch a half of what he was saying. But when his eyes fell upon me he dropped the pen on to the chart, and he sprang up with a look in his pale face which struck me cold.

"What the deuce are you doing here?" he shouted. When he was angry he had a voice like a peacock.

"I have the honour to report to you, sire," said I, "that I have delivered your despatch safely to the King of Spain."

"What!" he yelled, and his two eyes transfixed me like bayonets. Oh, those dreadful eyes, shifting from grey to blue, like steel in the sunshine. I can see them now when I have a bad dream.

"What has become of Charpentier?" he asked.

"He is captured," said Macdonald.

"By whom?"

"The Russians."

"The Cossacks?"

"No, a single Cossack."

"He gave himself up?"

"Without resistance."

"He is an intelligent officer. You will see that the medal of honour is awarded to him."

When I heard those words I had to rub my eyes to make sure that I was awake.

"As to you," cried the Emperor, taking a step forward as if he would have struck me, "you brain of a hare, what do you think that you were sent upon this mission for? Do you conceive that I would send a really important message by such a hand as yours, and through every village which the enemy holds? How you came through them passes my comprehension; but if your fellow messenger had had but as little sense as you, my whole plan of campaign would have been ruined. Can you not see, coglione, that this message contained false news, and that it was intended to deceive the enemy whilst I put a very different scheme into execution?"

When I heard those cruel words and saw the angry, white face which glared at me, I had to hold the back of a chair, for my mind was failing me and my knees would hardly bear me up. But then I took courage as I reflected that I was an honourable gentleman, and that my whole life had been spent in toiling for this man and for my beloved country.

"Sire," said I, and the tears would trickle down my cheeks whilst I spoke, "when you are dealing with a man like me you would find it wiser to deal openly. Had I known that you had wished the despatch to fall into the hands of the enemy, I would have seen that it came there. As I believed that I was to guard it, I was prepared to sacrifice my life for it. I do not believe, sire, that any man in the world ever met with more toils and perils than I have done in trying to carry out what I thought was your will."

I dashed the tears from my eyes as I spoke, and with such fire and spirit as I could command I gave him an account of it all, of my dash through Soissons, my brush with the dragoons, my adventure in Senlis, my rencontre with Count Boutkine in the cellar, my disguise, my meeting with the Cossack officer, my flight, and how at the last moment I was nearly cut down by a French dragoon. The Emperor, Berthier, and Macdonald listened with astonishment on their faces. When I had finished Napoleon stepped forward and he pinched me by the ear.

"There, there!" said he. "Forget anything which I may have said. I would have done better to trust you. You may go."

I turned to the door, and my hand was upon the handle, when the Emperor called upon me to stop.

"You will see," said he, turning to the Duke of Tarentum, "that Brigadier Gerard has the special medal of honour, for I believe that if he has the thickest head he has also the stoutest heart in my army."

HOW THE BRIGADIER HELD THE KING

I believe that the last story which I told you, my friends, was about how I received at the bidding of the Emperor the cross for valour which I had, if I may be allowed to say so, so long deserved.[1] Here upon the lapel of my coat you may see the ribbon, but the medal itself I keep in a leathern pouch at home, and I never venture to take it out unless one of the modern peace generals, or some foreigner of distinction who finds himself in our little town, takes advantage of the opportunity to pay his respects to the well-known Brigadier Gerard. Then I place it upon my breast, and I give my moustache the old Marengo twist which brings a grey point into either eye. Yet with it all I fear that neither they, nor you either, my friends, will ever realize the man that I was. You know me only as a civilian—with an air and a manner, it is true—but still merely as a civilian. Had you seen me as I stood in the doorway of the inn at Alamo, on the 1st of July, in the year 1810, you would then have known what the hussar may attain to.

For a month I had lingered in that accursed village, and all on account of a lance thrust in my ankle, which made it impossible for me to put my foot to the ground. There were three of us at first: old Bouvet, of the Hussars of Bercheny, Jacques Regnier, of the Cuirassiers, and a funny little voltigeur captain whose name I forget; but they all got well and hurried on to the front, while I sat gnawing my fingers and tearing my hair, and even, I must confess, weeping from time to time as I thought of my Hussars of Conflans, and the deplorable condition in which they must find themselves when deprived of their colonel. I was not a chief of brigade yet, you understand, although I already carried myself like one, but I was the youngest colonel in the whole service, and my regiment was wife and children to me. It went to my heart that they should be so bereaved. It is true that Villaret, the senior major, was an excellent soldier; but still, even among the best there are degrees of merit.

Ah, that happy July day of which I speak, when first I limped to the door and stood in the golden Spanish sunshine! It was but the evening before that I had heard from the regiment. They were at Pastores, on the other side of the mountains, face to face with the English—not forty miles from me by road. But how was I to get to them? The same thrust which had pierced my ankle had slain my charger. I took advice both from Gomez, the landlord, and from an old priest who had slept that night in the inn, but neither of them could do more than assure me that there was not so much as a colt left upon the whole country side. The landlord would not hear of my crossing the mountains without an escort, for he assured me that El Cuchillo, the Spanish guerilla chief, was out that way with his band, and that it meant a death by torture to fall into his hands. The old priest observed, however, that he did not think a French hussar would be deterred by that, and if I had had any doubts, they would of course have been decided by his remark.

But a horse! How was I to get one? I was standing in the doorway, plotting and planning, when I heard the clink of shoes, and, looking up, I saw a great bearded man, with a blue cloak frogged across in military fashion, coming towards me. He was riding a big black horse with one white stocking on his near fore-leg.

"Halloa, comrade!" said I, as he came up to me.

"Halloa! "said he.

"I am Colonel Gerard, of the Hussars," said I. "I have lain here wounded for a month, and I am now ready to rejoin my regiment at Pastores."

"I am Monsieur Vidal, of the commissariat," he answered, "and I am myself upon my way to Pastores. I should be glad to have your company, colonel, for I hear that the mountains are far from safe."

"Alas," said I, "I have no horse. But if you will sell me yours, I will promise that an escort of hussars shall be sent back for you."

He would not hear of it, and it was in vain that the landlord told him dreadful stories of the doings of El Cuchillo, and that I pointed out the duty which he owed to the army and to the country. He would not even argue, but called loudly for a cup of wine. I craftily asked him to dismount and to drink with me, but he must have seen something in my face for he shook his head; and then, as I approached him with some thought of seizing him by the leg, he jerked his heels into his horse's flanks, and was off in a cloud of dust.

My faith! it was enough to make a man mad to see this fellow riding away so gaily to join his beef-barrels, and his brandy-casks, and then to think of my five hundred beautiful hussars without their leader. I was gazing after him with bitter thoughts in my mind, when who should touch me on the elbow but the little priest whom I have mentioned.

"It is I who can help you," he said. "I am myself travelling south."

I put my arms about him and, as my ankle gave way at the same moment, we nearly rolled upon the ground together.

"Get me to Pastores," I cried, "and you shall have a rosary of golden beads." I had taken one from the Convent of Spiritu Santo. It shows how necessary it is to take what you can when you are upon a campaign, and how the most unlikely things may become useful.

"I will take you," he said, in very excellent French, "not because I hope for any reward, but because it is my way always to do what I can to serve my fellow-man, and that is why I am so beloved wherever I go."

With that he led me down the village to an old cow-house, in which we found a tumble-down sort of diligence, such as they used to run early in this century, between some of our remote villages. There were three old mules, too, none of which were strong enough to carry a man, but together they might draw the coach. The sight of their gaunt ribs and spavined legs gave me more delight than the whole two hundred and twenty hunters of the Emperor which I have seen in their stalls at Fontainebleau. In ten minutes the owner was harnessing them into the coach, with no very good will, however, for he was in mortal dread of this terrible Cuchillo. It was only by promising him riches in this world, while the priest threatened him with perdition in the next, that we at last got him safely upon the box with the reins between his fingers. Then he was in such a hurry to get off, out of fear lest we should find ourselves in the dark in the passes, that he hardly gave me time to renew my vows to the innkeeper's daughter. I cannot at this moment recall her name, but we wept together as we parted, and I can remember that she was a very beautiful woman. You will understand, my friends, that when a man like me, who has fought the men and kissed the women in fourteen separate kingdoms, gives a word of praise to the one or the other, it has a little meaning of its own.

The little priest had seemed a trifle grave when we kissed good-bye, but he soon proved himself the best of companions in the diligence. All the way he amused me with tales of his little parish up in the mountains, and I in my turn told him stories about my camp; but, my faith, I had to pick my steps, for when I said a word too much he would fidget in his seat and his face would show the pain that I had given him. And of course it is not the act of a gentleman to talk in anything but a proper manner to a religious man, though, with all the care in the world, one's words may get out of hand sometimes.

He had come from the North of Spain, as he told me, and was going to see his mother in a village of Estremadura, and as he spoke about her little peasant home, and her joy in seeing him, it brought my own mother so vividly to my thought that the tears started to my eyes. In his simplicity he showed me the little gifts which he was taking to her, and so kindly was his manner that I could readily believe him when he said that he was loved wherever he went. He examined my own uniform with as much curiosity as a child, admiring the plume of my busby, and passing his fingers through the sable with which my dolman was trimmed. He drew my sword, too, and then when I told him how many men I had cut down with it, and set my finger on the notch made by the shoulder-bone of the Russian Emperor's aide-de-camp, he shuddered and placed the weapon under the leathern cushion, declaring that it made him sick to look at it.

Well, we had been rolling and creaking on our way whilst this talk had been going forward, and as we reached the base of the mountains we could hear the rumbling of cannon far away upon the right. This came from Massena, who was, as I knew, besieging Ciudad Rodrigo. There was nothing I should have wished better than to have gone straight to him, for if, as some said, he had Jewish blood in his veins, he was the best Jew that I have heard of since Joshua's time. If you are in sight of his beaky nose and bold, black eyes, you are not likely to miss much of what is going on. Still, a siege is always a poor sort of a pick-and-shovel business, and there were better prospects with my hussars in front of the English. Every mile that passed, my heart grew lighter and lighter, until I found myself shouting and singing like a young ensign fresh from Saint Cyr, just to think of seeing all my fine horses and my gallant fellows once more.

As we penetrated the mountains the road grew rougher and the pass more savage. At first we had met a few muleteers, but now the whole country seemed deserted, which is not to be wondered at when you think that the French, the English, and the guerillas had each in turn had command over it. So bleak and wild was it, one great brown wrinkled cliff succeeding another, and the pass growing narrower and narrower, that I ceased to look out, but sat in silence, thinking of this and that, of women whom I had loved and of horses which I had handled. I was suddenly brought back from my dreams, however, by observing the difficulties of my companion, who was trying with a sort of brad-awl, which he had drawn out, to bore a hole through the leathern strap which held up his water-flask. As he worked with twitching fingers the strap escaped his grasp, and the wooden bottle fell at my feet. I stooped to pick it up, and as I did so the priest silently leaped upon my shoulders and drove his brad-awl into my eye!

My friends, I am, as you know, a man steeled to face every danger. When one has served from the affair of Zurich to that last fatal day of Waterloo, and has had the special medal, which I keep at home in a leathern pouch, one can afford to confess when one is frightened. It may console some of you, when your own nerves play you tricks, to remember that you have heard even me, Brigadier Gerard, say that I have been scared. And besides my terror at this horrible attack, and the maddening pain of my wound, there was a sudden feeling of loathing such as you might feel were some filthy tarantula to strike its fangs into you.

I clutched the creature in both hands, and, hurling him on to the floor of the coach, I stamped on him with my heavy boots. He had drawn a pistol from the front of his soutane, but I kicked it out of his hand, and again I fell with my knees upon his chest. Then, for the first time, he screamed horribly, while I, half blinded, felt about for the sword which he had so cunningly concealed. My hand had just lighted upon it, and I was dashing the blood from my face to see where he lay that I might transfix him, when the whole coach turned partly over upon its side, and my weapon was jerked out of my grasp by the shock. Before I could recover myself the door was burst open, and I was dragged by the heels on to the road. But even as I was torn out on to the flint stones and realized that thirty ruffians were standing around me, I was filled with joy, for my pelisse had been pulled over my head in the struggle and was covering one of my eyes, and it was with my wounded eye that I was seeing this gang of brigands. You see for yourself by this pucker and scar how the thin blade passed between socket and ball, but it was only at that moment, when I was dragged from the coach, that I understood that my sight was not gone for ever. The creature's intention doubtless, was to drive it through into my brain, and indeed he loosened some portion of the inner bone of my head, so that I afterwards had more trouble from that wound than from any one of the seventeen which I have received.

They dragged me out, these sons of dogs, with curses and execrations, beating me with their fists and kicking me as I lay upon the ground. I had frequently observed that the mountaineers wore cloth swathed round their feet, but never did I imagine that I should have so much cause to be thankful for it. Presently, seeing the blood upon my head, and that I lay quiet, they thought that I was unconscious, whereas I was storing every ugly face among them into my memory, so that I might see them all safely hanged if ever my chance came round. Brawny rascals they were, with yellow handkerchiefs round their heads, and great red sashes stuffed with weapons. They had rolled two rocks across the path, where it took a sharp turn, and it was these which had torn off one of the wheels of the coach and upset us. As to this reptile, who had acted the priest so cleverly and had told me so much of his parish and his mother, he, of course, had known where the ambuscade was laid, and had attempted to put me beyond all resistance at the moment when we reached it.

I cannot tell you how frantic their rage was when they drew him out of the coach and saw the state to which I had reduced him. If he had not got all his deserts, he had, at least, something as a souvenir of his meeting with Etienne Gerard, for his legs dangled aimlessly about, and though the upper part of his body was convulsed with rage and pain, he sat straight down upon his feet when they tried to set him upright. But all the time his two little black eyes, which had seemed so kindly and so innocent in the coach, were glaring at me like a wounded cat, and he spat, and spat, and spat in my direction. My faith! when the wretches jerked me on to my feet again, and when I was dragged off up one of the mountain paths, I understood that a time was coming when I was to need all my courage and resource. My enemy was carried upon the shoulders of two men behind me, and I could hear his hissing and his reviling, first in one ear and then in the other, as I was hurried up the winding track.

I suppose that it must have been for an hour that we ascended, and what with my wounded ankle and the pain from my eye, and the fear lest this wound should have spoiled my appearance, I have made no journey to which I look back with less pleasure. I have never been a good climber at any time, but it is astonishing what you can do, even with a stiff ankle, when you have a copper-coloured brigand at each elbow and a nine-inch blade within touch of your whiskers.

We came at last to a place where the path wound over a ridge, and descended upon the other side through thick pine trees into a valley which opened to the south. In time of peace I have little doubt that the villains were all smugglers, and that these were the secret paths by which they crossed the Portuguese frontier. There were many mule tracks, and once I was surprised to see the marks of a large horse where a stream had softened the track. These were explained when, on reaching a place where there was a clearing in the fir wood, I saw the animal itself haltered to a fallen tree. My eyes had hardly rested upon it, when I recognised the great black limbs and the white near fore-leg. It was the very horse which I had begged for in the morning.

What, then, had become of Commissariat Vidal? Was it possible that there was another Frenchman in as perilous a plight as myself? The thought had hardly entered my head when our party stopped and one of them uttered a peculiar cry. It was answered from among the brambles which lined the base of a cliff at one side of a clearing, and an instant later ten or a dozen more brigands came out from amongst them, and the two parties greeted each other. The new-comers surrounded my friend of the brad-awl with cries of grief and sympathy, and then turning upon me they brandished their knives and howled at me like the gang of assassins that they were. So frantic were their gestures that I was convinced that my end had come, and was just bracing myself to meet it in a manner which should be worthy of my past reputation, when one of them gave an order and I was dragged roughly across the little glade to the brambles from which this new band had emerged.

A narrow pathway led through them to a deep grotto in the side of the cliff. The sun was already setting outside, and in the cave itself it would have been quite dark but for a pair of torches which blazed from a socket on either side. Between them there was sitting at a rude table a very singular-looking person, whom I saw instantly, from the respect with which the others addressed him, could be none other than the brigand chief who had received, on account of his dreadful character, the sinister name of El Cuchillo.

The man whom I had injured had been carried in and placed upon the top of a barrel, his helpless legs dangling about in front of him, and his cat's eyes still darting glances of hatred at me. I understood from the snatches of talk which I could follow between the chief and him, that he was the lieutenant of the band, and that part of his duties was to lie in wait with his smooth tongue and his peaceful garb for travellers like myself. When I thought of how many gallant officers may have been lured to their death by this monster of hypocrisy, it gave me a glow of pleasure to think that I had brought his villainies to an end—though I feared that it would be at the price of a life which neither the Emperor nor the army could well spare.

As the injured man, still supported upon the barrel by two comrades, was explaining in Spanish all that had befallen him, I was held by several of the villains in front of the table at which the chief was seated, and had an excellent opportunity of observing him. I have seldom seen any man who was less like my idea of a brigand, and especially of a brigand with such a reputation that in a land of cruelty he had earned so dark a nickname. His face was bluff and broad and bland, with ruddy cheeks and comfortable little tufts of side-whiskers, which gave him the appearance of a well-to-do grocer of the Rue St Antoine. He had not any of those flaring sashes or gleaming weapons which distinguished his followers, but on the contrary he wore a good broad-cloth coat like a respectable father of a family, and save for his brown leggings there was nothing to indicate a life among the mountains. His surroundings, too, corresponded with himself, and beside his snuff-box upon the table there stood a great brown book, which looked like a commercial ledger. Many other books were ranged along a plank between two powder casks, and there was a great litter of papers, some of which had verses scribbled upon them. All this I took in while he, leaning indolently back in his chair, was listening to the report of his lieutenant. Having heard everything, he ordered the cripple to be carried out again, and I was left with my three guards, waiting to hear my fate. He took up his pen, and, tapping his forehead with the handle of it, he pursed up his lips and looked out of the corner of his eyes at the roof of the grotto.

"I suppose," said he, at last, speaking very excellent French, "that you are not able to suggest a rhyme for the word Covilha."

I answered him that my acquaintance with the Spanish language was so limited that I was unable to oblige him.

"It is a rich language," said he, "but less prolific in rhymes than either the German or the English. That is why our best work has been done in blank verse, a form of composition which, though hardly known in your literature, is capable of reaching great heights. But I fear that such subjects are somewhat outside the range of a hussar."

I was about to answer that if they were good enough for a guerilla, they could not be too much for the light cavalry, but he was already stooping over his half-finished verse. Presently he threw down the pen with an exclamation of satisfaction, and declaimed a few lines which drew a cry of approval from the three ruffians who held me. His broad face blushed like a young girl who receives her first compliment.

"The critics are in my favour, it appears," said he; "we amuse ourselves in our long evenings by singing our own ballads, you understand. I have some little facility in that direction, and I do not at all despair of seeing some of my poor efforts in print before long, and with 'Madrid' upon the title page, too. But we must get back to business. May I ask what your name is?"

"Etienne Gerard."

"Rank?"

"Colonel."

"Corps?"

"The Third Hussars of Conflans."

"You are young for a colonel."

"My career has been an eventful one."

"Tut, that makes it the sadder," said he, with his bland smile.

I made no answer to that, but I tried to show him by my bearing that I was ready for the worst which could befall me.

"By the way, I rather fancy that we have had some of your corps here," said he, turning over the pages of his big brown register. "We endeavour to keep a record of our operations. Here is a heading under June 24th. Have you not a young officer named Soubiron, a tall, slight youth with light hair?"

"Certainly."

"I see that we buried him upon that date."

"Poor lad!" I cried. "And how did he die?"

"We buried him."

"But before you buried him?"

"You misunderstand me, Colonel. He was not dead before we buried him."

"You buried him alive!"

For a moment I was too stunned to act. Then I hurled myself upon the man, as he sat with that placid smile of his upon his lips, and I would have torn his throat out had the three wretches not dragged me away from him. Again and again I made for him, panting and cursing, shaking off this man and that, straining and wrenching, but never quite free. At last, with my jacket torn nearly off my back and blood dripping from my wrists, I was hauled backwards in the bight of a rope and cords passed round my ankles and my arms.

"You sleek hound," I cried. "If ever I have you at my sword's point, I will teach you to maltreat one of my lads. You will find, you blood-thirsty beast, that my Emperor has long arms, and though you lie here like a rat in its hole, the time will come when he will tear you out of it, and you and your vermin will perish together."

My faith, I have a rough side to my tongue, and there was not a hard word that I had learned in fourteen campaigns which I did not let fly at him, but he sat with the handle of his pen tapping against his forehead and his eyes squinting up at the roof as if he had conceived the idea of some new stanza. It was this occupation of his which showed me how I might get my point into him.

"You spawn!" said I; "you think that you are safe here, but your life may be as short as that of your absurd verses, and God knows it could not be shorter than that."

Ah, you should have seen him bound from his chair when I said the words. This vile monster, who dispensed death and torture as a grocer serves out his figs, had one raw nerve then which I could prod at pleasure. His face grew livid, and those little bourgeois side-whiskers quivered and thrilled with passion.

"Very good, Colonel. You have said enough," he cried, in a choking voice. "You say that you have had a very distinguished career. I promise you also a very distinguished ending. Colonel Etienne Gerard of the Third Hussars shall have a death of his own."

"And I only beg," said I, "that you will not commemorate it in verse." I had one or two little ironies to utter, but he cut me short by a furious gesture which caused my three guards to drag me from the cave.

Our interview, which I have told you as nearly as I can remember it, must have lasted some time, for it was quite dark when we came out, and the moon was shining very clearly in the heavens. The brigands had lighted a great fire of the dried branches of the fir trees; not, of course, for warmth, since the night was already very sultry, but to cook their evening meal. A huge copper pot hung over the blaze, and the rascals were lying all round in the yellow glare, so that the scene looked like one of those pictures which Junot stole out of Madrid. There are some soldiers who profess to care nothing for art and the like, but I have always been drawn towards it myself, in which respect I show my good taste and my breeding. I remember, for example, that when Lefebvre was selling the plunder after the fall of Danzig, I bought a very fine picture, called "Nymphs Surprised in a Wood," and I carried it with me through two campaigns, until my charger had the misfortune to put his hoof through it.

I only tell you this, however, to show you that I was never a mere rough soldier like Rapp or Ney. As I lay in that brigand's camp, I had little time or inclination to think about such matters. They had thrown me down under a tree, the three villains squatting round and smoking their cigarettes within hands' touch of me. What to do I could not imagine. In my whole career I do not suppose that I have ten times been in as hopeless a situation. "But courage," thought I. "Courage, my brave boy! You were not made a Colonel of Hussars at twenty-eight because you could dance a cotillon. You are a picked man, Etienne; a man who has come through more than two hundred affairs, and this little one is surely not going to be the last." I began eagerly to glance about for some chance of escape, and as I did so I saw something which filled me with great astonishment.

I have already told you that a large fire was burning in the centre of the glade. What with its glare, and what with the moonlight, everything was as clear as possible. On the other side of the glade there was a single tall fir tree which attracted my attention because its trunk and lower branches were discoloured, as if a large fire had recently been lit underneath it. A clump of bushes grew in front of it which concealed the base. Well, as I looked towards it, I was surprised to see projecting above the bush, and fastened apparently to the tree, a pair of fine riding boots with the toes upwards. At first I thought that they were tied there, but as I looked harder I saw that they were secured by a great nail which was hammered through the foot of each. And then, suddenly, with a thrill of horror, I understood that these were not empty boots; and moving my head a little to the right, I was able to see who it was that had been fastened there, and why a fire had been lit beneath the tree. It is not pleasant to speak or to think of horrors, my friends, and I do not wish to give any of you bad dreams to-night — but I cannot take you among the Spanish guerillas without showing you what kind of men they were, and the sort of warfare that they waged. I will only say that I understood why Monsieur Vidal's horse was waiting masterless in the grove, and that I hoped he had met this terrible fate with sprightliness and courage, as a good Frenchman ought.

It was not a very cheering sight for me, as you can imagine. When I had been with their chief in the grotto I had been so carried away by my rage at the cruel death of young Soubiron, who was one of the brightest lads who ever threw his thigh over a charger, that I had never given a thought to my own position. Perhaps it would have been more politic had I spoken the ruffian fair, but it was too late now. The cork was drawn, and I must drain the wine. Besides, if the harmless commissariat man were put to such a death, what hope was there for me, who had snapped the spine of their lieutenant. No, I was doomed in any case, so it was as well perhaps that I should have put the best face on the matter. This beast could bear witness that Etienne Gerard had died as he had lived, and that one prisoner at least had not quailed before him. I lay there thinking of the various girls who would mourn for me, and of my dear old mother, and of the deplorable loss which I should be both to my regiment and to the Emperor, and I am not ashamed to confess to you that I shed tears as I thought of the general consternation which my premature end would give rise to.

But all the time I was taking the very keenest notice of everything which might possibly help me. I am not a man who would lie like a sick horse waiting for the farrier sergeant and the pole-axe. First I would give a little tug at my ankle cords, and then another at those which were round my wrists, and all the time that I was trying to loosen them I was peering round to see if I could find something which was in my favour. There was one thing which was very evident. A hussar is but half formed without a horse, and there was my other half quietly grazing within thirty yards of me. Then I observed yet another thing. The path by which we had come over the mountains was so steep that a horse could only be led across it slowly and with difficulty, but in the other direction the ground appeared to be more open, and to lead straight down into a gently sloping valley. Had I but my feet in yonder stirrups and my sabre in my hand, a single bold dash might take me out of the power of these vermin of the rocks.

I was still thinking it over and straining with my wrists and my ankles, when their chief came out from his grotto, and after some talk with his lieutenant, who lay groaning near the fire, they both nodded their heads and looked across at me. He then said some few words to the band, who clapped their hands and laughed uproariously. Things looked ominous, and I was delighted to feel that my hands were so far free that I could easily slip them through the cords if I wished. But with my ankles, I feared that I could do nothing, for when I strained it brought such pain into my lance wound, that I had to gnaw my moustache to keep from crying out. I could only lie still, half free and half bound, and see what turn things were likely to take.

For a little I could not make out what they were after. One of the rascals climbed up a well-grown fir-tree upon one side of the glade, and tied a rope round the top of the trunk. He then fastened another rope in the same fashion to a similar tree upon the other side. The two loose ends were now dangling down, and I waited with some curiosity, and just a little trepidation also, to see what they would do next. The whole band pulled upon one of the ropes until they had bent the strong young tree down into a semicircle, and they then fastened it to a stump, so as to hold it so. When they had bent the other tree down in a similar fashion, the two summits were within a few feet of each other, though, as you understand, they would each spring back into their original position the instant that they were released. I already saw the diabolical plan which these miscreants had formed.

"I presume that you are a strong man, Colonel," said the chief, coming towards me with his hateful smile.

"If you will have the kindness to loosen these cords," I answered, "I will show you how strong I am."

"We were all interested to see whether you were as strong as these two young saplings," said he. "It is our intention, you see, to tie one end of each rope round your ankles and then to let the trees go. If you are stronger than the trees, then, of course, no harm would be done; if, on the other hand, the trees are stronger than you, why, in that case, Colonel, we may have a souvenir of you upon each side of our little glade."

He laughed as he spoke, and at the sight of it the whole forty of them laughed also. Even now if I am in my darker humour, or if I have a touch of my old Lithuanian ague, I see in my sleep that ring of dark savage faces, with their cruel eyes, and the firelight flashing upon their strong white teeth.

It is astonishing—and I have heard many make the same remark—how acute one's senses become at such a crisis as this. I am convinced that at no moment is one living so vividly, so acutely, as at the instant when a violent and foreseen death overtakes one. I could smell the resinous fagots, I could see every twig upon the ground, I could hear every rustle of the branches, as I have never smelled or seen or heard save at such times of danger. And so it was that long before anyone else, before even the time when the chief had addressed me, I had heard a low, monotonous sound, far away indeed, and yet coming nearer at every instant. At first it was but a murmur, a rumble, but by the time he had finished speaking, while the assassins were untying my ankles in order to lead me to the scene of my murder, I heard, as plainly as ever I heard anything in my life, the clinking of horseshoes and the jingling of bridle chains, with the clank of sabres against stirrup-irons. Is it likely that I, who had lived with the light cavalry since the first hair shaded my lip, would mistake the sound of troopers on the march?

"Help, comrades, help!" I shrieked, and though they struck me across the mouth and tried to drag me up to the trees I kept on yelling. "Help me, my brave boys! Help me, my children! They are murdering your colonel!"

For the moment my wounds and my troubles had brought on a delirium, and I looked for nothing less than my five hundred hussars, kettle-drums and all, to appear at the opening of the glade.

But that which really appeared was very different to anything which I had conceived. Into the clear space there came galloping a fine young man upon a most beautiful roan horse. He was fresh-faced and pleasant looking, with the most debonair bearing in the world and the most gallant way of carrying himself—a way which reminded me somewhat of my own. He wore a singular coat which had once been red all over, but which was now stained to the colour of a withered oak leaf wherever the weather could reach it. His shoulder-straps, however, were of golden lace, and he had a bright metal helmet upon his head, with a coquettish white plume upon one side of its crest. He trotted his horse up the glade, while behind him rode four cavaliers in the same dress —all clean-shaven, with round, comely faces, looking to me more like monks than dragoons. At a short, gruff order they halted with a rattle of arms, while their leader cantered forward, the fire beating upon his eager face and the beautiful head of his charger. I knew, of course, by the strange coats that they were English. It was the first sight that I had ever had of them, but from their stout bearing and their masterful way I could see at a glance that what I had always been told was true, and that they were excellent people to fight against.

"Well, well, well!" cried the young officer, in sufficiently bad French, "what game are you up to here? Who was that who was yelling for help, and what are you trying to do to him?"

It was at that moment that I learned to bless those months which Obriant, the descendant of the Irish kings, had spent in teaching me the tongue of the English. My ankles had just been freed, so that I had only to slip my hands out of the cords, and with a single rush I had flown across, picked up my sabre where it lay by the fire, and hurled myself on to the saddle of poor Vidal's horse. Yes, for all my wounded ankle, I never put foot to stirrup, but was in the seat in a single bound. I tore the halter from the tree, and before these villains could so much as snap a pistol at me I was beside the English officer.

"I surrender to you, sir," I cried; though I daresay my English was not very much better than his French. "If you will look at that tree to the left you will see what these villains do to the honourable gentlemen who fall into their hands."

The fire had flared up at that moment, and there was poor Vidal exposed before them, as horrible an object as one could see in a nightmare. "Godam!" cried the officer, and "Godam!" cried each of the four troopers, which is the same as with us when we cry "Mon Dieu!" Out rasped the five swords, and the four men closed up. One, who wore a sergeant's chevrons, laughed and clapped me on the shoulder.

"Fight for your skin, froggy," said he.

Ah, it was so fine to have a horse between my thighs and weapon in my grip. I waved it above my head and shouted in my exultation. The chief had come forward with that odious smiling face of his.

"Your excellency will observe that this Frenchman is our prisoner," said he.

"You are a rascally robber," said the Englishman, shaking his sword at him. "It is a disgrace to us to have such allies. By my faith, if Lord Wellington were of my mind we would swing you up on the nearest tree."

"But my prisoner?" said the brigand, in his suave voice.

"He shall come with us to the British camp."

"Just a word in your ear before you take him."

He approached the young officer, and then, turning as quick as a flash, he fired his pistol in my face. The bullet scored its way through my hair and burst a hole on each side of my busby. Seeing that he had missed me, he raised the pistol and was about to hurl it at me when the English sergeant, with a single back-handed cut, nearly severed his head from his body. His blood had not reached the ground, nor the last curse died on his lips, before the whole horde was upon us, but with a dozen bounds and as many slashes we were all safely out of the glade, and galloping down the winding track which led to the valley.

It was not until we had left the ravine far behind us and were right out in the open fields that we ventured to halt, and to see what injuries we had sustained. For me, wounded and weary as I was, my heart was beating proudly, and my chest was nearly bursting my tunic to think that I, Etienne Gerard, had left this gang of murderers so much by which to remember me. My faith, they would think twice before they ventured to lay hands upon one of the Third Hussars. So carried away was I that I made a small oration to these brave Englishmen, and told them who it was that they had helped to rescue. I would have spoken of glory also, and of the sympathies of brave men, but the officer cut me short.

"That's all right," said he. "Any injuries, Sergeant?"

"Trooper Jones's horse hit with a pistol bullet on the fetlock."

"Trooper Jones to go with us. Sergeant Halliday, with troopers Harvey and Smith, to keep to the right until they touch the vedettes of the German Hussars."

So these three jingled away together, while the officer and I, followed at some distance by the trooper whose horse had been wounded, rode straight down in the direction of the English camp. Very soon we had opened our hearts, for we each liked the look of the other from the beginning. He was of the nobility, this brave lad, and he had been sent out scouting by Lord Wellington to see if there were any signs of our advancing through the mountains. It is one advantage of a wandering life like mine, that you learn to pick up those bits of knowledge which distinguish the man of the world. I have, for example, hardly ever met a Frenchman who could repeat an English title correctly. If I had not travelled I should not be able to say with confidence that this young man's real name was Milor the Hon. Sir Russell, Bart., this last being an honourable distinction, so that it was as the Bart that I usually addressed him, just as in Spanish one might say "the Don."

As we rode beneath the moonlight in the lovely Spanish night, we spoke our minds to each other, as if we were brothers. We were both of an age, you see, both of the light cavalry also (the Sixteenth Light Dragoons was his regiment), and both with the same hopes and ambitions. Never have I learned to know a man so quickly as I did the Bart. He gave me the name of a girl whom he had loved at a garden called Vauxhall, and, for my own part, I spoke to him of little Coralie, of the Opera. He took a lock of hair from his bosom, and I a garter. Then we nearly quarrelled over hussar and dragoon, for he was absurdly proud of his regiment, and you should have seen him curl his lip and clap his hand to his hilt when I said that I hoped it might never be its misfortune to come in the way of the Third. Finally, he began to speak about what the English call sport, and he told such stories of the money which he had lost over which of two cocks could kill the other, or which of two men could strike the other the most in a fight for a prize, that I was filled with astonishment. He was ready to bet upon anything in the most wonderful manner, and when I chanced to see a shooting star he was anxious to bet that he would see more than me, twenty-five francs a star, and it was only when I explained that my purse was in the hands of the brigands that he would give over the idea.

Well, we chatted away in this very amiable fashion until the day began to break, when suddenly we heard a great volley of musketry from somewhere in the front of us. It was very rocky and broken ground, and I thought, although I could see nothing, that a general engagement had broken out. The Bart laughed at my idea, however, and explained that the sound came from the English camp, where every man emptied his piece each morning so as to make sure of having a dry priming.

"In another mile we shall be up with the outposts," said he.

I glanced round at this, and I perceived that we had trotted along at so good a pace during the time that we were keeping up our pleasant chat that the dragoon with the lame horse was altogether out of sight. I looked on every side, but in the whole of that vast rocky valley there was no one save only the Bart and I — both of us armed, you understand, and both of us well mounted. I began to ask myself whether after all it was quite necessary that I should ride that mile which would bring me to the British outposts.

Now, I wish to be very clear with you on this point, my friends, for I would not have you think that I was acting dishonourably or ungratefully to the man who had helped me away from the brigands. You must remember that of all duties the strongest is that which a commanding officer owes to his men. You must also bear in mind that war is a game which is played under fixed rules, and when these rules are broken one must at once claim the forfeit. If, for example, I had given a parole, then I should have been an infamous wretch had I dreamed of escaping. But no parole had been asked of me. Out of over-confidence, and the chance of the lame horse dropping behind, the Bart had permitted me to get up on equal terms with him. Had it been I who had taken him, I should have used him as courteously as he had me, but, at the same time, I should have respected his enterprise so far as to have deprived him of his sword, and seen that I had at least one guard beside myself. I reined up my horse and explained this to him, asking him at the same time whether he saw any breach of honour in my leaving him.

He thought about it, and several times repeated that which the English say when they mean "Mon Dieu!"

"You would give me the slip, would you?" said he.

"If you can give no reason against it."

"The only reason that I can think of," said the Bart, "is that I should instantly cut your head off if you were to attempt it."

"Two can play at that game, my dear Bart," said I.

"Then we'll see who can play at it best," he cried, pulling out his sword.

I had drawn mine also, but I was quite determined not to hurt this admirable young man who had been my benefactor.

"Consider," said I, "you say that I am your prisoner. I might with equal reason say that you are mine. We are alone here, and though I have no doubt that you are an excellent swordsman, you can hardly hope to hold your own against the best blade in the six light cavalry brigades."

His answer was a cut at my head. I parried and shore off half of his white plume. He thrust at my breast. I turned his point and cut away the other half of his cockade.

"Curse your monkey tricks!" he cried, as I wheeled my horse away from him.

"Why should you strike at me?" said I. "You see that I will not strike back."

"That's all very well," said he; "but you've got to come along with me to the camp."

"I shall never see the camp," said I.

"I'll lay you nine to four you do," he cried, as he made at me, sword in hand.

But those words of his put something new into my head. Could we not decide the matter in some better way than by fighting? The Bart was placing me in such a position that I should have to hurt him, or he would certainly hurt me. I avoided his rush, though his sword point was within an inch of my neck.

"I have a proposal," I cried. "We shall throw dice as to which is the prisoner of the other."

He smiled at this. It appealed to his love of sport.

"Where are your dice?" he cried.

"I have none."

"Nor I. But I have cards."

"Cards let it be," said I.

"And the game?"

"I leave it to you."

"Écarté, then — the best of three."

I could not help smiling as I agreed, for I do not suppose that there were three men in France who were my masters at the game. I told the Bart as much as we dismounted. He smiled also as he listened.

"I was counted the best player at Watier's," said he. "With even luck you deserve to get off if you beat me."

So we tethered our two horses and sat down one on either side of a great flat rock. The Bart took a pack of cards out of his tunic, and I had only to see him shuffle to convince me that I had no novice to deal with. We cut, and the deal fell to him.

My faith, it was a stake worth playing for. He wished to add a hundred gold pieces a game, but what was money when the fate of Colonel Etienne Gerard hung upon the cards? I felt as though all those who had reason to be interested in the game: my mother, my hussars, the Sixth Corps d'Armée, Ney, Massena, even the Emperor himself, were forming a ring round us in that desolate valley. Heavens, what a blow to one and all of them should the cards go against me! But I was confident, for my écarté play was as famous as my swordsmanship, and save old Bouvet of the Hussars of Bercheny, who won seventy-six out of one hundred and fifty games off me, I have always had the best of a series.

The first game I won right off, though I must confess that the cards were with me, and that my adversary could have done no more. In the second, I never played better and saved a trick by a finesse, but the Bart voled me once, marked the king, and ran out in the second hand. My faith, we were so excited that he laid his helmet down beside him and I my busby.

"I'll lay my roan mare against your black horse," said he.

"Done!" said I.

"Sword against sword."

"Done!" said I.

"Saddle, bridle, and stirrups!" he cried.

"Done!" I shouted.

I had caught this spirit of sport from him. I would have laid my hussars against his dragoons had they been ours to pledge.

And then began the game of games. Oh, he played, this Englishman—he played in a way that was worthy of such a stake. But I, my friends, I was superb! Of the five which I had to make to win, I gained three on the first hand. The Bart bit his moustache and drummed his hands, while I already felt myself at the head of my dear little rascals. On the second, I turned the king, but lost two tricks—and my score was four to his two. When I saw my next hand I could not but give a cry of delight. "If I cannot gain my freedom on this," thought I, "I deserve to remain for ever in chains."

Give me the cards, landlord, and I will lay them out on the table for you.

Here was my hand: knave and ace of clubs, queen and knave of diamonds, and king of hearts. Clubs were trumps, mark you, and I had but one point between me and freedom. As you may think, I declined his proposal. He knew that it was the crisis and he undid his tunic. I threw my dolman on the ground. He led the ten of spades. I took it with my ace of trumps. One point in my favour. The correct play was to clear the trumps, and I led the knave. Down came the queen upon it, and the game was equal. He led the eight of spades, and I could only discard my queen of diamonds. Then came the seven of spades, and the hair stood straight up on my head. We each threw down a king at the final. He had won two points, and my beautiful hand had been mastered by his inferior one. I could have rolled on the ground as I thought of it. They used to play very good écarté at Watier's in the year '10. I say it—I, Brigadier Gerard.

The last game was now four all. This next hand must settle it one way or the other. He undid his sash, and I put away my sword belt. He was cool, this Englishman, and I tried to be so also, but the perspiration would trickle into my eyes. The deal lay with him, and I may confess to you, my friends, that my hands shook so that I could hardly pick my cards from the rock. But when I raised them, what was the first thing that my eyes rested upon. It was the king, the king, the glorious king of trumps! My mouth was open to declare it when the words were frozen upon my lips by the appearance of my comrade.

He held his cards in his hand, but his jaw had fallen, and his eyes were staring over my shoulder with the most dreadful expression of consternation and surprise. I whisked round, and I was myself amazed at what I saw.

Three men were standing quite close to us—fifteen metres at the furthest. The middle one was of a good height, and yet not too tall—about the same height, in fact, that I am myself. He was clad in a dark uniform with a small cocked hat, and some sort of white plume upon the side. But I had little thought of his dress. It was his face, his gaunt cheeks, his beak-like nose, his masterful blue eyes, his thin, firm slit of a mouth which made one feel that this was a wonderful man, a man of a million. His brows were tied into a knot, and he cast such a glance at my poor Bart from under them that one by one the cards came fluttering down from his nerveless fingers. Of the two other men, one, who had a face as brown and hard as though it had been carved out of old oak, wore a bright red coat, while the other, a fine portly man with bushy sidewhiskers, was in a blue jacket with gold facings. Some little distance behind, three orderlies were holding as many horses, and an escort of lancers was waiting in the rear.

"Heh, Crauford, what the deuce is this?" asked the thin man.

"D'you hear, sir?" cried the man with the red coat. "Lord Wellington wants to know what this means."

My poor Bart broke into an account of all that had occurred, but that rock-face never softened for an instant.

"Pretty fine, 'pon my word, General Crauford," he broke in. "The discipline of this force must be maintained, sir. Report yourself at headquarters as a prisoner."

It was dreadful to me to see the Bart mount his horse and ride off with hanging head. I could not endure it. I threw myself before this English General. I pleaded with him for my friend. I told him how I, Colonel Gerard, would witness what a dashing young officer he was. Ah, my eloquence might have melted the hardest heart; I brought tears to my own eyes, but none to his. My voice broke, and I could say no more.

"What weight do you put on your mules, sir, in the French service?" he asked. Yes, that was all this phlegmatic Englishman had to answer to these burning words of mine. That was his reply to what would have made a Frenchman weep upon my shoulder.

"What weight on a mule?" asked the man with the red coat.

"Two hundred and ten pounds," said I.

"Then you load them deucedly badly," said Lord Wellington. "Remove the prisoner to the rear."

His Lancers closed in upon me, and I — I was driven mad, as I thought that the game had been in my hands, and that I ought at that moment to be a free man. I held the cards up in front of the General.

"See, my lord!" I cried; "I played for my freedom and I won, for, as you perceive, I hold the king."

For the first time a slight smile softened his gaunt face.

"On the contrary," said he, as he mounted his horse, "it was I who won, for, as you perceive, my king holds you."

HOW THE KING HELD THE BRIGADIER

MURAT was undoubtedly an excellent cavalry officer, but he had too much swagger, which spoils many a good soldier. Lasalle, too, was a very dashing leader, but he ruined himself with wine and folly. Now I, Etienne Gerard, was always totally devoid of swagger, and at the same time I was very abstemious, except, maybe, at the end of a campaign, or when I met an old comrade-in-arms. For these reasons I might, perhaps, had it not been for a certain diffidence, have claimed to be the most valuable officer in my own branch of the Service. It is true that I never rose to be more than a chief of brigade, but then, as everyone knows, no one had a chance of rising to the top unless he had the good fortune to be with the Emperor in his early campaigns. Except Lasalle, and Lobau, and Drouet, I can hardly remember any one of the generals who had not already made his name before the Egyptian business. Even I, with all my brilliant qualities, could only attain the head of my brigade, and also the special medal of honour, which I received from the Emperor himself, and which I keep at home in a leathern pouch. But though I never rose higher than this, my qualities were very well known by those who had served with me, and also by the English. After they had captured me in the way which I described to you the other night, they kept a very good guard over me at Oporto, and I promise you that they did not give such a formidable opponent a chance of slipping through their fingers. It was on the 10th of August that I was escorted on board the transport which was to take us to England, and behold me before the end of the month in the great prison which had been built for us at Dartmoor! "L'hôtel Français, et Pension," we used to call it, for you understand that we were all brave men there, and that we did not lose our spirits because we were in adversity.

It was only those officers who refused to give their parole who were confined at Dartmoor, and most of the prisoners were seamen, or from the ranks. You ask me, perhaps, why it was that I did not give this parole, and so enjoy the same good treatment as most of my brother officers. Well, I had two reasons, and both of them were sufficiently strong.

In the first place, I had so much confidence in myself, that I was quite convinced that I could escape. In the second, my family, though of good repute, has never been wealthy, and I could not bring myself to take anything from the small income of my mother. On the other hand, it would never do for a man like me to be outshone by the bourgeois society of an English country town, or to be without the means of showing courtesies and attentions to those ladies whom I should attract. It was for these reasons that I preferred to be buried in the dreadful prison of Dartmoor. I wish now to tell you of my adventures in England, and of how far Milor Wellington's words were true when he said that his king would hold me.

And first of all I may say that if it were not that I have set off to tell you about what befell myself, I could keep you here until morning with my stories about Dartmoor itself, and about the singular things which occurred there. It was one of the very strangest places in the whole world, for there, in the middle of that great desolate waste, were herded together seven or eight thousand men—warriors you understand, men of experience and courage. Around there were a double wall and a ditch, and warders and soldiers, but, my faith! you could not coop men like that up like rabbits in a hutch! They would escape by twos and tens and twenties, and then the cannon would boom, and the search parties run, and we, who were left behind, would laugh and dance and shout "Vive l'Empereur," until the warders would turn their muskets upon us in their passion. And then we would have our little mutinies too, and up would come the infantry and the guns from Plymouth, and that would set us yelling "Vive l'Empereur" once more, as though we wished them to hear us in Paris. We had lively moments at Dartmoor, and we contrived that those who were about us should be lively also.

You must know that the prisoners there had their own Courts of Justice, in which they tried their own cases, and inflicted their own punishments. Stealing and quarrelling were punished—but most of all treachery. When I came there first there was a man, Meunier, from Rheims, who had given information of some plot to escape. Well, that night, owing to some form or other which had to be gone through, they did not take him out from among the other prisoners, and though he wept and screamed, and grovelled upon the ground, they left him there amongst the comrades whom he had betrayed. That night there was a trial with a whispered accusation and a whispered defence, a gagged prisoner, and a judge whom none could see. In the morning, when they came for their man with papers for his release, there was not as much of him left as you could put upon your thumb nail. They were ingenious people, these prisoners, and they had their own way of managing.

We officers, however, lived in a separate wing, and a very singular group of people we were. They had left us our uniforms, so that there was hardly a corps which had served under Victor, or Massena, or Ney, which was not represented there, and some had been there from the time when Junot was beaten at Vimiera. We had chasseurs in their green tunics, and hussars, like myself, and blue-coated dragoons, and white-fronted lancers, and voltigeurs, and grenadiers, and men of the artillery and engineers. But the greater part were naval officers, for the English had had the better of us upon the seas. I could never understand this until I journeyed myself from Oporto to Plymouth, when I lay for seven days upon my back, and could not have stirred had I seen the eagle of the regiment carried off before my eyes. It was in perfidious weather like this that Nelson took advantage of us.

I had no sooner got into Dartmoor than I began to plan to get out again, and you can readily believe that with wits sharpened by twelve years of warfare, it was not very long before I saw my way.

You must know, in the first place, that I had a very great advantage in having some knowledge of the English language. I learned it during the months that I spent before Danzig, from Adjutant Obriant, of the Regiment Irlandais, who was sprung from the ancient kings of the country. I was quickly able to speak it with some facility, for I do not take long to master anything to which I set my mind. In three months I could not only express my meaning, but I could use the idioms of the people. It was Obriant who taught me to say "Be jabers," just as we might say "Ma foi"; and also "The curse of Crummle!" which means "Ventre bleu!" Many a time I have seen the English smile with pleasure when they have heard me speak so much like one of themselves.

We officers were put two in a cell, which was very little to my taste, for my room-mate was a tall, silent man named Beaumont, of the Flying Artillery, who had been taken by the English cavalry at Astorga.

It is seldom I meet a man of whom I cannot make a friend, for my disposition and manners are—as you know them. But this fellow had never a smile for my jests, nor an ear for my sorrows, but would sit looking at me with his sullen eyes, until sometimes I thought that his two years of captivity had driven him crazy. Ah, how I longed that old Bouvet, or any of my comrades of the hussars was there, instead of this mummy of a man. But such as he was I had to make the best of him, and it was very evident that no escape could be made unless he were my partner in it, for what could I possibly do without his observing me? I hinted at it, therefore, and then by degrees I spoke more plainly, until it seemed to me that I had prevailed upon him to share my lot.

I tried the walls, and I tried the floor, and I tried the ceiling, but though I tapped and probed, they all appeared to be very thick and solid. The door was of iron, shutting with a spring lock, and provided with a small grating, through which a warder looked twice in every night. Within there were two beds, two stools, two washstands—nothing more. It was enough for my wants, for when had I had as much during those twelve years spent in camps? But how was I to get out? Night after night I thought of my five hundred hussars, and had dreadful nightmares, in which I fancied that the whole regiment needed shoeing, or that my horses were all bloated with green fodder, or that they were foundered from bogland, or that six squadrons were clubbed in the presence of the Emperor. Then I would awake in a cold sweat, and set to work picking and tapping at the walls once more; for I knew very well that there is no difficulty which cannot be overcome by a ready brain and pair of cunning hands.

There was a single window in our cell, which was too small to admit a child. It was further defended by a thick iron bar in the centre. It was not a very promising point of escape, as you will allow, but I became more and more convinced that our efforts must be directed towards it. To make matters worse, it only led out into the exercise yard, which was surrounded by two high walls. Still, as I said to my sullen comrade, it is time to talk of the Vistula when you are over the Rhine. I got a small piece of iron, therefore, from the fittings of my bed, and I set to work to loosen the plaster at the top and the bottom of the bar. Three hours I would work, and then leap into my bed upon the sound of the warder's step. Then another three hours and then very often another yet, for I found that Beaumont was so slow and clumsy at it that it was on myself only that I could rely. I pictured to myself my Third of Hussars waiting just outside that window, with kettledrums and standards and leopard-skin schabraques all complete. Then I would work and work like a madman, until my iron was crusted with my own blood, as if with rust. And so, night by night, I loosened that stony plaster, and hid it away in the stuffing of my pillow, until the hour came when the iron shook; and then with one good wrench it came off in my hand, and my first step had been made towards freedom.

You will ask me what better off I was, since, as I have said, a child could not have fitted through the opening. I will tell you. I had gained two things—a tool and a weapon. With the one I might loosen the stone which flanked the window. With the other I might defend myself when I had scrambled through. So now I turned my attention to that stone, and I picked and picked with the sharpened end of my bar until I had worked out the mortar all round. You understand, of course that during the day I replaced everything in its position, and that the warder was never permitted to see a speck upon the floor. At the end of three weeks I had separated the stone, and had the rapture of drawing it through, and seeing a hole left with ten stars shining through it, where there had been but four before. All was ready for us now, and I replaced the stone, smearing the edges of it round with a little fat and soot, so as to hide the cracks where the mortar should have been. In three nights the moon would be gone, and that seemed the best time for our attempt.

I had now no doubt at all about getting into the yard, but I had very considerable misgivings as to how I was to get out again. It would be too humiliating, after trying here, and trying there, to have to go back to my hole again in despair, or to be arrested by the guards outside, and thrown into those damp underground cells which are reserved for prisoners who are caught in escaping. I set to work, therefore, to plan what I should do. I have never, as you know, had the chance of showing what I could do as a general. Sometimes, after a glass or two of wine, I have found myself capable of thinking out surprising combinations, and have felt that if Napoleon had intrusted me with an army corps, things might have gone differently with him. But however that may be, there is no doubt that in the small stratagems of war, and in that quickness of invention which is so necessary for an officer of light cavalry, I could hold my own against anyone. It was now that I had need of it, and I felt sure that it would not fail me.

The inner wall which I had to scale was built of bricks, 12ft high, with a row of iron spikes, three inches apart, upon the top. The outer I had only caught a glimpse of once or twice, when the gate of the exercise yard was open. It appeared to be about the same height, and was also spiked at the top. The space between the walls was over twenty feet, and I had reason to believe that there were no sentries there, except at the gates. On the other hand, I know that there was a line of soldiers outside. Behold the little nut, my friends, which I had to open with no crackers, save these two hands.

One thing upon which I relied was the height of my comrade Beaumont. I have already said that he was a very tall man, six feet at least, and it seemed to me that if I could mount upon his shoulders, and get my hands upon the spikes, I could easily scale the wall. Could I pull my big companion up after me? That was the question, for when I set forth with a comrade, even though it be one for whom I bear no affection, nothing on earth would make me abandon him. If I climbed the wall and he could not follow me, I should be compelled to return to him. He did not seem to concern himself much about it, however, so I hoped that he had confidence in his own activity.

Then another very important matter was the choice of the sentry who should be on duty in front of my window at the time of our attempt. They were changed every two hours to insure their vigilance, but I, who watched them closely each night out of my window, knew that there was a great difference between them. There were some who were so keen that a rat could not cross the yard unseen, while others thought only of their own ease, and could sleep as soundly leaning upon a musket as if they were at home upon a feather bed. There was one especially, a fat, heavy man, who would retire into the shadow of the wall and doze so comfortably during his two hours, that I have dropped pieces of plaster from my window at his very feet, without his observing it. By good luck, this fellow's watch was due from twelve to two upon the night which we had fixed upon for our enterprise.

As the last day passed, I was so filled with nervous agitation that I could not control myself, but ran ceaselessly about my cell, like a mouse in a cage. Every moment I thought that the warder would detect the looseness of the bar, or that the sentry would observe the unmortared stone, which I could not conceal outside, as I did within. As for my companion, he sat brooding upon the end of his bed, looking at me in a sidelong fashion from time to time, and biting his nails like one who is deep in thought.

"Courage, my friend!" I cried, slapping him upon the shoulder. "You will see your guns before another month be past."

"That is very well," said he. "But whither will you fly when you get free?"

"To the coast," I answered. "All comes right for a brave man, and I shall make straight for my regiment."

"You are more likely to make straight for the underground cells, or for the Portsmouth hulks," said he.

"A soldier takes his chances," I remarked. "It is only the poltroon who reckons always upon the worst."

I raised a flush in each of his sallow cheeks at that, and I was glad of it, for it was the first sign of spirit which I had ever observed in him. For a moment he put his hand out towards his water jug, as though he would have hurled it at me, but then he shrugged his shoulders and sat in silence once more, biting his nails, and scowling down at the floor. I could not but think, as I looked at him, that perhaps I was doing the Flying Artillery a very bad service by bringing him back to them.

I never in my life have known an evening pass as slowly as that one. Towards nightfall a wind sprang up, and as the darkness deepened it blew harder and harder, until a terrible gale was whistling over the moor. As I looked out of my window I could not catch a glimpse of a star, and the black clouds were flying low across the heavens. The rain was pouring down, and what with its hissing and splashing, and the howling and screaming of the wind, it was impossible for me to hear the steps of the sentinels. "If I cannot hear them," thought I, "then it is unlikely that they can hear me"; and I waited with the utmost impatience until the time when the inspector should have come round for his nightly peep through our grating. Then having peered through the darkness, and seen nothing of the sentry, who was doubtless crouching in some corner out of the rain, I felt that the moment was come. I removed the bar, pulled out the stone, and motioned to my companion to pass through.

"After you, colonel," said he.

"Will you not go first?" I asked.

"I had rather you showed me the way."

"Come after me, then, but come silently, as you value your life."

In the darkness I could hear the fellow's teeth chattering, and I wondered whether a man ever had such a partner in such a desperate enterprise. I seized the bar, however, and mounting upon my stool, I thrust my head and shoulders into the hole. I had wriggled through as far as my waist, when my companion seized me suddenly by the knees, and yelled at the top of his voice: "Help! Help! A prisoner is escaping!"

Ah, my friends, what did I not feel at that moment! Of course, I saw in an instant the game of this vile creature. Why should he risk his skin in climbing walls when he might be sure of a free pardon from the English for having prevented the escape of one so much more distinguished than himself? I had recognised him as a poltroon and a sneak, but I had not understood the depth of baseness to which he could descend. One who has spent his life among gentlemen and men of honour does not think of such things until they happen.

The blockhead did not seem to understand that he was lost more certainly than I. I writhed back in the darkness, and seizing him by the throat I struck him twice with my iron bar. At the first blow he yelped as a little cur does when you tread upon its paw. At the second, down he fell with a groan upon the floor. Then I seated myself upon my bed, and waited resignedly for whatever punishment my gaolers might inflict upon me.

But a minute passed and yet another, with no sound save the heavy snoring breathing of the senseless wretch upon the floor. Was it possible, then, that amid the fury of the storm his warning cries had passed unheeded? At first it was but a tiny hope, another minute and it was probable, another and it was certain. There was no sound in the corridor, none in the courtyard. I wiped the cold sweat from my brow, and asked myself what I should do next.

One thing seemed certain. The man on the floor must die. If I left him I could not tell how short a time it might be before he gave the alarm. I dare not strike a light, so I felt about in the darkness until my hand came upon something wet, which I knew to be his head. I raised my iron bar, but there was something, my friends, which prevented me from bringing it down. In the heat of fight I have slain many men—men of honour too, who had done me no injury. Yet here was this wretch, a creature too foul to live, who had tried to work me so great a mischief, and yet I could not bring myself to crush his skull in. Such deeds are very well for a Spanish partida—or for that matter a sans-culotte of the Faubourg St Antoine—but not for a soldier and a gentleman like me.

However, the heavy breathing of the fellow made me hope that it might be a very long time before he recovered his senses. I gagged him therefore, and bound him with strips of blanket to the bed, so that in his weakened condition there was good reason to think that, in any case, he might not get free before the next visit of the warder. But now again I was faced with new difficulties, for you will remember that I had relied upon his height to help me over the walls. I could have sat down and shed tears of despair had not the thought of my mother and of the Emperor come to sustain me. "Courage!" said I. "If it were anyone but Etienne Gerard he would be in a bad fix now; that is a young man who is not so easily caught."

I set to work therefore upon Beaumont's sheet as well as my own, and by tearing them into strips and then plaiting them together, I made a very excellent rope. This I tied securely to the centre of my iron bar, which was a little over a foot in length. Then I slipped out into the yard, where the rain was pouring and the wind screaming louder than ever. I kept in the shadow of the prison wall, but it was as black as the ace of spades, and I could not see my own hand in front of me. Unless I walked into the sentinel I felt that I had nothing to fear from him. When I had come under the wall I threw up my bar, and to my joy it stuck the very first time between the spikes at the top. I climbed up my rope, pulled it after me, and dropped down on the other side. Then I scaled the second wall, and was sitting astride among the spikes upon the top, when I saw something twinkle in the darkness beneath me. It was the bayonet of the sentinel below, and so close was it (the second wall being rather lower than the first) that I could easily, by leaning over, have unscrewed it from its socket. There he was, humming a tune to himself, and cuddling up against the wall to keep himself warm, little thinking that a desperate man within a few feet of him was within an ace of stabbing him to the heart with his own weapon. I was already bracing myself for the spring when the fellow, with an oath, shouldered his musket, and I heard his steps squelching through the mud as he resumed his beat. I slipped down my rope, and, leaving it hanging, I ran at the top of my speed across the moor.

Heavens, how I ran! The wind buffeted my face and buzzed in my nostrils. The rain pringled upon my skin and hissed past my ears. I stumbled into holes. I tripped over bushes. I fell among brambles. I was torn and breathless and bleeding. My tongue was like leather, my feet like lead, and my heart beating like a kettle-drum. Still I ran, and I ran, and I ran.

But I had not lost my head, my friends. Everything was done with a purpose. Our fugitives always made for the coast. I was determined to go inland, and the more so as I had told Beaumont the opposite. I would fly to the north, and they would seek me in the south. Perhaps you will ask me how I could tell which was which on such a night. I answer that it was by the wind. I had observed in the prison that it came from the north, and so, as long as I kept my face to it, I was going in the right direction.

Well, I was rushing along in this fashion when, suddenly, I saw two yellow lights shining out of the darkness in front of me. I paused for a moment, uncertain what I should do. I was still in my hussar uniform, you understand, and it seemed to me that the very first thing that I should aim at was to get some dress which should not betray me. If these lights came from a cottage, it was probable enough that I might find what I wanted there. I approached therefore, feeling very sorry that I had left my iron bar behind; for I was determined to fight to the death before I should be retaken.

But very soon I found that there was no cottage there. The lights were two lamps hung upon each side of a carriage, and by their glare I saw that a broad road lay in front of me. Crouching among the bushes, I observed that there were two horses to the equipage, that a small post-boy was standing at their heads, and that one of the wheels was lying in the road beside him. I can see them now, my friends: the steaming creatures, the stunted lad with his hands to their bits, and the big, black coach all shining with the rain, and balanced upon its three wheels. As I looked, the window was lowered, and a pretty little face under a bonnet peeped out from it.

"What shall I do?" the lady cried to the post-boy, in a voice of despair. "Sir Charles is certainly lost, and I shall have to spend the night upon the moor."

"Perhaps I can be of some assistance to madame," said I, scrambling out from among the bushes into the glare of the lamps. A woman in distress is a sacred thing to me, and this one was beautiful. You must not forget that, although I was a colonel, I was only eight-and-twenty years of age.

My word, how she screamed, and how the post-boy stared! You will understand that after that long race in the darkness, with my shako broken in, my face smeared with dirt, and my uniform all stained and torn with brambles, I was not entirely the sort of gentleman whom one would choose to meet in the middle of a lonely moor. Still, after the first surprise, she soon understood that I was her very humble servant, and I could even read in her pretty eyes that my manner and bearing had not failed to produce an impression upon her.

"I am sorry to have startled you, madame," said I. "I chanced to overhear your remark, and I could not refrain from offering you my assistance." I bowed as I spoke. You know my bow, and can realize what its effect was upon the lady.

"I am much indebted to you, sir," said she. "We have had a terrible journey since we left Tavistock. Finally, one of our wheels came off, and here we are helpless in the middle of the moor. My husband, Sir Charles, has gone on to get help, and I much fear that he must have lost his way."

I was about to attempt some consolation, when I saw beside the lady a black travelling coat, faced with astrakhan, which her companion must have left behind him. It was exactly what I needed to conceal my uniform. It is true that I felt very much like a highway robber, but then, what would you have? Necessity has no law, and I was in an enemy's country.

"I presume, madame, that this is your husband's coat," I remarked. "You will, I am sure, forgive me, if I am compelled to—" I pulled it through the window as I spoke.

I could not bear to see the look of surprise and fear and disgust which came over her face.

"Oh, I have been mistaken in you!" she cried. "You came to rob me, then, and not to help me. You have the bearing of a gentleman, and yet you steal my husband's coat."

"Madame," said I, "I beg that you will not condemn me until you know everything. It is quite necessary that I should take this coat, but if you will have the goodness to tell me who it is who is fortunate enough to be your husband, I shall see that the coat is sent back to him."

Her face softened a little, though she still tried to look severe. "My husband," she answered, "is Sir Charles Meredith, and he is travelling to Dartmoor Prison, upon important Government business. I only ask you, sir, to go upon your way, and to take nothing which belongs to him."

"There is only one thing which belongs to him that I covet," said I.

"And you have taken it from the carriage," she cried.

"No," I answered. "It still remains there."

She laughed in her frank English way.

"If, instead of paying me compliments, you were to return my husband's coat—" she began.

"Madame," I answered, "what you ask is quite impossible. If you will allow me to come into the carriage I will explain to you how necessary this coat is to me."

Heavens knows into what foolishness I might have plunged myself had we not, at this instant, heard a faint hallo in the distance, which was answered by a shout from the little postboy. In the rain and the darkness I saw a lantern some distance from us, but approaching rapidly.

"I am sorry, madame, that I am forced to leave you," said I. "You can assure your husband that I shall take every care of his coat." Hurried as I was, I ventured to pause a moment to salute the lady's hand, which she snatched through the window with an admirable pretence of being offended at my presumption. Then, as the lantern was quite close to me, and the post-boy seemed inclined to interfere with my flight, I tucked my precious overcoat under my arm, and dashed off into the darkness.

And now I set myself to the task of putting as broad a stretch of moor between the prison and myself as the remaining hours of darkness would allow. Setting my face to the wind once more, I ran until I fell from exhaustion. Then, after five minutes of panting among the heather, I made another start, until again my knees gave way beneath me. I was young and hard, with muscles of steel, and a frame which had been toughened by twelve years of camp and field. Thus I was able to keep up this wild flight for another three hours, during which I still guided myself, you understand, by keeping the wind in my face. At the end of that time I calculated that I had put nearly twenty miles between the prison and myself. Day was about to break, so I crouched down among the heather upon the top of one of those small hills which abound in that country, with the intention of hiding myself until nightfall. It was no new thing for me to sleep in the wind and the rain, so, wrapping myself up in my thick warm cloak, I soon sank into a doze.

But it was not a refreshing slumber. I tossed and tumbled amid a series of vile dreams, in which everything seemed to go wrong with me. At last, I remember, I was charging an unshaken square of Hungarian Grenadiers, with a single squadron upon spent horses, just as I did at Elchingen. I stood in my stirrups to shout "Vive l'Empereur!" and as I did so, there came the answering roar from my hussars, "Vive l'Empereur!" I sprang from my rough bed, with the words still ringing in my ears, and then, as I rubbed my eyes, and wondered if I were mad, the same cry came again, five thousand voices in one long-drawn yell. I looked out from my screen of brambles, and saw in the clear light of morning the very last thing that I should have either expected or chosen.

It was Dartmoor Prison! There it stretched, grim and hideous, within a furlong of me. Had I run on for a few more minutes in the dark, I should have butted my shako against the wall. I was so taken aback at the sight, that I could scarcely realize what had happened. Then it all became clear to me, and I struck my head with my hands in my despair. The wind had veered from north to south during the night, and I, keeping my face always towards it, had run ten miles out, and ten miles in, winding up where I had started. When I thought of my hurry, my falls, my mad rushing and jumping, all ending in this, it seemed so absurd, that my grief changed suddenly to amusement, and I fell among the brambles, and laughed, and laughed, until my sides were sore. Then I rolled myself up in my cloak, and considered seriously what I should do.

One lesson which I have learned in my roaming life, my friends, is never to call anything a misfortune until you have seen the end of it. Is not every hour a fresh point of view? In this case I soon perceived that accident had done for me as much as the most profound cunning. My guards naturally commenced their search from the place where I had taken Sir Charles Meredith's coat, and from my hiding-place I could see them hurrying along the road to that point. Not one of them ever dreamed that I could have doubled back from there, and I lay quite undisturbed in the little bush-covered cup at the summit of my knoll. The prisoners had, of course, learned of my escape, and all day exultant yells, like that which had aroused me in the morning, resounded over the moor, bearing a welcome message of sympathy and companionship to my ears. How little did they dream that on the top of that very mound, which they could see from their windows, was lying the comrade whose escape they were celebrating. As for me—I could look down upon this herd of idle warriors, as they paced about the great exercise yard, or gathered in little groups, gesticulating joyfully over my success. Once I heard a howl of execration and I saw Beaumont, his head all covered with bandages, being led across the yard by two of the warders. I cannot tell you the pleasure which this sight gave me, for it proved that I had not killed him, and also that the others knew the true story of what had passed. They had all known me too well to think that I could have abandoned him.

All that long day I lay behind my screen of bushes, listening to the bells which struck the hours below.

My pockets were filled with bread which I had saved out of my allowance, and on searching my borrowed overcoat I came upon a silver flask, full of excellent brandy and water, so that I was able to get through the day without hardship. The only other things in the pockets were a red silk handkerchief, a tortoise-shell snuff-box, and a blue envelope, with a red seal, addressed to the Governor of Dartmoor Prison. As to the first two, I determined to send them back when I should return the coat itself. The letter caused me more perplexity, for the Governor had always shown me every courtesy, and it offended my sense of honour that I should interfere with his correspondence. I had almost made up my mind to leave it under a stone upon the roadway within musket-shot of the gate. This would guide them in their search for me, however, and so, on the whole, I saw no better way than just to carry the letter with me in the hope that I might find some means of sending it back to him. Meanwhile I packed it safely away in my innermost pocket.

There was a warm sun to dry my clothes, and when night fell I was ready for my journey. I promise you that there were no mistakes this time. I took the stars for my guides, as every hussar should be taught to do, and I put eight good leagues between myself and the prison. My plan now was to obtain a complete suit of clothes from the first person whom I could waylay, and I should then find my way to the north coast, where there were many smugglers and fishermen who would be ready to earn the reward which was paid by the Emperor to those who brought escaping prisoners across the Channel. I had taken the panache from my shako so that it might escape notice, but even with my fine overcoat I feared that sooner or later my uniform would betray me. My first care must be to provide myself with a complete disguise.

When day broke, I saw a river upon my right and a small town upon my left—the blue smoke reeking up above the moor. I should have liked well to have entered it, because it would have interested me to see something of the customs of the English, which differ very much from those of other nations. Much as I should have wished, however, to have seen them eat their raw meat and sell their wives, it would have been dangerous until I had got rid of my uniform. My cap, my moustache, and my speech would all help to betray me. I continued to travel towards the north therefore, looking about me continually, but never catching a glimpse of my pursuers.

About mid-day I came to where, in a secluded valley, there stood a single small cottage without any other building in sight. It was a neat little house, with a rustic porch and a small garden in front of it, with a swarm of cocks and hens. I lay down among the ferns and watched it, for it seemed to be exactly the kind of place where I might obtain what I wanted. My bread was finished, and I was exceedingly hungry after my long journey; I determined, therefore, to make a short reconnaissance, and then to march up to this cottage, summon it to surrender, and help myself to all that I needed. It could, at least, provide me with a chicken and with an omelette. My mouth watered at the thought.

As I lay there, wondering who could live in this lonely place, a brisk little fellow came out through the porch, accompanied by another older man, who carried two large clubs in his hands.

These he handed to his young companion, who swung them up and down, and round and round, with extraordinary swiftness. The other, standing beside him, appeared to watch him with great attention, and occasionally to advise him. Finally he took a rope, and began skipping like a girl, the other still gravely observing him. As you may think, I was utterly puzzled as to what these people could be, and could only surmise that the one was a doctor, and the other a patient who had submitted himself to some singular method of treatment.

Well, as I lay watching and wondering, the older man brought out a greatcoat, and held it while the other put it on and buttoned it to his chin. The day was a warmish one, so that this proceeding amazed me even more than the other. "At least," thought I, "it is evident that his exercise is over"; but, far from this being so, the man began to run, in spite of his heavy coat, and as it chanced, he came right over the moor in my direction. His companion had re-entered the house, so that this arrangement suited me admirably. I would take the small man's clothing, and hurry on to some village where I could buy provisions. The chickens were certainly tempting, but still there were at least two men in the house, so perhaps it would be wiser for me, since I had no arms, to keep away from it.

I lay quietly then among the ferns. Presently I heard the steps of the runner, and there he was quite close to me, with his huge coat, and the perspiration running down his face. He seemed to be a very solid man — but small — so small that I feared that his clothes might be of little use to me. When I jumped out upon him he stopped running, and looked at me in the greatest astonishment.

"Blow my dickey," said he, "give it a name, guv'nor! Is it a circus, or what?" That was how he talked, though I cannot pretend to tell you what he meant by it.

"You will excuse me, sir," said I, "but I am under the necessity of asking you to give me your clothes."

"Give you what?" he cried.

"Your clothes."

"Well, if this don't lick cock-fighting!" said he. "What am I to give you my clothes for?"

"Because I need them."

"And suppose I won't?"

"Be jabers," said I, "I shall have no choice but to take them."

He stood with his hands in the pockets of his greatcoat, and a most amused smile upon his square-jawed, cleanshaven face.

"You'll take them, will you?" said he. "You're a very leery cove, by the look of you, but I can tell you that you've got the wrong sow by the ear this time. I know who you are. You're a runaway Frenchy, from the prison yonder, as anyone could tell with half an eye. But you don't know who I am, else you wouldn't try such a plant as that. Why, man, I'm the Bristol Bustler, nine stone champion, and them's my training quarters down yonder."

He stared at me as if this announcement of his would have crushed me to the earth, but I smiled at him in my turn, and looked him up and down, with a twirl of my moustache.

"You may be a very brave man, sir," said I, "but when I tell you that you are opposed to Colonel Etienne Gerard, of the Hussars of Conflans, you will see the necessity of giving up your clothes without further parley."

"Look here, mounseer, drop it!" he cried; "this'll end by your getting pepper."

"Your clothes, sir, this instant!" I shouted, advancing fiercely upon him.

For answer he threw off his heavy greatcoat, and stood in a singular attitude, with one arm out, and the other across his chest, looking at me with a curious smile. For myself, I knew nothing of the methods of fighting which these people have, but on horse or on foot, with arms or without them, I am always ready to take my own part. You understand that a soldier cannot always choose his own methods, and that it is time to howl when you are living among wolves. I rushed at him, therefore, with a warlike shout, and kicked him with both my feet. At the same moment my heels flew into the air, I saw as many flashes as at Austerlitz, and the back of my head came down with a crash upon a stone. After that I can remember nothing more.

When I came to myself I was lying upon a truckle-bed, in a bare, half-furnished room. My head was ringing like a bell, and when I put up my hand, there was a lump like a walnut over one of my eyes. My nose was full of a pungent smell, and I soon found that a strip of paper soaked in vinegar was fastened across my brow. At the other end of the room this terrible little man was sitting with his knee bare, and his elderly companion was rubbing it with some liniment. The latter seemed to be in the worst of tempers, and he kept up a continual scolding, which the other listened to with a gloomy face.

"Never heard tell of such a thing in my life," he was saying. "In training for a month with all the weight of it on my shoulders, and then when I get you as fit as a trout, and within two days of fighting the likeliest man on the list, you let yourself into a by-battle with a foreigner."

"There, there! Stow your gab!" said the other, sulkily. "You're a very good trainer, Jim, but you'd be better with less jaw."

"I should think it was time to jaw," the elderly man answered. "If this knee don't get well before Wednesday, they'll have it that you fought a cross, and a pretty job you'll have next time you look for a backer."

"Fought a cross!" growled the other. "I've won nineteen battles, and no man ever so much as dared to say the word 'cross' in my hearin'. How the deuce was I to get out of it when the cove wanted the very clothes off my back?"

"Tut, man, you know that the beak and the guards were within a mile of you. You could have set them on to him as well then as now. You'd have got your clothes back again all right."

"Well, strike me!" said the Bustler, "I don't often break my trainin', but when it comes to givin' up my clothes to a Frenchy who couldn't hit a dint in a pat o' butter, why, it's more than I can swaller."

"Pooh, man, what are the clothes worth? D'you know that Lord Rufton alone has five thousand pounds on you? When you jump the ropes on Wednesday, you'll carry every penny of fifty thousand into the ring. A pretty thing to turn up with a swollen knee and a story about a Frenchman!"

"I never thought he'd ha' kicked," said the Bustler.

"I suppose you expected he'd fight Broughton's rules, and strict P.R.? Why, you silly, they don't know what fighting is in France."

"My friends," said I, sitting up on my bed, "I do not understand very much of what you say, but when you speak like that it is foolishness. We know so much about fighting in France, that we have paid our little visit to nearly every capital in Europe, and very soon we are coming to London. But we fight like soldiers, you understand, and not like gamins in the gutter. You strike me on the head. I kick you on the knee. It is child's play. But if you will give me a sword, and take another one, I will show you how we fight over the water."

They both stared at me in their solid, English way.

"Well, I'm glad you're not dead, mounseer," said the elder one at last. "There wasn't much sign of life in you when the Bustler and me carried you down. That head of yours ain't thick enough to stop the crook of the hardest hitter in Bristol."

"He's a game cove, too, and he came for me like a bantam," said the other, still rubbing his knee. "I got my old left-right in, and he went over as if he had been pole-axed. It wasn't my fault, mounseer. I told you you'd get pepper if you went on."

"Well, it's something to say all your life, that you've been handled by the finest light-weight in England," said the older man, looking at me with an expression of congratulation upon his face. "You've had him at his best, too—in the pink of condition, and trained by Jim Hunter."

"I am used to hard knocks," said I, unbuttoning my tunic, and showing my two musket wounds. Then I bared my ankle also, and showed the place in my eye where the guerilla had stabbed me.

"He can take his gruel," said the Bustler.

"What a glutton he'd have made for the middle-weights," remarked the trainer; "with six months' coaching he'd astonish the fancy. It's a pity he's got to go back to prison."

I did not like that last remark at all. I buttoned up my coat and rose from the bed.

"I must ask you to let me continue my journey," said I.

"There's no help for it, mounseer," the trainer answered. "It's a hard thing to send such a man as you back to such a place, but business is business, and there's a twenty pound reward. They were here this morning, looking for you, and I expect they'll be round again."

His words turned my heart to lead.

"Surely, you would not betray me," I cried. "I will send you twice twenty pounds on the day that I set foot upon France. I swear it upon the honour of a French gentleman."

But I only got head-shakes for a reply. I pleaded, I argued, I spoke of the English hospitality and the fellowship of brave men, but I might as well have been addressing the two great wooden clubs which stood balanced upon the floor in front of me. There was no sign of sympathy upon their bull-faces.

"Business is business, mounseer," the old trainer repeated. "Besides, how am I to put the Bustler into the ring on Wednesday if he's jugged by the beak for aidin' and abettin' a prisoner of war? I've got to look after the Bustler, and I take no risks."

This, then, was the end of all my struggles and strivings. I was to be led back again like a poor silly sheep who has broken through the hurdles. They little knew me who could fancy that I should submit to such a fate. I had heard enough to tell me where the weak point of these two men was, and I showed, as I have often showed before, that Etienne Gerard is never so terrible as when all hope seems to have deserted him. With a single spring I seized one of the clubs and swung it over the head of the Bustler.

"Come what may," I cried, "*you* shall be spoiled for Wednesday."

The fellow growled out an oath, and would have sprung at me, but the other flung his arms round him and pinned him to the chair.

"Not if I know it, Bustler," he screamed. "None of your games while I am by. Get away out of this, Frenchy. We only want to see your back. Run away, run away, or he'll get loose!"

It was good advice, I thought, and I ran to the door, but as I came out into the open air my head swam round and I had to lean against the porch to save myself from falling. Consider all that I had been through, the anxiety of my escape, the long, useless flight in the storm, the day spent amid wet ferns, with only bread for food, the second journey by night, and now the injuries which I had received in attempting to deprive the little man of his clothes. Was it wonderful that even I should reach the limits of my endurance? I stood there in my heavy coat and my poor battered shako, my chin upon my chest, and my eyelids over my eyes. I had done my best, and I could do no more. It was the sound of horses' hoofs which made me at last raise my head, and there was the grey-moustached Governor of Dartmoor Prison not ten paces in front of me, with six mounted warders behind him.

"So, Colonel," said he, with a bitter smile, "we have found you once more."

When a brave man has done his utmost, and has failed, he shows his breeding by the manner in which he accepts his defeat. For me, I took the letter which I had in my pocket, and stepping forward, I handed it with such grace of manner as I could summon to the Governor.

"It has been my misfortune, sir, to detain one of your letters," said I.

He looked at me in amazement, and beckoned to the warders to arrest me. Then he broke the seal of the letter. I saw a curious expression come over his face as he read it.

"This must be the letter which Sir Charles Meredith lost," said he.

"It was in the pocket of his coat."

"You have carried it for two days?"

"Since the night before last."

"And never looked at the contents?"

I showed him by my manner that he had committed an indiscretion in asking a question which one gentleman should not have put to another.

To my surprise he burst out into a roar of laughter.

"Colonel," said he, wiping the tears from his eyes, "you have really given both yourself and us a great deal of unnecessary trouble. Allow me to read the letter which you carried with you in your flight."

And this was what I heard: —

"On receipt of this you are directed to release Colonel Etienne Gerard, of the 3rd Hussars, who has been exchanged against Colonel Mason, of the Horse Artillery, now in Verdun."

And as he read it, he laughed again, and the warders laughed, and the two men from the cottage laughed, and then, as I heard this universal merriment, and thought of all my hopes and fears, and my struggles and dangers, what could a debonair soldier do but lean against the porch once more, and laugh as heartily as any of them? And of them all was it not I who had the best reason to laugh, since in front of me I could see my dear France, and my mother, and the Emperor, and my horsemen; while behind lay the gloomy prison, and the heavy hand of the English king?

HOW THE BRIGADIER SLEW
THE BROTHERS OF AJACCIO

WHEN I told you some little time ago how it was that I won the special medal for valour, I finished, as you will doubtless remember, by repeating the saying of the Emperor that I had the stoutest heart in all his armies. In making that remark, Napoleon was showing the insight for which he was so famous. He disfigured his sentence, however, by adding something about the thickness of my head. We will pass that over. It is ungenerous to dwell upon the weaker moments of a great man. I will only say this, that when the Emperor needed an agent he was always very ready to do me the honour of recalling the name of Etienne Gerard, though it occasionally escaped him when rewards were to be distributed. Still, I was a colonel at twenty-eight, and the chief of a brigade at thirty-one, so that I have no reason to be dissatisfied with my career. Had the wars lasted another two or three years I might have grasped my bâton, and the man who had his hand upon that was only one stride from a throne. Murat had changed his hussar's cap for a crown, and another light cavalry man might have done as much. However, all those dreams were driven away by Waterloo, and, although I was not able to write my name upon history, it is sufficiently well known by all who served with me in the great wars of the Empire.

What I want to tell you to-night is about the very singular affair which first started me upon my rapid upward course, and which had the effect of establishing a secret bond between the Emperor and myself. There is just one little word of warning which I must give you before I begin. When you hear me speak, you must always bear in mind that you are listening to one who has seen history from the inside. I am talking about what my ears have heard and my eyes have seen, so you must not try to confute me by quoting the opinions of some student or man of the pen, who has written a book of history or memoirs. There is much which is unknown by such people, and much which never will be known by the world. For my own part, I could tell you some very surprising things were it discreet to do so. The facts which I am about to relate to you to-night were kept secret by me during the Emperor's lifetime, because I gave him my promise that it should be so, but I do not think that there can be any harm now in my telling the remarkable part which I played.

You must know, then, that at the time of the Treaty of Tilsit I was a simple lieutenant in the 10th Hussars, without money or interest. It is true that my appearance and my gallantry were in my favour, and that I had already won a reputation as being one of the best swordsmen in the army; but among the host of brave men who surrounded the Emperor it needed more than this to insure a rapid career. I was confident, however, that my chance would come, though I never dreamed that it would take so remarkable a form.

When the Emperor returned to Paris, after the declaration of peace in the year 1807, he spent much of his time with the Empress and the Court at Fontainebleau. It was the time when he was at the pinnacle of his career. He had in three successive campaigns humbled Austria, crushed Prussia, and made the Russians very glad to get upon the right side of the Niemen. The old Bulldog over the Channel was still growling, but he could not get very far from his kennel. If we could have made a perpetual peace at that moment, France would have taken a higher place than any nation since the days of the Romans. So I have heard the wise folk say, though for my part I had other things to think of. All the girls were glad to see the army back after its long absence, and you may be sure that I had my share of any favours that were going. You

may judge how far I was a favourite in those days when I say that
even now, in my sixtieth year—but why should I dwell upon that
which is already sufficiently well known?

Our regiment of hussars was quartered with the horse chasseurs of the guard at Fontainebleau. It is, as you know, but a little
place, buried in the heart of the forest, and it was wonderful at this
time to see it crowded with Grand Dukes and Electors and Princes,
who thronged round Napoleon like puppies round their master,
each hoping that some bone might be thrown to him. There was
more German than French to be heard in the street, for those who
had helped us in the late war had come to beg for a reward, and
those who had opposed us had come to try and escape their punishment. And all the time our little man, with his pale face and his
cold, grey eyes, was riding to the hunt every morning, silent and
brooding, all of them following in his train, in the hope that some
word would escape him. And then, when the humour seized him,
he would throw a hundred square miles to that man, or tear as
much off the other, round off one kingdom by a river, or cut off
another by a chain of mountains. That was how he used to do business, this little artilleryman, whom we had raised so high with our
sabres and our bayonets. He was very civil to us always, for he knew
where his power came from. We knew also, and showed it by the
way in which we carried ourselves. We were agreed, you understand, that he was the finest leader in the world, but we did not
forget that he had the finest men to lead.

Well, one day I was seated in my quarters playing cards with
young Morat, of the horse chasseurs, when the door opened and
in walked Lasalle, who was our Colonel. You know what a fine,
swaggering fellow he was, and the sky-blue uniform of the Tenth
suited him to a marvel. My faith, we youngsters were so taken by
him that we all swore and diced and drank and played the deuce
whether we liked it or no, just that we might resemble our
Colonel! We forgot that it was not because he drank or gambled
that the Emperor was going to make him the head of the light
cavalry, but because he had the surest eye for the nature of a posi-

tion or for the strength of a column, and the best judgment as to
when infantry could be broken, or whether guns were exposed,
of any man in the army. We were too young to understand all that,
however, so we waxed our moustaches and clinked our spurs and
let the ferrules of our scabbards wear out by trailing them along
the pavement in the hope that we should all become Lasalles.
When he came clanking into my quarters, both Morat and I
sprang to our feet.

"My boy," said he, clapping me on the shoulder, "the Emperor
wants to see you at four o'clock."

The room whirled round me at the words, and I had to lean my
hands upon the edge of the card-table.

"What?" I cried. "The Emperor!"

"Precisely," said he, smiling at my astonishment.

"But the Emperor does not know of my existence, Colonel," I
protested. "Why should he send for me?"

"Well, that's just what puzzles me," cried Lasalle, twirling his
moustache. "If he wanted the help of a good sabre, why should he
descend to one of my lieutenants when he might have found all
that he needed at the head of the regiment? However," he added,
clapping me upon the shoulder again in his hearty fashion,
"every man has his chance. I have had mine, otherwise I should
not be Colonel of the Tenth. I must not grudge you yours.
Forwards, my boy, and may it be the first step towards changing
your busby for a cocked hat."

It was but two o'clock, so he left me, promising to come back
and to accompany me to the palace. My faith, what a time I passed,
and how many conjectures did I make as to what it was that the
Emperor could want of me! I paced up and down my little room in
a fever of anticipation. Sometimes I thought that perhaps he had
heard of the guns which we had taken at Austerlitz; but then there
were so many who had taken guns at Austerlitz, and two years had
passed since the battle. Or it might be that he wished to reward me
for my affair with the *aide-de-camp* of the Russian Emperor. But
then again a cold fit would seize me, and I would fancy that he had

sent for me to reprimand me. There were a few duels which he might have taken in ill part, and there were one or two little jokes in Paris since the peace.

But, no! I considered the words of Lasalle. "If he had need of a brave man," said Lasalle.

It was obvious that my Colonel had some idea of what was in the wind. If he had not known that it was to my advantage, he would not have been so cruel as to congratulate me. My heart glowed with joy as this conviction grew upon me, and I sat down to write to my mother and to tell her that the Emperor was waiting, at that very moment, to have my opinion upon a matter of importance. It made me smile as I wrote it to think that, wonderful as it appeared to me, it would probably only confirm my mother in her opinion of the Emperor's good sense.

At half-past three I heard a sabre come clanking against every step of my wooden stair. It was Lasalle, and with him was a little gentleman, very neatly dressed in black with dapper ruffles and cuffs. We did not know many civilians, we of the army, but, my word, this was one whom we could not afford to ignore! I had only to glance at those twinkling eyes, the comical, upturned nose, and the straight, precise mouth, to know that I was in the presence of the one man in France whom even the Emperor had to consider.

"This is Monsieur Etienne Gerard, Monsieur de Talleyrand," said Lasalle.

I saluted, and the statesman took me in from the top of my panache to the rowel of my spur, with a glance that played over me like a rapier point.

"Have you explained to the Lieutenant the circumstances under which he is summoned to the Emperor's presence?" he asked, in his dry, creaking voice.

They were such a contrast, these two men, that I could not help glancing from one to the other of them: the little, black, sly politician, and the big, sky-blue hussar, with one fist on his hip and the other on the hilt of his sabre. They both took their seats as I looked, Talleyrand without a sound, and Lasalle with a clash and jingle like a prancing charger.

"It's this way, youngster," said he, in his brusque fashion; "I was with the Emperor in his private cabinet this morning when a note was brought in to him. He opened it, and as he did so he gave such a start that it fluttered down on to the floor. I handed it up to him again, but he was staring at the wall in front of him as if he had seen a ghost. 'Fratelli dell' Ajaccio,' he muttered; and then again, 'Fratelli dell' Ajaccio.' I don't pretend to know more Italian than a man can pick up in two campaigns, and I could make nothing of this. It seemed to me that he had gone out of his mind; and you would have said so also, Monsieur de Talleyrand, if you had seen the look in his eyes. He read the note, and then he sat for half an hour or more without moving."

"And you?" asked Talleyrand.

"Why, I stood there not knowing what I ought to do. Presently he seemed to come back to his senses.

"'I suppose, Lasalle,' said he, 'that you have some gallant young officers in the Tenth?'

"'They are all that, sire,' I answered.

"'If you had to pick one who was to be depended upon for action, but who would not think too much—you understand me, Lasalle—which would you select?' he asked.

"I saw that he needed an agent who would not penetrate too deeply into his plans.

"'I have one,' said I, 'who is all spurs and moustaches, with never a thought beyond women and horses.'

"'That is the man I want,' said Napoleon. 'Bring him to my private cabinet at four o'clock.'

"So, youngster, I came straight away to you at once, and mind that you do credit to the 10th Hussars."

I was by no means flattered by the reasons which had led to my Colonel's choice, and I must have shown as much in my face, for he roared with laughter and Talleyrand gave a dry chuckle also.

"Just one word of advice before you go, Monsieur Gerard," said he: "you are now coming into troubled waters, and you might find a worse pilot than myself. We have none of us any idea as to what this little affair means, and, between ourselves, it is very important to us, who have the destinies of France upon our shoulders, to keep ourselves in touch with all that goes on. You understand me, Monsieur Gerard?"

I had not the least idea what he was driving at, but I bowed and tried to look as if it was clear to me.

"Act very guardedly, then, and say nothing to anybody," said Talleyrand. "Colonel de Lasalle and I will not show ourselves in public with you, but we will await you here, and we will give you our advice when you have told us what has passed between the Emperor and yourself. It is time that you started now, for the Emperor never forgives unpunctuality."

Off I went on foot to the palace, which was only a hundred paces off. I made my way to the antechamber, where Duroc, with his grand new scarlet and gold coat, was fussing about among the crowd of people who were waiting. I heard him whisper to Monsieur de Caulaincourt that half of them were German Dukes who expected to be made Kings, and the other half German Dukes who expected to be made paupers. Duroc, when he heard my name, showed me straight in, and I found myself in the Emperor's presence.

I had, of course, seen him in camp a hundred times, but I had never been face to face with him before. I have no doubt that if you had met him without knowing in the least who he was, you would simply have said that he was a sallow little fellow with a good forehead and fairly well-turned calves. His tight white cashmere breeches and white stockings showed off his legs to advantage. But even a stranger must have been struck by the singular look of his eyes, which could harden into an expression which would frighten a grenadier. It is said that even Auguereau, who was a man who had never known what fear was, quailed before Napoleon's gaze, at a time, too, when the Emperor was but an unknown soldier. He looked mildly enough at me, however, and motioned me to remain by the door. De Meneval was writing to his dictation, looking up at him between each sentence with his spaniel eyes.

"That will do. You can go," said the Emperor, abruptly. Then, when the secretary had left the room, he strode across with his hands behind his back, and he looked me up and down without a word. Though he was a small man himself, he was very fond of having fine-looking fellows about him, and so I think that my appearance gave him pleasure. For my own part, I raised one hand to the salute and held the other upon the hilt of my sabre, looking straight ahead of me, as a soldier should.

"Well, Monsieur Gerard," said he, at last, tapping his forefinger upon one of the brandebourgs of gold braid upon the front of my pelisse, "I am informed that you are a very deserving young officer. Your Colonel gives me an excellent account of you."

I wished to make a brilliant reply, but I could think of nothing save Lasalle's phrase that I was all spurs and moustaches, so it ended in my saying nothing at all. The Emperor watched the struggle which must have shown itself upon my features, and when, finally, no answer came he did not appear to be displeased.

"I believe that you are the very man that I want," said he. "Brave and clever men surround me upon every side. But a brave man who—" He did not finish his sentence, and for my own part I could not understand what he was driving at. I contented myself with assuring him that he could count upon me to the death.

"You are, as I understand, a good swordsman?" said he.

"Tolerable, sire," I answered.

"You were chosen by your regiment to fight the champion of the Hussars of Chambarant?" said he.

I was not sorry to find that he knew so much of my exploits.

"My comrades, sire, did me that honour," said I.

"And for the sake of practice you insulted six fencing masters in the week before your duel?"

"I had the privilege of being out seven times in as many days, sire," said I.

"And escaped without a scratch?"

"The fencing master of the 23rd Light Infantry touched me on the left elbow, sire."

"Let us have no more child's play of the sort, monsieur," he cried, turning suddenly to that cold rage of his which was so appalling. "Do you imagine that I place veteran soldiers in these positions that you may practise quarte and tierce upon them? How am I to face Europe if my soldiers turn their points upon each other? Another word of your duelling, and I break you between these fingers."

I saw his plump white hands flash before my eyes as he spoke, and his voice had turned to the most discordant hissing and growling. My word, my skin pringled all over as I listened to him, and I would gladly have changed my position for that of the first man in the steepest and narrowest breach that ever swallowed up a storming party. He turned to the table, drank off a cup of coffee, and then when he faced me again every trace of this storm had vanished, and he wore that singular smile which came from his lips but never from his eyes.

"I have need of your services, Monsieur Gerard," said he. "I may be safer with a good sword at my side, and there are reasons why yours should be the one which I select. But first of all I must bind you to secrecy. Whilst I live what passes between us to-day must be known to none but ourselves."

I thought of Talleyrand and of Lasalle, but I promised.

"In the next place, I do not want your opinions or conjectures, and I wish you to do exactly what you are told."

I bowed.

"It is your sword that I need, and not your brains. I will do the thinking. Is that clear to you?"

"Yes, sire."

"You know the Chancellor's Grove, in the forest?"

I bowed.

"You know also the large double fir-tree where the hounds assembled on Tuesday?"

Had he known that I met a girl under it three times a week, he would not have asked me. I bowed once more without remark.

"Very good. You will meet me there at ten o'clock to-night."

I had got past being surprised at anything which might happen. If he had asked me to take his place upon the Imperial throne I could only have nodded my busby.

"We shall then proceed into the wood together," said the Emperor. "You will be armed with a sword, but not with pistols. You must address no remark to me, and I shall say nothing to you. We will advance in silence. You understand?"

"I understand, sire."

"After a time we shall see a man, or more probably two men, under a certain tree. We shall approach them together. If I signal to you to defend me, you will have your sword ready. If, on the other hand, I speak to these men, you will wait and see what happens. If you are called upon to draw, you must see that neither of them, in the event of there being two, escapes from us. I shall myself assist you."

"But, sire," I cried, "I have no doubt that two would not be too many for my sword; but would it not be better that I should bring a comrade than that you should be forced to join in such a struggle?"

"Ta, ta, ta," said he. "I was a soldier before I was an Emperor. Do you think, then, that artillerymen have not swords as well as the hussars? But I ordered you not to argue with me. You will do exactly what I tell you. If swords are once out, neither of these men is to get away alive."

"They shall not, sire," said I.

"Very good. I have no more instructions for you. You can go."

I turned to the door, and then an idea occurring to me I turned.

"I have been thinking, sire—" said I.

He sprang at me with the ferocity of a wild beast. I really thought he would have struck me.

"Thinking!" he cried. "You, *you!* Do you imagine I chose you out because you could think? Let me hear of your doing such a thing again! You, the one man—but, there! You meet me at the fir-tree at ten o'clock."

My faith, I was right glad to get out of the room. If I have a good horse under me, and a sword clanking against my stirrup-iron, I know where I am. And in all that relates to green fodder or dry, barley and oats and rye, and the handling of squadrons upon the march, there is no one who can teach me very much. But when I meet a Chamberlain and a Marshal of the Palace, and have to pick my words with an Emperor, and find that everybody hints instead of talking straight out, I feel like a troop-horse who has been put in a lady's calèche. It is not my trade, all this mincing and pretending. I have learned the manners of a gentleman, but never those of a courtier. I was right glad then to get into the fresh air again, and I ran away up to my quarters like a schoolboy who has just escaped from the seminary master.

But as I opened the door, the very first thing that my eye rested upon was a long pair of sky-blue legs with hussar boots, and a short pair of black ones with knee-breeches and buckles. They both sprang up together to greet me.

"Well, what news?" they cried, the two of them.

"None," I answered.

"The Emperor refused to see you?"

"No, I have seen him."

"And what did he say?"

"Monsieur de Talleyrand," I answered, "I regret to say that it is quite impossible for me to tell you anything about it. I have promised the Emperor."

"Pooh, pooh, my dear young man," said he, sidling up to me, as a cat does when it is about to rub itself against you. "This is all among the friends, you understand, and goes no further than these four walls. Besides, the Emperor never meant to include me in this promise."

"It is but a minute's walk to the palace, Monsieur de Talleyrand," I answered; "if it would not be troubling you too much to ask you to step up to it and bring back the Emperor's written statement that he did not mean to include you in this promise, I shall be happy to tell you every word that passed."

He showed his teeth at me then like the old fox that he was.

"Monsieur Gerard appears to be a little puffed up," said he. "He is too young to see things in their just proportion. As he grows older he may understand that it is not always very discreet for a subaltern of cavalry to give such very abrupt refusals."

I did not know what to say to this, but Lasalle came to my aid in his downright fashion.

"The lad is quite right," said he. "If I had known that there was a promise I should not have questioned him. You know very well, Monsieur de Talleyrand, that if he had answered you, you would have laughed in your sleeve and thought as much about him as I think of the bottle when the burgundy is gone. As for me, I promise you that the Tenth would have had no room for him, and that we should have lost our best swordsman if I had heard him give up the Emperor's secret."

But the statesman became only the more bitter when he saw that I had the support of my Colonel.

"I have heard, Colonel de Lasalle," said he, with an icy dignity, "that your opinion is of great weight upon the subject of light cavalry. Should I have occasion to seek information about that branch of the army, I shall be very happy to apply to you. At present, however, the matter concerns diplomacy, and you will permit me to form my own views upon that question. As long as the welfare of France and the safety of the Emperor's person are largely committed to my care, I will use every means in my power to secure them, even if it should be against the Emperor's own temporary wishes. I have the honour, Colonel de Lasalle, to wish you a very good day!"

He shot a most unamiable glance in my direction, and, turning upon his heel, he walked with little, quick, noiseless steps out of the room.

I could see from Lasalle's face that he did not at all relish finding himself at enmity with the powerful Minister. He rapped out an oath or two, and then, catching up his sabre and his cap, he clattered away down the stairs. As I looked out of the window I saw the two of them, the big blue man and the little black one, going up the street together. Talleyrand was walking very rigidly, and Lasalle was waving his hands and talking, so I suppose that he was trying to make his peace.

The Emperor had told me not to think, and I endeavoured to obey him. I took up the cards from the table where Morat had left them, and I tried to work out a few combinations at écarté. But I could not remember which were trumps, and I threw them under the table in despair. Then I drew my sabre and practised giving point until I was weary, but it was all of no use at all. My mind *would* work, in spite of myself. At ten o'clock I was to meet the Emperor in the forest. Of all extraordinary combinations of events in the whole world, surely this was the last which would have occurred to me when I rose from my couch that morning. But the responsibility— the dreadful responsibility! It was all upon my shoulders. There was no one to halve it with me. It made me cold all over. Often as I have faced death upon the battlefield, I have never known what real fear was until that moment. But then I considered that after all I could but do my best like a brave and honourable gentleman, and above all obey the orders which I had received, to the very letter. And, if all went well, this would surely be the foundation of my fortunes. Thus, swaying between my fears and my hopes, I spent the long, long evening until it was time for me to keep my appointment.

I put on my military overcoat, as I did not know how much of the night I might have to spend in the woods, and I fastened my sword outside it. I pulled off my hussar boots also, and wore a pair of shoes and gaiters, that I might be lighter upon my feet. Then I stole out of my quarters and made for the forest, feeling very much easier in my mind, for I am always at my best when the time of thought has passed and the moment for action arrived.

I passed the barracks of the Chasseurs of the Guards, and the line of cafés all filled with uniforms. I caught a glimpse as I went by of the blue and gold of some of my comrades, amid the swarm of dark infantry coats and the light green of the Guides. There they sat, sipping their wine and smoking their cigars, little dreaming what their comrade had on hand. One of them, the chief of my squadron, caught sight of me in the lamplight, and came shouting after me into the street. I hurried on, however, pretending not to hear him, so he, with a curse at my deafness, went back at last to his wine bottle.

It is not very hard to get into the forest at Fontainebleau. The scattered trees steal their way into the very streets, like the tirailleurs in front of a column. I turned into a path, which led to the edge of the woods, and then I pushed rapidly forward towards the old fir-tree. It was a place which, as I have hinted, I had my own reasons for knowing well, and I could only thank the Fates that it was not one of the nights upon which Léonie would be waiting for me. The poor child would have died of terror at sight of the Emperor. He might have been too harsh with her — and worse still, he might have been too kind.

There was a half moon shining, and, as I came up to our trysting-place, I saw that I was not the first to arrive. The Emperor was pacing up and down, his hands behind him and his face sunk somewhat forward upon his breast. He wore a grey great-coat with a capote over his head. I had seen him in such a dress in our winter campaign in Poland, and it was said that he used it because the hood was such an excellent disguise. He was always fond, whether in the camp or in Paris, of walking round at night, and overhearing the talk in the cabarets or round the fires. His figure, however, and his way of carrying his head and his hands, were so well known that he was always recognised, and then the talkers would just say whatever they thought would please him best.

My first thought was that he would be angry with me for having kept him waiting, but as I approached him, we heard the big church clock of Fontainebleau clang out the hour of ten. It was evident, therefore, that it was he who was too soon, and not I too late. I remembered his order that I should make no remark, so contented myself with halting within four paces of him, clicking my spurs together, grounding my sabre, and saluting. He glanced at me, and then without a word he turned and walked slowly through the forest, I keeping always about the same distance behind him. Once or twice he seemed to me to look apprehensively to right and to left, as if he feared that someone was observing us. I looked also, but although I have the keenest sight, it was quite impossible to see anything except the ragged patches of moonshine between the great black shadows of the trees. My ears are as quick as my eyes, and once or twice I thought that I heard a twig crack; but you know how many sounds there are in a forest at night, and how difficult it is even to say what direction they come from.

We walked for rather more than a mile, and I knew exactly what our destination was, long before we got there. In the centre of one of the glades there is the shattered stump of what must at some time have been a most gigantic tree. It is called the Abbot's Beech, and there are so many ghostly stories about it, that I know many a brave soldier who would not care about mounting sentinel over it. However, I cared as little for such folly as the Emperor did, so we crossed the glade and made straight for the old broken trunk. As we approached, I saw that two men were waiting for us beneath it.

When I first caught sight of them they were standing rather behind it, as if they were not anxious to be seen, but as we came nearer they emerged from its shadow and walked forward to meet us. The Emperor glanced back at me, and slackened his pace a little, so that I came within arm's length of him. You may think that I had my hilt well to the front, and that I had a very good look at these two people who were approaching us. The one was tall, remarkably so, and of a very spare frame, while the other was rather below the usual height, and had a brisk, determined way of walking. They each wore black cloaks, which were slung right across their figures, and hung down upon one side, like the mantles of Murat's dragoons. They had flat black caps, like those which I have since seen in Spain, which threw their faces into darkness, though I could see the gleam of their eyes from beneath them. With the moon behind them and their long black shadows walking in front, they were such figures as one might expect to meet at night near the Abbot's Beech. I can remember that they had a stealthy way of moving, and that as they approached, the moonshine formed two white diamonds between their legs and the legs of their shadows.

The Emperor had paused, and these two strangers came to a stand also within a few paces of us. I had drawn up close to my companion's elbow, so that the four of us were facing each other without a word spoken. My eyes were particularly fixed upon the taller one, because he was slightly the nearer to me, and I became certain as I watched him that he was in the last state of nervousness. His lean figure was quivering all over, and I heard a quick, thin panting like that of a tired dog. Suddenly one of them gave a short, hissing signal. The tall man bent his back and his knees like a diver about to spring, but before he could move, I had jumped with drawn sabre in front of him. At the same instant the smaller man bounded past me, and buried a long poniard in the Emperor's heart.

My God! the horror of that moment! It is a marvel that I did not drop dead myself. As in a dream, I saw the grey coat whirl convulsively round, and caught a glimpse in the moonlight of three inches of red point which jutted out from between the shoulders. Then down he fell with a dead man's gasp upon the grass, and the assassin, leaving his weapon buried in his victim, threw up both his hands and shrieked with joy. But I—I drove my sword through his midriff with such frantic force, that the mere blow of the hilt against the end of his breast-bone sent him six paces before he fell, and left my reeking blade ready for the other. I sprang round upon him with such a lust for blood upon me as I had never felt, and never have felt, in all my days. As I turned, a dagger flashed before my eyes, and I felt the cold wind of it pass my neck and the villain's wrist jar upon my shoulder. I shortened my sword, but he winced away from me, and an instant afterwards was in full flight, bounding like a deer across the glade in the moonlight.

But he was not to escape me thus. I knew that the murderer's poniard had done its work. Young as I was, I had seen enough of war to know a mortal blow. I paused but for an instant to touch the cold hand.

"Sire! Sire!" I cried, in an agony; and then as no sound came back and nothing moved, save an ever-widening dark circle in the moonlight, I knew that all was indeed over. I sprang madly to my feet, threw off my great-coat, and ran at the top of my speed after the remaining assassin.

Ah, how I blessed the wisdom which had caused me to come in shoes and gaiters! And the happy thought which had thrown off my coat. He could not get rid of his mantle, this wretch, or else he was too frightened to think of it. So it was that I gained upon him from the beginning. He must have been out of his wits, for he never tried to bury himself in the darker parts of the woods, but he flew on from glade to glade, until he came to the heath-land which leads up to the great Fontainebleau quarry. There I had him in full sight, and knew that he could not escape me. He ran well, it is true—ran as a coward runs when his life is at stake. But I ran as Destiny runs when it gets behind a man's heels. Yard by yard I drew in upon him. He was rolling and staggering. I could hear the rasping and crackling of his breath. The great gulf of the quarry suddenly yawned in front of his path, and glancing at me over his shoulder, he gave a shriek of despair. The next instant he had vanished from my sight.

Vanished utterly, you understand. I rushed to the spot, and gazed down into the black abyss. Had he hurled himself over? I had almost made up my mind that he had done so, when a gentle sound rising and falling came out of the darkness beneath me. It was his breathing once more, and it showed me where he must be. He was hiding in the tool-house.

At the edge of the quarry and beneath the summit there is a small platform upon which stands a wooden hut for the use of the labourers. It was into this, then, that he had darted. Perhaps he had thought, the fool, that, in the darkness, I would not venture to follow him. He little knew Etienne Gerard. With a spring I was on the platform, with another I was through the doorway, and then, hearing him in the corner, I hurled myself down upon the top of him.

He fought like a wild cat, but he never had a chance with his shorter weapon. I think that I must have transfixed him with that first mad lunge, for, though he struck and struck, his blows had no power in them, and presently his dagger tinkled down upon the floor. When I was sure that he was dead, I rose up and passed out into the moonlight. I climbed up on to the heath again, and wandered across it as nearly out of my mind as a man could be. With the blood singing in my ears, and my naked sword still clutched in my hand, I walked aimlessly on until, looking round me, I found that I had come as far as the glade of the Abbot's Beech, and saw in the distance that gnarled stump which must ever be associated with the most terrible moment of my life. I sat down upon a fallen trunk with my sword across my knees and my head between my hands, and I tried to think about what had happened and what would happen in the future.

The Emperor had committed himself to my care. The Emperor was dead. Those were the two thoughts which clanged in my head, until I had no room for any other ones. He had come with me and he was dead. I had done what he had ordered when living. I had revenged him when dead. But what of all that? The world would look upon me as responsible. They might even look upon me as the assassin. What could I prove? What witnesses had I? Might I not have been the accomplice of these wretches? Yes, yes, I was eternally dishonoured—the lowest, most despicable creature in all France. This then was the end of my fine military ambitions— of the hopes of my mother. I laughed bitterly at the thought. And what was I to do now? Was I to go into Fontainebleau, to wake up the palace, and to inform them that the great Emperor had been murdered within a pace of me? I could not do it—no, I could not do it! There was but one course for an honourable gentleman whom Fate had placed in so cruel a position. I would fall upon my dishonoured sword, and so share, since I could not avert, the Emperor's fate. I rose with my nerves strung to this last piteous deed, and as I did so, my eyes fell upon something which struck the breath from my lips. The Emperor was standing before me!

He was not more than ten yards off, with the moon shining straight upon his cold, pale face. He wore his grey overcoat, but the hood was turned back, and the front open, so that I could see the green coat of the Guides, and the white breeches. His hands were clasped behind his back, and his chin sunk forward upon his breast, in the way that was usual with him.

"Well," said he in his hardest and most abrupt voice, "what account do you give of yourself?"

I believe that, if he had stood in silence for another minute, my brain would have given way. But those sharp military accents were exactly what I needed to bring me to myself. Living or dead, here was the Emperor standing before me and asking me questions. I sprang to the salute.

"You have killed one, I see," said he, jerking his head towards the beech.

"Yes, sire."

"And the other escaped?"

"No, sire, I killed him also."

"What!" he cried. "Do I understand that you have killed them both?" He approached me as he spoke with a smile which set his teeth gleaming in the moonlight.

"One body lies there, sire," I answered. "The other is in the tool-house at the quarry."

"Then the Brothers of Ajaccio are no more," he cried, and after a pause, as if speaking to himself: "The shadow has passed me for ever." Then he bent forward and laid his hand upon my shoulder.

"You have done very well, my young friend," said he. "You have lived up to your reputation."

He was flesh and blood, then, this Emperor. I could feel the little, plump palm that rested upon me. And yet I could not get over what I had seen with my own eyes, and so I stared at him in such bewilderment that he broke once more into one of his smiles.

"No, no, Monsieur Gerard," said he, "I am not a ghost, and you have not seen me killed. You will come here, and all will be clear to you."

He turned as he spoke, and led the way towards the great beech stump.

The bodies were still lying upon the ground, and two men were standing beside them. As we approached I saw from the turbans that they were Roustem and Mustafa; the two Mameluke servants.

The Emperor paused when he came to the grey figure upon the ground, and turning back the hood which shrouded the features, he showed a face which was very different from his own.

"Here lies a faithful servant who has given up his life for his master," said he. "Monsieur de Goudin resembles me in figure and in manner, as you must admit."

What a delirium of joy came upon me when these few words made everything clear to me. He smiled again as he saw the delight which urged me to throw my arms round him and to embrace him, but he moved a step away, as if he had divined my impulse.

"You are unhurt?" he asked.

"I am unhurt, sire. But in another minute I should in my despair—"

"Tut, tut!" he interrupted. "You did very well. He should himself have been more on his guard. I saw everything which passed."

"You saw it, sire!"

"You did not hear me follow you through the wood, then? I hardly lost sight of you from the moment that you left your quarters until poor De Goudin fell. The counterfeit Emperor was in front of you and the real one behind. You will now escort me back to the palace."

He whispered an order to his Mamelukes, who saluted in silence and remained where they were standing. For my part, I followed the Emperor with my pelisse bursting with pride. My word, I have always carried myself as a hussar should, but Lasalle himself never strutted and swung his dolman as I did that night! Who should clink his spurs and clatter his sabre if it were not I—I, Etienne Gerard—the confidant of the Emperor, the chosen swordsman of the light cavalry, the man who slew the would-be assassins of Napoleon? But he noticed my bearing and turned upon me like a blight.

"Is that the way to carry yourself on a secret mission?" he hissed, with that cold glare in his eyes. "Is it thus that you will make your comrades believe that nothing remarkable has occurred? Have done with this nonsense, monsieur, or you will find yourself transferred to the sappers, where you would have harder work and duller plumage."

That was the way with the Emperor. If ever he thought that anyone might have a claim upon him, he took the first opportunity to show him the gulf that lay between. I saluted and was silent, but I must confess to you that it hurt me after all that had passed between us. He led on to the palace, where we passed through the side door and up into his own cabinet. There were a couple of grenadiers at the staircase, and their eyes started out from under their fur caps, I promise you, when they saw a young lieutenant of hussars going up to the Emperor's room at midnight. I stood by the door, as I had done in the afternoon, while he flung himself down in an arm-chair, and remained silent so long that it seemed to me that he had forgotten all about me. I ventured at last upon a slight cough to remind him.

"Ah, Monsieur Gerard," said he, "you are very curious, no doubt, as to the meaning of all this?"

"I am quite content, sire, if it is your pleasure not to tell me," I answered.

"Ta, ta, ta," said he, impatiently. "These are only words. The moment that you were outside that door you would begin making inquiries about what it means. In two days your brother officers would know about it, in three days it would be all over Fontainebleau, and it would be in Paris on the fourth. Now, if I tell you enough to appease your curiosity, there is some reasonable hope that you may be able to keep the matter to yourself."

He did not understand me, this Emperor, and yet I could only bow and be silent.

"A few words will make it clear to you," said he, speaking very swiftly and pacing up and down the room. "They were Corsicans, these two men. I had known them in my youth. We had belonged to the same society—Brothers of Ajaccio, as we called ourselves. It was founded in the old Paoli days, you understand, and we had some strict rules of our own which were not infringed with impunity."

A very grim look came over his face as he spoke, and it seemed to me that all that was French had gone out of him, and that it was the pure Corsican, the man of strong passions and of strange revenges, who stood before me. His memory had gone back to those early days of his, and for five minutes, wrapped in thought, he paced up and down the room with his quick little tiger steps. Then with an impatient wave of his hands he came back to his palace and to me.

"The rules of such a society," he continued, "are all very well for a private citizen. In the old days there was no more loyal brother than I. But circumstances change, and it would be neither for my welfare nor for that of France that I should now submit myself to them. They wanted to hold me to it, and so brought their fate upon their own heads. These were the two chiefs of the order, and they had come from Corsica to summon me to meet them at the spot which they named. I knew what such a summons meant. No man had ever returned from obeying one. On the other hand, if I did not go, I was sure that disaster would follow. I am a brother myself, you remember, and I know their ways."

Again there came that hardening of his mouth and cold glitter of his eyes.

"You perceive my dilemma, Monsieur Gerard," said he. "How would you have acted yourself, under such circumstances?"

"Given the word to the 10th Hussars, sire," I cried. "Patrols could have swept the woods from end to end, and brought these two rascals to your feet."

He smiled, but he shook his head.

"I had very excellent reasons why I did not wish them taken alive," said he. "You can understand that an assassin's tongue might be as dangerous a weapon as an assassin's dagger. I will not disguise from you that I wished to avoid scandal at all cost. That was why I ordered you to take no pistols with you. That also is why my Mamelukes will remove all traces of the affair, and nothing more will be heard about it. I thought of all possible plans, and I am convinced that I selected the best one. Had I sent more than one guard with De Goudin into the woods, then the brothers would not have appeared. They would not change their plans or miss their chance for the sake of a single man. It was Colonel Lasalle's accidental presence at the moment when I received the summons which led to my choosing one of his hussars for the mission. I selected you, Monsieur Gerard, because I wanted a man who could handle a sword, and who would not pry more deeply into the affair than I desired. I trust that, in this respect, you will justify my choice as well as you have done in your bravery and skill."

"Sire," I answered, "you may rely upon it."

"As long as I live," said he, "you never open your lips upon this subject."

"I dismiss it entirely from my mind, sire. I will efface it from my recollection as if it had never been. I will promise you to go out of your cabinet at this moment exactly as I was when I entered it at four o'clock."

"You cannot do that," said the Emperor, smiling. "You were a lieutenant at that time. You will permit me, Captain, to wish you a very good-night."

HOW THE BRIGADIER CAME
TO THE CASTLE OF GLOOM

You do very well, my friends, to treat me with some little reverence, for in honouring me you are honouring both France and yourselves. It is not merely an old, grey-moustached officer whom you see eating his omelette or draining his glass, but it is a piece of history, and of the most glorious history which our own or any country has ever had. In me you see one of the last of those wonderful men, the men who were veterans when they were yet boys, who learned to use a sword earlier than a razor, and who during a hundred battles had never once let the enemy see the colour of their knapsacks. For twenty years we were teaching Europe how to fight, and even when they had learned their lesson it was only the thermometer, and never the bayonet, which could break the Grand Army down. Berlin, Naples, Vienna, Madrid, Lisbon, Moscow—we stabled our horses in them all. Yes, my friends, I say again that you do well to send your children to me with flowers, for these ears have heard the trumpet calls of France, and these eyes have seen her standards in lands where they may never be seen again.

Even now, when I doze in my arm-chair, I can see those great warriors stream before me—the green-jacketed chasseurs, the giant cuirassiers, Poniatowsky's lancers, the white-mantled dragoons, the nodding bearskins of the horse grenadiers. And then there comes the thick, low rattle of the drums, and through wreaths of dust and smoke I see the line of high bonnets, the row of brown faces, the swing and toss of the long, red plumes amid the sloping lines of steel. And there rides Ney with his red head, and

Lefebvre with his bulldog jaw, and Lannes with his Gascon swagger; and then amidst the gleam of brass and the flaunting feathers I catch a glimpse of *him,* the man with the pale smile, the rounded shoulders, and the far-off eyes. There is an end of my sleep, my friends, for up I spring from my chair, with a cracked voice calling and a silly hand outstretched, so that Madame Titaux has one more laugh at the old fellow who lives among the shadows.

Although I was a full Chief of the Brigade when the wars came to an end, and had every hope of soon being made a General of Division, it is still rather to my earlier days that I turn when I wish to talk of the glories and the trials of a soldier's life. For you will understand that when an officer has so many men and horses under him, he has his mind full of recruits and remounts, fodder and farriers, and quarters, so that even when he is not in the face of the enemy, life is a very serious matter for him. But when he is only a lieutenant or a captain, he has nothing heavier than his epaulettes upon his shoulders, so that he can clink his spurs and swing his dolman, drain his glass and kiss his girl, thinking of nothing save of enjoying a gallant life. That is the time when he is likely to have adventures, and it is most often to that time that I shall turn in the stories which I may have for you. So it will be to-night when I tell you of my visit to the Castle of Gloom; of the strange mission of Sub-Lieutenant Duroc, and of the horrible affair of the man who was once known as Jean Carabin, and afterwards as the Baron Straubenthal.

You must know, then, that in the February of 1807, immediately after the taking of Danzig, Major Legendre and I were commissioned to bring four hundred remounts from Prussia into Eastern Poland.

The hard weather, and especially the great battle at Eylau, had killed so many of the horses that there was some danger of our beautiful Tenth of Hussars becoming a battalion of light infantry. We knew, therefore, both the Major and I, that we should be very welcome at the front. We did not advance very rapidly, however, for the snow was deep, the roads detestable, and we had but twenty returning invalids to assist us. Besides, it is impossible, when you have a daily change of forage, and sometimes none at all, to move horses faster than a walk. I am aware that in the story-books the cavalry whirls past at the maddest of gallops; but for my own part, after twelve campaigns, I should be very satisfied to know that my brigade could always walk upon the march and trot in the presence of the enemy. This I say of the hussars and chasseurs, mark you, so that it is far more the case with cuirassiers or dragoons.

For myself I am fond of horses, and to have four hundred of them, of every age and shade and character, all under my own hands, was a very great pleasure to me. They were from Pomerania for the most part, though some were from Normandy and some from Alsace, and it amused us to notice that they differed in character as much as the people of those provinces. We observed also, what I have often proved since, that the nature of a horse can be told by his colour, from the coquettish light bay full of fancies and nerves, to the hardy chestnut, and from the docile roan to the pig-headed rusty-black. All this has nothing in the world to do with my story, but how is an officer of cavalry to get on with his tale when he finds four hundred horses waiting for him at the outset? It is my habit, you see, to talk of that which interests myself, and so I hope that I may interest you.

We crossed the Vistula opposite Marienwerder, and had got as far as Riesenberg, when Major Legendre came into my room in the post-house with an open paper in his hand.

"You are to leave me," said he, with despair upon his face.

It was no very great grief to me to do that, for he was, if I may say so, hardly worthy to have such a subaltern. I saluted, however, in silence.

"It is an order from General Lasalle," he continued; "you are to proceed to Rossel instantly, and to report yourself at the head-quarters of the regiment."

No message could have pleased me better. I was already very well thought of by my superior officers, although I may say that none of them had quite done me justice. It was evident to me, therefore, that this sudden order meant that the regiment was about to see service once more, and that Lasalle understood how incomplete my squadron would be without me. It is true that it came at an inconvenient moment, for the keeper of the post-house had a daughter—one of those ivory-skinned, black haired Polish girls—whom I had hoped to have some further talk with. Still, it is not for the pawn to argue when the fingers of the player move him from the square; so down I went, saddled my big black charger, Rataplan, and set off instantly upon my lonely journey.

My word, it was a treat for those poor Poles and Jews, who have so little to brighten their dull lives, to see such a picture as that before their doors. The frosty morning air made Rataplan's great black limbs and the beautiful curves of his back and sides gleam and shimmer with every gambade. As for me, the rattle of hoofs upon a road, and the jingle of bridle chains which comes with every toss of a saucy head, would even now set my blood dancing though my veins. You may think, then, how I carried myself in my five-and-twentieth year—I, Etienne Gerard, the picked horseman and surest blade in the ten regiments of hussars. Blue was our colour in the Tenth—a sky-blue dolman and pelisse with a scarlet front—and it was said of us in the army that we could set a whole population running, the women towards us, and the men away. There were bright eyes in the Riesenberg windows that morning, which seemed to beg me to tarry; but what can a soldier do, save to kiss his hand and shake his bridle as he rides upon his way?

It was a bleak season to ride through the poorest and ugliest country in Europe, but there was a cloudless sky above, and a bright, cold sun, which shimmered on the huge snowfields. My breath reeked into the frosty air, and Rataplan sent up two feathers of steam from his nostrils, while the icicles drooped from the side-irons of his bit. I let him trot to warm his limbs, while for my own part I had too much to think of to give much heed to the cold. To north and south stretched the great plains, mottled over with dark clumps of fir and lighter patches of larch. A few cottages peeped out here and there, but it was only three months since the Grand Army had passed that way, and you know what that meant to a country. The Poles were our friends, it was true, but out of a hundred thousand men, only the Guard had waggons, and the rest had to live as best they might. It did not surprise me, therefore, to see no signs of cattle and no smoke from the silent houses. A weal had been left across the country where the great host had passed, and it was said that even the rats were starved wherever the Emperor had led his men.

By midday I had got as far as the village of Saalfeldt, but as I was on the direct road for Osterode, where the Emperor was wintering, and also for the main camp of the seven divisions of infantry, the highway was choked with carriages and carts. What with artillery caissons and waggons and couriers, and the ever-thickening stream of recruits and stragglers, it seemed to me that it would be a very long time before I should join my comrades. The plains, however, were five feet deep in snow, so there was nothing for it but to plod upon our way. It was with joy, therefore, that I found a second road which branched away from the other, trending through a fir-wood towards the north. There was a small auberge at the cross-roads, and a patrol of the Third Hussars of Conflans — the very regiment of which I was afterwards colonel — were mounting their horses at the door. On the steps stood their officer, a slight, pale young man, who looked more like a young priest from a seminary than a leader of the devil-may-care rascals before him.

"Good day, sir," said he, seeing that I pulled up my horse.

"Good-day," I answered. "I am Lieutenant Etienne Gerard, of the Tenth."

I could see by his face that he had heard of me. Everybody had heard of me since my duel with the six fencing-masters. My manner, however, served to put him at his ease with me.

"I am Sub-Lieutenant Duroc, of the Third," said he.

"Newly joined?" I asked.

"Last week."

I had thought as much, from his white face and from the way in which he let his men lounge upon their horses. It was not so long, however, since I had learned myself what it was like when a schoolboy has to give orders to veteran troopers. It made me blush, I remember, to shout abrupt commands to men who had seen more battles than I had years, and it would have come more natural for me to say, "With your permission, we shall now wheel into line," or, "If you think it best, we shall trot." I did not think the less of the lad, therefore, when I observed that his men were somewhat out of hand, but I gave them a glance which stiffened them in their saddles.

"May I ask, monsieur, whether you are going by this northern road?" I asked.

"My orders are to patrol it as far as Arensdorf," said he.

"Then I will, with your permission, ride so far with you," said I. "It is very clear that the longer way will be the faster."

So it proved, for this road led away from the army into a country which was given over to Cossacks and marauders, and it was as bare as the other was crowded. Duroc and I rode in front, with our six troopers clattering in the rear. He was a good boy, this Duroc, with his head full of the nonsense that they teach at St Cyr, knowing more about Alexander and Pompey than how to mix a horse's fodder or care for a horse's feet. Still, he was, as I have said, a good boy, unspoiled as yet by the camp. It pleased me to hear him prattle away about his sister Marie and about his mother in Amiens. Presently we found ourselves at the village of Hayenau. Duroc rode up to the post-house and asked to see the master.

"Can you tell me," said he, "whether the man who calls himself the Baron Straubenthal lives in these parts?"

The postmaster shook his head, and we rode upon our way.

I took no notice of this, but when, at the next village, my comrade repeated the same question, with the same result, I could not help asking who this Baron Straubenthal might be.

"He is a man," said Duroc, with a sudden flush upon his boyish face, "to whom I have a very important message to convey."

Well, this was not satisfactory, but there was something in my companion's manner which told me that any further questioning would be distasteful to him. I said nothing more, therefore, but

Duroc would still ask every peasant whom we met whether he could give him any news of the Baron Straubenthal.

For my own part I was endeavouring, as an officer of light cavalry should, to form an idea of the lay of the country, to note the course of the streams, and to mark the places where there should be fords. Every step was taking us farther from the camp round the flanks of which we were travelling. Far to the south a few plumes of grey smoke in the frosty air marked the position of some of our outposts. To the north, however, there was nothing between ourselves and the Russian winter quarters. Twice on the extreme horizon I caught a glimpse of the glitter of steel, and pointed it out to my companion. It was too distant for us to tell whence it came, but we had little doubt that it was from the lance-heads of marauding Cossacks.

The sun was just setting when we rode over a low hill and saw a small village upon our right, and on our left a high black castle, which jutted out from amongst the pine-woods. A farmer with his cart was approaching us — a matted-haired, downcast fellow, in a sheepskin jacket.

"What village is this?" asked Duroc.

"It is Arensdorf," he answered, in his barbarous German dialect.

"Then here I am to stay the night," said my young companion. Then, turning to the farmer, he asked his eternal question, "Can you tell me where the Baron Straubenthal lives?"

"Why, it is he who owns the Castle of Gloom," said the farmer, pointing to the dark turrets over the distant fir forest.

Duroc gave a shout like the sportsman who sees his game rising in front of him. The lad seemed to have gone off his head — his eyes shining, his face deathly white, and such a grim set about his mouth as made the farmer shrink away from him. I can see him now, leaning forward on his brown horse, with his eager gaze fixed upon the great black tower.

"Why do you call it the Castle of Gloom?" I asked.

"Well, it's the name it bears upon the countryside," said the farmer. "By all accounts there have been some black doings up yonder. It's not for nothing that the wickedest man in Poland has been living there these fourteen years past."

"A Polish nobleman?" I asked.

"Nay, we breed no such men in Poland," he answered.

"A Frenchman, then?" cried Duroc.

"They say that he came from France."

"And with red hair?"

"As red as a fox."

"Yes, yes, it is my man," cried my companion, quivering all over in his excitement. "It is the hand of Providence which has led me here. Who can say that there is not justice in this world? Come, Monsieur Gerard, for I must see the men safely quartered before I can attend to this private matter."

He spurred on his horse, and ten minutes later we were at the door of the inn of Arensdorf, where his men were to find their quarters for the night.

Well, all this was no affair of mine, and I could not imagine what the meaning of it might be. Rossel was still far off, but I determined to ride on for a few hours and take my chance of some wayside barn in which I could find shelter for Rataplan and myself. I had mounted my horse, therefore, after tossing off a cup of wine, when young Duroc came running out of the door and laid his hand upon my knee.

"Monsieur Gerard," he panted, "I beg of you not to abandon me like this!"

"My good sir," said I, "if you would tell me what is the matter and what you would wish me to do, I should be better able to tell you if I could be of any assistance to you."

"You can be of the very greatest," he cried. "Indeed, from all that I have heard of you, Monsieur Gerard, you are the one man whom I should wish to have by my side to-night."

"You forget that I am riding to join my regiment."

"You cannot, in any case, reach it to-night. To-morrow will bring you to Rossel. By staying with me you will confer the very greatest kindness upon me, and you will aid me in a matter which concerns my own honour and the honour of my family. I am compelled, however, to confess to you that some personal danger may possibly be involved."

It was a crafty thing for him to say. Of course, I sprang from Rataplan's back and ordered the groom to lead him back into the stables.

"Come into the inn," said I, "and let me know exactly what it is that you wish me to do."

He led the way into a sitting-room, and fastened the door lest we should be interrupted. He was a well-grown lad, and as he stood in the glare of the lamp, with the light beating upon his earnest face and upon his uniform of silver grey, which suited him to a marvel, I felt my heart warm towards him. Without going so far as to say that he carried himself as I had done at his age, there was at least similarity enough to make me feel in sympathy with him.

"I can explain it all in a few words," said he. "If I have not already satisfied your very natural curiosity, it is because the subject is so painful a one to me that I can hardly bring myself to allude to it. I cannot, however, ask for your assistance without explaining to you exactly how the matter lies.

"You must know, then, that my father was the well-known banker, Christophe Duroc, who was murdered by the people during the September massacres. As you are aware, the mob took possession of the prisons, chose three so-called judges to pass sentence upon the unhappy aristocrats, and then tore them to pieces when they were passed out into the street. My father had been a benefactor of the poor all his life. There were many to plead for him. He had the fever, too, and was carried in, half-dead, upon a blanket. Two of the judges were in favour of acquitting him; the third, a young Jacobin, whose huge body and brutal mind had made him a leader among these wretches, dragged him, with his own hands, from the litter, kicked him again and again with his heavy boots, and hurled him out of the door, where in an instant he was torn limb from limb under circumstances which are too horrible for me to describe. This, as you perceive, was murder, even under their own unlawful laws, for two of their own judges had pronounced in my father's favour.

"Well, when the days of order came back again, my elder brother began to make inquiries about this man. I was only a child then, but it was a family matter, and it was discussed in my presence. The fellow's name was Carabin. He was one of Sansterre's Guard, and a noted duellist. A foreign lady named the Baroness Straubenthal having been dragged before the Jacobins, he had gained her liberty for her on the promise that she with her money and estates should be his. He had married her, taken her name and title, and escaped out of France at the time of the fall of Robespierre. What had become of him we had no means of learning.

"You will think, doubtless, that it would be easy for us to find him, since we had both his name and his title. You must remember, however, that the Revolution left us without money, and that without money such a search is very difficult. Then came the Empire, and it became more difficult still, for, as you are aware, the Emperor considered that the 18th Brumaire brought all accounts to a settlement, and that on that day a veil had been drawn across the past. None the less, we kept our own family story and our own family plans.

"My brother joined the army, and passed with it through all Southern Europe, asking everywhere for the Baron Straubenthal. Last October he was killed at Jena, with his mission still unfulfilled. Then it became my turn, and I have the good fortune to hear of the very man of whom I am in search at one of the first Polish villages which I have to visit, and within a fortnight of joining my regiment. And then, to make the matter even better, I find myself in the company of one whose name is never mentioned throughout the army save in connection with some daring and generous deed."

This was all very well, and I listened to it with the greatest interest, but I was none the clearer as to what young Duroc wished me to do.

"How can I be of service to you?" I asked.

"By coming up with me."

"To the Castle?"

"Precisely."

"When?"

"At once."

"But what do you intend to do?"

"I shall know what to do. But I wish you to be with me, all the same."

Well, it was never in my nature to refuse an adventure, and, besides, I had every sympathy with the lad's feelings. It is very well to forgive one's enemies, but one wishes to give them something to forgive also. I held out my hand to him, therefore.

"I must be on my way for Rossel tomorrow morning, but to-night I am yours," said I.

We left our troopers in snug quarters, and, as it was but a mile to the Castle, we did not disturb our horses. To tell the truth, I hate to see a cavalry man walk, and I hold that just as he is the most gallant thing upon earth when he has his saddle-flaps between his knees, so he is the most clumsy when he has to loop up his sabre and his sabre-tasche in one hand and turn in his toes for fear of catching the rowels of his spurs. Still, Duroc and I were of the age when one can carry things off, and I dare swear that no woman at least would have quarrelled with the appearance of the two young hussars, one in blue and one in grey, who set out that night from the Arensdorf post-house. We both carried our swords, and for my own part I slipped a pistol from my holster into the inside of my pelisse, for it seemed to me that there might be some wild work before us.

The track which led to the Castle wound through pitch-black fir-wood, where we could see nothing save the ragged patch of stars above our head. Presently, however, it opened up, and there was the Castle right in front of us, about as far as a carbine would carry. It was a huge, uncouth place, and bore every mark of being exceedingly old, with turrets at every corner, and a square keep on the side which was nearest to us. In all its great shadow there was no sign of light save for a single window, and no sound came from it. To me there was something awful in its size and its silence, which corresponded so well with its sinister name. My companion pressed on eagerly, and I followed him along the ill-kept path which led to the gate.

There was no bell or knocker upon the great, iron-studded door, and it was only by pounding with the hilts of our sabres that we could attract attention. A thin, hawk-faced man, with a beard up to his temples, opened it at last. He carried a lantern in one hand, and in the other a chain which held an enormous black hound. His manner at the first moment was threatening, but the sight of our uniforms and of our faces turned it into one of sulky reserve.

"The Baron Straubenthal does not receive visitors at so late an hour," said he, speaking in very excellent French.

"You can inform Baron Straubenthal that I have come eight hundred leagues to see him, and that I will not leave until I have done so," said my companion. I could not have said it with a better voice and manner.

The fellow took a sidelong look at us, and tugged at his black beard in his perplexity.

"To tell the truth, gentlemen," said he, "the Baron has a cup or two of wine in him at this hour, and you would certainly find him a more entertaining companion if you were to come again in the morning."

He had opened the door a little wider as he spoke, and I saw by the light of the lamp in the hall behind him that three other rough fellows were standing there, one of whom held another of these monstrous hounds. Duroc must have seen it also, but it made no difference to his resolution.

"Enough talk," said he, pushing the man to one side. "It is with your master that I have to deal."

The fellows in the hall made way for him as he strode in among them, so great is the power of one man who knows what he wants over several who are not sure of themselves. My companion tapped one of them upon the shoulder with as much assurance as though he owned him.

"Show me to the Baron," said he.

The man shrugged his shoulders, and answered something in Polish. The fellow with the beard, who had shut and barred the front door, appeared to be the only one among them who could speak French.

"Well, you shall have your way," said he, with a sinister smile. "You shall see the Baron. And perhaps, before you have finished, you will wish that you had taken my advice."

We followed him down the hall, which was stone-flagged and very spacious, with skins scattered upon the floor, and the heads of wild beasts upon the walls. At the farther end he threw open a door, and we entered.

It was a small room, scantily furnished, with the same marks of neglect and decay which met us at every turn. The walls were hung with discoloured tapestry, which had come loose at one corner, so as to expose the rough stonework behind. A second door, hung with a curtain, faced us upon the other side. Between lay a square table, strewn with dirty dishes and the sordid remains of a meal. Several bottles were scattered over it. At the head of it, and facing us, there sat a huge man, with a lion-like head, and great shock of orange-coloured hair. His beard was of the same glaring hue; matted and tangled and coarse as a horse's mane. I have seen some strange faces in my time, but never one more brutal than that, with its small, vicious, blue eyes, its white, crumpled cheeks, and the thick, hanging lip which protruded over his monstrous beard. His head swayed about on his shoulders, and he looked at us with the vague, dim gaze of a drunken man. Yet he was not so drunk but that our uniforms carried their message to him.

"Well, my brave boys," he hiccoughed. "What is the latest news from Paris, eh? You're going to free Poland, I hear, and have meantime all become slaves yourselves—slaves to a little aristocrat with his grey coat and his three-cornered hat. No more citizens either, I am told, and nothing but monsieur and madame. My faith, some more heads will have to roll into the sawdust basket some of these mornings."

Duroc advanced in silence, and stood by the ruffian's side.

"Jean Carabin," said he.

The Baron started, and the film of drunkenness seemed to be clearing from his eyes.

"Jean Carabin," said Duroc, once more.

He sat up and grasped the arms of his chair.

"What do you mean be repeating that name, young man?" he asked.

"Jean Carabin, you are a man whom I have long wished to meet."

"Supposing that I once had such a name, how can it concern you, since you must have been a child when I bore it?"

"My name is Duroc."

"Not the son of—?"

"The son of the man you murdered."

The Baron tried to laugh, but there was terror in his eyes.

"We must let bygones be bygones, young man," he cried. "It was our life or theirs in those days: the aristocrats or the people. Your father was of the Gironde. He fell. I was of the mountain. Most of my comrades fell. It was all the fortune of war. We must forget all this and learn to know each other better, you and I." He held out a red, twitching hand as he spoke.

"Enough," said young Duroc. "If I were to pass my sabre through you as you sit in that chair, I should do what is just and right. I dishonour my blade by crossing it with yours. And yet you are a Frenchman, and have even held a commission under the same flag as myself. Rise, then, and defend yourself!"

"Tut, tut!" cried the Baron. "It is all very well for you young bloods—"

Duroc's patience could stand no more. He swung his open hand into the centre of the great orange beard. I saw a lip fringed with blood, and two glaring eyes above it.

"You shall die for that blow."

"That is better," said Duroc.

"My sabre!" cried the other; "I will not keep you waiting, I promise you!" and he hurried from the room.

I have said that there was a second door covered with a curtain. Hardly had the Baron vanished when there ran from behind it a woman, young and beautiful. So swiftly and noiselessly did she move that she was between us in an instant, and it was only the shaking curtains which told us whence she had come.

"I have seen it all," she cried. "Oh, sir, you have carried yourself splendidly." She stooped to my companion's hand, and kissed it again and again ere he could disengage it from her grasp.

"Nay, madame, why should you kiss my hand?" he cried.

"Because it is the hand which struck him on his vile, lying mouth. Because it may be the hand which will avenge my mother. I am his step-daughter. The woman whose heart he broke was my mother. I loathe him, I fear him. Ah, there is his step!" In an instant she had vanished as suddenly as she had come. A moment later, the Baron entered with a drawn sword in his hand, and the fellow who had admitted us at his heels.

"This is my secretary," said he. "He will be my friend in this affair. But we shall need more elbow-room than we can find here. Perhaps you will kindly come with me to a more spacious apartment."

It was evidently impossible to fight in a chamber which was blocked by a great table. We followed him out, therefore, into the dimly-lit hall. At the farther end a light was shining through an open door.

"We shall find what we want in here," said the man with the dark beard. It was large, empty room, with rows of barrels and cases round the walls. A strong lamp stood upon a shelf in the corner. The floor was level and true, so that no swordsman could ask for more. Duroc drew his sabre and sprang into it. The Baron stood back with a bow and motioned me to follow my companion. Hardly were my heels over the threshold when the heavy door crashed behind us and the key screamed in the lock. We were taken in a trap.

For a moment we could not realize it. Such incredible baseness was outside all our experiences. Then, as we understood how foolish we had been to trust for an instant a man with such a history, a flush of rage came over us, rage against his villainy and against our own stupidity. We rushed at the door together, beating it with our fists and kicking with our heavy boots. The sound of our blows and our execrations must have resounded through the Castle. We called to this villain, hurling at him every name which might pierce even into his hardened soul. But the door was enormous — such a door as one finds in mediæval castles — made of huge beams clamped together with iron. It was as easy to break as a square of the Old Guard. And our cries appeared to be of as little avail as our blows, for they only brought for answer the clattering echoes from the high roof above us. When you have done some soldiering, you soon learn to put up with what cannot be altered. It was I, then, who first recovered my calmness, and prevailed upon Duroc to join with me in examining the apartment which had become our dungeon.

There was only one window, which had no glass in it and was so narrow that one could not so much as get one's head through. It was high up, and Duroc had to stand upon a barrel in order to see from it.

"What can you see?" I asked.

"Fir-woods, and an avenue of snow between them," said he. "Ah!" he gave a cry of surprise.

I sprang upon the barrel beside him. There was, as he said, a long, clear strip of snow in front. A man was riding down it, flogging his horse and galloping like a madman. As we watched, he grew smaller and smaller, until he was swallowed up by the black shadows of the forest.

"What does that mean?" asked Duroc.

"No good for us," said I. "He may have gone for some brigands to cut our throats. Let us see if we cannot find a way out of this mouse-trap before the cat can arrive."

The one piece of good fortune in our favour was that beautiful lamp. It was nearly full of oil, and would last us until morning. In the dark our situation would have been far more difficult. By its light we proceeded to examine the packages and cases which lined the walls. In some places there was only a single line of them, while in one corner they were piled nearly to the ceiling. It seemed that we were in the storehouse of the Castle, for there were a great number of cheeses, vegetables of various kinds, bins full of dried fruits, and a line of wine barrels. One of these had a spigot in it, and as I had eaten little during the day, I was glad of a cup of claret and some food. As to Duroc, he would take nothing, but paced up and down the room in a fever of impatience. "I'll have him yet!" he cried, every now and then. "The rascal shall not escape me!"

This was all very well, but it seemed to me, as I sat on a great round cheese eating my supper, that this youngster was thinking rather too much of his own family affairs and too little of the fine scrape into which he had got me. After all, his father had been dead fourteen years, and nothing could set that right; but here was Etienne Gerard, the most dashing lieutenant in the whole Grand Army, in imminent danger of being cut off at the very outset of his brilliant career. Who was ever to know the heights to which I might have risen if I were knocked on the head in this hole-and-corner business, which had nothing whatever to do with France or the Emperor? I could not help thinking what a fool I had been, when I had a fine war before me and everything which a man could desire, to go off upon a hare-brained expedition of this sort, as if it were not enough to have a quarter of a million Russians to fight against, without plunging into all sorts of private quarrels as well.

"That is all very well," I said at last, as I heard Duroc muttering his threats. "You may do what you like to him when you get the upper hand. At present the question rather is, what is *he* going to do to us?"

"Let him do his worst!" cried the boy. "I owe a duty to my father."

"That is mere foolishness," said I. "If you owe a duty to your father, I owe one to my mother, which is to get us out of this business safe and sound."

My remark brought him to his senses.

"I have thought too much of myself!" he cried. "Forgive me, Monsieur Gerard. Give me your advice as to what I should do."

"Well," said I, "it is not for our health that they have shut us up here among the cheeses. They mean to make an end of us if they can. That is certain. They hope that no one knows that we have come here, and that none will trace us if we remain. Do your hussars know where you have gone to?"

"I said nothing."

"Hum! It is clear that we cannot be starved here. They must come to us if they are to kill us. Behind a barricade of barrels we could hold our own against the five rascals whom we have seen. That is, probably, why they have sent that messenger for assistance."

"We must get out before he returns."

"Precisely, if we are to get out at all."

"Could we not burn down this door?" he cried.

"Nothing could be easier," said I. "There are several casks of oil in the corner. My only objection is that we should ourselves be nicely toasted, like two little oyster pâtés."

"Can you not suggest something?" he cried, in despair. "Ah, what is that?"

There had been a low sound at our little window, and a shadow came between the stars and ourselves. A small, white hand was stretched into the lamplight. Something glittered between the fingers.

"Quick! Quick!" cried a woman's voice.

We were on the barrel in an instant.

"They have sent for the Cossacks. Your lives are at stake. Ah, I am lost! I am lost!"

There was the sound of rushing steps, a hoarse oath, a blow, and the stars were once more twinkling through the window. We stood helpless upon our barrel with our blood cold with horror.

Half a minute afterwards we heard a smothered scream, ending in a choke. A great door slammed somewhere in the silent night.

"Those ruffians have seized her. They will kill her," I cried.

Duroc sprang down with the inarticulate shouts of one whose reason had left him. He struck the door so frantically with his naked hands that he left a blotch of blood with every blow.

"Here is the key!" I shouted, picking one from the floor. "She must have thrown it in at the instant that she was torn away."

My companion snatched it from me with a shriek of joy. A moment later he dashed it down upon the boards. It was so small that it was lost in the enormous lock. Duroc sank upon one of the boxes with his head between his hands. He sobbed in his despair. I could have sobbed, too, when I thought of the woman and how helpless we were to save her.

But I am not easily baffled. After all, this key must have been sent to us for a purpose. The lady could not bring us that of the door, because this murderous step-father of hers would most certainly have it in his pocket. Yet this other must have a meaning, or why should she risk her life to place it in our hands? It would say little for our wits if we could not find out what that meaning might be.

I set to work moving all the cases out from the wall, and Duroc, gaining new hope from my courage, helped me with all his strength. It was no light task, for many of them were large and heavy. On we went, working like maniacs, slinging barrels, cheeses, and boxes pell-mell into the middle of the room. At last there only remained one huge barrel of vodki, which stood in the corner. With our united strength we rolled it out, and there was a little low wooden door in the wainscot behind it. The key fitted, and with a cry of delight we saw it swing open before us. With the lamp in my hand, I squeezed my way in, followed by my companion.

We were in the powder-magazine of the castle—a rough, walled cellar, with barrels all round it, and one with the top staved in in the centre. The powder from it lay in a black heap upon the floor. Beyond there was another door, but it was locked.

"We are no better off than before," cried Duroc. "We have no key."

"We have a dozen," I cried.

I pointed to the line of powder barrels.

"You would blow this door open?"

"Precisely."

"But you would explode the magazine."

It was true, but I was not at the end of my resources.

"We will blow open the store-room door," I cried.

I ran back and seized a tin box which had been filled with candles. It was about the size of my shako—large enough to hold several pounds of powder. Duroc filled it while I cut off the end of a candle. When we had finished, it would have puzzled a colonel of engineers to make a better petard. I put three cheeses on the top of each other and placed it above them, so as to lean against the lock. Then we lit our candle-end and ran for shelter, shutting the door of the magazine behind us.

It is no joke, my friends, to lie among all those tons of powder, with the knowledge that if the flame of the explosion should penetrate through one thin door our blackened limbs would be shot higher than the Castle keep. Who could have believed that a half-inch of candle could take so long to burn? My ears were straining all the time for the thudding of the hoofs of the Cossacks who were coming to destroy us. I had almost made up my mind that the candle must have gone out when there was a smack like a bursting bomb, our door flew to bits, and pieces of cheese, with a shower of turnips, apples, and splinters of cases, were shot in among us. As we rushed out we had to stagger through an impenetrable smoke, with all sorts of débris beneath our feet, but there was a glimmering square where the dark door had been. The petard had done its work.

In fact, it had done more for us than we had even ventured to hope. It had shattered gaolers as well as gaol. The first thing that I saw as I came out into the hall was a man with a butcher's axe in his hand, lying flat upon his back, with a gaping wound across his forehead. The second was a huge dog, with two of its legs broken, twisting in agony upon the floor. As it raised itself up I saw the two broken ends flapping like flails. At the same instant I heard a cry, and there was Duroc, thrown against the wall, with the other hound's teeth in his throat. He pushed it off with his left hand, while again and again he passed his sabre through its body, but it was not until I blew out its brains with my pistol that the iron jaws relaxed, and the fierce, bloodshot eyes were glazed in death.

There was no time for us to pause. A woman's scream from in front—a scream of mortal terror—told us that even now we might be too late. There were two other men in the hall, but they cowered away from our drawn swords and furious faces. The blood was streaming from Duroc's neck and dyeing the grey fur of his pelisse. Such was the lad's fire, however, that he shot in front of me, and it was only over his shoulder that I caught a glimpse of the scene as we rushed into the chamber in which we had first seen the master of the Castle of Gloom.

The Baron was standing in the middle of the room, with his tangled mane bristling like an angry lion. He was, as I have said, a huge man, with enormous shoulders; and as he stood there, with his face flushed with rage and his sword advanced, I could not but think that, in spite of all his villanies, he had a proper figure for a grenadier. The lady lay cowering in a chair behind him. A weal across one of her white arms and a dog-whip upon the floor were enough to show that our escape had hardly been in time to save her from his brutality. He gave a howl like a wolf as we broke in, and was upon us in an instant, hacking and driving, with a curse at every blow.

I have already said that the room gave no space for swordsmanship. My young companion was in front of me in the narrow passage between the table and the wall, so that I could only look on without being able to aid him. The lad knew something of his weapon, and was as fierce and active as a wild cat, but in so narrow a space the weight and strength of the giant gave him the advantage. Besides, he was an admirable swordsman. His parade and riposte were as quick as lightening. Twice he touched Duroc upon the shoulder, and then, as the lad slipped up on a lunge, he whirled up his sword to finish him before he could recover his feet. I was quicker than he, however, and took the cut upon the pommel of my sabre.

"Excuse me," said I, "but you have still to deal with Etienne Gerard."

He drew back and leaned against the tapestry-covered wall, breathing in little, hoarse gasps, for his foul living was against him.

"Take your breath," said I. "I will await your convenience."

"You have no cause of quarrel against me," he panted.

"I owe you some little attention," said I, "for having shut me up in your store-room. Besides, if all other were wanting, I see cause enough upon that lady's arm."

"Have your way, then!" he snarled, and leaped at me like a madman. For a minute I saw only the blazing blue eyes, and the red glazed point which stabbed and stabbed, rasping off to right or to left, and yet ever back at my throat and my breast. I had never thought that such good sword-play was to be found at Paris in the days of the Revolution. I do not suppose that in all my little affairs I have met six men who had a better knowledge of their weapon. But he knew that I was his master. He read death in my eyes, and I could see that he read it. The flush died from his face. His breath came in shorter and in thicker gasps. Yet he fought on, even after the final thrust had come, and died still hacking and cursing, with foul cries upon his lips, and his blood clotting upon his orange beard. I who speak to you have seen so many battles, that my old memory can scarce contain their names, and yet of all the terrible sights which these eyes have rested upon, there is none which I care to think of less than of that orange beard with the crimson stain in the centre, from which I had drawn my sword point.

It was only afterwards that I had time to think of all this. His monstrous body had hardly crashed down upon the floor before the woman in the corner sprang to her feet, clapping her hands together and screaming out her delight. For my part I was disgusted to see a woman take such delight in a deed of blood, and I gave no thought as to the terrible wrongs which must have befallen her before she could so far forget the gentleness of her sex. It was on my tongue to tell her sharply to be silent, when a strange, choking smell took the breath from my nostrils, and a sudden, yellow glare brought out the figures upon the faded hangings.

"Duroc, Duroc!" I shouted, tugging at his shoulder. "The Castle is on fire!"

The boy lay senseless upon the ground, exhausted by his wounds. I rushed out into the hall to see whence the danger came. It was our explosion which had set alight to the dry framework of the door. Inside the store-room some of the boxes were already blazing. I glanced in, and as I did so my blood was turned to water by the sight of the powder barrels beyond, and of the loose heap upon the floor. It might be seconds, it could not be more than minutes, before the flames would be at the edge of it. These eyes will be closed in death, my friends, before they cease to see those crawling lines of fire and the black heap beyond.

How little I can remember what followed. Vaguely I can recall how I rushed into the chamber of death, how I seized Duroc by one limp hand and dragged him down the hall, the woman keeping pace with me and pulling at the other arm. Out of the gateway we rushed, and on down the snow-covered path until we were on the fringe of the fir forest. It was at that moment that I heard a crash behind me, and, glancing round, saw a great spout of fire shoot up into the wintry sky. An instant later there seemed to come a second crash far louder than the first. I saw the fir trees and the stars whirling round me, and I fell unconscious across the body of my comrade.

It was some weeks before I came to myself in the post-house of Arensdorf, and longer still before I could be told all that had befallen me. It was Duroc, already able to go soldiering, who came to my bedside and gave me an account of it. He it was who told me how a piece of timber had struck me on the head and had laid me almost dead upon the ground. From him, too, I learned how the Polish girl had run to Arensdorf, how she had roused our hussars, and how she had only just brought them back in time to save us from the spears of the Cossacks who had been summoned from their bivouac by that same black-bearded secretary whom we had seen galloping so swiftly over the snow. As to the brave lady who had twice saved our lives, I could not learn very much about her at that moment from Duroc, but when I chanced to meet him in Paris two years later, after the campaign of Wagram, I was not very much surprised to find that I needed no introduction to his bride, and that by the queer turns of fortune he had himself, had he chosen to use it, that very name and title of the Baron Straubenthal, which showed him to be the owner of the blackened ruins of the Castle of Gloom.

HOW THE BRIGADIER TOOK THE FIELD
AGAINST THE MARSHAL MILLEFLEURS

MASSENA was a thin, sour little fellow, and after his hunting accident he had only one eye, but when it looked out from under his cocked hat there was not much upon a field of battle which escaped it. He could stand in front of a battalion, and with a single sweep tell you if a buckle or a gaiter button were out of place. Neither the officers nor the men were very fond of him, for he was, as you know, a miser, and soldiers love that their leaders should be free-handed. At the same time, when it came to work they had a very high respect for him, and they would rather fight under him than under anyone except the Emperor himself, and Lannes, when he was alive. After all, if he had a tight grasp upon his money-bags, there was a day also, you must remember, when that same grip was upon Zurich and Genoa. He clutched on to his positions as he did to his strong box, and it took a very clever man to loosen him from either.

When I received his summons I went gladly to his headquarters, for I was always a great favourite of his, and there was no officer of whom he thought more highly. That was the best of serving with those good old generals, that they knew enough to be able to pick out a fine soldier when they saw one. He was seated alone in his tent, with his chin upon his hand, and his brow as wrinkled as if he had been asked for a subscription. He smiled, however, when he saw me before him.

"Good day, Colonel Gerard."

"Good day, Marshal."

"How is the Third of Hussars?"

"Seven hundred incomparable men upon seven hundred excellent horses."

"And your wounds—are they healed?"

"My wounds never heal, Marshal," I answered.

"And why?"

"Because I have always new ones."

"General Rapp must look to his laurels," said he, his face all breaking into wrinkles as he laughed. "He has had twenty-one from the enemy's bullets, and as many from Larrey's knives and probes. Knowing that you were hurt, Colonel, I have spared you of late."

"Which hurt me most of all."

"Tut, tut! Since the English got behind these accursed lines of Torres Vedras, there has been little for us to do. You did not miss much during your imprisonment at Dartmoor. But now we are on the eve of action."

"We advance?"

"No, retire."

My face must have shown my dismay. What, retire before this sacred dog of a Wellington—he who had listened unmoved to my words, and had sent me to his land of fogs! I could have sobbed as I thought of it.

"What would you have?" cried Massena, impatiently. "When one is in check, it is necessary to move the king."

"Forwards," I suggested.

He shook his grizzled head.

"The lines are not to be forced," said he. "I have already lost General St Croix and more men than I can replace. On the other hand, we have been here at Santarem for nearly six months. There is not a pound of flour nor a jug of wine on the country-side. We must retire."

"There is flour and wine in Lisbon," I persisted.

"Tut, you speak as if an army could charge in and charge out again like your regiment of hussars. If Soult were here with thirty thousand men—but he will not come. I sent for you, however,

Colonel Gerard, to say that I have a very singular and important expedition which I intend to place under your direction."

I pricked up my ears, as you can imagine. The Marshal unrolled a great map of the country and spread it upon the table. He flattened it out with his little, hairy hands.

"This is Santarem," he said, pointing.

I nodded.

"And here, twenty-five miles to the east, is Almeixal, celebrated for its vintages and for its enormous Abbey."

Again I nodded; I could not think what was coming.

"Have you heard of the Marshal Millefleurs?" asked Massena.

"I have served with all the Marshals," said I, "but there is none of that name."

"It is but the nickname which the soldiers have given him," said Massena. "If you had not been away from us for some months, it would not be necessary for me to tell you about him. He is an Englishman, and a man of good breeding. It is on account of his manners that they have given him his title. I wish you to go to this polite Englishman at Almeixal."

"Yes, Marshal."

"And to hang him to the nearest tree."

"Certainly, Marshal."

I turned briskly upon my heels, but Massena recalled me before I could reach the opening of his tent.

"One moment, Colonel," said he; "you had best learn how matters stand before you start. You must know, then, that this Marshal Millefleurs, whose real name is Alexis Morgan, is a man of very great ingenuity and bravery. He was an officer in the English Guards, but having been broken for cheating at cards, he left the army. In some manner he gathered a number of English deserters round him and took to the mountains. French stragglers and Portuguese brigands joined him, and he found himself at the head of five hundred men. With these he took possession of the Abbey of Almeixal, sent the monks about their business, fortified the place, and gathered in the plunder of all the country round."

"For which it is high time he was hanged," said I, making once more for the door.

"One instant!" cried the Marshal, smiling at my impatience. "The worst remains behind. Only last week the Dowager Countess of La Ronda, the richest woman in Spain, was taken by these ruffians in the passes as she was journeying from King Joseph's Court to visit her grandson. She is now a prisoner in the Abbey, and is only protected by her—"

"Grandmotherhood," I suggested.

"Her power of paying a ransom," said Massena. "You have three missions, then: to rescue this unfortunate lady; to punish this villain; and, if possible, to break up this nest of brigands. It will be a proof of the confidence which I have in you when I say that I can only spare you half a squadron with which to accomplish all this."

My word, I could hardly believe my ears! I thought that I should have had my regiment at the least.

"I would give you more," said he, "but I commence my retreat to-day, and Wellington is so strong in horse that every trooper becomes of importance. I cannot spare you another man. You will see what you can do, and you will report yourself to me at Abrantes not later than to-morrow night."

It was very complimentary that he should rate my powers so high, but it was also a little embarrassing. I was to rescue an old lady, to hang an Englishman, and to break up a band of five hundred assassins—all with fifty men. But after all, the fifty men were Hussars of Conflans, and they had an Etienne Gerard to lead them. As I came out into the warm Portuguese sunshine my confidence had returned to me, and I had already begun to wonder whether the medal which I had so often deserved might not be waiting for me at Almeixal.

You may be sure that I did not take my fifty men at haphazard. They were all old soldiers of the German wars, some of them with three stripes, and most of them with two. Oudet and Papilette, two of the best sub-officers in the regiment, were at their head. When I had them formed up in fours, all in silver grey and upon chestnut horses, with their leopard skin shabracks and their little red panaches, my heart beat high at the sight. I could not look at their weather-stained faces, with the great moustaches which bristled over their chin-straps, without feeling a glow of confidence, and, between ourselves, I have no doubt that was exactly how they felt when they saw their young Colonel on his great black war-horse riding at their head.

Well, when we got free of the camp and over the Tagus, I threw out my advance and my flankers, keeping my own place at the head of the main body. Looking back from the hills above Santarem, we could see the dark lines of Massena's army, with the flash and twinkle of the sabres and bayonets as he moved his regiments into position for their retreat. To the south lay the scattered red patches of the English outposts, and behind the grey smoke-cloud which rose from Wellington's camp — thick, oily smoke, which seemed to our poor starving fellows to bear with it the rich smell of seething camp-kettles. Away to the west lay a curve of blue sea flecked with the white sails of the English ships.

You will understand that as we were riding to the east, our road lay away from both armies. Our own marauders, however, and the scouting parties of the English, covered the country, and it was necessary with my small troop that I should take every precaution. During the whole day we rode over desolate hill-sides, the lower portions covered by the budding vines, but the upper turning from green to grey, and jagged along the skyline like the back of a starved horse. Mountain streams crossed our path, running west to the Tagus, and once we came to a deep strong river, which might have checked us had I not found the ford by observing where houses had been built opposite each other upon either bank. Between them, as every scout should know, you will find your ford. There was none to give us information, for neither man nor beast, nor any living thing except great clouds of crows, was to be seen during our journey.

The sun was beginning to sink when we came to a valley clear in the centre, but shrouded by huge oak trees upon either side. We could not be more than a few miles from Almeixal, so it seemed to me to be best to keep among the groves, for the spring had been an early one and the leaves were already thick enough to conceal us. We were riding then in open order among the great trunks, when one of my flankers came galloping up.

"There are English across the valley, Colonel," he cried, as he saluted.

"Cavalry or infantry?"

"Dragoons, Colonel," said he; "I saw the gleam of their helmets, and heard the neigh of a horse."

Halting my men, I hastened to the edge of the wood. There could be no doubt about it. A party of English cavalry was travelling in a line with us, and in the same direction I caught a glimpse of their red coats and of their flashing arms glowing and twinkling among the tree-trunks. Once, as they passed through a small clearing, I could see their whole force, and I judged that they were of about the same strength as my own—a half squadron at the most.

You who have heard some of my little adventures will give me credit for being quick in my decisions, and prompt in carrying them out. But here I must confess that I was in two minds. On the one hand there was the chance of a fine cavalry skirmish with the English. On the other hand, there was my mission at the Abbey of Almeixal, which seemed already to be so much above my power. If I were to lose any of my men, it was certain that I should be unable to carry out my orders. I was sitting my horse, with my chin in my gauntlet, looking across at the rippling gleams of light from the further wood, when suddenly one of these red-coated Englishmen rode out from the cover, pointing at me and breaking into a shrill whoop and halloa as if I had been a fox. Three others joined him, and one who was a bugler sounded a call which brought the whole of them into the open. They were, as I had thought, a half squadron, and they formed a double line with a front of twenty-five, their officer—the one who had whooped at me—at their head.

For my own part, I had instantly brought my own troopers into the same formation, so that there we were, hussars and dragoons, with only two hundred yards of grassy sward between us. They carried themselves well, those red-coated troopers, with their silver helmets, their high white plumes, and their long, gleaming swords; while, on the other hand, I am sure that they would acknowledge that they had never looked upon finer light horsemen than the fifty hussars of Conflans who were facing them. They were heavier, it is true, and they may have seemed the smarter, for Wellington used to make them burnish their metal work, which was not usual among us. On the other hand, it is well known that the English tunics were too tight for the sword-arm, which gave our men an advantage. As to bravery, foolish, inexperienced people of every nation always think that their own soldiers are braver than any others. There is no nation in the world which does not entertain this idea. But when one has seen as much as I have done, one understands that there is no very marked difference, and that although nations differ very much in discipline, they are all equally brave — except that the French have rather more courage than the rest.

Well, the cork was drawn and the glasses ready, when suddenly the English officer raised his sword to me as if in a challenge, and cantered his horse across the grassland. My word, there is no finer sight upon earth than that of a gallant man upon a gallant steed! I could have halted there just to watch him as he came with such careless grace, his sabre down by his horse's shoulder, his head thrown back, his white plume tossing — youth and strength and courage, with the violet evening sky above and the oak trees behind. But it was not for me to stand and stare. Etienne Gerard may have his faults, but, my faith, he was never accused of being backward in taking his own part. The old horse, Rataplan, knew me so well that he had started off before ever I gave the first shake to the bridle.

There are two things in this world that I am very slow to forget, the face of a pretty woman, and the legs of a fine horse. Well, as we drew together, I kept on saying, "Where have I seen those great roan shoulders? Where have I seen that dainty fetlock?" Then suddenly I remembered, and as I looked up at the reckless eyes and the challenging smile, whom should I recognise but the man who had saved me from the brigands and played me for my freedom — he whose correct title was Milor the Hon. Sir Russell Bart!

"Bart!" I shouted.

He had his arm raised for a cut, and three parts of his body open to my point, for he did not know very much about the use of the sword. As I brought my hilt to the salute he dropped his hand and stared at me.

"Halloa!" said he. "It's Gerard!" You would have thought by his manner that I had met him by appointment. For my own part I would have embraced him had he but come an inch of the way to meet me.

"I thought we were in for some sport," said he. "I never dreamed that it was you."

I found this tone of disappointment somewhat irritating. Instead of being glad at having met a friend, he was sorry at having missed an enemy.

"I should have been happy to join in your sport, my dear Bart," said I. "But I really cannot turn my sword upon a man who saved my life."

"Tut, never mind about that."

"No, it is impossible. I should never forgive myself."

"You make too much of a trifle."

"My mother's one desire is to embrace you. If ever you should be in Gascony — "

"Lord Wellington is coming there with 60,000 men."

"Then one of them will have a chance of surviving," said I, laughing. "In the meantime, put your sword in your sheath!"

Our horses were standing head to tail, and the Bart put out his hand and patted me on the thigh.

"You're a good chap, Gerard," said he. "I only wish you had been born on the right side of the Channel."

"I was," said I.

"Poor fellow!" he cried, with such an earnestness of pity that he set me laughing again. "But look here, Gerard," he continued, "this is all very well, but it is not business, you know. I don't know what Massena would say to it, but our Chief would jump out of his riding-boots if he saw us. We weren't sent out here for a picnic—either of us."

"What would you have?"

"Well, we had a little argument about our hussars and dragoons, if you remember. I've got fifty of the Sixteenth all chewing their carbine bullets behind me. You've got as many fine-looking boys over yonder, who seem to be fidgeting in their saddles. If you and I took the right flanks we should not spoil each other's beauty—though a little blood-letting is a friendly thing in this climate."

There seemed to me to be a good deal of sense in what he said. For the moment Mr Alexis Morgan and the Countess of La Ronda and the Abbey of Almeixal went right out of my head, and I could only think of the fine level turf and of the beautiful skirmish which we might have.

"Very good, Bart," said I. "We have seen the front of your dragoons. We shall now have a look at their backs."

"Any betting?" he asked.

"The stake," said I, "is nothing less than the honour of the Hussars of Conflans."

"Well, come on!" he answered. "If we break you, well and good—if you break us, it will be all the better for Marshal Millefleurs."

When he said that I could only stare at him in astonishment.

"Why for Marshal Millefleurs?" I asked.

"It is the name of a rascal who lives out this way. My dragoons have been sent by Lord Wellington to see him safely hanged."

"Name of a name!" I cried. "Why, my hussars have been sent by Massena for that very object."

We burst out laughing at that, and sheathed our swords. There was a whirr of steel from behind us as our troopers followed our example.

"We are allies," he cried.

"For a day."

"We must join forces."

"There is no doubt of it."

And so, instead of fighting, we wheeled our half squadrons round and moved in two little columns down the valley, the shakos and the helmets turned inwards, and the men looking their neighbours up and down, like old fighting dogs with tattered ears who have learned to respect each other's teeth. The most were on the broad grin, but there were some on either side who looked black and challenging, especially the English sergeant and my own sub-officer Papilette. They were men of habit, you see, who could not change all their ways of thinking in a moment. Besides, Papilette had lost his only brother at Busaco. As for the Bart and me, we rode together at the head and chatted about all that had occurred to us since that famous game of écarté of which I have told you. For my own part, I spoke to him of my adventures in England. They are a very singular people, these English. Although he knew that I had been engaged in twelve campaigns, yet I am sure that the Bart thought more highly of me because I had had an affair with the Bristol Bustler. He told me, too, that the Colonel who presided over his court-martial for playing cards with a prisoner, acquitted him of neglect of duty, but nearly broke him because he thought that he had not cleared his trumps before leading his suit. Yes, indeed, they are a singular people.

At the end of the valley the road curved over some rising ground before winding down into another wider valley beyond. We called a halt when we came to the top; for there, right in front of us, at the distance of about three miles, was a scattered, grey town, with a single enormous building upon the flank of the mountain which overlooked it. We could not doubt that we were at last in sight of the Abbey that held the gang of rascals whom we had come to disperse. It was only now, I think, that we fully understood what a task lay in front of us, for the place was a veritable fortress, and it was evident that cavalry should never have been sent out upon such an errand.

"That's got nothing to do with us," said the Bart; "Wellington and Massena can settle that between them."

"Courage!" I answered. "Piré took Leipzig with fifty hussars."

"Had they been dragoons," said the Bart, laughing, "he would have had Berlin. But you are senior officer: give us a lead, and we'll see who will be the first to flinch."

"Well," said I, "whatever we do must be done at once, for my orders are to be on my way to Abrantes by to-morrow night. But we must have some information first, and here is someone who should be able to give it to us."

There was a square, whitewashed house standing by the roadside, which appeared, from the bush hanging over the door, to be one of those wayside tabernas which are provided for the muleteers. A lantern was hung in the porch, and by its light we saw two men, the one in the brown habit of a Capuchin monk, and the other girt with an apron, which showed him to be the landlord. They were conversing together so earnestly that we were upon them before they were aware of us. The innkeeper turned to fly, but one of the Englishmen seized him by the hair, and held him tight.

"For mercy's sake, spare me," he yelled. "My house has been gutted by the French and harried by the English, and my feet have been burned by the brigands. I swear by the Virgin that I have neither money nor food in my inn, and the good Father Abbot, who is starving upon my doorstep, will be witness to it."

"Indeed, sir," said the Capuchin, in excellent French, "what this worthy man says is very true. He is one of the many victims to these cruel wars, although his loss is but a feather-weight compared to mine. Let him go," he added, in English, to the trooper, "he is too weak to fly, even if he desired to."

In the light of the lantern I saw that this monk was a magnificent man, dark and bearded, with the eyes of a hawk, and so tall that his cowl came up to Rataplan's ears. He wore the look of one who had been through much suffering, but he carried himself like a king, and we could form some opinion of his learning when we each heard him talk our own language as fluently as if he were born to it.

"You have nothing to fear," said I, to the trembling innkeeper. "As to you, father, you are, if I am not mistaken, the very man who can give us the information which we require."

"All that I have is at your service, my son. But," he added with a wan smile, "my Lenten fare is always somewhat meagre, and this year it has been such that I must ask you for a crust of bread if I am to have the strength to answer your questions."

We bore two days' rations in our haversacks, so that he soon had the little he had asked for. It was dreadful to see the wolfish way in which he seized the piece of dried goat's flesh which I was able to offer him.

"Time presses, and we must come to the point," said I. "We want your advice as to the weak points of yonder Abbey, and concerning the habits of the rascals who infest it."

He cried out something which I took to be Latin, with his hands clasped and his eyes upturned. "The prayer of the just availeth much," said he, "and yet I had not dared to hope that mine would have been so speedily answered. In me you see the unfortunate Abbot of Almeixal, who has been cast out by this rabble of three armies with their heretical leader. Oh! to think of what I have lost!" his voice broke, and the tears hung upon his lashes.

"Cheer up, sir," said the Bart. "I'll lay nine to four that we have you back again by to-morrow night."

"It is not of my own welfare that I think," said he, "nor even of that of my poor, scattered flock. But it is of the holy relics which are left in the sacrilegious hands of these robbers."

"It's even betting whether they would ever bother their heads about them," said the Bart. "But show us the way inside the gates, and we'll soon clear the place out for you."

In a few short words the good Abbot gave us the very points that we wished to know. But all that he said only made our task more formidable. The walls of the Abbey were forty feet high. The lower windows were barricaded, and the whole building loopholed for musketry fire. The gang preserved military discipline, and their sentries were too numerous for us to hope to take them by surprise. It was more than ever evident that a battalion of grenadiers and a couple of breaching pieces were what was needed. I raised my eyebrows, and the Bart began to whistle.

"We must have a shot at it, come what may," said he.

The men had already dismounted, and, having watered their horses, were eating their suppers. For my own part I went into the sitting-room of the inn with the Abbot and the Bart, that we might talk about our plans.

I had a little cognac in my *sauve vie,* and I divided it among us —just enough to wet our moustaches.

"It is unlikely," said I, "that those rascals know anything about our coming. I have seen no signs of scouts along the road. My own plan is that we should conceal ourselves in some neighbouring wood, and then, when they open their gates, charge down upon them and take them by surprise."

The Bart was of opinion that this was the best that we could do, but, when we came to talk it over, the Abbot made us see that there were difficulties in the way.

"Save on the side of the town there is no place within a mile of the Abbey where you could shelter man or horse," said he. "As to the townsfolk, they are not to be trusted. I fear, my son, that your excellent plan would have little chance of success in the face of the vigilant guard which these men keep."

"I see no other way," answered I. "Hussars of Conflans are not so plentiful that I can afford to run half a squadron of them against a forty foot wall with five hundred infantry behind it."

"I am a man of peace," said the Abbot, "and yet I may, perhaps, give a word of counsel. I know these villains and their ways. Who should do so better, seeing that I have stayed for a month in this lonely spot, looking down in weariness of heart at the Abbey which was my own? I will tell you now what I should myself do if I were in your place."

"Pray tell us, father," we cried, both together.

"You must know that bodies of deserters, both French and English, are continually coming in to them, carrying their weapons with them. Now, what is there to prevent you and your men from pretending to be such a body, and so making your way into the Abbey?"

I was amazed at the simplicity of the thing, and I embraced the good Abbot. The Bart, however, had some objections to offer.

"That is all very well," said he, "but if these fellows are as sharp as you say, it is not very likely that they are going to let a hundred armed strangers into their crib. From all I have heard of Mr Morgan, or Marshal Millefleurs, or whatever the rascal's name is, I give him credit for more sense than that."

"Well, then," I cried, "let us send fifty in, and let them at daybreak throw open the gates to the other fifty, who will be waiting outside."

We discussed the question at great length and with much foresight and discretion. If it had been Massena and Wellington instead of two young officers of light cavalry, we could not have weighed it all with more judgement. At last we agreed, the Bart and I, that one of us should indeed go with fifty men under pretence of being deserters, and that in the early morning he should gain command of the gate and admit the others. The Abbot, it is true, was still of opinion that it was dangerous to divide our force, but finding that we were both of the same mind, he shrugged his shoulders and gave in.

"There is only one thing that I would ask," said he. "If you lay hands upon Marshal Millefleurs — this dog of a brigand — what will you do with him?"

"Hang him," I answered.

"It is too easy a death," cried the Capuchin, with a vindictive glow in his dark eyes. "Had I my way with him — but, oh, what thoughts are these for a servant of God to harbour!" He clapped his hands to his forehead like one who is half demented by his troubles, and rushed out of the room.

There was an important point which we had still to settle, and that was whether the French or the English party should have the honour of entering the Abbey first. My faith, it was asking a great deal of Etienne Gerard that he should give place to any man at such a time! But the poor Bart pleaded so hard, urging the few poor skirmishes which he had seen against my four-and-seventy engagements, that at last I consented that he should go. We had just clasped hands over the matter when there broke out such a shouting and cursing and yelling from the front of the inn, that out we rushed with our drawn sabres in our hands, convinced that the brigands were upon us.

You may imagine our feelings when, by the light of the lantern which hung from the porch, we saw a score of our hussars and dragoons all mixed in one wild heap, red coats and blue, helmets and busbies, pomelling each other to their hearts' content. We flung ourselves upon them, imploring, threatening, tugging at a lace collar, or at a spurred heel, until, at last, we had dragged them all apart. There they stood, flushed and bleeding, glaring at each other, and all panting together like a line of troop horses after a ten-mile chase. It was only with our drawn swords that we could keep them from each other's throats. The poor Capuchin stood in the porch in his long brown habit, wringing his hands and calling upon all the saints for mercy.

He was indeed, as I found upon inquiry, the innocent cause of all the turmoil, for, not understanding how soldiers look upon such things, he had made some remark to the English sergeant that it was a pity that his squadron was not as good as the French. The words were not out of his mouth before a dragoon knocked down the nearest hussar, and then, in a moment, they all flew at each other like tigers. We would trust them no more after that, but the Bart moved his men to the front of the inn, and I mine to the back, the English all scowling and silent, and our fellows shaking their fists and chattering, each after the fashion of their own people.

Well, as our plans were made, we thought it best to carry them out at once, lest some fresh cause of quarrel should break out between our followers. The Bart and his men rode off, therefore, he having first torn the lace from his sleeves, and the gorget and sash from his uniform, so that he might pass as a simple trooper. He explained to his men what it was that was expected of them, and though they did not raise a cry or wave their weapons as mine might have done, there was an expression upon their stolid and clean-shaven faces which filled me with confidence. Their tunics were left unbuttoned, their scabbards and helmets stained with dirt, and their harness badly fastened, so that they might look the part of deserters, without order or discipline. At six o'clock next morning they were to gain command of the main gate of the Abbey, while at that same hour my hussars were to gallop up to it from outside. The Bart and I pledged our words to it before he trotted off with his detachment. My sergeant, Papilette, with two troopers, followed the English at a distance, and returned in half an hour to say that, after some parley, and the flashing of lanterns upon them from the grille, they had been admitted into the Abbey.

So far, then, all had gone well. It was a cloudy night with a sprinkling of rain, which was in our favour, as there was the less chance of our presence being discovered. My vedettes I placed two hundred yards in every direction, to guard against a surprise, and also to prevent any peasant who might stumble upon us from carrying the news to the Abbey. Oudin and Papilette were to take turns of duty, while the others with their horses had snug quarters in a great wooden granary. Having walked round and seen that all was as it should be, I flung myself upon the bed which the innkeeper had set apart for me, and fell into a dreamless sleep.

No doubt you have heard my name mentioned as being the beau-ideal of a soldier, and that not only by friends and admirers like our fellow-townsfolk, but also by old officers of the great wars who have shared the fortunes of those famous campaigns with me. Truth and modesty compel me to say, however, that this is not so. There are some gifts which I lack—very few, no doubt—but, still, amid the vast armies of the Emperor there may have been some who were free from those blemishes which stood between me and perfection. Of bravery I say nothing. Those who have seen me in the field are best fitted to speak about that. I have often heard the soldiers discussing round the camp-fires as to who was the bravest man in the Grand Army. Some said Murat, and some said Lasalle, and some Ney; but for my own part, when they asked me, I merely shrugged my shoulders and smiled. It would have seemed mere conceit if I had answered that there was no man braver than

Brigadier Gerard. At the same time, facts are facts, and a man knows best what his own feelings are. But there are other gifts besides bravery which are necessary for a soldier, and one of them is that he should be a light sleeper. Now, from my boyhood onwards, I have been hard to wake, and it was this which brought me to ruin upon that night.

It may have been about two o'clock in the morning that I was suddenly conscious of a feeling of suffocation. I tried to call out, but there was something which prevented me from uttering a sound. I struggled to rise, but I could only flounder like a hamstrung horse. I was strapped at the ankles, strapped at the knees, and strapped again at the wrists. Only my eyes were free to move, and there at the foot of my couch, by the light of a Portuguese lamp, whom should I see but the Abbot and the innkeeper!

The latter's heavy, white face had appeared to me when I looked upon it the evening before to express nothing but stupidity and terror. Now, on the contrary, every feature bespoke brutality and ferocity. Never have I seen a more dreadful-looking villain. In his hand he held a long, dull-coloured knife. The Abbot, on the other hand, was as polished and dignified as ever. His Capuchin gown had been thrown open, however, and I saw beneath it a black-frogged coat, such as I have seen among the English officers. As our eyes met he leaned over the wooden end of the bed and laughed silently until it creaked again.

"You will, I am sure, excuse my mirth, my dear Colonel Gerard," said he. "The fact is, that the expression upon your face when you grasped the situation was just a little funny. I have no doubt that you are an excellent soldier, but I hardly think that you are fit to measure wits with the Marshal Millefleurs, as your fellows have been good enough to call me. You appear to have given me credit for singularly little intelligence, which argues, if I may be allowed to say so, a want of acuteness upon your own part. Indeed, with the single exception of my thick-headed compatriot, the British dragoon, I have never met anyone who was less competent to carry out such a mission."

You can imagine how I felt and how I looked, as I listened to this insolent harangue, which was all delivered in that flowery and condescending manner which had gained this rascal his nickname. I could say nothing, but they must have read my threat in my eyes, for the fellow who had played the part of the innkeeper whispered something to his companion.

"No, no, my dear Chenier, he will be infinitely more valuable alive," said he. "By the way, Colonel, it is just as well that you are a sound sleeper, for my friend here, who is a little rough in his ways, would certainly have cut your throat if you had raised any alarm. I should recommend you to keep in his good graces, for Sergeant Chenier, late of the 7th Imperial Light Infantry, is a much more dangerous person than Captain Alexis Morgan, of His Majesty's foot-guards."

Chenier grinned and shook his knife at me, while I tried to look the loathing which I felt at the thought that a soldier of the Emperor could fall so low.

"It may amuse you to know," said the Marshal, in that soft, suave voice of his, "that both your expeditions were watched from the time that you left your respective camps. I think that you will allow that Chenier and I played our parts with some subtlety. We had made every arrangement for your reception at the Abbey, though we had hoped to receive the whole squadron instead of half. When the gates are secured behind them, our visitors find themselves in a very charming little mediæval quadrangle, with no possible exit, commanded by musketry fire from a hundred windows. They may choose to be shot down; or they may choose to surrender. Between ourselves, I have not the slightest doubt that they have been wise enough to do the latter. But since you are naturally interested in the matter, we thought that you would care to come with us and to see for yourself. I think I can promise you that you will find your titled friend waiting for you at the Abbey with a face as long as your own."

The two villains began whispering together, debating, as far as I could hear, which was the best way of avoiding my vedettes.

"I will make sure that it is all clear upon the other side of the barn," said the Marshal at last. "You will stay here, my good Chenier, and if the prisoner gives any trouble you will know what to do."

So we were left together, this murderous renegade and I—he sitting at the end of the bed, sharpening his knife upon his boot in the light of the single smoky little oil-lamp. As to me, I only wonder now as I look back upon it, that I did not go mad with vexation and self-reproach as I lay helplessly upon the couch, unable to utter a word or move a finger, with the knowledge that my fifty gallant lads were so close to me, and yet with no means of letting them know the straits to which I was reduced. It was no new thing for me to be a prisoner; but to be taken by these renegades, and to be led into their Abbey in the midst of their jeers, befooled and outwitted by their insolent leaders—that was indeed more than I could endure. The knife of the butcher beside me would cut less deeply than that.

I twitched softly at my wrists, and then at my ankles, but whichever of the two had secured me was no bungler at his work. I could not move either of them an inch. Then I tried to work the handkerchief down over my mouth, but the ruffian beside me raised his knife with such a threatening snarl that I had to desist. I was lying still looking at his bull neck, and wondering whether it would ever be my good fortune to fit it for a cravat, when I heard returning steps coming down the inn passage and up the stair. What word would the villain bring back? If he found it impossible to kidnap me, he would probably murder me where I lay. For my own part, I was indifferent which it might be, and I looked at the doorway with the contempt and defiance which I longed to put into words. But you can imagine my feelings, my dear friends, when, instead of the tall figure and dark, sneering face of the Capuchin, my eyes fell upon the grey pelisse and huge moustaches of my good little sub-officer, Papilette!

The French soldier of those days had seen too much to be ever taken by surprise. His eyes had hardly rested upon my bound figure and the sinister face beside me before he had seen how the matter lay.

"Sacred name of a dog!" he growled, and out flashed his great sabre. Chenier sprang forward at him with his knife, and then, thinking better of it, he darted back and stabbed frantically at my heart. For my own part, I had hurled myself off the bed on the side opposite him, and the blade grazed my side before ripping its way through blanket and sheet. An instant later I heard the thud of a heavy fall, and then almost simultaneously a second object struck the floor—something lighter but harder, which rolled under the bed. I will not horrify you with details, my friends. Suffice it that Papilette was one of the strongest swordsmen in the regiment, and that his sabre was heavy and sharp. It left a red blotch upon my wrists and my ankles, as it cut the thongs which bound me.

When I had thrown off my gag, the first use which I made of my lips was to kiss the sergeant's scarred cheeks. The next was to ask him if all was well with the command. Yes, they had had no alarms. Oudin had just relieved him, and he had come to report. Had he seen the Abbot? No, he had seen nothing of him. Then we must form a cordon and prevent his escape. I was hurrying out to give the orders, when I heard a slow and measured step enter the door below, and come creaking up the stairs.

Papilette understood it all in an instant. "You are not to kill him," I whispered, and thrust him into the shadow on one side of the door; I crouched on the other. Up he came, up and up, and every footfall seemed to be upon my heart. The brown skirt of his gown was not over the threshold before we were both on him, like two wolves on a buck. Down we crashed, the three of us, he fighting like a tiger, and with such amazing strength that he might have broken away from the two of us. Thrice he got to his feet, and thrice we had him over again, until Papilette made him feel that there was a point to his sabre. He had sense enough then to know that the game was up, and to lie still while I lashed him with the very cords which had been around my own limbs.

"There has been a fresh deal, my fine fellow," said I, "and you will find that I have some of the trumps in *my* hand this time."

"Luck always comes to the aid of a fool," he answered. "Perhaps it is as well, otherwise the world would fall too completely into the power of the astute. So, you have killed Chenier, I see. He was an insubordinate dog, and always smelt abominably of garlic. Might I trouble you to lay me upon the bed? The floor of these Portuguese tabernas is hardly a fitting couch for anyone who has prejudices in favour of cleanliness."

I could not but admire the coolness of the man, and the way in which he preserved the same insolent air of condescension in spite of this sudden turning of the tables. I dispatched Papilette to summon a guard, whilst I stood over our prisoner with my drawn sword, never taking my eyes off him for an instant, for I must confess that I had conceived a great respect for his audacity and resource.

"I trust," said he, "that your men will treat me in a becoming manner."

"You will get your deserts—you may depend upon that."

"I ask nothing more. You may not be aware of my exalted birth, but I am so placed that I cannot name my father without treason, nor my mother without a scandal. I cannot *claim* Royal honours, but these things are so much more graceful when they are conceded without a claim. The thongs are cutting my skin. Might I beg you to loosen them?"

"You do not give me credit for much intelligence," I remarked, repeating his own words.

"*Touché,*" he cried, like a pinked fencer. "But here come your men, so it matters little whether you loosen them or not."

I ordered the gown to be stripped from him and placed him under a strong guard. Then, as morning was already breaking, I had to consider what my next step was to be. The poor Bart and his Englishmen had fallen victims to the deep scheme which might, had we adopted all the crafty suggestions of our adviser, have ended in the capture of the whole instead of the half of our force. I must extricate them if it were still possible. Then there was the old lady, the Countess of La Ronda, to be thought of. As to the Abbey, since its garrison was on the alert it was hopeless to think of capturing that. All turned now upon the value which they placed upon their leader. The game depended upon my playing that one card. I will tell you how boldly and how skilfully I played it.

It was hardly light before my bugler blew the assembly, and out we trotted on to the plain. My prisoner was placed on horseback in the very centre of the troops. It chanced that there was a large tree just out of musket-shot from the main gate of the Abbey, and under this we halted. Had they opened the great doors in order to attack us, I should have charged home on them; but, as I had expected, they stood upon the defensive, lining the long wall and pouring down a torrent of hootings and taunts and derisive laughter upon us. A few fired their muskets, but finding that we were out of reach they soon ceased to waste their powder. It was the strangest sight to see that mixture of uniforms, French, English, and Portuguese, cavalry, infantry and artillery, all wagging their heads and shaking their fists at us.

My word, their hubbub soon died away when we opened our ranks, and showed whom we had got in the midst of us! There was silence for a few seconds, and then such a howl of rage and grief! I could see some of them dancing like madmen upon the wall. He must have been a singular person, this prisoner of ours, to have gained the affection of such a gang.

I had brought a rope from the inn, and we slung it over the lower bough of the tree.

"You will permit me, monsieur, to undo your collar," said Papilette, with mock politeness.

"If your hands are perfectly clean," answered our prisoner, and set the whole half-squadron laughing.

There was another yell from the wall, followed by a profound hush as the noose was tightened round Marshal Millefleurs' neck. Then came a shriek from a bugle, the Abbey gates flew open, and three men rushed out waving white cloths in their hands. Ah, how my heart bounded with joy at the sight of them. And yet I would not advance an inch to meet them, so that all the eagerness might seem to be upon their side. I allowed my trumpeter, however, to wave a handkerchief in reply, upon which the three envoys came running towards us. The Marshal, still pinioned, and with the rope round his neck, sat his horse with a half smile, as one who is slightly bored and yet strives out of courtesy not to show it. If I were in such a situation I could not wish to carry myself better, and surely I can say no more than that.

They were a singular trio, these ambassadors. The one was a Portuguese caçadore in his dark uniform, the second a French chasseur in the lightest green, and the third a big English artillery-man in blue and gold. They saluted, all three, and the Frenchman did the talking.

"We have thirty-seven English dragoons in our hands," said he. "We give you our most solemn oath that they shall all hang from the Abbey wall within five minutes of the death of our Marshal."

"Thirty-seven!" I cried. "You have fifty-one."

"Fourteen were cut down before they could be secured."

"And the officer?"

"He would not surrender his sword save with his life. It was not our fault. We would have saved him if we could."

Alas for my poor Bart! I had met him but twice, and yet he was a man very much after my heart. I have always had a regard for the English for the sake of that one friend. A braver man and a worse swordsman I have never met.

I did not, as you may think, take these rascals' word for anything. Papilette was dispatched with one of them, and returned to say that it was too true. I had now to think of the living.

"You will release the thirty-seven dragoons if I free your leader?"

"We will give you ten of them."

"Up with him!" I cried.

"Twenty," shouted the chasseur.

"No more words," said I. "Pull on the rope!"

"All of them," cried the envoy, as the cord tightened round the Marshal's neck.

"With horses and arms?"

They could see that I was not a man to jest with.

"All complete," said the chasseur, sulkily.

"And the Countess of La Ronda as well?" said I.

But here I met with firmer opposition. No threats of mine could induce them to give up the Countess. We tightened the cord. We moved the horse. We did all but leave the Marshal suspended. If once I broke his neck the dragoons were dead men. It was as precious to me as to them.

"Allow me to remark," said the Marshal, blandly, "that you are exposing me to a risk of quinsy. Do you not think, since there is a difference of opinion upon this point, that it would be an excellent idea to consult the lady herself? We would neither of us, I am sure, wish to over-ride her own inclinations."

Nothing could be more satisfactory. You can imagine how quickly I grasped at so simple a solution. In ten minutes she was before us, a most stately dame, with her grey curls peeping out from under her mantilla. Her face was as yellow as though it reflected the countless doubloons of her treasury.

"This gentleman," said the Marshal, "is exceedingly anxious to convey you to a place where you will never see us more. It is for you to decide whether you would wish to go with him, or whether you prefer to remain with me."

She was at his horse's side in an instant. "My own Alexis," she cried, "nothing can ever part us."

He looked at me with a sneer upon his handsome face.

"By the way, you made a small slip of the tongue, my dear Colonel," said he. "Except by courtesy, no such person exists as the Dowager Countess of La Ronda. The lady whom I have the honour to present to you is my very dear wife, Mrs Alexis Morgan—or shall I say Madame la Marèchale Millefleurs?"

It was at this moment that I came to the conclusion that I was dealing with the cleverest, and also the most unscrupulous, man whom I had ever met. As I looked upon this unfortunate old woman my soul was filled with wonder and disgust. As for her, her eyes were raised to his face with such a look as a young recruit might give to the Emperor.

"So be it," said I, at last; "give me the dragoons and let me go."

They were brought out with their horses and weapons, and the rope was taken from the Marshal's neck.

"Good-bye, my dear Colonel," said he. "I am afraid that you will have rather a lame account to give of your mission, when you find your way back to Massena, though, from all I hear, he will probably be too busy to think of you. I am free to confess that you have extricated yourself from your difficulties with greater ability than I had given you credit for. I presume that there is nothing which I can do for you before you go?"

"There is one thing."

"And that is?"

"To give fitting burial to this young officer and his men."

"I pledge my word to it."

"And there is one other."

"Name it."

"To give me five minutes in the open with a sword in your hand and a horse between your legs."

"Tut, tut!" said he. "I should either have to cut short your promising career, or else to bid adieu to my own bonny bride. It is unreasonable to ask such a request of a man in the first joys of matrimony."

I gathered my horsemen together and wheeled them into column.

"Au revoir," I cried, shaking my sword at him. "The next time you may not escape so easily."

"Au revoir," he answered. "When you are weary of the Emperor, you will always find a commission waiting for you in the service of the Marshal Millefleurs."

HOW THE BRIGADIER WAS
TEMPTED BY THE DEVIL

THE spring is at hand, my friends. I can see the little green spear-heads breaking out once more upon the chestnut trees, and the café tables have all been moved into the sunshine. It is more pleasant to sit there, and yet I do not wish to tell my little stories to the whole town. You have heard my doings as a lieutenant, as a squadron officer, as a colonel, as the chief of a brigade. But now I suddenly become something higher and more important. I become history.

If you have read of those closing years of the life of the Emperor which were spent in the Island of St Helena, you will remember that, again and again, he implored permission to send out one single letter which should be unopened by those who held him. Many times he made this request, and even went so far as to promise that he would provide for his own wants and cease to be an expense to the British Government if it were granted to him. But his guardians knew that he was a terrible man, this pale, fat gentleman in the straw hat, and they dared not grant him what he asked. Many have wondered who it was to whom he could have had anything so secret to say. Some have supposed that it was to his wife, and some that it was to his father-in-law; some that it was to the Emperor Alexander, and some to Marshal Soult. What will you think of me, my friends, when I tell you it was to me — to me, the Brigadier Gerard — that the Emperor wished to write! Yes, humble as you see me, with only my 100 francs a month of half-pay between me and hunger, it is none the less true that I was

151

always in the Emperor's mind, and that he would have given his left hand for five minutes' talk with me. I will tell you to-night how this came about.

It was after the Battle of Fére-Champenoise, where the conscripts in their blouses and their sabots made such a fine stand, that we, the more long-headed of us, began to understand that it was all over with us. Our reserve ammunition had been taken in the battle, and we were left with silent guns and empty caissons. Our cavalry, too, was in a deplorable condition, and my own brigade had been destroyed in the great charge at Craonne. Then came the news that the enemy had taken Paris, that the citizens had mounted the white cockade; and finally, most terrible of all, that Marmont and his corps had gone over to the Bourbons. We looked at each other and asked how many more of our generals were going to turn against us. Already there were Jourdan, Marmont, Murat, Bernadotte, and Jomini — though nobody minded much about Jomini, for his pen was always sharper than his sword. We had been ready to fight Europe, but it looked now as though we were to fight Europe and half of France as well.

We had come to Fontainebleau by a long, forced march, and there we were assembled, the poor remnants of us, the corps of Ney, the corps of my cousin Gerard, and the corps of Macdonald: twenty-five thousand in all, with seven thousand of the guard. But we had our prestige, which was worth fifty thousand, and our Emperor, who was worth fifty thousand more. He was always among us, serene, smiling, confident, taking his snuff and playing with his little riding-whip. Never in the days of his greatest victories have I admired him as much as I did during the Campaign of France.

One evening I was with a few of my officers drinking a glass of wine of Suresnes. I mention that it was wine of Suresnes just to show you that times were not very good with us. Suddenly I was disturbed by a message from Berthier that he wished to see me. When I speak of my old comrades-in-arms, I will, with your permission, leave out all the fine foreign titles which they had picked up during the wars. They are excellent for a Court, but you never heard them in the camp, for we could not afford to do away with our Ney, our Rapp, or our Soult—names which were as stirring to our ears as the blare of our trumpets blowing the reveille. It was Berthier, then, who sent to say that he wished to see me.

He had a suite of rooms at the end of the gallery of Francis the First, not very far from those of the Emperor. In the antechamber were waiting two men whom I knew well: Colonel Despienne, of the 57th of the line, and Captian Tremeau, of the Voltigeurs. They were both old soldiers—Tremeau had carried a musket in Egypt— and they were also both famous in the army for their courage and their skill with weapons. Tremeau had become a little stiff in the wrist, but Despienne was capable at his best of making me exert myself. He was a tiny fellow, about three inches short of the proper height for a man—he was exactly three inches shorter than myself —but both with the sabre and with the small-sword he had several times almost held his own against me when we used to exhibit at Verron's Hall of Arms in the Palais Royal. You may think that it made us sniff something in the wind when we found three such men called together into one room. You cannot see the lettuce and the dressing without suspecting a salad.

"Name of a pipe!" said Tremeau, in his barrack-room fashion. "Are we then expecting three champions of the Bourbons?"

To all of us the idea appeared not improbable. Certainly in the whole army we were the very three who might have been chosen to meet them.

"The Prince of Neufchâtel desires to speak with the Brigadier Gerard," said a footman, appearing at the door.

In I went, leaving my two companions consumed with impatience behind me. It was a small room, but very gorgeously furnished. Berthier was seated opposite to me at a little table, with a pen in his hand and a note-book open before him. He was looking weary and slovenly—very different from that Berthier who used to give the fashion to the army, and who had so often set us poorer officers tearing our hair by trimming his pelisse with fur, one campaign, and with grey astrakhan the next. On his clean-shaven, comely face there was an expression of trouble, and he looked at me as I entered his chamber in a way which had in it something furtive and displeasing.

"Chief of Brigade Gerard!" said he.

"At your service, your Highness!" I answered.

"I must ask you, before I go further, to promise me, upon your honour as a gentleman and a soldier, that what is about to pass between us shall never be mentioned to any third person."

My word, this was a fine beginning! I had no choice but to give the promise required.

"You must know, then, that it is all over with the Emperor," said he, looking down at the table and speaking very slowly, as if he had a hard task in getting out the words. "Jourdan at Rouen and Marmont at Paris have both mounted the white cockade, and it is rumoured that Talleyrand has talked Ney into doing the same. It is evident that further resistance is useless, and that it can only bring misery upon our country. I wish to ask you, therefore, whether you are prepared to join me in laying hands upon the Emperor's person, and bringing the war to a conclusion by delivering him over to the allies."

I assure you that when I heard this infamous proposition put forward by the man who had been the earliest friend of the Emperor, and who had received greater favours from him than any of his followers, I could only stand and stare at him in amazement. For his part he tapped his pen-handle against his teeth, and looked at me with a slanting head.

"Well?" he asked.

"I am a little deaf upon one side," said I, coldly. "There are some things which I cannot hear. I beg that you will permit me to return to my duties."

"Nay, but you must not be headstrong," said he, rising up and laying his hand upon my shoulder. "You are aware that the Senate has declared against Napoleon, and that the Emperor Alexander refuses to treat with him."

"Sir," I cried, with passion, "I would have you know that I do not care the dregs of a wine-glass for the Senate or for the Emperor Alexander either."

"Then for what do you care?"

"For my own honour and for the service of my glorious master, the Emperor Napoleon."

"That is all very well," said Berthier, peevishly, shrugging his shoulders. "Facts are facts, and as men of the world, we must look them in the face. Are we to stand against the will of the nation? Are we to have civil war on the top of all our misfortunes? And, besides, we are thinning away. Every hour comes the news of fresh desertions. We have still time to make our peace, and, indeed, to earn the highest reward, by giving up the Emperor."

I shook so with passion that my sabre clattered against my thigh.

"Sir," I cried, "I never thought to have seen the day when a Marshal of France would have so far degraded himself as to put forward such a proposal. I leave you to your own conscience; but as for me, until I have the Emperor's own order, there shall always be the sword of Etienne Gerard between his enemies and himself."

I was so moved by my own words and by the fine position which I had taken up, that my voice broke, and I could hardly refrain from tears. I should have liked the whole army to have seen me as I stood with my head so proudly erect and my hand upon my heart proclaiming my devotion to the Emperor in his adversity. It was one of the supreme moments of my life.

"Very good," said Berthier, ringing a bell for the lackey. "You will show the Chief of Brigade Gerard into the salon."

The footman led me into an inner room, where he desired me to be seated. For my own part, my only desire was to get away, and I could not understand why they should wish to detain me. When one has had no change of uniform during a whole winter's campaign, one does not feel at home in a palace.

I had been there about a quarter of an hour when the footman opened the door again, and in came Colonel Despienne. Good heavens, what a sight he was! His face was as white as a guardsman's gaiters, his eyes projecting, the veins swollen upon his fore-head, and every hair of his moustache bristling like those of an angry cat. He was too angry to speak, and could only shake his hands at the ceiling and make a gurgling in his throat. "Parricide! Viper!" those were the words that I could catch as he stamped up and down the room.

Of course it was evident to me that he had been subjected to the same infamous proposals as I had, and that he had received them in the same spirit. His lips were sealed to me, as mine were to him, by the promise which we had taken, but I contented myself with muttering "Atrocious! Unspeakable!"—so that he might know that I was in agreement with him.

Well, we were still there, he striding furiously up and down, and I seated in the corner, when suddenly a most extraordinary uproar broke out in the room which we had just quitted. There was a snarling, worrying growl, like that of a fierce dog which has got his grip. Then came a crash and a voice calling for help. In we rushed, the two of us, and, my faith, we were none too soon.

Old Tremeau and Berthier were rolling together upon the floor, with the table upon the top of them. The Captain had one of his great, skinny, yellow hands upon the Marshal's throat, and already his face was lead-coloured, and his eyes were starting from their sockets. As to Tremeau, he was beside himself, with foam upon the corners of his lips, and such a frantic expression upon him that I am convinced, had we not loosened his iron grip, finger by finger, that it would never have relaxed while the Marshal lived. His nails were white with the power of his grasp.

"I have been tempted by the devil!" he cried, as he staggered to his feet. "Yes, I have been tempted by the devil!"

As to Berthier, he could only lean against the wall, and pant for a couple of minutes, putting his hands up to his throat and rolling his head about. Then, with an angry gesture, he turned to the heavy blue curtain which hung behind his chair.

"There, sire!" he cried, furiously, "I told you exactly what would come of it."

The curtain was torn to one side and the Emperor stepped out into the room. We sprang to the salute, we three old soldiers, but it was all like a scene in a dream to us, and our eyes were as far out as Berthier's had been. Napoleon was dressed in his green coated chasseur uniform, and he held his little silver-headed switch in his hand. He looked at us each in turn, with a smile upon his face—that frightful smile in which neither eyes nor brow joined—and each in turn had, I believe, a pringling on his skin, for that was the effect which the Emperor's gaze had upon most of us. Then he walked across to Berthier and put his hand upon his shoulder.

"You must not quarrel with blows, my dear Prince," said he; "they are your title to nobility." He spoke in that soft, caressing manner which he could assume. There was no one who could make the French tongue sound so pretty as the Emperor, and no one who could make it more harsh and terrible.

"I believe he would have killed me," cried Berthier, still rolling his head about.

"Tut, tut! I should have come to your help had these officers not heard your cries. But I trust that you are not really hurt!" He spoke with earnestness, for he was in truth very fond of Berthier—more so than of any man, unless it were of poor Duroc.

Berthier laughed, though not with a very good grace.

"It is new for me to receive my injuries from French hands," said he.

"And yet it was in the cause of France," returned the Emperor. Then, turning to us, he took old Tremeau by the ear. "Ah, old grumbler," said he, "you were one of my Egyptian grenadiers, were you not, and had your musket of honour at Marengo. I remember you very well, my good friend. So the old fires are not yet extinguished! They still burn up when you think that your Emperor is wronged. And you, Colonel Despienne, you would not even listen to the tempter. And you, Gerard, your faithful sword is ever to be between me and my enemies. Well, well, I have had some traitors about me, but now at last we are beginning to see who are the true men."

You can fancy, my friends, the thrill of joy which it gave us when the greatest man in the whole world spoke to us in this fashion. Tremeau shook until I thought he would have fallen, and the tears ran down his gigantic moustache. If you had not seen it, you could never believe the influence which the Emperor had upon those coarse-grained, savage old veterans.

"Well, my faithful friends," said he, "if you will follow me into this room, I will explain to you the meaning of this little farce which we have been acting. I beg, Berthier, that you will remain in this chamber, and so make sure that no one interrupts us."

It was new for us to be doing business, with a Marshal of France as sentry at the door. However, we followed the Emperor as we were ordered, and he led us into the recess of the window, gathering us around him and sinking his voice as he addressed us.

"I have picked you out of the whole army," said he, "as being not only the most formidable but also the most faithful of my soldiers. I was convinced that you were all three men who would never waver in your fidelity to me. If I have ventured to put that fidelity to the proof, and to watch you whilst attempts were at my orders made upon your honour, it was only because, in the days when I have found the blackest treason amongst my own flesh and blood, it is necessary that I should be doubly circumspect. Suffice it that I am well convinced now that I can rely upon your valour."

"To the death, sire!" cried Tremeau, and we both repeated it after him.

Napoleon drew us all yet a little closer to him, and sank his voice still lower.

"What I say to you now I have said to no one—not to my wife or my brothers; only to you. It is all up with us, my friends. We have come to our last rally. The game is finished, and we must make provision accordingly."

My heart seemed to have changed to a nine-pounder ball as I listened to him. We had hoped against hope, but now when he, the man who was always serene and who always had reserves— when he, in that quiet, impassive voice of his, said that everything was over, we realized that the clouds had shut for ever, and the last gleam gone. Tremeau snarled and gripped at his sabre, Despienne ground his teeth, and for my own part I threw out my chest and clicked my heels to show the Emperor that there were some spirits which could rise to adversity.

"My papers and my fortune must be secured," whispered the Emperor. "The whole course of the future may depend upon my having them safe. They are our base for the next attempt—for I am sure that these poor Bourbons would find that my footstool is too large to make a throne for them. Where am I to keep these precious things? My belongings will be searched—so will the houses of my supporters. They must be secured and concealed by men whom I can trust with that which is more precious to me than my life. Out of the whole of France, you are those whom I have chosen for this sacred trust.

"In the first place, I will tell you what these papers are. You shall not say that I have made you blind agents in the matter. They are the official proof of my divorce from Josephine, of my legal marriage to Marie Louise, and of the birth of my son and heir, the King of Rome. If we cannot prove each of these, the future claim of my family to the throne of France falls to the ground. Then there are securities to the value of forty millions of francs—an immense sum, my friends, but of no more value than this riding switch when compared to the other papers of which I have spoken. I tell you these things that you may realize the enormous importance of the task which I am committing to your care. Listen, now, while I inform you where you are to get these papers, and what you are to do with them.

"They were handed over to my trusty friend, the Countess Walewski, at Paris, this morning. At five o'clock she starts for Fontainebleau in her blue berline. She should reach here between half-past nine and ten. The papers will be concealed in the berline, in a hiding-place which none know but herself. She has been warned that her carriage will be stopped outside the town by three mounted officers, and she will hand the packet over to your care. You are the younger man, Gerard, but you are of the senior grade. I confide to your care this amethyst ring, which you will show the lady as a token of your mission, and which you will leave with her as a receipt for her papers.

"Having received the packet, you will ride with it into the forest as far as the ruined dove-house — the Colombier. It is possible that I may meet you there — but if it seems to me to be dangerous, I will send my body-servant, Mustapha, whose directions you may take as being mine. There is no roof to the Colombier, and to-night will be a full moon. At the right of the entrance you will find three spades leaning against the wall. With these you will dig a hole three feet deep in the north-eastern corner — that is, in the corner to the left of the door, and nearest to Fontainebleau. Having buried the papers, you will replace the soil with great care, and you will then report to me at the palace."

These were the Emperor's directions, but given with an accuracy and minuteness of detail such as no one but himself could put into an order. When he had finished, he made us swear to keep his secret as long as he lived, and as long as the papers should remain buried. Again and again he made us swear it before he dismissed us from his presence.

Colonel Despienne had quarters at the "Sign of the Pheasant," and it was there that we supped together. We were all three men who had been trained to take the strangest turns of fortune as part of our daily life and business, yet we were all flushed and moved by the extra-ordinary interview which we had had, and by the thought of the great adventure which lay before us. For my own part, it had been my fate three several times to take my orders from the lips of the Emperor himself, but neither the incident of the Ajaccio murderers nor the famous ride which I made to Paris appeared to offer such opportunities as this new and most intimate commission.

"If things go right with the Emperor," said Despienne, "we shall all live to be marshals yet."

We drank with him to our future cocked hats and our bâtons.

It was agreed between us that we should make our way separately to our rendezvous, which was to be the first milestone upon the Paris road. In this way we should avoid the gossip which might get about if three men who were so well known were to be seen riding out together. My little Violette had cast a shoe that morning, and the farrier was at work upon her when I returned, so that my comrades were already there when I arrived at the trysting-place. I had taken with me not only my sabre, but also my new pair of English rifled pistols, with a mallet for knocking in the charges. They had cost me a hundred and fifty francs at Trouvel's, in the Rue de Rivoli, but they would carry far further and straighter than the others. It was with one of them that I had saved old Bouvet's life at Leipzig.

The night was cloudless, and there was a brilliant moon behind us, so that we always had three black horsemen riding down the white road in front of us. The country is so thickly wooded, however, that we could not see very far. The great palace clock had already struck ten, but there was no sign of the Countess. We began to fear that something might have prevented her from starting.

And then suddenly we heard her in the distance. Very faint at first were the birr of wheels and the tat-tat-tat of the horses' feet. Then they grew louder and clearer and louder yet, until a pair of yellow lanterns swung round the curve, and in their light we saw the two big brown horses tearing along with the high, blue carriage at the back of them. The postillion pulled them up panting and foaming within a few yards of us. In a moment we were at the window and had raised our hands in a salute to the beautiful pale face which looked out at us.

"We are the three officers of the Emperor, madame," said I, in a low voice leaning my face down to the open window. "You have already been warned that we should wait upon you."

The countess had a very beautiful, cream-tinted complexion of a sort which I particularly admire, but she grew whiter and whiter as she looked at me. Harsh lines deepened upon her face until she seemed, even as I looked at her, to turn from youth into age.

"It is evident to me," she said, "that you are three impostors."

If she had struck me across the face with her delicate hand she could not have startled me more. It was not her words only, but the bitterness with which she hissed them out.

"Indeed, madame," said I. "You do us less than justice. These are the Colonel Despienne and Captain Tremeau. For myself, my name is Brigadier Gerard, and I have only to mention it to assure anyone who has heard of me that—"

"Oh, you villains!" she interrupted. "You think that because I am only a woman I am very easily to be hood-winked! You miserable impostors!"

I looked at Despienne, who had turned white with anger, and at Tremeau, who was tugging at his moustache.

"Madame," said I, coldly, "when the Emperor did us the honour to intrust us with this mission, he gave me this amethyst ring as a token. I had not thought that three honourable gentlemen would have needed such corroboration, but I can only confute your unworthy suspicions by placing it in your hands."

She held it up in the light of the carriage lamp, and the most dreadful expression of grief and of horror contorted her face.

"It is his!" she screamed, and then, "Oh, my God, what have I done? What have I done?"

I felt that something terrible had befallen. "Quick, madame, quick!" I cried. "Give us the papers!"

"I have already given them."

"Given them! To whom?"

"To three officers."

"When?"

"Within the half-hour."

"Where are they?"

"God help me, I do not know. They stopped the berline, and I handed them over to them without hesitation, thinking that they had come from the Emperor."

It was a thunder-clap. But those are the moments when I am at my finest.

"You remain here," said I, to my comrades. "If three horsemen pass you, stop them at any hazard. The lady will describe them to you. I will be with you presently." One shake of the bridle, and I was flying into Fontainbleau as only Violette could have carried me. At the palace I flung myself off, rushed up the stairs, brushed aside the lackeys who would have stopped me, and pushed my way into the Emperor's own cabinet. He and Macdonald were busy with pencil and compasses over a chart. He looked up with an angry frown at my sudden entry, but his face changed colour when he saw that it was I.

"You can leave us, Marshal," said he, and then, the instant that the door was closed: "What news about the papers?"

"They are gone," said I, and in a few curt words I told him what had happened. His face was calm, but I saw the compasses quiver in his hand.

"You must recover them, Gerard!" he cried. "The destinies of my dynasty are at stake. Not a moment is to be lost! To horse, sir, to horse!"

"Who are they, sire?"

"I cannot tell. I am surrounded with treason. But they will take them to Paris. To whom should they carry them but to the villain Talleyrand? Yes, yes, they are on the Paris road, and may yet be overtaken. With the three best mounts in my stables and — "

I did not wait to hear the end of the sentence. I was already clattering down the stair. I am sure that five minutes had not passed before I was galloping Violette out of the town with the bridle of one of the Emperor's own Arab chargers in either hand. They wished me to take three, but I should have never dared to look my Violette in the face again. I feel that the spectacle must have been superb when I dashed up to my comrades and pulled the horses on to their haunches in the moonlight.

"No one has passed?"

"No one."

"Then they are on the Paris road. Quick! Up and after them!"

They did not take long, those good soldiers. In a flash they were upon the Emperor's horses, and their own left masterless by the roadside. Then away we went upon our long chase, I in the centre, Despienne upon my right, and Tremeau a little behind, for he was the heavier man. Heavens, how we galloped! The twelve flying hoofs roared and roared along the hard, smooth road. Poplars and moon, black bars and silver streaks, for mile after mile our course lay along the same chequered track, with our shadows in front and our dust behind. We could hear the rasping of bolts and the creaking of shutters from the cottages as we thundered past them, but we were only three dark blurs upon the road by the time that the folk could look after us. It was just striking midnight as we raced into Corbail; but an ostler with a bucket in each hand was throwing his black shadow across the golden fan which was cast from the open door of the inn.

"Three riders!" I gasped. "Have they passed?"

"I have just been watering their horses," said he. "I should think they—"

"On, on, my friends!" and away we flew, striking fire from the cobblestones of the little town. A gendarme tried to stop us, but his voice was drowned by our rattle and clatter. The houses slid past, and we were out on the country road again, with a clear twenty miles between ourselves and Paris. How could they escape us, with the finest horses in France behind them? Not one of the three had turned a hair, but Violette was always a head and shoulders to the front. She was going within herself, too, and I knew by the spring of her that I had only to let her stretch herself, and the Emperor's horses would see the colour of her tail.

"There they are!" cried Despienne.

"We have them!" growled Tremeau.

"On, comrades, on!" I shouted, once more.

A long stretch of white road lay before us in the moonlight. Far away down it we could see three cavaliers, lying low upon their horses' necks. Every instant they grew larger and clearer as we gained upon them. I could see quite plainly that the two upon either side were wrapped in mantles and rode upon chestnut horses, whilst the man between them was dressed in a chasseur uniform and mounted upon a grey. They were keeping abreast, but it was easy enough to see from the way in which he gathered his legs for each spring that the centre horse was far the fresher of the three. And the rider appeared to be the leader of the party, for we continually saw the glint of his face in the moonshine as he looked back to measure the distance between us. At first it was only a glimmer, then it was cut across with a moustache, and at last when we began to feel their dust in our throats I could give a name to my man.

"Halt, Colonel de Montluc!" I shouted. "Halt, in the Emperor's name!"

I had known him for years as a daring officer and an unprincipled rascal. Indeed there was a score between us, for he had shot my friend, Treville, at Warsaw, pulling his trigger, as some said, a good second before the drop of the handkerchief.

Well, the words were hardly out of my mouth when his two comrades wheeled round and fired their pistols at us. I heard Despienne give a terrible cry, and at the same instant both Tremeau and I let drive at the same man. He fell forward with his hands swinging on each side of his horse's neck. His comrade spurred on to Tremeau, sabre in hand, and I heard the crash which comes when a strong cut is met by a stronger parry. For my own part I never turned my head, but I touched Violette with the spur for the first time and flew after the leader. That he should leave his comrades and fly was proof enough that I should leave mine and follow.

He had gained a couple of hundred paces, but the good little mare set that right before we could have passed two milestones. It was in vain that he spurred and thrashed like a gunner driver on a soft road. His hat flew off with his exertions, and his bald head gleamed in the moonshine. But do what he might, he still heard the rattle of the hoofs growing louder and louder behind him. I could not have been twenty yards from him, and the shadow head was touching the shadow haunch, when he turned with a curse in his saddle and emptied both his pistols, one after the other, into Violette.

I have been wounded myself so often that I have to stop and think before I can tell you the exact number of times. I have been hit by musket balls, by pistol bullets, and by bursting shell, besides being pierced by bayonet, lance, sabre, and finally by a bradawl, which was the most painful of any. Yet out of all these injuries I have never known the same deadly sickness as came over me when I felt the poor, silent, patient creature, which I had come to love more than anything in the world except my mother and the Emperor, reel and stagger beneath me. I pulled my second pistol from my holster and fired point-blank between the fellow's broad shoulders. He slashed his horse across the flank with his whip, and for a moment I thought that I had missed him. But then on the green of his chasseur jacket I saw an ever-widening black smudge, and he began to sway in his saddle, very slightly at first, but more and more with every bound, until at last over he went, with his foot caught in the stirrup and his shoulders thud-thud-thudding along the road, until the drag was too much for the tired horse, and I closed my hand upon the foam-spattered bridle-chain. As I pulled him up it eased the stirrup leather, and the spurred heel clinked loudly as it fell.

"Your papers!" I cried, springing from my saddle. "This instant!"

But even as I said it, the huddle of the green body and the fantastic sprawl of the limbs in the moonlight told me clearly enough that it was all over with him. My bullet had passed through his heart, and it was only his own iron will which had held him so long in the saddle. He had lived hard, this Montluc, and I will do him justice to say that he died hard also.

But it was the papers—always the papers—of which I thought. I opened his tunic and I felt in his shirt. Then I searched his holsters and his sabre-tasche. Finally I dragged off his boots, and undid his horse's girth so as to hunt under the saddle. There was not a nook or crevice which I did not ransack. It was useless. They were not upon him.

When this stunning blow came upon me I could have sat down by the roadside and wept. Fate seemed to be fighting against me, and that is an enemy from whom even a gallant hussar might not be ashamed to flinch. I stood with my arm over the neck of my poor wounded Violette, and I tried to think it all out, that I might act in the wisest way. I was aware that the Emperor had no great respect for my wits, and I longed to show him that he had done me an injustice. Montluc had not the papers. And yet Montluc had sacrificed his companions in order to make his escape. I could make nothing of that. On the other hand, it was clear that, if he had not got them, one or other of his comrades had. One of them was certainly dead. The other I had left fighting with Tremeau, and if he escaped from the old swordsman he had still to pass me. Clearly, my work lay behind me.

I hammered fresh charges into my pistols after I had turned this over in my head. Then I put them back in the holsters, and I examined my little mare, she jerking her head and cocking her ears the while, as if to tell me that an old soldier like herself did not make a fuss about a scratch or two. The first shot had merely grazed her off shoulder, leaving a skin-mark, as if she had brushed a wall. The second was more serious. It had passed through the muscle of her neck, but already it had ceased to bleed. I reflected that if she weakened I could mount Montluc's grey, and meanwhile I led him along beside us, for he was a fine horse, worth fifteen hundred francs at the least, and it seemed to me that no one had a better right to him than I.

Well, I was all impatience now to get back to the others, and I had just given Violette her head, when suddenly I saw something glimmering in a field by the roadside. It was the brasswork upon the chasseur hat which had flown from Montluc's head; and at the sight of it a thought made me jump in the saddle. How could the hat have flown off? With its weight, would it not have simply dropped? And here it lay, fifteen paces from the roadway! Of course, he must have thrown it off when he had made sure that I would overtake him. And if he threw it off—I did not stop to reason any more, but sprang from the mare with my heart beating the *pas-de-charge*. Yes, it was all right this time. There, in the crown of the hat was stuffed a roll of papers in a parchment wrapper bound round with yellow ribbon. I pulled it out with the one hand, and holding the hat in the other, I danced for joy in the moonlight. The Emperor would see that he had not made a mistake when he put his affairs into the charge of Etienne Gerard.

I had a safe pocket on the inside of my tunic just over my heart, where I kept a few little things which were dear to me, and into this I thrust my precious roll. Then I sprang upon Violette, and was pushing forward to see what had become of Tremeau, when I saw a horseman riding across the field in the distance. At the same instant I heard the sound of hoofs approaching me, and there in the moonlight was the Emperor upon his white charger, dressed in his grey overcoat and his three-cornered hat, just as I had seen him so often upon the field of battle.

"Well!" he cried, in the sharp, sergeant-major way of his. "Where are my papers?"

I spurred forward and presented them without a word. He broke the ribbon and ran his eyes rapidly over them. Then, as we sat our horses head to tail, he threw his left arm across me with his hand upon my shoulder. Yes, my friends, simple as you see me, I have been embraced by my great master.

"Gerard," he cried, "you are a marvel!"

I did not wish to contradict him, and it brought a flush of joy upon my cheeks to know that he had done me justice at last.

"Where is the thief, Gerard?" he asked.

"Dead, sire."

"You killed him?"

"He wounded my horse, sire, and would have escaped had I not shot him."

"Did you recognise him?"

"De Montluc is his name, sire—a Colonel of Chasseurs."

"Tut," said the Emperor. "We have got the poor pawn, but the hand which plays the game is still out of our reach." He sat in silent thought for a little, with his chin sunk upon his chest. "Ah,

Talleyrand, Talleyrand," I heard him mutter. "If I had been in your place and you in mine, you would have crushed a viper when you held it under your heel. For five years I have known you for what you are, and yet I have let you live to sting me. Never mind, my brave," he continued, turning to me, "there will come a day of reckoning for everybody, and when it arrives, I promise you that my friends will be remembered as well as my enemies."

"Sire," said I, for I had had time for thought as well as he, "if your plans about these papers have been carried to the ears of your enemies, I trust that you do not think that it was owing to any indiscretion upon the part of myself or of my comrades."

"It would be hardly reasonable for me to do so," he answered, "seeing that this plot was hatched in Paris, and that you only had your orders a few hours ago."

"Then how—?"

"Enough," he cried sternly. "You take an undue advantage of your position."

That was always the way with the Emperor. He would chat with you as with a friend and a brother, and then when he had wiled you into forgetting the gulf which lay between you, he would suddenly, with a word or with a look, remind you that it was as impassable as ever. When I have fondled my old hound until he has been encouraged to paw my knees, and I have then thrust him down again, it has made me think of the Emperor and his ways.

He reined his horse round, and I followed him in silence and with a heavy heart. But when he spoke again his words were enough to drive all thought of myself out of my mind.

"I could not sleep until I knew how you had fared," said he. "I have paid a price for my papers. There are not so many of my old soldiers left that I can afford to lose two in one night."

When he said "two" it turned me cold.

"Colonel Despienne was shot, sire," I stammered.

"And Captain Tremeau cut down. Had I been a few minutes earlier I might have saved him. The other escaped across the fields."

I remembered that I had seen a horseman a moment before I had met the Emperor. He had taken to the fields to avoid me, but if I had known, and Violette been unwounded, the old soldier would not have gone unavenged. I was thinking sadly of his sword-play, and wondering whether it was his stiffening wrist which had been fatal to him, when Napoleon spoke again.

"Yes, Brigadier," said he, "you are now the only man who will know where these papers are concealed."

It must have been imagination, my friends, but for an instant I may confess that it seemed to me that there was a tone in the Emperor's voice which was not altogether one of sorrow. But the dark thought had hardly time to form itself in my mind before he let me see that I was doing him an injustice.

"Yes, I have paid a price for my papers," he said, and I heard them crackle as he put his hand up to his bosom. "No man has ever had more faithful servants — no man since the beginning of the world."

As he spoke we came upon the scene of the struggle. Colonel Despienne and the man whom we had shot lay together some distance down the road, while their horses grazed contentedly beneath the poplars. Captain Tremeau lay in front of us upon his back, with his arms and legs stretched out, and his sabre broken short off in his hand. His tunic was open, and a huge blood-clot hung like a dark handkerchief out of a slit in his white shirt. I could see the gleam of his clenched teeth from under his immense moustache.

The Emperor sprang from his horse and bent down over the dead man.

"He was with me since Rivoli," said he, sadly. "He was one of my old grumblers in Egypt."

And the voice brought the man back from the dead. I saw his eyelids shiver. He twitched his arm, and moved the sword-hilt a few inches. He was trying to raise it in a salute. Then the mouth opened, and the hilt tinkled down on to the ground.

"May we all die as gallantly," said the Emperor, as he rose, and from my heart I added "Amen."

There was a farm within fifty yards of where we were standing, and the farmer, roused from his sleep by the clatter of hoofs and the cracking of pistols, had rushed out to the roadside. We saw him now, dumb with fear and astonishment, staring open-eyed at the Emperor. It was to him that we committed the care of the four dead men and of the horses also. For my own part, I thought it best to leave Violette with him and to take De Montluc's grey with me, for he could not refuse to give me back my own mare, whilst there might be difficulties about the other. Besides, my little friend's wound had to be considered, and we had a long return ride before us.

The Emperor did not at first talk much upon the way. Perhaps the deaths of Despienne and Tremeau still weighed heavily upon his spirits. He was always a reserved man, and in those times, when every hour brought him the news of some success of his enemies or defection of his friends, one could not expect him to be a merry companion. Nevertheless, when I reflected that he was carrying in his bosom those papers which he valued so highly, and which only a few hours ago appeared to be for ever lost, and when I further thought that it was I, Etienne Gerard, who had placed them there, I felt that I had deserved some little consideration. The same idea may have occurred to him, for when we had at last left the Paris high road, and had entered the forest, he began of his own accord to tell me that which I should have most liked to have asked him.

"As to the papers," said he, "I have already told you that there is no one now, except you and me, who knows where they are to be concealed. My Mameluke carried the spades to the pigeon-house, but I have told him nothing. Our plans, however, for bringing the packet from Paris have been formed since Monday. There were three in the secret, a woman and two men. The woman I would trust with my life; which of the two men has betrayed us I do not know, but I think that I may promise to find out."

We were riding in the shadow of the trees at the time, and I could hear him slapping his riding-whip against his boot, and taking pinch after pinch of snuff, as was his way when he was excited.

"You wonder, no doubt," said he, after a pause, "why these rascals did not stop the carriage at Paris instead of at the entrance to Fontainebleau."

In truth, the objection had not occurred to me, but I did not wish to appear to have less wits than he gave me credit for, so I answered that it was indeed surprising.

"Had they done so they would have made a public scandal, and run a chance of missing their end. Short of taking the berline to pieces, they could not have discovered the hiding-place. He planned it well — he could always plan well — and he chose his agents well also. But mine were the better."

It is not for me to repeat to you, my friends, all that was said to me by the Emperor as we walked our horses amid the black shadows and through the moon-silvered glades of the great forest. Every word of it is impressed upon my memory, and before I pass away it is likely that I will place it all upon paper, so that others may read it in the days to come. He spoke freely of his past, and something also of his future; of the devotion of Macdonald, of the treason of Marmont, of the little King of Rome, concerning whom he talked with as much tenderness as any bourgeois father of a single child; and, finally, of his father-in-law, the Emperor of Austria, who would, he thought, stand between his enemies and himself. For myself, I dared not say a word, remembering how I had already brought a rebuke upon myself; but I rode by his side, hardly able to believe that this was indeed the great Emperor, the man whose glance sent a thrill through me, who was now pouring out his thoughts to me in short, eager sentences, the words rattling and racing like the hoofs of a galloping squadron. It is possible that, after the word-splittings and diplomacy of a Court, it was a relief to him to speak his mind to a plain soldier like myself.

In this way the Emperor and I — even after years it sends a flush of pride into my cheeks to be able to put those words together — the Emperor and I walked our horses through the Forest of Fontainebleau, until we came at last to the Colombier. The three spades were propped against the wall upon the right-hand side of the ruined door, and at the sight of them the tears sprang to my eyes as I thought of the hands for which they were intended. The Emperor seized one and I another.

"Quick!" said he. "The dawn will be upon us before we get back to the palace."

We dug the hole, and placing the papers in one of my pistol holsters to screen them from the damp, we laid them at the bottom and covered them up. We then carefully removed all marks of the ground having been disturbed, and we placed a large stone upon the top. I dare say that since the Emperor was a young gunner, and helped to train his pieces against Toulon, he had not worked so hard with his hands. He was mopping his forehead with his silk handkerchief long before we had come to the end of our task.

The first grey cold light of morning was stealing through the tree trunks when we came out together from the old pigeon-house. The Emperor laid his hand upon my shoulder as I stood ready to help him to mount.

"We have left the papers there," said he, solemnly, "and I desire that you shall leave all thought of them there also. Let the recollection of them pass entirely from your mind, to be revived only when you receive a direct order under my own hand and seal. From this time onwards you forget all that has passed."

"I forget it, sire," said I.

We rode together to the edge of town, where he desired that I should separate from him. I had saluted, and was turning my horse, when he called me back.

"It is easy to mistake the points of the compass in the forest," said he. "Would you not say that it was in the northeastern corner that we buried them?"

"Buried what, sire?"

"The papers, of course," he cried, impatiently.

"What papers, sire?"

"Name of a name! Why, the papers that you have recovered for me."

"I am really at a loss to know what your Majesty is talking about."

He flushed with anger for a moment, and then he burst out laughing.

"Very good, Brigadier!" he cried. "I begin to believe that you are as good a diplomatist as you are a soldier, and I cannot say more than that."

So that was my strange adventure in which I found myself the friend and confident agent of the Emperor. When he returned from Elba he refrained from digging up the papers until his position should be secure, and they still remained in the corner of the old pigeon-house after his exile to St Helena. It was at this time that he was desirous of getting them into the hands of his own supporters, and for that purpose he wrote me, as I afterwards learned, three letters, all of which were intercepted by his guardians. Finally, he offered to support himself and his own establishment—which he might very easily have done out of the gigantic sum which belonged to him—if they would only pass one of his letters unopened. This request was refused, and so, up to his death in '21, the papers still remained where I have told you. How they came to be dug up by Count Bertrand and myself, and who eventually obtained them, is a story which I would tell you, were it not that the end has not yet come.

Some day you will hear of those papers and you will see how, after he has been so long in his grave, that great man can still set Europe shaking. When that day comes, you will think of Etienne Gerard, and you will tell your children that you have heard the story from the lips of the man who was the only one living of all who took part in that strange history—the man who was tempted by Marshal Berthier, who led that wild pursuit upon the Paris road, who was honoured by the embrace of the Emperor, and who rode with him by moonlight in the Forest of Fontainebleau. The buds are bursting and the birds are calling, my friends. You may find better things to do in the sunlight than listening to the stories of an old, broken soldier. And yet you may well treasure what I say, for the buds will have burst and the birds sung in many seasons before France will see such another ruler as he whose servants we were proud to be.

HOW THE BRIGADIER PLAYED
FOR A KINGDOM

IT has sometimes struck me that some of you, when you have heard me tell these little adventures of mine, may have gone away with the impression that I was conceited. There could not be a greater mistake than this, for I have always observed that really fine soldiers are free from this failing. It is true that I have had to depict myself sometimes as brave, sometimes as full of resource, always as interesting; but, then, it really was so, and I had to take the facts as I found them. It would be an unworthy affectation if I were to pretend that my career has been anything but a fine one. The incident which I will tell you to-night, however, is one which you will understand that only a modest man would describe. After all, when one has attained such a position as mine, one can afford to speak of what an ordinary man might be tempted to conceal.

You must know, then, that after the Russian campaign the remains of our poor army were quartered along the western bank of the Elbe, where they might thaw their frozen blood and try, with the help of the good German beer, to put a little between their skin and their bones. There were some things which we could not hope to regain, for I daresay that three large commissariat fourgons would not have sufficed to carry the fingers and the toes which the army had shed during that retreat. Still, lean and crippled as we were, we had much to be thankful for when we thought of our poor comrades whom we had left behind, and of the snowfields—the horrible, horrible snowfields. To this day, my friends, I do not care to see red and white together. Even my red cap thrown down upon my white counterpane has given me dreams in which I have seen those monstrous plains, the reeling, tortured army, and the crimson smears which glared upon the snow behind them. You will coax no story out of me about that business, for the thought of it is enough to turn my wine to vinegar and my tobacco to straw.

Of the half-million who crossed the Elbe in the autumn of the year '12, about forty thousand infantry were left in the spring of '13. But they were terrible men, these forty thousand: men of iron, eaters of horses, and sleepers in the snow; filled, too, with rage and bitterness against the Russians. They would hold the Elbe until the great army of conscripts, which the Emperor was raising in France, should be ready to help them to cross it once more.

But the cavalry was in a deplorable condition. My own hussars were at Borna, and when I paraded them first, I burst into tears at the sight of them. My fine men and my beautiful horses—it broke my heart to see the state to which they were reduced. "But, courage," I thought, "they have lost much, but their Colonel is still left to them." I set to work, therefore, to repair their disasters, and had already constructed two good squadrons, when an order came that all colonels of cavalry should repair instantly to the depots of the regiments in France to organize the recruits and the remounts for the coming campaign.

You will think, doubtless, that I was overjoyed at this chance of visiting home once more. I will not deny that it was a pleasure to me to know that I should see my mother again, and there were a few girls who would be very glad at the news; but there were others in the army who had a stronger claim. I would have given my place to any who had wives and children whom they might not see again. However, there is no arguing when the blue paper with the little red seal arrives, so within an hour I was off upon my great ride from the Elbe to the Vosges. At last, I was to have a period of quiet. War lay behind my mare's tail and peace in front of her nostrils. So I thought, as the sound of the bugles died in the distance, and the long, white road curled away in front of me through plain and forest and mountain, with France somewhere beyond the blue haze which lay upon the horizon.

It is interesting, but it is also fatiguing, to ride in the rear of an army. In the harvest time our soldiers could do without supplies, for they had been trained to pluck the grain in the fields as they passed, and to grind it for themselves in their bivouacs. It was at that time of year, therefore, that those swift marches were performed which were the wonder and the despair of Europe. But now the starving men had to be made robust once more, and I was forced to draw into the ditch continually as the Coburg sheep and the Bavarian bullocks came streaming past with waggon loads of Berlin beer and good French cognac. Sometimes, too, I would hear the dry rattle of the drums and the shrill whistle of the fifes, and long columns of our good little infantry men would swing past me with the white dust lying thick upon their blue tunics. These were old soldiers drawn from the garrisons of our German fortresses, for it was not until May that the new conscripts began to arrive from France.

Well, I was rather tired of this eternal stopping and dodging, so that I was not sorry when I came to Altenburg to find that the road divided, and that I could take the southern and quieter branch. There were few wayfarers between there and Greiz, and the road wound through groves of oaks and beeches, which shot their branches across the path. You will think it strange that a Colonel of hussars should again and again pull up his horse in order to admire the beauty of the feathery branches and the little, green, new-budded leaves, but if you had spent six months among the fir trees of Russia you would be able to understand me.

There was something, however, which pleased me very much less than the beauty of the forests, and that was the words and looks of the folk who lived in the woodland villages. We had always been excellent friends with the Germans, and during the last six years they had never seemed to bear us any malice for having made a little free with their country. We had shown kindnesses to the men and received them from the women, so that good, comfortable Germany was a second home to all of us. But now there was something which I could not understand in the behaviour of the people. The travellers made no answer to my salute; the foresters turned their heads away to avoid seeing me; and in the villages the folk would gather into knots in the roadway and would scowl at me as I passed. Even women would do this, and it was something new for me in those days to see anything but a smile in a woman's eyes when they were turned upon me.

It was in the hamlet of Schmolin, just ten miles out of Altenburg, that the thing became most marked. I had stopped at the little inn there just to damp my moustache and to wash the dust out of poor Violette's throat. It was my way to give some little compliment, or possibly a kiss, to the maid who served me; but this one would have neither the one nor the other, but darted a glance at me like a bayonet-thrust. Then when I raised my glass to the folk who drank their beer by the door they turned their backs on me, save only one fellow, who cried, "Here's a toast for you, boys! Here's to the letter T!" At that they all emptied their beer mugs and laughed; but it was not a laugh that had good-fellowship in it.

I was turning this over in my head and wondering what their boorish conduct could mean, when I saw, as I rode from the village, a great T new carved upon a tree. I had already seen more than one in my morning's ride, but I had given no thought to them until the words of the beer-drinker gave them an importance. It chanced that a respectable-looking person was riding past me at the moment, so I turned to him for information.

"Can you tell me, sir," said I, "what this letter T is?"

He looked at it and then at me in the most singular fashion. "Young man," said he, "it is not the letter N." Then before I could ask further he clapped his spurs into his horse's ribs and rode, stomach to earth, upon his way.

At first his words had no particular significance in my mind, but as I trotted onwards Violette chanced to half turn her dainty head, and my eyes were caught by the gleam of the brazen N's at the end of the bridle-chain. It was the Emperor's mark. And those T's meant something which was opposite to it. Things had been happening in Germany, then, during our absence, and the giant sleeper had begun to stir. I thought of the mutinous faces that I had seen, and I felt that if I could only have looked into the hearts of these people I might have had some strange news to bring into France with me. It made me the more eager to get my remounts, and to see ten strong squadrons behind my kettledrums once more.

While these thoughts were passing through my head I had been alternately walking and trotting, as a man should who has a long journey before and a willing horse beneath him. The woods were very open at this point, and beside the road there lay a great heap of fagots. As I passed there came a sharp sound from among them, and, glancing round, I saw a face looking out at me — a hot, red face, like that of a man who is beside himself with excitement and anxiety. A second glance told me that it was the very person with whom I had talked an hour before in the village.

"Come nearer!" he hissed. "Nearer still! Now dismount and pretend to be mending the stirrup leather. Spies may be watching us, and it means death to me if I am seen helping you."

"Death!" I whispered. "From whom?"

"From the Tugendbund. From Lutzow's night-riders. You Frenchmen are living on a powder-magazine, and the match has been struck which will fire it."

"But this is all strange to me," said I, still fumbling at the leathers of my horse. "What is this Tugendbund?"

"It is the secret society which has planned the great rising which is to drive you out of Germany, just as you have been driven out of Russia."

"And these T's stand for it?"

"They are the signal. I should have told you all this in the village, but I dared not be seen speaking to you. I galloped through the woods to cut you off, and concealed both my horse and myself."

"I am very much indebted to you," said I, "and the more so as you are the only German that I have met to-day from whom I have had common civility."

"All that I possess I have gained through contracting for the French armies," said he. "Your Emperor has been a good friend to me. But I beg that you will ride on now, for we have talked long enough. Beware only of Lutzow's night-riders!"

"Banditti? "I asked.

"All that is best in Germany," said he. "But for God's sake ride forwards, for I have risked my life and exposed my good name in order to carry you this warning."

Well, if I had been heavy with thought before, you can think how I felt after my strange talk with the man among the fagots. What came home to me even more than his words was his shivering, broken voice, his twitching face, and his eyes glancing swiftly to right and left, and opening in horror whenever a branch cracked upon a tree. It was clear that he was in the last extremity of terror, and it is possible that after I had left him I heard a distant gunshot and a shouting from somewhere behind me. It may have been some sportsman halloaing to his dogs, but I never again heard or saw the man who had given me my warning.

I kept a good look-out after this, riding swiftly where the country was open, and slowly where there might be an ambuscade. It was serious for me, since 500 good miles of German soil lay in front of me; but somehow I did not take it very much to heart, for the Germans had always seemed to me to be a kindly, gentle people, whose hands closed more readily round a pipe-stem than a swordhilt—not out of want of valour, you understand, but because they are genial, open souls, who would rather be on good terms with all men. I did not know then that beneath that homely surface there lurks a devilry as fierce as, and far more persistent than, that of the Castilian or the Italian.

And it was not long before I had shown to me that there was something far more serious abroad than rough words and hard looks. I had come to a spot where the road runs upwards through a wild tract of heathland and vanishes into an oak wood. I may have been half-way up the hill when, looking forward, I saw something gleaming under the shadow of the tree-trunks, and a man came out with a coat which was so slashed and spangled with gold that he blazed like a fire in the sunlight. He appeared to be very drunk, for he reeled and staggered as he came towards me. One of his hands was held up to his ear and clutched a great red handkerchief, which was fixed to his neck.

I had reined up the mare and was looking at him with some disgust, for it seemed strange to me that one who wore so gorgeous a uniform should show himself in such a state in broad daylight. For his part, he looked hard in my direction and came slowly onwards, stopping from time to time and swaying about as he gazed at me. Suddenly, as I again advanced, he screamed out his thanks to Christ, and, lurching forwards, he fell with a crash upon the dusty road. His hands flew forward with the fall, and I saw that what I had taken for a red cloth was a monstrous wound, which had left a great gap in his neck, from which a dark blood-clot hung, like an epaulette upon his shoulder.

"My God!" I cried, as I sprang to his aid. "And I thought you were drunk!"

"Not drunk, but dying," said he. "But thank Heaven that I have seen a French officer while I have still strength to speak."

I laid him among the heather and poured some brandy down his throat. All round us was the vast countryside, green and peaceful, with nothing living in sight save only the mutilated man beside me.

"Who has done this?" I asked, "and what are you? You are French, and yet the uniform is strange to me."

"It is that of the Emperor's new guard of honour. I am the Marquis of Château St Arnaud, and I am the ninth of my blood who has died in the service of France. I have been pursued and wounded by the night-riders of Lutzow, but I hid among the brushwood yonder, and waited in the hope that a Frenchman might pass. I could not be sure at first if you were friend or foe, but I felt that death was very near, and that I must take the chance."

"Keep your heart up, comrade," said I; "I have seen a man with a worse wound who has lived to boast of it."

"No, no," he whispered; "I am going fast." He laid his hand upon mine as he spoke, and I saw that his fingernails were already blue. "But I have papers here in my tunic which you must carry at once to the Prince of Saxe-Felstein, at his Castle of Hof. He is still true to us, but the Princess is our deadly enemy. She is striving to make him declare against us. If he does so, it will determine all those who are wavering, for the King of Prussia is his uncle and the King of Bavaria his cousin. These papers will hold him to us if they can only reach him before he takes the last step. Place them in his hands to-night, and, perhaps, you will have saved all Germany for the Emperor. Had my horse not been shot, I might, wounded as I am—" he choked, and the cold hand tightened into a grip which left mine as bloodless as itself. Then, with a groan, his head jerked back, and it was all over with him.

Here was a fine start for my journey home. I was left with a commission of which I knew little, which would lead me to delay the pressing needs of my hussars, and which at the same time was of such importance that it was impossible for me to avoid it. I opened the Marquis's tunic, the brilliance of which had been devised by the Emperor in order to attract those young aristocrats from whom he hoped to raise these new regiments of his Guard. It was a small packet of papers which I drew out, tied up with silk, and addressed to the Prince of Saxe-Felstein. In the corner, in a sprawling, untidy hand, which I knew to be the Emperor's own, was written: "Pressing and most important." It was an order to me, those four words—an order as clear as if it had come straight from the firm lips with the cold grey eyes looking into mine. My troopers might wait for their horses, the dead Marquis might lie where I had laid him amongst the heather, but if the mare and her rider had a breath left in them the papers should reach the Prince that night.

I should not have feared to ride by the road through the wood, for I have learned in Spain that the safest time to pass through a guerilla country is after an outrage, and that the moment of danger is when all is peaceful. When I came to look upon my map, however, I saw that Hof lay further to the south of me, and that I might reach it more directly by keeping to the moors. Off I set, therefore, and had not gone fifty yards before two carbine shots rang out of the brushwood and a bullet hummed past me like a bee. It was clear that the night-riders were bolder in their ways than the brigands of Spain, and that my mission would have ended where it had begun if I had kept to the road.

It was a mad ride, that—a ride with a loose rein, girth-deep in heather and in gorse, plunging through bushes, flying down hill-sides, with my neck at the mercy of my dear little Violette. But she— she never slipped, she never faltered, as swift and as surefooted as if she knew that her rider carried the fate of all Germany beneath the buttons of his pelisse. And I—I had long borne the name of being the best horseman in the six brigades of light cavalry, but I never rode as I rode then. My friend the Bart has told me of how they hunt the fox in England, but the swiftest fox would have been captured by me that day. The wild pigeons which flew overhead did not take a straighter course than Violette and I below. As an officer, I have always been ready to sacrifice myself for my men, though the Emperor would not have thanked me for it, for he had many men, but only one—well, cavalry leaders of the first class are rare.

But here I had an object which was indeed worth a sacrifice, and I thought no more of my life than of the clods of earth that flew from my darling's heels.

We struck the road once more as the light was failing, and galloped into the little village of Lobenstein. But we had hardly got upon the cobble-stones when off came one of the mare's shoes, and I had to lead her to the village smithy. His fire was low, and his day's work done, so that it would be an hour at the least before I could hope to push on to Hof. Cursing at the delay, I strode into the village inn and ordered a cold chicken and some wine to be served for my dinner. It was but a few more miles to Hof, and I had every hope that I might deliver my papers to the Prince on that very night, and be on my way for France next morning with despatches for the Emperor in my bosom. I will tell you now what befell me in the inn of Lobenstein.

The chicken had been served and the wine drawn, and I had turned upon both as a man may who has ridden such a ride, when I was aware of a murmur and a scuffling in the hall outside my door. At first I thought that it was some brawl between peasants in their cups, and I left them to settle their own affairs. But of a sudden there broke from among the low, sullen growl of the voices such a sound as would send Etienne Gerard leaping from his death-bed. It was the whimpering cry of a woman in pain. Down clattered my knife and my fork, and in an instant I was in the thick of the crowd which had gathered outside my door.

The heavy-cheeked landlord was there and his flaxen-haired wife, the two men from the stables, a chambermaid, and two or three villagers. All of them, women and men, were flushed and angry, while there in the centre of them, with pale cheeks and terror in her eyes, stood the loveliest woman that ever a soldier would wish to look upon. With her queenly head thrown back, and a touch of defiance mingled with her fear, she looked as she gazed round her like a creature of a different race from the vile, coarse-featured crew who surrounded her. I had not taken two steps from my door before she sprang to meet me, her hand resting upon my arm and her blue eyes sparkling with joy and triumph.

"A French soldier and a gentleman!" she cried. "Now at last I am safe."

"Yes, madam, you are safe," said I, and I could not resist taking her hand in mine in order that I might reassure her. "You have only to command me," I added, kissing the hand as a sign that I meant what I was saying.

"I am Polish," she cried; "the Countess Palotta is my name. They abuse me because I love the French. I do not know what they might have done to me had Heaven not sent you to my help."

I kissed her hand again lest she should doubt my intentions. Then I turned upon the crew with such an expression as I know how to assume. In an instant the hall was empty.

"Countess," said I, "you are now under my protection. You are faint, and a glass of wine is necessary to restore you." I offered her my arm and escorted her into my room, where she sat by my side at the table and took the refreshment which I offered her.

How she blossomed out in my presence, this woman, like a flower before the sun! She lit up the room with her beauty. She must have read my admiration in my eyes, and it seemed to me that I also could see something of the sort in her own. Ah! my friends, I was no ordinary-looking man when I was in my thirtieth year. In the whole light cavalry it would have been hard to find a finer pair of whiskers. Murat's may have been a shade longer, but the best judges are agreed that Murat's were a shade too long. And then I had a manner. Some women are to be approached in one way and some in another, just as a siege is an affair of fascines and gabions in hard weather and of trenches in soft. But the man who can mix daring with timidity, who can be outrageous with an air of humility and presumptuous with a tone of deference, that is the man whom mothers have to fear. For myself, I felt that I was the guardian of this lonely lady, and knowing what a dangerous man I had to deal with, I kept strict watch upon myself. Still, even a guardian has his privileges, and I did not neglect them.

But her talk was as charming as her face. In a few words she explained that she was travelling to Poland, and that her brother who had been her escort had fallen ill upon the way. She had more than once met with ill-treatment from the country folk because she could not conceal her good-will towards the French. Then turning from her own affairs she questioned me about the army, and so came round to myself and my own exploits. They were familiar to her, she said, for she knew several of Poniatowski's officers, and they had spoken of my doings. Yet she would be glad to hear them from my own lips. Never have I had so delightful a conversation. Most women make the mistake of talking rather too much about their own affairs, but this one listened to my tales just as you are listening now, ever asking for more and more and more. The hours slipped rapidly by, and it was with horror that I heard the village clock strike eleven, and so learned that for four hours I had forgotten the Emperor's business.

"Pardon me, my dear lady," I cried, springing to my feet, "but I must on instantly to Hof."

She rose also, and looked at me with a pale, reproachful face. "And me?" she said. "What is to become of me?"

"It is the Emperor's affair. I have already stayed far too long. My duty calls me, and I must go."

"You must go? And I must be abandoned alone to these savages? Oh, why did I ever meet you? Why did you ever teach me to rely upon your strength?" Her eyes glazed over, and in an instant she was sobbing upon my bosom.

Here was a trying moment for a guardian! Here was a time when he had to keep a watch upon a forward young officer. But I was equal to it. I smoothed her rich brown hair and whispered such consolations as I could think of in her ear, with one arm round her, it is true, but that was to hold her lest she should faint. She turned her tear-stained face to mine. "Water," she whispered. "For God's sake, water!"

I saw that in another moment she would be senseless. I laid the drooping head upon the sofa, and then rushed furiously from the room, hunting from chamber to chamber for a carafe. It was some minutes before I could get one and hurry back with it. You can imagine my feelings to find the room empty and the lady gone.

Not only was she gone, but her cap and silver-mounted riding switch which had lain upon the table were gone also. I rushed out and roared for the landlord. He knew nothing of the matter, had never seen the woman before, and did not care if he never saw her again. Had the peasants at the door seen anyone ride away? No, they had seen nobody. I searched here and searched there, until at last I chanced to find myself in front of a mirror, where I stood with my eyes staring and my jaw as far dropped as the chin-strap of my shako would allow.

Four buttons of my pelisse were open, and it did not need me to put my hand up to know that my precious papers were gone. Oh! the depth of cunning that lurks in a woman's heart. She had robbed me, this creature, robbed me as she clung to my breast. Even while I smoothed her hair and whispered kind words into her ear, her hands had been at work beneath my dolman. And here I was, at the very last step of my journey, without the power of carrying out this mission which had already deprived one good man of his life, and was likely to rob another one of his credit. What would the Emperor say when he heard that I had lost his despatches? Would the army believe it of Etienne Gerard? And when they heard that a woman's hand had coaxed them from me, what laughter there would be at mess-table and at camp-fire! I could have rolled upon the ground in my despair.

But one thing was certain — all this affair of the fracas in the hall and the persecution of the so-called Countess was a piece of acting from the beginning. This villainous innkeeper must be in the plot. From him I might learn who she was and where my papers had gone. I snatched my sabre from the table and rushed out in search of him. But the scoundrel had guessed what I would do, and had made his preparations for me. It was in the corner of the yard that I found him, a blunderbuss in his hands and a mastiff held upon a leash by his son. The two stable-hands, with pitch-forks, stood upon either side, and the wife held a great lantern behind him, so as to guide his aim.

"Ride away, sir, ride away!" he cried, with a crackling voice. "Your horse is ready, and no one will meddle with you if you go your way; but if you come against us, you are alone against three brave men."

I had only the dog to fear, for the two forks and the blunderbuss were shaking about like branches in a wind. Still, I considered that, though I might force an answer with my sword-point at the throat of this fat rascal, still I should have no means of knowing whether that answer was the truth. It would be a struggle, then, with much to lose and nothing certain to gain. I looked them up and down, therefore, in a way that set their foolish weapons shaking worse than ever, and then, throwing myself upon my mare, I galloped away with the shrill laughter of the landlady jarring upon my ears.

I had already formed my resolution. Although I had lost my papers, I could make a very good guess as to what their contents would be, and this I would say from my own lips to the Prince of

Saxe-Felstein, as though the Emperor had commissioned me to convey it in that way. It was a bold stroke and a dangerous one, but if I went too far I could afterwards be disavowed. It was that or nothing, and when all Germany hung on the balance the game should not be lost if the nerve of one man could save it.

It was midnight when I rode into Hof, but every window was blazing, which was enough in itself, in that sleepy country, to tell the ferment of excitement in which the people were. There was hooting and jeering as I rode through the crowded streets, and once a stone sang past my head, but I kept upon my way, neither slowing nor quickening my pace, until I came to the palace. It was lit from base to battlement, and the dark shadows, coming and going against the yellow glare, spoke of the turmoil within. For my part, I handed my mare to a groom at the gate, and striding in I demanded, in such a voice as an ambassador should have, to see the Prince instantly, upon business which would brook no delay.

The hall was dark, but I was conscious as I entered of a buzz of innumerable voices, which hushed into silence as I loudly proclaimed my mission. Some great meeting was being held then—a meeting which, as my instincts told me, was to decide this very question of war and peace. It was possible that I might still be in time to turn the scale for the Emperor and for France. As to the major-domo, he looked blackly at me, and showing me into a small ante-chamber he left me. A minute later he returned to say that the Prince could not be disturbed at present, but that the Princess would take my message.

The Princess! What use was there in giving it to her? Had I not been warned that she was German in heart and soul, and that it was she who was turning her husband and her State against us?

"It is the Prince that I must see," said I.

"Nay, it is the Princess," said a voice at the door, and a woman swept into the chamber. "Von Rosen, you had best stay with us. Now, sir, what is it that you have to say to either Prince or Princess of Saxe-Felstein?"

At the first sound of the voice I had sprung to my feet. At the first glance I had thrilled with anger. Not twice in a lifetime does one meet that noble figure, that queenly head, those eyes as blue as the Garonne, and as chilling as her winter waters.

"Time presses, sir!" she cried, with an impatient tap of her foot. "What have you to say to me?"

"What have I to say to you?" I cried. "What can I say, save that you have taught me never to trust a woman more? You have ruined and dishonoured me for ever."

She looked with arched brows at her attendant.

"Is this the raving of fever, or does it come from some less innocent cause?" said she. "Perhaps a little blood-letting—"

"Ah, you can act!" I cried. "You have shown me that already."

"Do you mean that we have met before?"

"I mean that you have robbed me within the last two hours."

"This is past all bearing," she cried, with an admirable affectation of anger. "You claim, as I understand, to be an ambassador, but there are limits to the privileges which such an office brings with it."

"You brazen it admirably," said I. "Your Highness will not make a fool of me twice in one night." I sprang forward and, stooping down, caught up the hem of her dress. "You would have done well to change it after you had ridden so far and so fast," said I.

It was like the dawn upon a snow-peak to see her ivory cheeks flush suddenly to crimson.

"Insolent!" she cried. "Call for the foresters and have him thrust from the palace!"

"I will see the Prince first."

"You will never see the Prince. Ah! Hold him, Von Rosen, hold him!"

She had forgotten the man with whom she had to deal—was it likely that I would wait until they could bring their rascals? She had shown me her cards too soon. Her game was to stand between me and her husband. Mine was to speak face to face with him at any cost. One spring took me out of the chamber. In another I had crossed the hall. An instant later I had burst into the great room from which the murmur of the meeting had come. At the far end I saw a figure upon a high chair under a daïs. Beneath him was a line of high dignitaries, and then on every side I saw vaguely the heads of a vast assembly. Into the centre of the room I strode, my sabre clanking, my shako under my arm.

"I am the messenger of the Emperor," I shouted. "I bear his message to his Highness the Prince of Saxe-Felstein."

The man beneath the daïs raised his head, and I saw that his face was thin and wan, and that his back was bowed as though some huge burden was balanced between his shoulders.

"Your name, sir?" he asked.

"Colonel Etienne Gerard, of the Third Hussars."

Every face in the gathering was turned upon me, and I heard the rustle of the innumerable necks and saw countless eyes without meeting one friendly one amongst them. The woman had swept past me, and was whispering, with many shakes of her head and dartings of her hands, into the Prince's ear. For my own part I threw out my chest and curled my moustache, glancing round in my own debonair fashion at the assembly. They were men, all of them, professors from the college, a sprinkling of their students, soldiers, gentlemen, artisans, all very silent and serious. In one corner there sat a group of men in black, with riding-coats drawn over their shoulders. They leaned their heads to each other, whispering under their breath, and with every movement I caught the clank of their sabres or the clink of their spurs.

"The Emperor's private letter to me informs me that it is the Marquis Château St Arnaud who is bearing his despatches," said the Prince.

"The Marquis has been foully murdered," I answered, and a buzz rose up from the people as I spoke. Many heads were turned, I noticed, towards the dark men in the cloaks.

"Where are your papers?" asked the Prince.

"I have none."

A fierce clamour rose instantly around me. "He is a spy! He plays a part!" they cried. "Hang him!" roared a deep voice from the corner, and a dozen others took up the shout. For my part, I drew out my handkerchief and flicked the dust from the fur of my pelisse. The Prince held out his thin hands, and the tumult died away.

"Where, then, are your credentials, and what is your message?"

"My uniform is my credential, and my message is for your private ear."

He passed his hand over his forehead with the gesture of a weak man who is at his wits' end what to do. The Princess stood beside him with her hand upon his throne, and again whispered in his ear.

"We are here in council together, some of my trusty subjects and myself," said he. "I have no secrets from them, and whatever message the Emperor may send to me at such a time concerns their interests no less than mine."

There was a hum of applause at this, and every eye was turned once more upon me. My faith, it was an awkward position in which I found myself, for it is one thing to address eight hundred hussars, and another to speak to such an audience on such a subject. But I fixed my eyes upon the Prince, and tried to say just what I should have said if we had been alone, shouting it out, too, as though I had my regiment on parade.

"You have often expressed friendship for the Emperor," I cried. "It is now at last that this friendship is about to be tried. If you will stand firm, he will reward you as only he can reward. It is an easy thing for him to turn a Prince into a King and a province into a power. His eyes are fixed upon you, and though you can do little to harm him, you can ruin yourself. At this moment he is crossing the Rhine with two hundred thousand men. Every fortress in the country is in his hands. He will be upon you in a week, and if you have played him false, God help both you and your people. You think that he is weakened because a few of us got the chilblains last winter. Look there!" I cried, pointing to a great star which blazed through the window. "That is the Emperor's star. When it wanes, he will wane — but not before."

You would have been proud of me, my friends, if you could have seen and heard me, for I clashed my sabre as I spoke, and swung my dolman as though my regiment was picketed outside in the courtyard. They listened to me in silence, but the back of the Prince bowed more and more as though the burden which weighed upon it was greater than his strength. He looked round with haggard eyes.

"We have heard a Frenchman speak for France," said he. "Let us have a German speak for Germany."

The folk glanced at each other, and whispered to their neighbours. My speech, as I think, had its effect, and no man wished to be the first to commit himself in the eyes of the Emperor. The Princess looked round her with blazing eyes, and her clear voice broke the silence.

"Is a woman to give this Frenchman his answer?" she cried. "Is it possible, then, that among the night-riders of Lutzow there is none who can use his tongue as well as his sabre?"

Over went a table with a crash, and a young man had bounded upon one of the chairs. He had the face of one inspired — pale, eager, with wild hawk eyes, and tangled hair. His sword hung straight from his side, and his riding-boots were brown with mire.

"It is Korner!" the people cried. "It is young Korner, the poet! Ah, he will sing, he will sing."

And he sang! It was soft, at first, and dreamy, telling of old Germany, the mother of nations, of the rich, warm plains, and the grey cities, and the fame of dead heroes. But then verse after verse rang like a trumpet-call. It was of the Germany of now, the Germany which had been taken unawares and overthrown, but which was up again, and snapping the bonds upon her giant limbs. What was life that one should covet it? What was glorious death that one should shun it? The mother, the great mother, was calling. Her sigh was in the night wind. She was crying to her own children for help. Would they come? Would they come? Would they come?

Ah, that terrible song, the spirit face and the ringing voice! Where were I, and France, and the Emperor? They did not shout, these people, they howled. They were up on the chairs and the tables. They were raving, sobbing, the tears running down their faces. Korner had sprung from the chair, and his comrades were round him with their sabres in the air. A flush had come into the pale face of the Prince, and he rose from his throne.

"Colonel Gerard," said he, "you have heard the answer which you are to carry to your Emperor. The die is cast, my children. Your Prince and you must stand or fall together."

He bowed to show that all was over, and the people with a shout made for the door to carry the tidings into the town. For my own part, I had done all that a brave man might, and so I was not sorry to be carried out amid the stream. Why should I linger in the palace? I had had my answer and must carry it, such as it was. I wished neither to see Hof nor its people again until I entered it at the head of a vanguard. I turned from the throng, then, and walked silently and sadly in the direction in which they had led the mare.

It was dark down there by the stables, and I was peering round for the ostler, when suddenly my two arms were seized from behind. There were hands at my wrists and at my throat, and I felt the cold muzzle of a pistol under my ear.

"Keep your lips closed, you French dog," whispered a fierce voice. "We have him, captain."

"Have you the bridle?"

"Here it is."

"Sling it over his head."

I felt the cold coil of leather tighten round my neck. An ostler with a stable lantern had come out and was gazing upon the scene. In its dim light I saw stern faces breaking everywhere through the gloom, with the black caps and dark cloaks of the night-riders.

"What would you do with him, captain?" cried a voice.

"Hang him at the Palace Gate."

"An ambassador?"

"An ambassador without papers."

"But the Prince?"

"Tut, man, do you not see that the Prince will then be committed to our side? He will be beyond all hope of forgiveness. At present he may swing round to-morrow as he has done before. He may eat his words, but a dead hussar is more than he can explain."

"No, no, Von Strelitz, we cannot do it," said another voice.

"Can we not? I shall show you that!" and there came a jerk on the bridle which nearly pulled me to the ground. At the same instant a sword flashed and the leather was cut through within two inches of my neck.

"By Heaven, Korner, this is rank mutiny," cried the captain. "You may hang yourself before you are through with it."

"I have drawn my sword as a soldier and not as a brigand," said the young poet. "Blood may dim its blade, but never dishonour. Comrades, will you stand by and see this French gentleman mishandled?"

A dozen sabres flew from their sheaths, and it was evident that my friends and my foes were about equally balanced. But the angry voices and the gleam of steel had brought the folk running from all parts.

"The Princess!" they cried. "The Princess is coming!"

And even as they spoke I saw her in front of us, her sweet face framed in the darkness. I had cause to hate her, for she had cheated and befooled me, and yet it thrilled me then and thrills me now to think that my arms have embraced her, and that I have felt the scent of her hair in my nostrils. I know not whether she lies under her German earth, or whether she still lingers, a grey-haired woman in her Castle of Hof, but she lives ever, young and lovely, in the heart and the memory of Etienne Gerard.

"For shame!" she cried, sweeping up to me, and tearing with her own hands the noose from my neck. "You are fighting in God's own quarrel, and yet you would begin with such a devil's deed as this. This man is mine, and he who touches a hair of his head will answer for it to me."

They were glad enough to slink off into the darkness before those scornful eyes. Then she turned once more to me.

"You can follow me, Colonel Gerard," she said. "I have a word that I would speak to you."

I walked behind her to the chamber into which I had originally been shown. She closed the door, and then looked at me with the archest twinkle in her eyes.

"Is it not confiding of me to trust myself with you?" said she. "You will remember that it is the Princess of Saxe-Felstein and not the poor Countess Palotta of Poland."

"Be the name what it might," I answered, "I helped a lady whom I believed to be in distress, and I have been robbed of my papers and almost of my honour as a reward."

"Colonel Gerard," said she, "we have been playing a game, you and I, and the stake was a heavy one. You have shown by delivering a message which was never given to you that you would stand at nothing in the cause of your country. My heart is German as yours is French, and I also would go all lengths, even to deceit and to theft, if at this crisis I can help my suffering fatherland. You see how frank I am."

"You tell me nothing that I have not seen."

"But now that the game is played and won, why should we bear malice? I will say this, that if ever I were in such a plight as that which I pretended in the inn of Lobenstein, I should never wish to meet a more gallant protector or a truer-hearted gentleman than Colonel Etienne Gerard. I had never thought that I could feel for a Frenchman as I felt for you when I slipped the papers from your breast."

"But you took them, none the less."

"They were necessary to me and to Germany. I knew the arguments which they contained and the effect which they would have upon the Prince. If they had reached him all would have been lost."

"Why should your Highness descend to such expedients when a score of these brigands, who wished to hang me at your castle gate, would have done the work as well?"

"They are not brigands, but the best blood of Germany," she cried, hotly. "If you have been roughly used you will remember the indignities to which every German has been subjected, from the Queen of Prussia downwards. As to why I did not have you waylaid upon the road, I may say that I had parties out on all sides, and that I was waiting at Lobenstein to hear of their success. When instead of their news you yourself arrived I was in despair, for there was only the one weak woman betwixt you and my husband. You see the straits to which I was driven before I used the weapon of my sex."

"I confess that you have conquered me, your Highness, and it only remains for me to leave you in possession of the field."

"But you will take your papers with you." She held them out to me as she spoke. "The Prince has crossed the Rubicon now, and nothing can bring him back. You can return these to the Emperor and tell him that we refused to receive them. No one can accuse you then of having lost your despatches. Good-bye, Colonel Gerard, and the best I can wish you is that when you reach France you may remain there. In a year's time there will be no place for a Frenchman upon this side of the Rhine."

And thus it was that I played the Princess of Saxe-Felstein with all Germany for a stake, and lost my game to her. I had much to think of as I walked my poor, tired Violette along the highway which leads westward from Hof. But amid all the thoughts there came back to me always the proud, beautiful face of the German woman, and the voice of the soldier-poet as he sang from the chair. And I understood then that there was something terrible in this strong, patient Germany—this mother root of nations—and I saw that such a land, so old and so beloved, never could be conquered. And as I rode I saw that the dawn was breaking, and that the great star at which I had pointed through the palace window was dim and pale in the western sky.

THE ADVENTURES OF BRIGADIER GERARD

THE CRIME OF THE BRIGADIER

In all the great hosts of France there was only one officer towards whom the English of Wellington's Army retained a deep, steady, and unchangeable hatred. There were plunderers among the French, and men of violence, gamblers, duellists, and roués. All these could be forgiven, for others of their kidney were to be found among the ranks of the English. But one officer of Massena's force had committed a crime which was unspeakable, unheard of, abominable; only to be alluded to with curses late in the evening, when a second bottle had loosened the tongues of men. The news of it was carried back to England, and country gentlemen who knew little of the details of the war grew crimson with passion when they heard of it, and yeomen of the shires raised freckled fists to Heaven and swore. And yet who should be the doer of this dreadful deed but our friend the Brigadier, Etienne Gerard, of the Hussars of Conflans, gay-riding, plume-tossing, debonnaire, the darling of the ladies and of the six brigades of light cavalry.

But the strange part of it is that this gallant gentleman did this hateful thing, and made himself the most unpopular man in the Peninsula, without ever knowing that he had done a crime for which there is hardly a name amid all the resources of our language. He died of old age, and never once in that imperturbable self-confidence which adorned or disfigured his character knew that so many thousand Englishmen would gladly have hanged him with their own hands. On the contrary, he numbered this adventure among those other exploits which he has given to the world, and many a time he chuckled and hugged himself as he narrated it to the eager circle who gathered round him in that humble café where, between his dinner and his dominoes, he would tell, amid tears and laughter, of that inconceivable Napoleonic past when France, like an angel of wrath, rose up, splendid and terrible, before a cowering continent. Let us listen to him as he tells the story in his own way and from his own point of view.

You must know, my friends, said he, that it was towards the end of the year eighteen hundred and ten that I and Massena and the others pushed Wellington backwards until we had hoped to drive him and his army into the Tagus. But when we were still twenty-five miles from Lisbon we found that we were betrayed, for what had this Englishman done but build an enormous line of works and forts at a place called Torres Vedras, so that even we were unable to get through them! They lay across the whole Peninsula, and our army was so far from home that we did not dare to risk a reverse, and we had already learned at Busaco that it was no child's play to fight against these people. What could we do then but sit down in front of these lines and blockade them to the best of our power? There we remained for six months, amid such anxieties that Massena said afterwards that he had not one hair which was not white upon his body. For my own part, I did not worry much about our situation, but I looked after our horses, who were in much need of rest and green fodder. For the rest, we drank the wine of the country and passed the time as best we might. There was a lady at Santarem — but my lips are sealed. It is the part of a gallant man to say nothing, though he may indicate that he could say a great deal.

One day Massena sent for me, and I found him in his tent with a great plan pinned upon the table. He looked at me in silence with that single piercing eye of his, and I felt by his expression that the matter was serious. He was nervous and ill at ease, but my bearing seemed to reassure him. It is good to be in contact with brave men.

"Colonel Etienne Gerard," said he, "I have always heard that you are a very gallant and enterprising officer."

It was not for me to confirm such a report, and yet it would be folly to deny it, so I clinked my spurs together and saluted.

"You are also an excellent rider."

I admitted it.

"And the best swordsman in the six brigades of light cavalry."

Massena was famous for the accuracy of his information.

"Now," said he, "if you will look at this plan you will have no difficulty in understanding what it is that I wish you to do. These are the lines of Torres Vedras. You will perceive that they cover a vast space, and you will realize that the English can only hold a position here and there. Once through the lines you have twenty-five miles of open country which lie between them and Lisbon. It is very important to me to learn how Wellington's troops are distributed throughout that space, and it is my wish that you should go and ascertain."

His words turned me cold.

"Sir," said I, "it is impossible that a colonel of light cavalry should condescend to act as a spy."

He laughed and clapped me on the shoulder.

"You would not be a Hussar if you were not a hot-head," said he. "If you will listen you will understand that I have not asked you to act as a spy. What do you think of that horse?"

He had conducted me to the opening of his tent, and there was a Chasseur who led up and down a most admirable creature. He was a dapple grey, not very tall, a little over fifteen hands perhaps, but with the short head and splendid arch of the neck which comes with the Arab blood. His shoulders and haunches were so muscular, and yet his legs so fine, that it thrilled me with joy just to gaze upon him. A fine horse or a beautiful woman, I cannot look at them unmoved, even now when seventy winters have chilled my blood. You can think how it was in the year '10.

"This," said Massena, "is Voltigeur, the swiftest horse in our army. What I desire is that you should start to-night, ride round the lines upon the flank, make your way across the enemy's rear, and return upon the other flank bringing me news of his dispositions.

You will wear a uniform, and will, therefore, if captured, be safe from the death of a spy. It is probable that you will get through the lines unchallenged, for the posts are very scattered. Once through, in daylight you can outride anything which you meet, and if you keep off the roads you may escape entirely unnoticed. If you have not reported yourself by to-morrow night, I will understand that you are taken, and I will offer them Colonel Petrie in exchange."

Ah, how my heart swelled with pride and joy as I sprang into the saddle and galloped this grand horse up and down to show the Marshal the mastery which I had of him! He was magnificent—we were both magnificent, for Massena clapped his hands and cried out in his delight. It was not I, but he, who said that a gallant beast deserves a gallant rider. Then, when for the third time, with my panache flying and my dolman streaming behind me, I thundered past him, I saw upon his hard old face that he had no longer any doubt that he had chosen the man for his purpose. I drew my sabre, raised the hilt to my lips in salute, and galloped on to my own quarters. Already the news had spread that I had been chosen for a mission, and my little rascals came swarming out of their tents to cheer me. Ah! it brings the tears to my old eyes when I think how proud they were of their Colonel. And I was proud of them also. They deserved a dashing leader.

The night promised to be a stormy one, which was very much to my liking. It was my desire to keep my departure most secret, for it was evident that if the English heard that I had been detached from the army they would naturally conclude that something important was about to happen. My horse was taken, therefore, beyond the picket line, as if for watering, and I followed and mounted him there. I had a map, a compass, and a paper of instructions from the Marshal, and with these in the bosom of my tunic and my sabre at my side I set out upon my adventure.

A thin rain was falling and there was no moon, so you may imagine that it was not very cheerful. But my heart was light at the thought of the honour which had been done me and the glory which awaited me. This exploit should be one more in that brilliant series which was to change my sabre into a bâton. Ah, how we dreamed, we foolish fellows, young, and drunk with success! Could I have foreseen that night as I rode, the chosen man of sixty thousand, that I should spend my life planting cabbages on a hundred francs a month! Oh, my youth, my hopes, my comrades! But the wheel turns and never stops. Forgive me, my friends, for an old man has his weakness.

My route, then, lay across the face of the high ground of Torres Vedras, then over a streamlet, past a farmhouse which had been burned down and was now only a landmark, then through a forest of young cork oaks, and so to the monastery of San Antonio, which marked the left of the English position. Here I turned south and rode quietly over the downs, for it was at this point that Massena thought that it would be most easy for me to find my way unobserved through the position. I went very slowly, for it was so dark that I could not see my hand in front of me. In such cases I leave my bridle loose and let my horse pick its own way. Voltigeur went confidently forward, and I was very content to sit upon his back and to peer about me, avoiding every light. For three hours we advanced in this cautious way, until it seemed to me that I must have left all danger behind me. I then pushed on more briskly, for I wished to be in the rear of the whole army by daybreak. There are many vineyards in these parts which in winter become open plains, and a horseman finds few difficulties in his way.

But Massena had underrated the cunning of these English, for it appears that there was not one line of defence but three, and it was the third, which was the most formidable, through which I was at that instant passing. As I rode, elated at my own success, a lantern flashed suddenly before me, and I saw the glint of polished gun-barrels and the gleam of a red coat.

"Who goes there?" cried a voice—such a voice! I swerved to the right and rode like a madman, but a dozen squirts of fire came out of the darkness, and the bullets whizzed all round my ears. That was no new sound to me, my friends, though I will not talk like a foolish conscript and say that I have ever liked it. But at least it had never kept me from thinking clearly, and so I knew that there was nothing for it but to gallop hard and try my luck elsewhere. I rode round the English picket, and then, as I heard nothing more of them, I concluded rightly that I had at last come through their defences. For five miles I rode south, striking a tinder from time to time to look at my pocket compass. And then in an instant—I feel the pang once more as my memory brings back the moment—my horse, without a sob or stagger, fell stone dead beneath me!

I had never known it, but one of the bullets from that infernal picket had passed through his body. The gallant creature had never winced nor weakened, but had gone while life was in him. One instant I was secure on the swiftest, most graceful horse in Massena's army. The next he lay upon his side, worth only the price of his hide, and I stood there that most helpless, most ungainly of creatures, a dismounted Hussar. What could I do with my boots, my spurs, my trailing sabre? I was far inside the enemy's lines. How could I hope to get back again? I am not ashamed to say that I, Etienne Gerard, sat upon my dead horse and sank my face in my hands in my despair. Already the first streaks were whitening the east. In half an hour it would be light. That I should have won my way past every obstacle and then at this last instant be left at the mercy of my enemies, my mission ruined, and myself a prisoner—was it not enough to break a soldier's heart?

But courage, my friends! We have these moments of weakness, the bravest of us; but I have a spirit like a slip of steel, for the more you bend it the higher it springs. One spasm of despair, and then a brain of ice and a heart of fire. All was not yet lost. I who had come through so many hazards would come through this one also. I rose from my horse and considered what had best be done.

And first of all it was certain that I could not get back. Long before I could pass the lines it would be broad daylight. I must hide myself for the day, and then devote the next night to my escape. I took the saddle, holsters, and bridle from poor Voltigeur, and I concealed them among some bushes, so that no one finding him could know that he was a French horse. Then, leaving him lying there, I wandered on in search of some place where I might be safe for the day. In every direction I could see camp fires upon the sides of the hills, and already figures had begun to move around them. I must hide quickly, or I was lost.

But where was I to hide? It was a vineyard in which I found myself, the poles of the vines still standing, but the plants gone. There was no cover there. Besides, I should want some food and water before another night had come. I hurried wildly onwards through the waning darkness, trusting that chance would be my friend. And I was not disappointed. Chance is a woman, my friends, and she has her eye always upon a gallant Hussar.

Well, then, as I stumbled through the vineyard, something loomed in front of me, and I came upon a great square house with another long, low building upon one side of it. Three roads met there, and it was easy to see that this was the posada, or wine shop. There was no light in the windows, and everything was dark and silent, but, of course, I knew that such comfortable quarters were certainly occupied, and probably by someone of importance. I have learned, however, that the nearer the danger may really be the safer place, and so I was by no means inclined to trust myself away from this shelter. The low building was evidently the stable, and into this I crept, for the door was unlatched. The place was full of bullocks and sheep, gathered there, no doubt, to be out of the clutches of marauders. A ladder led to a loft, and up this I climbed and concealed myself very snugly among some bales of hay upon the top. This loft had a small open window, and I was able to look down upon the front of the inn and also upon the road. There I crouched and waited to see what would happen.

It was soon evident that I had not been mistaken when I had thought that this might be the quarters of some person of importance. Shortly after daybreak an English light dragoon arrived with a despatch, and from then onwards the place was in a turmoil, officers continually riding up and away. Always the same name was upon their lips: "Sir Stapleton—Sir Stapleton." It was hard for me to lie there with a dry moustache and watch the great flagons which were brought out by the landlord to these English officers. But it amused me to look at their fresh-coloured, clean-shaven, careless faces, and to wonder what they would think if they knew that so celebrated a person was lying so near to them. And then, as I lay and watched, I saw a sight which filled me with surprise.

It is incredible the insolence of these English! What do you suppose Milord Wellington had done when he found that Massena had blockaded him and that he could not move his army? I might give you many guesses. You might say that he had raged, that he had despaired, that he had brought his troops together and spoken to them about glory and the fatherland before leading them to one last battle. No, Milord did none of these things. But he sent a fleet ship to England to bring him a number of fox-dogs, and he with his officers settled himself down to chase the fox. It is true what I tell you. Behind the lines of Torres Vedras these mad Englishmen made the fox chase three days in the week. We had heard of it in the camp, and now I was myself to see that it was true.

For, along the road which I have described, there came these very dogs, thirty or forty of them, white and brown, each with its tail at the same angle, like the bayonets of the Old Guard. My faith, but it was a pretty sight! And behind and amidst them there rode three men with peaked caps and red coats, whom I understood to be the hunters. After them came many horsemen with uniforms of various kinds, stringing along the roads in twos and threes, talking together and laughing. They did not seem to be going above a trot, and it appeared to me that it must indeed be a slow fox which they hoped to catch. However, it was their affair, not mine, and soon they had all passed my window and were out of sight. I waited and I watched, ready for any chance which might offer.

Presently an officer, in a blue uniform not unlike that of our flying artillery, came cantering down the road—an elderly, stout man he was, with grey side-whiskers. He stopped and began to talk with an orderly officer of dragoons, who waited outside the inn, and it was then that I learned the advantage of the English which had been taught me. I could hear and understand all that was said.

"Where is the meet?" said the officer, and I thought that he was hungering for his bifstek. But the other answered him that it was near Altara, so I saw that it was a place of which he spoke.

"You are late, Sir George," said the orderly.

"Yes, I had a court-martial. Has Sir Stapleton Cotton gone?"

At this moment a window opened, and a handsome young man in a very splendid uniform looked out of it.

"Halloa, Murray!" said he. "These cursed papers keep me, but I will be at your heels."

"Very good, Cotton. I am late already, so I will ride on."

"You might order my groom to bring round my horse," said the young General at the window to the orderly below, while the other went on down the road.

The orderly rode away to some outlying stable, and then in a few minutes there came a smart English groom with a cockade in his hat, leading by the bridle a horse — and, oh, my friends, you have never known the perfection to which a horse can attain until you have seen a first-class English hunter. He was superb: tall, broad, strong, and yet as graceful and agile as a deer. Coal black he was in colour, and his neck, and his shoulder, and his quarters, and his fetlocks — how can I describe him all to you? The sun shone upon him as on polished ebony, and he raised his hoofs in a little, playful dance so lightly and prettily, while he tossed his mane and whinnied with impatience. Never have I seen such a mixture of strength and beauty and grace. I had often wondered how the English Hussars had managed to ride over the Chasseurs of the Guards in the affair at Astorga, but I wondered no longer when I saw the English horses.

There was a ring for fastening bridles at the door of the inn, and the groom tied the horse there while he entered the house. In an instant I had seen the chance which Fate had brought to me. Were I in that saddle I should be better off than when I started. Even Voltigeur could not compare with this magnificent creature. To think is to act with me. In one instant I was down the ladder and at the door of the stable. The next I was out and the bridle was in my hand. I bounded into the saddle. Somebody, the master or the man, shouted wildly behind me. What cared I for his shouts! I touched the horse with my spurs and he bounded forward with such a spring that only a rider like myself could have sat him. I gave him his head and let him go — it did not matter to me where, so long as we left this inn far behind us. He thundered away across the vineyards, and in a very few minutes I had placed miles between myself and my pursuers. They could no longer tell in that wild country in which direction I had gone. I knew that I was safe, and so, riding to the top of a small hill, I drew my pencil and note-book from my pocket and proceeded to make plans of those camps which I could see and to draw the outline of the country.

He was a dear creature upon whom I sat, but it was not easy to draw upon his back, for every now and then his two ears would cock, and he would start and quiver with impatience. At first I could not understand this trick of his, but soon I observed that he only did it when a peculiar noise — "yoy, yoy, yoy" — came from somewhere among the oak woods beneath us. And then suddenly this strange cry changed into a most terrible screaming, with the frantic blowing of a horn. Instantly he went mad — this horse. His eyes blazed. His mane bristled. He bounded from the earth and bounded again, twisting and turning in a frenzy. My pencil flew one way and my notebook another. And then, as I looked down into the valley, an extraordinary sight met my eyes. The hunt was streaming down it. The fox I could not see, but the dogs were in full cry, their noses down, their tails up, so close together that they might have been one great yellow and white moving carpet. And behind them rode the horsemen — my faith, what a sight! Consider every type which a great army could show. Some in hunting dress, but the most in uniforms: blue dragoons, red dragoons, red-trousered hussars, green riflemen, artillery men, gold-slashed lancers, and most of all red, red, red, for the infantry officers ride as hard as the cavalry. Such a crowd, some well mounted, some ill, but all flying along as best they might, the sub-altern as good as the general, jostling and pushing, spurring and driving, with every thought thrown to the winds save that they should have the blood of this absurd fox! Truly, they are an extraordinary people, the English!

But I had little time to watch the hunt or to marvel at these islanders, for of all these mad creatures the very horse upon which I sat was the maddest. You understand that he was himself a hunter, and that the crying of these dogs was to him what the call of a cavalry trumpet in the street yonder would be to me. It thrilled him. It drove him wild. Again and again he bounded into the air, and then, seizing the bit between his teeth, he plunged down the slope and galloped after the dogs. I swore, and tugged, and pulled, but I was powerless. This English General rode his horse with a snaffle only, and the beast had a mouth of iron. It was useless to pull him back. One might as well try to keep a Grenadier from a wine bottle. I gave it up in despair, and, settling down in the saddle, I prepared for the worst which could befall.

What a creature he was! Never have I felt such a horse between my knees. His great haunches gathered under him with every stride, and he shot forward ever faster and faster, stretched like a greyhound, while the wind beat in my face and whistled past my ears. I was wearing our undress jacket, a uniform simple and dark in itself—though some figures give distinction to any uniform— and I had taken the precaution to remove the long panache from my busby. The result was that, amidst the mixture of costumes in the hunt, there was no reason why mine should attract attention, or why these men, whose thoughts were all with the chase, should give any heed to me. The idea that a French officer might be riding with them was too absurd to enter their minds. I laughed as I rode, for, indeed, amid all the danger, there was something of comic in the situation.

I have said that the hunters were very unequally mounted, and so at the end of a few miles, instead of being one body of men, like a charging regiment, they were scattered over a considerable space, the better riders well up to the dogs and the others trailing away behind. Now, I was as good a rider as any, and my horse was the best of them all, and so you can imagine that it was not long before he carried me to the front. And when I saw the dogs streaming over the open, and the red-coated huntsman behind them, and only seven or eight horsemen between us, then it was that the strangest thing of all happened, for I, too, went mad—I, Etienne Gerard! In a moment it came upon me, this spirit of sport, this desire to excel, this hatred of the fox. Accursed animal, should he then defy us? Vile robber, his hour was come! Ah, it is a great feeling, this feeling of sport, my friends, this desire to trample the fox under the hoofs of your horse. I have made the fox chase with the English. I have also, as I may tell you some day, fought the box-fight with the Bustler, or Bristol. And I say to you that this sport is a wonderful thing—full of interest as well as madness.

The farther we went the faster galloped my horse, and soon there were but three men as near the dogs as I was. All thought of fear of discovery had vanished. My brain throbbed, my blood ran hot—only one thing upon earth seemed worth living for, and that was to overtake this infernal fox. I passed one of the horsemen—a Hussar like myself. There were only two in front of me now: the one in a black coat, the other the blue artilleryman whom I had seen at the inn. His grey whiskers streamed in the wind, but he rode magnificently. For a mile or more we kept in this order, and then, as we galloped up a steep slope, my lighter weight brought me to the front. I passed them both, and when I reached the crown I was riding level with the little, hard-faced English huntsman. In front of us were the dogs, and then, a hundred paces beyond them, was a brown wisp of a thing, the fox itself, stretched to the uttermost. The sight of him fired my blood. "Aha, we have you then, assassin!" I cried, and shouted my encouragement to the huntsman. I waved my hand to show him that there was one upon whom he could rely.

And now there were only the dogs between me and my prey. These dogs, whose duty it is to point out the game, were now rather a hindrance than a help to us, for it was hard to know how to pass them. The huntsman felt the difficulty as much as I, for he rode behind them, and could make no progress towards the fox. He was a swift rider, but wanting in enterprise. For my part, I felt that it would be unworthy of the Hussars of Conflans if I could not overcome such a difficulty as this. Was Etienne Gerard to be stopped by a herd of fox-dogs? It was absurd. I gave a shout and spurred my horse.

"Hold hard, sir! Hold hard!" cried the huntsman.

He was uneasy for me, this good old man, but I reassured him by a wave and a smile. The dogs opened in front of me. One or two may have been hurt, but what would you have? The egg must be broken for the omelette. I could hear the huntsman shouting his congratulations behind me. One more effort, and the dogs were all behind me. Only the fox was in front.

Ah, the joy and pride of that moment! To know that I had beaten the English at their own sport. Here were three hundred all thirsting for the life of this animal, and yet it was I who was about to take it. I thought of my comrades of the light cavalry brigade, of my mother, of the Emperor, of France. I had brought honour to each and all. Every instant brought me nearer to the fox. The moment for action had arrived, so I unsheathed my sabre. I waved it in the air, and the brave English all shouted behind me.

Only then did I understand how difficult is this fox chase, for one may cut again and again at the creature and never strike him once. He is small, and turns quickly from a blow. At every cut I heard those shouts of encouragement from behind me, and they spurred me to yet another effort. And then at last the supreme moment of my triumph arrived. In the very act of turning I caught him fair with such another back-handed cut as that with which I killed the aide-de-camp of the Emperor of Russia. He flew into two pieces, his head one way and his tail another. I looked back and waved the blood-stained sabre in the air. For the moment I was exalted—superb!

Ah! how I should have loved to have waited to have received the congratulations of these generous enemies. There were fifty of them in sight, and not one who was not waving his hand and shouting. They are not really such a phlegmatic race, the English. A gallant deed in war or in sport will always warm their hearts. As to the old huntsman, he was the nearest to me, and I could see with my own eyes how overcome he was by what he had seen. He was like a man paralyzed, his mouth open, his hand, with outspread fingers, raised in the air. For a moment my inclination was to return and to embrace him. But already the call of duty was sounding in my ears, and these English, in spite of all the fraternity which exists among sportsmen, would certainly have made me prisoner. There was no hope for my mission now, and I had done all that I could do. I could see the lines of Massena's camp no very great distance off, for, by a lucky chance, the chase had taken us in that direction. I turned from the dead fox, saluted with my sabre, and galloped away.

But they would not leave me so easily, these gallant huntsmen. I was the fox now, and the chase swept bravely over the plain. It was only at the moment when I started for the camp that they could have known that I was a Frenchman, and now the whole swarm of them were at my heels. We were within gunshot of our pickets before they would halt, and then they stood in knots and would not go away, but shouted and waved their hands at me. No, I will not think that it was in enmity. Rather would I fancy that a glow of admiration filled their breasts, and that their one desire was to embrace the stranger who had carried himself so gallantly and well.

HOW BRIGADIER GERARD LOST HIS EAR

It was the old Brigadier who was talking in the café.

I have seen a great many cities, my friends. I would not dare to tell you how many I have entered as a conqueror with eight hundred of my little fighting devils clanking and jingling behind me. The cavalry were in front of the Grande Armée, and the Hussars of Conflans were in front of the cavalry, and I was in front of the Hussars. But of all the cities which we visited Venice is the most ill-built and ridiculous. I cannot imagine how the people who laid it out thought that the cavalry could manoeuvre. It would puzzle Murat or Lassalle to bring a squadron into that square of theirs. For this reason we left Kellermann's heavy brigade and also my own Hussars at Padua on the mainland. But Suchet with the infantry held the town, and he had chosen me as his aide-de-camp for that winter, because he was pleased about the affair of the Italian fencing-master at Milan. The fellow was a good swordsman, and it was fortunate for the credit of French arms that it was I who was opposed to him. Besides, he deserved a lesson, for if one does not like a *prima donna's* singing one can always be silent, but it is intolerable that a public affront should be put upon a pretty woman. So the sympathy was all with me, and after the affair had blown over and the man's widow had been pensioned Suchet chose me as his own galloper, and I followed him to Venice, where I had the strange adventure which I am about to tell you.

You have not been to Venice? No, for it is seldom that the French travel. We were great travellers in those days. From Moscow to Cairo we had travelled everywhere, but we went in larger parties than were convenient to those whom we visited, and we carried our passports in our limbers. It will be a bad day for Europe when the French start travelling again, for they are slow to leave their homes, but when they have done so no one can say how far they will go if they have a guide like our little man to point out the way. But the great days are gone and the great men are dead, and here am I, the last of them, drinking wine of Suresnes and telling old tales in a café.

But it is of Venice that I would speak. The folk there live like water-rats upon a mud-bank, but the houses are very fine, and the churches, especially that of St Mark, are as great as any I have seen. But above all they are proud of their statues and their pictures, which are the most famous in Europe. There are many soldiers who think that because one's trade is to make war one should never have a thought above fighting and plunder. There was old Bouvet, for example—the one who was killed by the Prussians on the day that I won the Emperor's medal; if you took him away from the camp and the canteen, and spoke to him of books or of art, he would sit and stare at you. But the highest soldier is a man like myself who can understand the things of the mind and the soul. It is true that I was very young when I joined the army, and that the quarter-master was my only teacher, but if you go about the world with your eyes open you cannot help learning a great deal.

Thus I was able to admire the pictures in Venice, and to know the names of the great men, Michael Titiens, and Angelus, and the others, who had painted them. No one can say that Napoleon did not admire them also, for the very first thing which he did when he captured the town was to send the best of them to Paris. We all took what we could get, and I had two pictures for my share. One of them, called "Nymphs Surprised," I kept for myself, and the other, "Saint Barbara," I sent as a present for my mother.

It must be confessed, however, that some of our men behaved very badly in this matter of the statues and the pictures. The people at Venice were very much attached to them, and as to the four bronze horses which stood over the gate of their great church, they loved them as dearly as if they had been their children. I have always been a judge of a horse, and I had a good look at these ones, but I could not see that there was much to be said for them. They were too coarse-limbed for light cavalry chargers and they had not the weight for the gun-teams. However, they were the only four horses, alive or dead, in the whole town, so it was not to be expected that the people would know any better. They wept bitterly when they were sent away, and ten French soldiers were found floating in the canals that night. As a punishment for these murders a great many more of their pictures were sent away, and the soldiers took to breaking the statues and firing their muskets at the stained-glass windows. This made the people furious, and there was very bad feeling in the town. Many officers and men disappeared during that winter, and even their bodies were never found.

For myself I had plenty to do, and I never found the time heavy on my hands. In every country it has been my custom to try to learn the language. For this reason I always look round for some lady who will be kind enough to teach it to me, and then we practise it together. This is the most interesting way of picking it up, and before I was thirty I could speak nearly every tongue in Europe; but it must be confessed that what you learn is not of much use for the ordinary purposes of life. My business, for example, has usually been with soldiers and peasants, and what advantage is it to be able to say to them that I love only them, and that I will come back when the wars are over?

Never have I had so sweet a teacher as in Venice. Lucia was her first name, and her second — but a gentleman forgets second names. I can say this with all discretion, that she was of one of the senatorial families of Venice and that her grandfather had been Doge of the town. She was of an exquisite beauty — and when I, Etienne Gerard, use such a word as "exquisite," my friends, it has a meaning. I have judgment, I have memories, I have the means of comparison. Of all the women who have loved me there are not twenty to whom I could apply such a term as that. But I say again that Lucia was exquisite. Of the dark type I do not recall her equal unless it were Dolores of Toledo. There was a little brunette whom I loved at Santarem when I was soldiering under Massena in Portugal—her name has escaped me. She was of a perfect beauty, but she had not the figure nor the grace of Lucia. There was Agnes also. I could not put one before the other, but I do none an injustice when I say that Lucia was the equal of the best.

It was over this matter of pictures that I had first met her, for her father owned a palace on the farther side of the Rialto Bridge upon the Grand Canal, and it was so packed with wall-paintings that Suchet sent a party of sappers to cut some of them out and send them to Paris. I had gone down with them, and after I had seen Lucia in tears it appeared to me that the plaster would crack if it were taken from the support of the wall. I said so, and the sappers were withdrawn. After that I was the friend of the family, and many a flask of Chianti have I cracked with the father and many a sweet lesson have I had from the daughter. Some of our French officers married in Venice that winter, and I might have done the same, for I loved her with all my heart; but Etienne Gerard has his sword, his horse, his regiment, his mother, his Emperor, and his career. A debonair Hussar has room in his life for love, but none for a wife. So I thought then, my friends, but I did not see the lonely days when I should long to clasp those vanished hands, and turn my head away when I saw old comrades with their tall children standing round their chairs. This love which I had thought was a joke and a plaything—it is only now that I understand that it is the moulder of one's life, the most solemn and sacred of all things. . . . Thank you, my friend, thank you! It is a good wine, and a second bottle cannot hurt.

And now I will tell you how my love for Lucia was the cause of one of the most terrible of all the wonderful adventures which have ever befallen me, and how it was that I came to lose the top of my right ear. You have often asked me why it was missing. Tonight for the first time I will tell you.

Suchet's head-quarters at that time was the old palace of the Doge Dandolo, which stands, on the lagoon not far from the place of San Marco. It was near the end of the winter, and I had returned one night from the Theatre Goldini, when I found a note from Lucia and a gondola waiting. She prayed me to come to her at once as she was in trouble. To a Frenchman and a soldier there was but one answer to such a note. In an instant I was in the boat and the gondolier was pushing out into the dark lagoon. I remember that as I took my seat in the boat I was struck by the man's great size. He was not tall, but he was one of the broadest men that I have ever seen in my life. But the gondoliers of Venice are a strong breed, and powerful men are common enough among them. The fellow took his place behind me and began to row.

A good soldier in an enemy's country should everywhere and at all times be on the alert. It has been one of the rules of my life, and if I have lived to wear grey hairs it is because I have observed it. And yet upon that night I was as careless as a foolish young recruit who fears lest he should be thought to be afraid. My pistols I had left behind in my hurry . . . My sword was at my belt, but it is not always the most convenient of weapons. I lay back in my seat in the gondola, lulled by the gentle swish of the water and the steady creaking of the oar. Our way lay through a network of narrow canals with high houses towering on either side and a thin slit of star-spangled sky above us. Here and there, on the bridges which spanned the canal, there was the dim glimmer of an oil lamp, and sometimes there came a gleam from some niche where a candle burned before the image of a saint. But save for this it was all black, and one could only see the water by the white fringe which curled round the long black nose of our boat. It was a place and a time for dreaming. I thought of my own past life, of all the great deeds in which I had been concerned, of the horses that I had handled, and of the women that I had loved. Then I thought also of my dear mother, and I fancied her joy when she heard the folk in the village talking about the fame of her son. Of the Emperor also I thought, and of France, the dear fatherland, the sunny France, mother of beautiful daughters and of gallant sons. My heart glowed within me as I thought of how we had brought her colours so many hundred leagues beyond her borders. To her greatness I would dedicate my life. I placed my hand upon my heart as I swore it, and at that instant the gondolier fell upon me from behind.

When I say that he fell upon me I do not mean merely that he attacked me, but that he really did tumble upon me with all his weight. The fellow stands behind you and above you as he rows, so that you can neither see him nor can you in any way guard against such an assault. One moment I had sat with my mind filled with sublime resolutions, the next I was flattened out upon the bottom of the boat, the breath dashed out of my body, and this monster pinning me down. I felt the fierce pants of his hot breath upon the back of my neck. In an instant he had torn away my sword, had slipped a sack over my head, and had tied a rope firmly round the outside of it. There I was at the bottom of the gondola as helpless as a trussed fowl. I could not shout, I could not move; I was a mere bundle. An instant later I heard once more the swishing of the water and the creaking of the oar. This fellow had done his work and had resumed his journey as quietly and unconcernedly as if he were accustomed to clap a sack over a colonel of Hussars every day of the week.

I cannot tell you the humiliation and also the fury which filled my mind as I lay there like a helpless sheep being carried to the butcher's. I, Etienne Gerard, the champion of the six brigades of light cavalry and the first swordsman of the Grand Army, to be overpowered by a single unarmed man in such a fashion! Yet I lay quiet, for there is a time to resist and there is a time to save one's strength. I had felt the fellow's grip upon my arms, and I knew that I would be a child in his hands. I waited quietly, therefore, with a heart which burned with rage, until my opportunity should come.

How long I lay there at the bottom of the boat I cannot tell; but it seemed to me to be a long time, and always there were the hiss of the waters and the steady creaking of the oar. Several times we turned corners, for I heard the long, sad cry which these gondoliers give when they wish to warn their fellows that they are coming. At last, after a considerable journey, I felt the side of the boat scrape up against a landing-place. The fellow knocked three times with his oar upon wood, and in answer to his summons I heard the rasping of bars and the turning of keys. A great door creaked back upon its hinges.

"Have you got him?" asked a voice, in Italian.

My monster gave a laugh and kicked the sack in which I lay.

"Here he is," said he.

"They are waiting." He added something which I could not understand.

"Take him, then," said my captor. He raised me in his arms, ascended some steps, and I was thrown down upon a hard floor. A moment later the bars creaked and the key whined once more. I was a prisoner inside a house.

From the voices and the steps there seemed now to be several people round me. I understand Italian a great deal better than I speak it, and I could make out very well what they were saying.

"You have not killed him, Matteo?"

"What matter if I have?"

"My faith, you will have to answer for it to the tribunal."

"They will kill him, will they not?"

"Yes, but it is not for you or me to take it out of their hands."

"Tut! I have not killed him. Dead men do not bite, and his cursed teeth met in my thumb as I pulled the sack over his head."

"He lies very quiet."

"Tumble him out and you will find he is lively enough."

The cord which bound me was undone and the sack drawn from over my head. With my eyes closed I lay motionless upon the floor.

"By the saints, Matteo, I tell you that you have broken his neck."

"Not I. He has only fainted. The better for him if he never came out of it again."

I felt a hand within my tunic.

"Matteo is right," said a voice. "His heart beats like a hammer. Let him lie and he will soon find his senses."

I waited for a minute or so and then I ventured to take a stealthy peep from between my lashes. At first I could see nothing, for I had been so long in darkness and it was but a dim light in which I found myself. Soon, however, I made out that a high and vaulted ceiling covered with painted gods and goddesses was arching over my head. This was no mean den of cut-throats into which I had been carried, but it must be the hall of some Venetian palace. Then, without movement, very slowly and stealthily I had a peep at the men who surrounded me. There was the gondolier, a swart, hard-faced, murderous ruffian, and beside him were three other men, one of them a little, twisted fellow with an air of authority and several keys in his hand, the other two tall young servants in a smart livery. As I listened to their talk I saw that the small man was the steward of the house, and that the others were under his orders.

There were four of them, then, but the little steward might be left out of the reckoning. Had I a weapon I should have smiled at such odds as those. But, hand to hand, I was no match for the one even without three others to aid him. Cunning, then, not force, must be my aid. I wished to look round for some mode of escape, and in doing so I gave an almost imperceptible movement of my head. Slight as it was it did not escape my guardians.

"Come, wake up, wake up!" cried the steward.

"Get on your feet, little Frenchman," growled the gondolier. "Get up, I say!" and for the second time he spurned me with his foot.

Never in the world was a command obeyed so promptly as that one. In an instant I had bounded to my feet and rushed as hard as I could run to the back of the hall. They were after me as I have seen the English hounds follow a fox, but there was a long passage down which I tore. It turned to the left and again to the left, and then I found myself back in the hall once more. They were almost within touch of me and there was no time for thought. I turned towards the staircase, but two men were coming down it. I dodged back and tried the door through which I had been brought, but it was fastened with great bars and I could not loosen them. The gondolier was on me with his knife, but I met him with a kick on the body which stretched him on his back. His dagger flew with a clatter across the marble floor. I had no time to seize it, for there were half-a-dozen of them now clutching at me. As I rushed through them the little steward thrust his leg before me and I fell with a crash, but I was up in an instant, and breaking from their grasp I burst through the very middle of them and made for a door at the other end of the hall. I reached it well in front of them, and I gave a shout of triumph as the handle turned freely in my hand, for I could see that it led to the outside and that all was clear for my escape. But I had forgotten this strange city in which I was. Every house is an island. As I flung open the door, ready to bound out into the street, the light of the hall shone upon the deep, still, black water which lay flush with the topmost step. I shrank back, and in an instant my pursuers were on me. But I am not taken so easily. Again I kicked and fought my way through them, though one of them tore a handful of hair from my head in his effort to hold me. The little steward struck me with a key and I was battered and bruised, but once more I cleared a way in front of me. Up the grand staircase I rushed, burst open the pair of huge folding doors which faced me, and learned at last that my efforts were in vain.

The room into which I had broken was brilliantly lighted. With its gold cornices, its massive pillars, and its painted walls and ceilings it was evidently the grand hall of some famous Venetian palace. There are many hundred such in this strange city, any one of which has rooms which would grace the Louvre or Versailles. In the centre of this great hall there was a raised daïs, and upon it in a half circle there sat twelve men all clad in black gowns, like those of a Franciscan monk, and each with a mask over the upper part of his face. A group of armed men — rough-looking rascals — were standing round the door, and amid them facing the daïs was a young fellow in the uniform of the light infantry. As he turned his head I recognised him. It was Captain Auret, of the 7th, a young Basque with whom I had drunk many a glass during the winter. He was deadly white, poor wretch, but he held himself manfully amid the assassins who surrounded him. Never shall I forget the sudden flash of hope which shone in his dark eyes when he saw a comrade burst into the room, or the look of despair which followed as he understood that I had come not to change his fate but to share it.

You can think how amazed these people were when I hurled myself into their presence. My pursuers had crowded in behind me and choked the doorway, so that all further flight was out of the question. It is at such instants that my nature asserts itself. With dignity I advanced towards the tribunal. My jacket was torn, my hair was dishevelled, my head was bleeding, but there was that in my eyes and in my carriage which made them realize that no common man was before them. Not a hand was raised to arrest me until I halted in front of a formidable old man whose long grey beard and masterful manner told me that both by years and by character he was the man in authority.

"Sir," said I, "you will, perhaps, tell me why I have been forcibly arrested and brought to this place. I am an honourable soldier, as is this other gentleman here, and I demand that you will instantly set us both at liberty."

There was an appalling silence to my appeal. It is not pleasant to have twelve masked faces turned upon you and to see twelve pairs of vindictive Italian eyes fixed with fierce intentness upon your face. But I stood as a debonair soldier should, and I could not but reflect how much credit I was bringing upon the Hussars of Conflans by the dignity of my bearing. I do not think that anyone could have carried himself better under such difficult circumstances. I looked with a fearless face from one assassin to another, and I waited for some reply.

It was the greybeard who at last broke the silence.

"Who is this man?" he asked.

"His name is Gerard," said the little steward at the door.

"Colonel Gerard," said I. "I will not deceive you. I am Etienne Gerard, *the* Colonel Gerard, five times mentioned in despatches and recommended for the sword of honour. I am aide-de-camp to General Suchet, and I demand my instant release, together with that of my comrade in arms."

The same terrible silence fell upon the assembly, and the same twelve pairs of merciless eyes were bent upon my face. Again it was the greybeard who spoke.

"He is out of his order. There are two names upon our list before him."

"He escaped from our hands and burst into the room."

"Let him await his turn. Take him down to the wooden cell."

"If he resist us, your excellency?"

"Bury your knives in his body. The tribunal will uphold you. Remove him until we have dealt with the others."

They advanced upon me, and for an instant I thought of resistance. It would have been a heroic death, but who was there to see it or to chronicle it? I might be only postponing my fate, and yet I had been in so many bad places and come out unhurt that I had learned always to hope and to trust my star. I allowed these rascals to seize me, and I was led from the room, the gondolier walking at my side with a long naked knife in his hand. I could see in his brutal eyes the satisfaction which it would give him if he could find some excuse for plunging it into my body.

They are wonderful places, these great Venetian houses, palaces and fortresses and prisons all in one. I was led along a passage and down a bare stone stair until we came to a short corridor from which three doors opened. Through one of these I was thrust and the spring lock closed behind me. The only light came dimly through a small grating which opened on the passage. Peering and feeling, I carefully examined the chamber in which I had been placed. I understood from what I had heard that I should soon have to leave it again in order to appear before this tribunal, but still it is not my nature to throw away any possible chances.

The stone floor of the cell was so damp and the walls for some feet high were so slimy and foul that it was evident they were beneath the level of the water. A single slanting hole high up near the ceiling was the only aperture for light or air. Through it I saw one bright star shining down upon me, and the sight filled me with comfort and with hope. I have never been a man of religion, though I have always had a respect for those who were, but I remember that night that the star shining down the shaft seemed to be an all-seeing eye which was upon me, and I felt as a young and frightened recruit might feel in battle when he saw the calm gaze of his colonel turned upon him.

Three of the sides of my prison were formed of stone, but the fourth was of wood, and I could see that it had only recently been erected. Evidently a partition had been thrown up to divide a single large cell into two smaller ones. There was no hope for me in the old walls, in the tiny window, or in the massive door. It was only in this one direction of the wooden screen that there was any possibility of exploring. My reason told me that if I should pierce it—which did not seem very difficult—it would only be to find myself in another cell as strong as that in which I then was. Yet I had always rather be doing something than doing nothing, so I bent all my attention and all my energies upon the wooden wall. Two planks were badly joined, and so loose that I was certain I could easily detach them. I searched about for some tool, and I found one in the leg of a small bed which stood in the corner. I forced the end of this into the chink of the planks, and I was about to twist them outwards when the sound of rapid footsteps caused me to pause and to listen.

I wish I could forget what I heard. Many a hundred men have I seen die in battle, and I have slain more myself than I care to think of, but all that was fair fight and the duty of a soldier. It was a very different matter to listen to a murder in this den of assassins. They were pushing someone along the passage, someone who resisted and who clung to my door as he passed. They must have taken him into the third cell, the one which was farthest from me. "Help! Help!" cried a voice, and then I heard a blow and a scream. "Help! Help!" cried the voice again, and then "Gerard! Colonel Gerard!" It was my poor captain of infantry whom they were slaughtering. "Murderers! Murderers!" I yelled, and I kicked at my door, but again I heard him shout and then everything was silent. A minute later there was a heavy splash, and I knew that no human eye would ever see Auret again. He had gone as a hundred others had gone whose names were missing from the roll-calls of their regiments during that winter in Venice.

The steps returned along the passage, and I thought that they were coming for me. Instead of that they opened the door of the cell next to mine and they took someone out of it. I heard the steps die away up the stair. At once I renewed my work upon the planks, and within a very few minutes I had loosened them in such a way that I could remove and replace them at pleasure. Passing through the aperture I found myself in the farther cell, which, as I expected, was the other half of the one in which I had been confined. I was not any nearer to escape than I had been before, for there was no other wooden wall which I could penetrate and the spring lock of the door had been closed. There were no traces to show who was my companion in misfortune. Closing the two loose planks behind me I returned to my own cell and waited there with all the courage which I could command for the summons which would probably be my death-knell.

It was a long time in coming, but at last I heard the sound of feet once more in the passage, and I nerved myself to listen to some other odious deed and to hear the cries of the poor victim. Nothing of the kind occurred, however, and the prisoner was placed in the cell without violence. I had no time to peep through my hole of communication, for next moment my own door was flung open and my rascally gondolier, with the other assassins, came into the cell.

"Come, Frenchman," said he. He held his blood-stained knife in his great hairy hand, and I read in his fierce eyes that he only looked for some excuse in order to plunge it into my heart. Resistance was useless. I followed without a word. I was led up the stone stair and back into that gorgeous chamber in which I had left the secret tribunal. I was ushered in, but to my surprise it was not on me that their attention was fixed. One of their own number, a tall, dark young man, was standing before them and was pleading with them in low, earnest tones. His voice quivered with anxiety and his hands darted in and out or writhed together in an agony of entreaty. "You cannot do it! You cannot do it!" he cried. "I implore the tribunal to reconsider this decision."

"Stand aside, brother," said the old man who presided. "The case is decided and another is up for judgment."

"For Heaven's sake be merciful!" cried the young man.

"We have already been merciful," the other answered. "Death would have been a small penalty for such an offence. Be silent and let judgment take its course."

I saw the young man throw himself in an agony of grief into his chair. I had no time, however, to speculate as to what it was which was troubling him, for his eleven colleagues had already fixed their stern eyes upon me. The moment of fate had arrived.

"You are Colonel Gerard?" said the terrible old man.

"I am."

"Aide-de-camp to the robber who calls himself General Suchet, who in turn represents that arch-robber Buonaparte?"

It was on my lips to tell him that he was a liar, but there is a time to argue and a time to be silent.

"I am an honourable soldier," said I. "I have obeyed my orders and done my duty."

The blood flushed into the old man's face and his eyes blazed through his mask.

"You are thieves and murderers, every man of you," he cried. "What are you doing here? You are Frenchmen. Why are you not in France? Did we invite you to Venice? By what right are you here? Where are our pictures? Where are the horses of St Mark? Who are you that you should pilfer those treasures which our fathers through so many centuries have collected? We were a great city when France was a desert. Your drunken, brawling, ignorant soldiers have undone the work of saints and heroes. What have you to say to it?"

He was, indeed, a formidable old man, for his white beard bristled with fury and he barked out the little sentences like a savage hound. For my part I could have told him that his pictures would be safe in Paris, that his horses were really not worth making a fuss about, and that he could see heroes—I say nothing of saints—without going back to his ancestors or even moving out of his chair. All this I could have pointed out, but one might as well argue with a Mamaluke about religion. I shrugged my shoulders and said nothing.

"The prisoner has no defence," said one of my masked judges.

"Has anyone any observation to make before judgment is passed?" The old man glared round him at the others.

"There is one matter, your excellency," said another. "It can scarce be referred to without re-opening a brother's wounds, but I would remind you that there is a very particular reason why an exemplary punishment should be inflicted in the case of this officer."

"I had not forgotten it," the old man answered. "Brother, if the tribunal has injured you in one direction, it will give you ample satisfaction in another."

The young man who had been pleading when I entered the room staggered to his feet.

"I cannot endure it," he cried. "Your excellency must forgive me. The tribunal can act without me. I am ill. I am mad." He flung his hands out with a furious gesture and rushed from the room.

"Let him go! Let him go!" said the president. "It is, indeed, more than can be asked of flesh and blood that he should remain under this roof. But he is a true Venetian, and when the first agony is over he will understand that it could not be otherwise."

I had been forgotten during this episode, and though I am not a man who is accustomed to being overlooked I should have been all the happier had they continued to neglect me. But now the old president glared at me again like a tiger who comes back to his victim.

"You shall pay for it all, and it is but justice that you should," said he. "You, an upstart adventurer and foreigner, have dared to raise your eyes in love to the grand-daughter of a Doge of Venice who was already betrothed to the heir of the Loredans. He who enjoys such privileges must pay a price for them."

"It cannot be higher than they are worth," said I.

"You will tell us that when you have made a part payment," said he. "Perhaps your spirit may not be so proud by that time. Matteo, you will lead this prisoner to the wooden cell. To-night is Monday. Let him have no food or water, and let him be led before the tribunal again on Wednesday night. We shall then decide upon the death which he is to die."

It was not a pleasant prospect, and yet it was a reprieve. One is thankful for small mercies when a hairy savage with a blood-stained knife is standing at one's elbow. He dragged me from the room and I was thrust down the stairs and back into my cell. The door was locked and I was left to my reflections.

My first thought was to establish connection with my neighbour in misfortune. I waited until the steps had died away, and then I cautiously drew aside the two boards and peeped through. The light was very dim, so dim that I could only just discern a figure huddled in the corner, and I could hear the low whisper of a voice which prayed as one prays who is in deadly fear. The boards must have made a creaking. There was a sharp exclamation of surprise.

"Courage, friend, courage!" I cried. "All is not lost. Keep a stout heart, for Etienne Gerard is by your side."

"Etienne!" It was a woman's voice which spoke—a voice which was always music to my ears. I sprang through the gap and I flung my arms round her. "Lucia! Lucia!" I cried.

It was "Etienne!" and "Lucia!" for some minutes, for one does not make speeches at moments like that. It was she who came to her senses first.

"Oh, Etienne, they will kill you. How came you into their hands?"

"In answer to your letter."

"I wrote no letter."

"The cunning demons! But you?"

"I came also in answer to your letter."

"Lucia, I wrote no letter."

"They have trapped us both with the same bait."

"I care nothing about myself, Lucia. Besides, there is no pressing danger with me. They have simply returned me to my cell."

"Oh, Etienne, Etienne, they will kill you. Lorenzo is there."

"The old greybeard?"

"No, no, a young dark man. He loved me, and I thought I loved him until . . . until I learned what love is, Etienne. He will never forgive you. He has a heart of stone."

"Let them do what they like. They cannot rob me of the past, Lucia. But you—what about you?"

"It will be nothing, Etienne. Only a pang for an instant and then all over. They mean it as a badge of infamy, dear, but I will carry it like a crown of honour since it was through you that I gained it."

Her words froze my blood with horror. All my adventures were insignificant compared to this terrible shadow which was creeping over my soul.

"Lucia! Lucia!" I cried. "For pity's sake tell me what these butchers are about to do. Tell me, Lucia! Tell me!"

"I will not tell you, Etienne, for it would hurt you far more than it would me. Well, well, I will tell you lest you should fear it was something worse. The president has ordered that my ear be cut off, that I may be marked for ever as having loved a Frenchman."

Her ear! The dear little ear which I had kissed so often. I put my hand to each little velvet shell to make certain that this sacrilege had not yet been committed. Only over my dead body should they reach them. I swore it to her between my clenched teeth.

"You must not care, Etienne. And yet I love that you should care all the same."

"They shall not hurt you—the fiends!"

"I have hopes, Etienne. Lorenzo is there. He was silent while I was judged, but he may have pleaded for me after I was gone."

"He did. I heard him."

"Then he may have softened their hearts."

I knew that it was not so, but how could I bring myself to tell her? I might as well have done so, for with the quick instinct of woman my silence was speech to her.

"They would not listen to him! You need not fear to tell me, dear, for you will find that I am worthy to be loved by such a soldier. Where is Lorenzo now?"

"He left the hall."

"Then he may have left the house as well."

"I believe that he did."

"He has abandoned me to my fate. Etienne, Etienne, they are coming!"

Afar off I heard those fateful steps and the jingle of distant keys. What were they coming for now, since there were no other prisoners to drag to judgment? It could only be to carry out the sentence upon my darling. I stood between her and the door, with the strength of a lion in my limbs. I would tear the house down before they should touch her.

"Go back! Go back!" she cried. "They will murder you, Etienne. My life, at least, is safe. For the love you bear me, Etienne, go back. It is nothing. I will make no sound. You will not hear that it is done."

She wrestled with me, this delicate creature, and by main force she dragged me to the opening between the cells. But a sudden thought had crossed my mind.

"We may yet be saved," I whispered. "Do what I tell you at once and without argument. Go into my cell. Quick!"

I pushed her through the gap and helped her to replace the planks. I had retained her cloak in my hands, and with this wrapped round me I crept into the darkest corner of her cell. There I lay when the door was opened and several men came in. I had reckoned that they would bring no lantern, for they had none with them before. To their eyes I was only a dark blur in the corner.

"Bring a light," said one of them.

"No, no; curse it!" cried a rough voice, which I knew to be that of the ruffian Matteo. "It is not a job that I like, and the more I saw it the less I should like it. I am sorry, signora, but the order of the tribunal has to be obeyed."

My impulse was to spring to my feet and to rush through them all and out by the open door. But how would that help Lucia? Suppose that I got clear away, she would be in their hands until I could come back with help, for single-handed I could not hope to clear a way for her. All this flashed through my mind in an instant, and I saw that the only course for me was to lie still, take what came, and wait my chance. The fellow's coarse hand felt about among my curls—those curls in which only a woman's fingers had ever wandered. The next instant he gripped my ear and a pain shot through me as if I had been touched with a hot iron. I bit my lip to stifle a cry, and I felt the blood run warm down my neck and back.

"There, thank Heaven, that's over," said the fellow, giving me a friendly pat on the head. "You're a brave girl, signora, I'll say that for you, and I only wish you'd have better taste than to love a Frenchman. You can blame him and not me for what I have done."

What could I do save to lie still and grind my teeth at my own helplessness? At the same time my pain and my rage were always soothed by the reflection that I had suffered for the woman whom I loved. It is the custom of men to say to ladies that they would willingly endure any pain for their sake, but it was my privilege to show that I had said no more than I meant. I thought also how nobly I would seem to have acted if ever the story came to be told, and how proud the regiment of Conflans might well be of their colonel. These thoughts helped me to suffer in silence while the blood still trickled over my neck and dripped upon the stone floor. It was that sound which nearly led to my destruction.

"She's bleeding fast," said one of the valets. "You had best fetch a surgeon or you will find her dead in the morning."

"She lies very still and she has never opened her mouth," said another. "The shock has killed her."

"Nonsense; a young woman does not die so easily." It was Matteo who spoke. "Besides, I did but snip off enough to leave the tribunal's mark upon her. Rouse up, signora, rouse up!"

He shook me by the shoulder, and my heart stood still for fear he should feel the epaulette under the mantle.

"How is it with you now?" he asked.

I made no answer.

"Curse it, I wish I had to do with a man instead of a woman, and the fairest woman in Venice," said the gondolier. "Here, Nicholas, lend me your handkerchief and bring a light."

It was all over. The worst had happened. Nothing could save me. I still crouched in the corner, but I was tense in every muscle, like a wild cat about to spring. If I had to die I was determined that my end should be worthy of my life.

One of them had gone for a lamp and Matteo was stooping over me with a handkerchief. In another instant my secret would be discovered. But he suddenly drew himself straight and stood motionless. At the same instant there came a confused murmuring sound through the little window far above my head. It was the rattle of oars and the buzz of many voices. Then there was a crash upon the door upstairs, and a terrible voice roared: "Open! Open in the name of the Emperor!"

The Emperor! It was like the mention of some saint which, by its very sound, can frighten the demons. Away they ran with cries of terror—Matteo, the valets, the steward, all of the murderous gang. Another shout and then the crash of a hatchet and the splintering of planks. There were the rattle of arms and the cries of French soldiers in the hall. Next instant feet came flying down the stair and a man burst frantically into my cell.

"Lucia!" he cried, "Lucia!" He stood in the dim light, panting and unable to find his words. Then he broke out again. "Have I not shown you how I love you, Lucia? What more could I do to prove it? I have betrayed my country, I have broken my vow, I have ruined my friends, and I have given my life in order to save you."

It was young Lorenzo Loredan, the lover whom I had superseded. My heart was heavy for him at the time, but after all it is every man for himself in love, and if one fails in the game it is some consolation to lose to one who can be a graceful and considerate winner. I was about to point this out to him, but at the first word I uttered he gave a shout of astonishment, and, rushing out, he seized the lamp which hung in the corridor and flashed it in my face.

"It is you, you villain!" he cried. "You French coxcomb. You shall pay me for the wrong which you have done me."

But the next instant he saw the pallor of my face and the blood which was still pouring from my head.

"What is this?" he asked. "How come you to have lost your ear?"

I shook off my weakness, and pressing my handkerchief to my wound I rose from my couch, the debonair colonel of Hussars.

"My injury, sir, is nothing. With your permission we will not allude to a matter so trifling and so personal."

But Lucia had burst through from her cell and was pouring out the whole story while she clasped Lorenzo's arm.

"This noble gentleman—he has taken my place, Lorenzo! He has borne it for me. He has suffered that I might be saved."

I could sympathize with the struggle which I could see in the Italian's face. At last he held out his hand to me.

"Colonel Gerard," he said, "you are worthy of a great love. I forgive you, for if you have wronged me you have made a noble atonement. But I wonder to see you alive. I left the tribunal before you were judged, but I understood that no mercy would be shown to any Frenchman since the destruction of the ornaments of Venice."

"He did not destroy them," cried Lucia. "He has helped to preserve those in our palace."

"One of them, at any rate," said I, as I stooped and kissed her hand.

This was the way, my friends, in which I lost my ear. Lorenzo was found stabbed to the heart in the Piazza of St Mark within two days of the night of my adventure. Of the tribunal and its ruffians, Matteo and three others were shot, the rest banished from the town. Lucia, my lovely Lucia, retired into a convent at Murano after the French had left the city, and there she still may be, some gentle lady abbess who has perhaps long forgotten the days when our hearts throbbed together, and when the whole great world seemed so small a thing beside the love which burned in our veins. Or perhaps it may not be so. Perhaps she has not forgotten. There may still be times when the peace of the cloister is broken by the memory of the old soldier who loved her in those distant days. Youth is past and passion is gone, but the soul of the gentleman can never change, and still Etienne Gerard would bow his grey head before her and would very gladly lose this other ear if he might do her a service.

HOW THE BRIGADIER SAVED THE ARMY

I have told you, my friends, how we held the English shut up for six months, from October, 1810, to March, 1811, within their lines of Torres Vedras. It was during this time that I hunted the fox in their company, and showed them that amidst all their sportsmen there was not one who could outride a Hussar of Conflans. When I galloped back into the French lines with the blood of the creature still moist upon my blade the outposts who had seen what I had done raised a frenzied cry in my honour, whilst these English hunters still yelled behind me, so that I had the applause of both armies. It made the tears rise to my eyes to feel that I had won the admiration of so many brave men. These English are generous foes. That very evening there came a packet under a white flag addressed "To the Hussar officer who cut down the fox." Within I found the fox itself in two pieces, as I had left it. There was a note also, short but hearty as the English fashion is, to say that as I had slaughtered the fox it only remained for me to eat it. They could not know that it was not our French custom to eat foxes, and it showed their desire that he who had won the honours of the chase should also partake of the game. It is not for a Frenchman to be outdone in politeness, and so I returned it to these brave hunters, and begged them to accept it as a side-dish for their next *déjeuner de la chasse*. It is thus that chivalrous opponents make war.

I had brought back with me from my ride a clear plan of the English lines, and this I laid before Massena that very evening.

I had hoped that it would lead him to attack, but all the marshals were at each other's throats, snapping and growling like so many hungry hounds. Ney hated Massena, and Massena hated Junot, and Soult hated them all. For this reason nothing was done. In the meantime food grew more and more scarce, and our beautiful cavalry was ruined for want of fodder. With the end of the winter we had swept the whole country bare, and nothing remained for us to eat, although we sent our forage parties far and wide. It was clear even to the bravest of us that the time had come to retreat. I was myself forced to admit it.

But retreat was not so easy. Not only were the troops weak and exhausted from want of supplies, but the enemy had been much encouraged by our long inaction. Of Wellington we had no great fear. We had found him to be brave and cautious, but with little enterprise. Besides, in that barren country his pursuit could not be rapid. But on our flanks and in our rear there had gathered great numbers of Portuguese militia, of armed peasants, and of guerillas. These people had kept a safe distance all the winter, but now that our horses were foundered they were as thick as flies all round our outposts, and no man's life was worth a sou when once he fell into their hands. I could name a dozen officers of my own acquaintance who were cut off during that time, and the luckiest was he who received a ball from behind a rock through his head or his heart. There were some whose deaths were so terrible that no report of them was ever allowed to reach their relatives. So frequent were these tragedies, and so much did they impress the imagination of the men, that it became very difficult to induce them to leave the camp. There was one especial scoundrel, a guerilla chief named Manuelo, "The Smiler," whose exploits filled our men with horror. He was a large, fat man of jovial aspect, and he lurked with a fierce gang among the mountains which lay upon our left flank. A volume might be written of this fellow's cruelties and brutalities, but he was certainly a man of power, for he organized his brigands in a manner which made it almost impossible for us to get through his country. This he did by imposing a severe discipline upon them and enforcing it by cruel penalties, a policy by which he made them formidable, but which had some unexpected results, as I will show you in my story. Had he not flogged his own lieutenant—but you will hear of that when the time comes.

There were many difficulties in connection with a retreat, but it was very evident that there was no other possible course, and so Massena began to quickly pass his baggage and his sick from Torres Novas, which was his head-quarters, to Coimbra, the first strong post on his line of communications. He could not do this unperceived, however, and at once the guerillas came swarming closer and closer upon our flanks. One of our divisions, that of Clausel, with a brigade of Montbrun's cavalry, was far to the south of the Tagus, and it became very necessary to let them know that we were about to retreat, for otherwise they would be left unsupported in the very heart of the enemy's country. I remember wondering how Massena would accomplish this, for simple couriers could not get through, and small parties would be certainly destroyed. In some way an order to fall back must be conveyed to these men, or France would be the weaker by fourteen thousand men. Little did I think that it was I, Colonel Gerard, who was to have the honour of a deed which might have formed the crowning glory of any other man's life, and which stands high among those exploits which have made my own so famous.

At that time I was serving on Massena's staff, and he had two other aides-de-camp, who were also very brave and intelligent officers. The name of one was Cortex and of the other Duplessis. They were senior to me in age, but junior in every other respect. Cortex was a small, dark man, very quick and eager. He was a fine soldier, but he was ruined by his conceit. To take him at his own valuation he was the first man in the army. Duplessis was a Gascon, like myself, and he was a very fine fellow, as all Gascon gentlemen are. We took it in turn, day about, to do duty, and it was Cortex who was in attendance upon the morning of which I speak. I saw him at breakfast, but afterwards neither he nor his horse was to be seen. All day Massena was in his usual gloom, and he spent much of his time staring with his telescope at the English lines and at the shipping in the Tagus. He said nothing of the mission upon which he had sent our comrade, and it was not for us to ask him any questions.

That night, about twelve o'clock, I was standing outside the Marshal's head-quarters when he came out and stood motionless for half an hour, his arms folded upon his breast, staring through the darkness towards the east. So rigid and intent was he that you might have believed the muffled figure and the cocked hat to have been the statue of the man. What he was looking for I could not imagine; but at last he gave a bitter curse, and, turning on his heel, he went back into the house, banging the door behind him.

Next day the second aide-de-camp, Duplessis, had an interview with Massena in the morning, after which neither he nor his horse was seen again. That night, as I sat in the anteroom, the Marshal passed me, and I observed him through the window standing and staring to the east exactly as he had done before. For fully half an hour he remained there, a black shadow in the gloom. Then he strode in, the door banged, and I heard his spurs and his scabbard jingling and clanking through the passage. At the best he was a savage old man, but when he was crossed I had almost as soon face the Emperor himself. I heard him that night cursing and stamping above my head, but he did not send for me, and I knew him too well to go unsought.

Next morning it was my turn, for I was the only aide-de-camp left. I was his favourite aide-de-camp. His heart went out always to a smart soldier. I declare that I think there were tears in his black eyes when he sent for me that morning.

"Gerard!" said he. "Come here!"

With a friendly gesture he took me by the sleeve and he led me to the open window which faced the east. Beneath us was the infantry camp, and beyond that the lines of the cavalry with the long rows of picketed horses. We could see the French outposts, and then a stretch of open country, intersected by vineyards. A range of hills lay beyond, with one well-marked peak towering above them. Round the base of these hills was a broad belt of forest. A single road ran white and clear, dipping and rising until it passed through a gap in the hills.

"This," said Massena, pointing to the mountain, "is the Sierra de Merodal. Do you perceive anything upon the top?"

I answered that I did not.

"Now?" he asked, and he handed me his field-glass.

With its aid I perceived a small mound or cairn upon the crest.

"What you see," said the Marshal, "is a pile of logs which was placed there as a beacon. We laid it when the country was in our hands, and now, although we no longer hold it, the beacon remains undisturbed. Gerard, that beacon must be lit to-night. France needs it, the Emperor needs it, the army needs it. Two of your comrades have gone to light it, but neither has made his way to the summit. To-day it is your turn, and I pray that you may have better luck."

It is not for a soldier to ask the reason for his orders, and so I was about to hurry from the room, but the Marshal laid his hand upon my shoulder and held me.

"You shall know all, and so learn how high is the cause for which you risk your life," said he. "Fifty miles to the south of us, on the other side of the Tagus, is the army of General Clausel. His camp is situated near a peak named the Sierra d'Ossa. On the summit of this peak is a beacon, and by this beacon he has a picket. It is agreed between us that when at midnight he shall see our signal fire he shall light his own as an answer, and shall then at once fall back upon the main army. If he does not start at once I must go without him. For two days I have endeavoured to send him his message. It must reach him to-day, or his army will be left behind and destroyed."

Ah, my friends, how my heart swelled when I heard how high was the task which Fortune had assigned to me! If my life were spared, here was one more splendid new leaf for my laurel crown. If, on the other hand, I died, then it would be a death worthy of such a career. I said nothing, but I cannot doubt that all the noble thoughts that were in me shone in my face, for Massena took my hand and wrung it.

"There is the hill and there the beacon," said he. "There is only this guerilla and his men between you and it. I cannot detach a large party for the enterprise and a small one would be seen and destroyed. Therefore to you alone I commit it. Carry it out in your own way, but at twelve o'clock this night let me see the fire upon the hill."

"If it is not there," said I, "then I pray you, Marshal Massena, to see that my effects are sold and the money sent to my mother." So I raised my hand to my busby and turned upon my heel, my heart glowing at the thought of the great exploit which lay before me.

I sat in my own chamber for some little time considering how I had best take the matter in hand. The fact that neither Cortex nor Duplessis, who were very zealous and active officers, had succeeded in reaching the summit of the Sierra de Merodal showed that the country was very closely watched by the guerillas. I reckoned out the distance upon a map. There were ten miles of open country to be crossed before reaching the hills. Then came a belt of forest on the lower slopes of the mountain, which may have been three or four miles wide. And then there was the actual peak itself, of no very great height, but without any cover to conceal me. Those were the three stages of my journey.

It seemed to me that once I had reached the shelter of the wood all would be easy, for I could lie concealed within its shadows and climb upwards under the cover of night. From eight till twelve would give me four hours of darkness in which to make the ascent. It was only the first stage, then, which I had seriously to consider.

Over that flat country there lay the inviting white road, and I remembered that my comrades had both taken their horses. That was clearly their ruin, for nothing could be easier than for the brigands to keep watch upon the road, and to lay an ambush for all who passed along it. It would not be difficult for me to ride across country, and I was well horsed at that time, for I had not only Violette and Rataplan, who were two of the finest mounts in the army, but I had the splendid black English hunter which I had taken from Sir Cotton. However, after much thought, I determined to go upon foot, since I should then be in a better state to take advantage of any chance which might offer. As to my dress, I covered my Hussar uniform with a long cloak, and I put a grey forage cap upon my head. You may ask me why I did not dress as a peasant, but I answer that a man of honour has no desire to die the death of a spy. It is one thing to be murdered, and it is another to be justly executed by the laws of war. I would not run the risk of such an end.

In the late afternoon I stole out of the camp and passed through the line of our pickets. Beneath my cloak I had a field-glass and a pocket pistol, as well as my sword. In my pocket were tinder, flint, and steel.

For two or three miles I kept under cover of the vineyards, and made such good progress that my heart was high within me, and I thought to myself that it only needed a man of some brains to take the matter in hand to bring it easily to success. Of course, Cortex and Duplessis galloping down the high road would be easily seen, but the intelligent Gerard lurking among the vines was quite another person. I dare say I had got as far as five miles before I met any check. At that point there is a small wine-house, round which I perceived some carts and a number of people, the first that I had seen. Now that I was well outside the lines I knew that every person was my enemy, so I crouched lower while I stole along to a point from which I could get a better view of what was going on. I then perceived that these people were peasants, who were loading two waggons with empty wine-casks. I failed to see how they could either help or hinder me, so I continued upon my way.

But soon I understood that my task was not so simple as had appeared. As the ground rose the vineyards ceased, and I came upon a stretch of open country studded with low hills. Crouching in a ditch I examined them with a glass, and I very soon perceived that there was a watcher upon every one of them, and that these people had a line of pickets and outposts thrown forward exactly like our own. I had heard of the discipline which was practised by this scoundrel whom they called "The Smiler," and this, no doubt, was an example of it. Between the hills there was a cordon of sentries, and though I worked some distance round to the flank I still found myself faced by the enemy. It was a puzzle what to do. There was so little cover that a rat could hardly cross without being seen. Of course, it would be easy enough to slip through at night, as I had done with the English at Torres Vedras, but I was still far from the mountain and I could not in that case reach it in time to light the midnight beacon. I lay in my ditch and I made a thousand plans, each more dangerous than the last. And then suddenly I had that flash of light which comes to the brave man who refuses to despair.

You remember I have mentioned that two waggons were loading up with empty casks at the inn. The heads of the oxen were turned to the east, and it was evident that those waggons were going in the direction which I desired. Could I only conceal myself upon one of them, what better and easier way could I find of passing through the lines of the guerillas? So simple and so good was the plan that I could not restrain a cry of delight as it crossed my mind, and I hurried away instantly in the direction of the inn. There, from behind some bushes, I had a good look at what was going on upon the road.

There were three peasants with red montero caps loading the barrels, and they had completed one waggon and the lower tier of the other. A number of empty barrels still lay outside the winehouse waiting to be put on. Fortune was my friend—I have always said that she is a woman and cannot resist a dashing young Hussar. As I watched, the three fellows went into the inn, for the day was hot and they were thirsty after their labour. Quick as a flash I darted out from my hiding-place, climbed on to the waggon, and crept into one of the empty casks. It had a bottom but no top, and it lay upon its side with the open end inwards. There I crouched like a dog in its kennel, my knees drawn up to my chin, for the barrels were not very large and I am a well-grown man. As I lay there out came the three peasants again, and presently I heard a crash upon the top of me which told that I had another barrel above me. They piled them upon the cart until I could not imagine how I was ever to get out again. However, it is time to think of crossing the Vistula when you are over the Rhine, and I had no doubt that if chance and my own wits had carried me so far they would carry me farther.

Soon, when the waggon was full, they set forth upon their way, and I within my barrel chuckled at every step, for it was carrying me whither I wished to go. We travelled slowly, and the peasants walked beside the waggons. This I knew, because I heard their voices close to me. They seemed to me to be very merry fellows, for they laughed heartily as they went. What the joke was I could not understand. Though I speak their language fairly well I could not hear anything comic in the scraps of their conversation which met my ear.

I reckoned that at the rate of walking of a team of oxen we covered about two miles an hour. Therefore, when I was sure that two and a half hours had passed—such hours, my friends, cramped, suffocated, and nearly poisoned with the fumes of the lees—when they had passed, I was sure that the dangerous open country was behind us, and that we were upon the edge of the forest and the mountain. So now I had to turn my mind upon how I was to get out of my barrel. I had thought of several ways, and was balancing one against the other when the question was decided for me in a very simple but unexpected manner.

The waggon stopped suddenly with a jerk, and I heard a number of gruff voices in excited talk. "Where, where?" cried one. "On our cart," said another. "Who is he?" said a third. "A French officer; I saw his cap and his boots." They all roared with laughter. "I was looking out of the window of the posada and I saw him spring into the cask like a toreador with a Seville bull at his heels." "Which cask, then?" "It was this one," said the fellow, and sure enough his fist struck the wood beside my head.

What a situation, my friends, for a man of my standing! I blush now, after forty years, when I think of it. To be trussed like a fowl and to listen helplessly to the rude laughter of these boors — to know, too, that my mission had come to an ignominious and even ridiculous end — I would have blessed the man who would have sent a bullet through the cask and freed me from my misery.

I heard the crashing of the barrels as they hurled them off the waggon, and then a couple of bearded faces and the muzzles of two guns looked in at me. They seized me by the sleeves of my coat, and they dragged me out into the daylight. A strange figure I must have looked as I stood blinking and gaping in the blinding sunlight. My body was bent like a cripple's, for I could not straighten my stiff joints, and half my coat was as red as an English soldier's from the lees in which I had lain. They laughed and laughed, these dogs, and as I tried to express by my bearing and gestures the contempt in which I held them their laughter grew all the louder. But even in these hard circumstances I bore myself like the man I am, and as I cast my eye slowly round I did not find that any of the laughers were very ready to face it.

That one glance round was enough to tell me exactly how I was situated. I had been betrayed by these peasants into the hands of an outpost of guerillas. There were eight of them, savage-looking, hairy creatures, with cotton handkerchiefs under their sombreros, and many-buttoned jackets with coloured sashes round the waist. Each had a gun and one or two pistols stuck in his girdle. The leader, a great bearded ruffian, held his gun against my ear while the others searched my pockets, taking from me my overcoat, my pistol, my glass, my sword, and, worst of all, my flint and steel and tinder. Come what might I was ruined, for I had no longer the means of lighting the beacon even if I should reach it.

Eight of them, my friends, with three peasants, and I unarmed! Was Etienne Gerard in despair? Did he lose his wits? Ah, you know me too well; but they did not know me yet, these dogs of brigands. Never have I made so supreme and astounding an effort as at this very instant when all seemed lost. Yet you might guess many times before you would hit upon the device by which I escaped them. Listen and I will tell you.

They had dragged me from the waggon when they searched me, and I stood, still twisted and warped, in the midst of them. But the stiffness was wearing off, and already my mind was very actively looking out for some method of breaking away. It was a narrow pass in which the brigands had their outpost. It was bounded on the one hand by a steep mountain side. On the other the ground fell away in a very long slope, which ended in a bushy valley many hundreds of feet below. These fellows, you understand, were hardy mountaineers, who could travel either up hill or down very much quicker than I. They wore abarcas, or shoes of skin, tied on like sandals, which gave them a foothold everywhere. A less resolute man would have despaired. But in an instant I saw and used the strange chance which Fortune had placed in my way. On the very edge of the slope was one of the wine-barrels. I moved slowly towards it, and then with a tiger spring I dived into it feet foremost, and with a roll of my body I tipped it over the side of the hill.

Shall I ever forget that dreadful journey—how I bounded and crashed and whizzed down that terrible slope? I had dug in my knees and elbows, bunching my body into a compact bundle so as to steady it; but my head projected from the end, and it was a marvel that I did not dash out my brains. There were long, smooth slopes, and then came steeper scarps where the barrel ceased to roll, and sprang into the air like a goat, coming down with a rattle and crash which jarred every bone in my body. How the wind whistled in my ears, and my head turned and turned until I was sick and giddy and nearly senseless! Then, with a swish and a great rasping and crackling of branches, I reached the bushes which I had seen so far below me. Through them I broke my way, down a slope beyond, and deep into another patch of underwood, where striking a sapling my barrel flew to pieces. From amid a heap of staves and hoops I crawled out, my body aching in every inch of it, but my heart singing loudly with joy and my spirit high within me, for I knew how great was the feat which I had accomplished, and I already seemed to see the beacon blazing on the hill.

A horrible nausea had seized me from the tossing which I had undergone, and I felt as I did upon the ocean when first I experienced those movements of which the English have taken so perfidious an advantage. I had to sit for a few moments with my head upon my hands beside the ruins of my barrel. But there was no time for rest. Already I heard shouts above me which told that my pursuers were descending the hill. I dashed into the thickest part of the underwood, and I ran and ran until I was utterly exhausted. Then I lay panting and listened with all my ears, but no sound came to them. I had shaken off my enemies.

When I had recovered my breath I travelled swiftly on, and waded knee-deep through several brooks, for it came into my head that they might follow me with dogs. On gaining a clear place and looking round me, I found to my delight that in spite of my adventures I had not been much out of my way. Above me towered the peak of Merodal, with its bare and bold summit shooting out of the groves of dwarf oaks which shrouded its flanks. These groves were the continuation of the cover under which I found myself, and it seemed to me that I had nothing to fear now until I reached the other side of the forest. At the same time I knew that every man's hand was against me, that I was unarmed, and that there were many people about me. I saw no one, but several times I heard shrill whistles, and once the sound of a gun in the distance.

It was hard work pushing one's way through the bushes, and so I was glad when I came to the larger trees and found a path which led between them. Of course, I was too wise to walk upon it, but I kept near it and followed its course. I had gone some distance, and had, as I imagined, nearly reached the limit of the wood, when a strange, moaning sound fell upon my ears. At first I thought it was the cry of some animal, but then there came words, of which I only caught the French exclamation, "Mon Dieu!" With great caution I advanced in the direction from which the sound proceeded, and this is what I saw.

On a couch of dried leaves there was stretched a man dressed in the same grey uniform which I wore myself. He was evidently horribly wounded, for he held a cloth to his breast which was crimson with his blood. A pool had formed all round his couch, and he lay in a haze of flies, whose buzzing and droning would certainly have called my attention if his groans had not come to my ear. I lay for a moment, fearing some trap, and then, my pity and loyalty rising above all other feelings, I ran forward and knelt by his side. He turned a haggard face upon me, and it was Duplessis, the man who had gone before me. It needed but one glance at his sunken cheeks and glazing eyes to tell me that he was dying.

"Gerard!" said he; "Gerard!"

I could but look my sympathy, but he, though the life was ebbing swiftly out of him, still kept his duty before him, like the gallant gentleman he was.

"The beacon, Gerard! You will light it?"

"Have you flint and steel?"

"It is here."

"Then I will light it to-night."

"I die happy to hear you say so. They shot me, Gerard. But you will tell the Marshal that I did my best."

"And Cortex?"

"He was less fortunate. He fell into their hands and died horribly. If you see that you cannot get away, Gerard, put a bullet into your own heart. Don't die as Cortex did."

I could see that his breath was failing, and I bent low to catch his words.

"Can you tell me anything which can help me in my task?" I asked.

"Yes, yes; De Pombal. He will help you. Trust De Pombal." With the words his head fell back and he was dead.

"Trust De Pombal. It is good advice." To my amazement a man was standing at the very side of me. So absorbed had I been in my comrade's words and intent on his advice that he had crept up without my observing him. Now I sprang to my feet and faced him. He was a tall, dark fellow, black-haired, black-eyed, black-bearded, with a long, sad face. In his hand he had a wine-bottle and over his shoulder was slung one of the trabucos or blunderbusses which these fellows bear. He made no effort to unsling it, and I understood that this was the man to whom my dead friend had commended me.

"Alas, he is gone!" said he, bending over Duplessis. "He fled into the wood after he was shot, but I was fortunate enough to find where he had fallen and to make his last hours more easy. This couch was my making, and I had brought this wine to slake his thirst."

"Sir," said I, "in the name of France I thank you. I am but a colonel of light cavalry, but I am Etienne Gerard, and the name stands for something in the French army. May I ask—"

"Yes, sir, I am Aloysius de Pombal, younger brother of the famous nobleman of that name. At present I am the first lieutenant in the band of the guerilla chief who is usually known as Manuelo, 'The Smiler.'"

My word, I clapped my hand to the place where my pistol should have been, but the man only smiled at the gesture.

"I am his first lieutenant, but I am also his deadly enemy," said he. He slipped off his jacket and pulled up his shirt as he spoke. "Look at this!" he cried, and he turned upon me a back which was all scored and lacerated with red and purple weals. "This is what 'The Smiler' has done to me, a man with the noblest blood of Portugal in my veins. What I will do to 'The Smiler' you have still to see."

There was such fury in his eyes and in the grin of his white teeth that I could no longer doubt his truth, with that clotted and oozing back to corroborate his words.

"I have ten men sworn to stand by me," said he. "In a few days I hope to join your army, when I have done my work here. In the meanwhile—." A strange change came over his face, and he suddenly slung his musket to the front: "Hold up your hands, you French hound!" he yelled. "Up with them, or I blow your head off!"

You start, my friends! You stare! Think, then, how I stared and started at this sudden ending of our talk. There was the black muzzle and there the dark, angry eyes behind it. What could I do? I was helpless. I raised my hands in the air. At the same moment voices sounded from all parts of the wood, there were crying and calling and rushing of many feet. A swarm of dreadful figures broke through the green bushes, a dozen hands seized me, and I, poor, luckless, frenzied I, was a prisoner once more. Thank God, there was no pistol which I could have plucked from my belt and snapped at my own head. Had I been armed at that moment I should not be sitting here in this café and telling you these old-world tales.

With grimy, hairy hands clutching me on every side I was led along the pathway through the wood, the villain De Pombal giving directions to my captors. Four of the brigands carried up the dead body of Duplessis. The shadows of evening were already falling when we cleared the forest and came out upon the mountain-side. Up this I was driven until we reached the headquarters of the guerillas, which lay in a cleft close to the summit of the mountain. There was the beacon which had cost me so much, a square stack of wood, immediately above our heads. Below were two or three huts which had belonged, no doubt, to goatherds, and which were now used to shelter these rascals. Into one of these I was cast, bound and helpless, and the dead body of my poor comrade was laid beside me.

I was lying there with the one thought still consuming me, how to wait a few hours and to get at that pile of fagots above my head, when the door of my prison opened and a man entered. Had my hands been free I should have flown at his throat, for it was none other than De Pombal. A couple of brigands were at his heels, but he ordered them back and closed the door behind him.

"You villain!" said I.

"Hush!" he cried. "Speak low, for I do not know who may be listening, and my life is at stake. I have some words to say to you, Colonel Gerard; I wish well to you, as I did to your dead companion. As I spoke to you beside his body I saw that we were surrounded, and that your capture was unavoidable. I should have shared your fate had I hesitated. I instantly captured you myself, so as to preserve the confidence of the band. Your own sense will tell you that there was nothing else for me to do. I do not know now whether I can save you, but at least I will try."

This was a new light upon the situation. I told him that I could not tell how far he spoke the truth, but that I would judge him by his actions.

"I ask nothing better," said he. "A word of advice to you! The chief will see you now. Speak him fair, or he will have you sawn between two planks. Contradict nothing he says. Give him such information as he wants. It is your only chance. If you can gain time something may come in our favour. Now, I have no more time. Come at once, or suspicion may be awakened." He helped me to rise, and then, opening the door, he dragged me out very roughly, and with the aid of the fellows outside he brutally pushed and thrust me to the place where the guerilla chief was seated, with his rude followers gathered round him.

A remarkable man was Manuelo, "The Smiler." He was fat and florid and comfortable, with a big, clean-shaven face and a bald head, the very model of a kindly father of a family. As I looked at his honest smile I could scarcely believe that this was, indeed, the infamous ruffian whose name was a horror through the English Army as well as our own. It is well known that Trent, who was a British officer, afterwards had the fellow hanged for his brutalities. He sat upon a boulder and he beamed upon me like one who meets an old acquaintance. I observed, however, that one of his men leaned upon a long saw, and the sight was enough to cure me of all delusions.

"Good evening, Colonel Gerard," said he. "We have been highly honoured by General Massena's staff: Major Cortex one day, Colonel Duplessis the next, and now Colonel Gerard. Possibly the Marshal himself may be induced to honour us with a visit. You have seen Duplessis, I understand. Cortex you will find nailed to a tree down yonder. It only remains to be decided how we can best dispose of yourself."

It was not a cheering speech; but all the time his fat face was wreathed in smiles, and he lisped out his words in the most mincing and amiable fashion. Now, however, he suddenly leaned forward, and I read a very real intensity in his eyes.

"Colonel Gerard," said he, "I cannot promise you your life, for it is not our custom, but I can give you an easy death or I can give you a terrible one. Which shall it be?"

"What do you wish me to do in exchange?"

"If you would die easy I ask you to give me truthful answers to the questions which I ask."

A sudden thought flashed through my mind.

"You wish to kill me," said I; "it cannot matter to you how I die. If I answer your questions, will you let me choose the manner of my own death?"

"Yes, I will," said he, "so long as it is before midnight to-night."

"Swear it!" I cried.

"The word of a Portuguese gentleman is sufficient," said he.

"Not a word will I say until you have sworn it."

He flushed with anger and his eyes swept round towards the saw. But he understood from my tone that I meant what I said, and that I was not a man to be bullied into submission. He pulled a cross from under his zammara or jacket of black sheepskin.

"I swear it," said he.

Oh, my joy as I heard the words! What an end—what an end for the first swordsman of France! I could have laughed with delight at the thought.

"Now, your questions!" said I.

"You swear in turn to answer them truly?"

"I do, upon the honour of a gentleman and a soldier." It was, as you perceive, a terrible thing that I promised, but what was it compared to what I might gain by compliance?

"This is a very fair and a very interesting bargain," said he, taking a note-book from his pocket. "Would you kindly turn your gaze towards the French camp?"

Following the direction of his gesture, I turned and looked down upon the camp in the plain beneath us. In spite of the fifteen miles, one could in that clear atmosphere see every detail with the utmost distinctness. There were the long squares of our tents and our huts, with the cavalry lines and the dark patches which marked the ten batteries of artillery. How sad to think of my magnificent regiment waiting down yonder, and to know that they would never see their colonel again! With one squadron of them I could have swept all these cut-throats off the face of the earth. My eager eyes filled with tears as I looked at the corner of the camp where I knew that there were eight hundred men, any one of whom would have died for his colonel. But my sadness vanished when I saw beyond the tents the plumes of smoke which marked the head-quarters at Torres Novas. There was Massena, and, please God, at the cost of my life his mission would that night be done. A spasm of pride and exultation filled my breast. I should have liked to have had a voice of thunder that I might call to them, "Behold it is I, Etienne Gerard, who will die in order to save the army of Clausel." It was, indeed, sad to think that so noble a deed should be done, and that no one should be there to tell the tale.

"Now," said the brigand chief, "you see the camp and you see also the road which leads to Coimbra. It is crowded with your fourgons and your ambulances. Does this mean that Massena is about to retreat?"

One could see the dark moving lines of waggons with an occasional flash of steel from the escort. There could, apart from my promise, be no indiscretion in admitting that which was already obvious.

"He will retreat," said I.

"By Coimbra?"

"I believe so."

"But the army of Clausel?"

I shrugged my shoulders.

"Every path to the south is blocked. No message can reach them. If Massena falls back the army of Clausel is doomed."

"It must take its chance," said I.

"How many men has he?"

"I should say about fourteen thousand."

"How much cavalry?"

"One brigade of Montbrun's Division."

"What regiments?"

"The 4th Chasseurs, the 9th Hussars, and a regiment of Cuirassiers."

"Quite right," said he, looking at his note-book. "I can tell you speak the truth, and Heaven help you if you don't." Then, division by division, he went over the whole army, asking the composition of each brigade. Need I tell you that I would have had my tongue torn out before I would have told him such things had I not a greater end in view? I would let him know all if I could but save the army of Clausel.

At last he closed his note-book and replaced it in his pocket. "I am obliged to you for this information, which shall reach Lord Wellington to-morrow," said he. "You have done your share of the bargain; it is for me now to perform mine. How would you wish to die? As a soldier you would, no doubt, prefer to be shot, but some think that a jump over the Merodal precipice is really an easier death. A good few have taken it, but we were, unfortunately, never able to get an opinion from them afterwards. There is the saw, too, which does not appear to be popular. We could hang you, no doubt, but it would involve the inconvenience of going down to the wood. However, a promise is a promise, and you seem to be an excellent fellow, so we will spare no pains to meet your wishes."

"You said," I answered, "that I must die before midnight. I will choose, therefore, just one minute before that hour."

"Very good," said he. "Such clinging to life is rather childish, but your wishes shall be met."

"As to the method," I added, "I love a death which all the world can see. Put me on yonder pile of fagots and burn me alive, as saints and martyrs have been burned before me. That is no common end, but one which an Emperor might envy."

The idea seemed to amuse him very much. "Why not?" said he. "If Massena has sent you to spy upon us, he may guess what the fire upon the mountains means."

"Exactly," said I. "You have hit upon my very reason. He will guess, and all will know, that I have died a soldier's death."

"I see no objection whatever," said the brigand, with his abominable smile. "I will send some goat's flesh and wine into your hut. The sun is sinking, and it is nearly eight o'clock. In four hours be ready for your end."

It was a beautiful world to be leaving. I looked at the golden haze below, where the last rays of the sinking sun shone upon the blue waters of the winding Tagus and gleamed upon the white sails of the English transports. Very beautiful it was, and very sad to leave; but there are things more beautiful than that. The death that is died for the sake of others, honour, and duty, and loyalty, and love—these are the beauties far brighter than any which the eye can see. My breast was filled with admiration for my own most noble conduct, and with wonder whether any soul would ever come to know how I had placed myself in the heart of the beacon which saved the army of Clausel. I hoped so and I prayed so, for what a consolation it would be to my mother, what an example to the army, what a pride to my Hussars! When De Pombal came at last into my hut with the food and the wine, the first request I made him was that he would write an account of my death and send it to the French camp. He answered not a word, but I ate my supper with a better appetite from the thought that my glorious fate would not be altogether unknown.

I had been there about two hours when the door opened again, and the chief stood looking in. I was in darkness, but a brigand with a torch stood beside him, and I saw his eyes and his teeth gleaming as he peered at me.

"Ready?" he asked.

"It is not yet time."

"You stand out for the last minute?"

"A promise is a promise."

"Very good. Be it so. We have a little justice to do among ourselves, for one of my fellows has been misbehaving. We have a strict rule of our own which is no respecter of persons, as De Pombal here could tell you. Do you truss him and lay him on the fagots, De Pombal, and I will return to see him die."

De Pombal and the man with the torch entered, while I heard the steps of the chief passing away. De Pombal closed the door.

"Colonel Gerard," said he, "you must trust this man, for he is one of my party. It is neck or nothing. We may save you yet. But I take a great risk, and I want a definite promise. If we save you, will you guarantee that we have a friendly reception in the French camp and that all the past will be forgotten?"

"I do guarantee it."

"And I trust your honour. Now, quick, quick, there is not an instant to lose! If this monster returns we shall die horribly, all three."

I stared in amazement at what he did. Catching up a long rope he wound it round the body of my dead comrade, and he tied a cloth round his mouth so as to almost cover his face.

"Do you lie there!" he cried, and he laid me in the place of the dead body. "I have four of my men waiting, and they will place this upon the beacon." He opened the door and gave an order. Several of the brigands entered and bore out Duplessis. For myself I remained upon the floor, with my mind in a turmoil of hope and wonder.

Five minutes later De Pombal and his men were back.

"You are laid upon the beacon," said he; "I defy anyone in the world to say it is not you, and you are so gagged and bound that no one can expect you to speak or move. Now, it only remains to carry forth the body of Duplessis and to toss it over the Merodal precipice."

Two of them seized me by the head and two by the heels and carried me, stiff and inert, from the hut. As I came into the open air I could have cried out in my amazement. The moon had risen above the beacon, and there, clear outlined against its silver light, was the figure of the man stretched upon the top. The brigands were either in their camp or standing round the beacon, for none of them stopped or questioned our little party. De Pombal led them in the direction of the precipice. At the brow we were out of sight, and there I was allowed to use my feet once more. De Pombal pointed to a narrow, winding track.

"This is the way down," said he, and then, suddenly, "Dios mio, what is that?"

A terrible cry had risen out of the woods beneath us. I saw that De Pombal was shivering like a frightened horse.

"It is that devil," he whispered. "He is treating another as he treated me. But on, on, for Heaven help us if he lays his hands upon us!"

One by one we crawled down the narrow goat track. At the bottom of the cliff we were back in the woods once more. Suddenly a yellow glare shone above us, and the black shadows of the tree-trunks started out in front. They had fired the beacon behind us. Even from where we stood we could see that impassive body amid the flames, and the black figures of the guerillas as they danced, howling like cannibals, round the pile. Ha! how I shook my fist at them, the dogs, and how I vowed that one day my Hussars and I would make the reckoning level!

De Pombal knew how the outposts were placed and all the paths which led through the forest. But to avoid these villains we had to plunge among the hills and walk for many a weary mile. And yet how gladly would I have walked those extra leagues if only for one sight which they brought to my eyes! It may have been two o'clock in the morning when we halted upon the bare shoulder of a hill over which our path curled. Looking back we saw the red glow of the embers of the beacon as if volcanic fires were bursting from the tall peak of Merodal. And then, as I gazed,

I saw something else—something which caused me to shriek with joy and to fall upon the ground, rolling in my delight. For, far away upon the southern horizon, there winked and twinkled one great yellow light, throbbing and flaming, the light of no house, the light of no star, but the answering beacon of Mount d'Ossa, which told that the army of Clausel knew what Etienne Gerard had been sent to tell them.

HOW THE BRIGADIER RODE TO MINSK

I would have a stronger wine to-night, my friends, a wine of Burgundy rather than of Bordeaux. It is that my heart, my old soldier heart, is heavy within me. It is a strange thing, this age which creeps upon one. One does not know, one does not understand; the spirit is ever the same, and one does not remember how the poor body crumbles. But there comes a moment when it is brought home, when quick as the sparkle of a whirling sabre it is clear to us, and we see the men we were and the men we are. Yes, yes, it was so to-day, and I would have a wine of Burgundy to-night. White Burgundy—Montrachet—Sir, I am your debtor!

It was this morning in the Champ de Mars. Your pardon, friends, while an old man tells his trouble. You saw the review. Was it not splendid? I was in the enclosure for veteran officers who have been decorated. This ribbon on my breast was my passport. The cross itself I keep at home in a leathern pouch. They did us honour, for we were placed at the saluting point, with the Emperor and the carriages of the Court upon our right.

It is years since I have been to a review, for I cannot approve of many things which I have seen. I do not approve of the red breeches of the infantry. It was in white breeches that the infantry used to fight. Red is for the cavalry. A little more, and they would ask our busbies and our spurs! Had I been seen at a review they might well have said that I, Etienne Gerard, had condoned it. So I have stayed at home. But this war of the Crimea is different. The men go to battle. It is not for me to be absent when brave men gather.

My faith, they march well, those little infantrymen! They are
not large, but they are very solid and they carry themselves well. I
took off my hat to them as they passed. Then there came the guns.
They were good guns, well horsed and well manned. I took off my
hat to them. Then came the Engineers, and to them also I took off
my hat. There are no braver men than the Engineers. Then came
the cavalry, Lancers, Cuirassiers, Chasseurs, and Spahis. To all of
them in turn I was able to take off my hat, save only to the Spahis.
The Emperor had no Spahis. But when all of the others had
passed, what think you came at the close? A brigade of Hussars,
and at the charge! Oh, my friends, the pride and the glory and the
beauty, the flash and the sparkle, the roar of the hoofs and the jingle of chains, the tossing manes, the noble heads, the rolling
cloud, and the dancing waves of steel! My heart drummed to them
as they passed. And the last of all, was it not my own old regiment?
My eyes fell upon the grey and silver dolmans, with the leopard-
skin shabraques, and at that instant the years fell away from me
and I saw my own beautiful men and horses, even as they had
swept behind their young colonel, in the pride of our youth and
our strength, just forty years ago. Up flew my cane. "Chargez! En
avant! Vive l'Empéreur!" It was the past calling to the present. But,
oh, what a thin, piping voice! Was this the voice that had once
thundered from wing to wing of a strong brigade? And the arm
that could scarce wave a cane, were these the muscles of fire and
steel which had no match in all Napoleon's mighty host? They
smiled at me. They cheered me. The Emperor laughed and
bowed. But to me the present was a dim dream, and what was real
were my eight hundred dead Hussars and the Etienne of long ago.
Enough—a brave man can face age and fate as he faced Cossacks
and Uhlans. But there are times when Montrachet is better than
the wine of Bordeaux.

It is to Russia that they go, and so I will tell you a story of
Russia. Ah, what an evil dream of the night it seems! Blood and
ice. Ice and blood. Fierce faces with snow upon the whiskers.
Blue hands held out for succour. And across the great white

plain the one long black line of moving figures, trudging, trudging, a hundred miles, another hundred, and still always the same white plain. Sometimes there were fir-woods to limit it, sometimes it stretched away to the cold blue sky, but the black line stumbled on and on. Those weary, ragged, starving men, the spirit frozen out of them, looked neither to right nor left, but with sunken faces and rounded backs trailed onwards and ever onwards, making for France as wounded beasts make for their lair. There was no speaking, and you could scarce hear the shuffle of feet in the snow. Once only I heard them laugh. It was outside Wilna, when an aide-de-camp rode up to the head of that dreadful column and asked if that were the Grand Army. All who were within hearing looked round, and when they saw those broken men, those ruined regiments, those fur-capped skeletons who were once the Guard, they laughed, and the laugh crackled down the column like a *feu de joie*. I have heard many a groan and cry and scream in my life, but nothing so terrible as the laugh of the Grand Army.

But why was it that these helpless men were not destroyed by the Russians? Why was it that they were not speared by the Cossacks or herded into droves, and driven as prisoners into the heart of Russia? On every side as you watched the black snake winding over the snow you saw also dark, moving shadows which came and went like cloud drifts on either flank and behind. They were the Cossacks, who hung round us like wolves round the flock. But the reason why they did not ride in upon us was that all the ice of Russia could not cool the hot hearts of some of our soldiers. To the end there were always those who were ready to throw themselves between these savages and their prey. One man above all rose greater as the danger thickened, and won a higher name amid disaster than he had done when he led our van to victory. To him I drink this glass—to Ney, the red-maned Lion, glaring back over his shoulder at the enemy who feared to tread too closely on his heels. I can see him now, his broad white face convulsed with fury, his light blue eyes sparkling like flints, his great voice roaring and crashing amid the roll of the musketry. His glazed and feather-less cocked hat was the ensign upon which France rallied during those dreadful days.

It is well known that neither I nor the regiment of Hussars of Conflans were at Moscow. We were left behind on the lines of communication at Borodino. How the Emperor could have advanced without us is incomprehensible to me, and, indeed, it was only then that I understood that his judgment was weakening and that he was no longer the man that he had been. However, a soldier has to obey orders, and so I remained at this village, which was poisoned by the bodies of thirty thousand men who had lost their lives in the great battle. I spent the late autumn in getting my horses into condition and reclothing my men, so that when the army fell back on Borodino my Hussars were the best of the cavalry, and were placed under Ney in the rear-guard. What could he have done without us during those dreadful days? "Ah, Gerard," said he one evening—but it is not for me to repeat the words. Suffice it that he spoke what the whole army felt. The rear-guard covered the army and the Hussars of Conflans covered the rear-guard. There was the whole truth in a sentence. Always the Cossacks were on us. Always we held them off. Never a day passed that we had not to wipe our sabres. That was soldiering indeed.

But there came a time between Wyasma and Smolensk when the situation became impossible. Cossacks and even cold we could fight, but we could not fight hunger as well. Food must be got at all costs. That night Ney sent for me to the waggon in which he slept. His great head was sunk on his hands. Mind and body he was wearied to death.

"Colonel Gerard," said he, "things are going very badly with us. The men are starving. We must have food at all costs."

"The horses," I suggested.

"Save your handful of cavalry there are none left."

"The band," said I.

He laughed, even in his despair.

"Why the band?" he asked.

"Fighting men are of value."

"Good," said he. "You would play the game down to the last card and so would I. Good, Gerard, good!" He clasped my hand in his. "But there is one chance for us yet, Gerard." He unhooked a lantern from the roof of the waggon and he laid it on a map which was stretched before him. "To the south of us," said he, "there lies the town of Minsk. I have word from a Russian deserter that much corn has been stored in the town-hall. I wish you to take as many men as you think best, set forth for Minsk, seize the corn, load any carts which you may collect in the town, and bring them to me between here and Smolensk. If you fail it is but a detachment cut off. If you succeed it is new life to the army."

He had not expressed himself well, for it was evident that if we failed it was not merely the loss of a detachment. It is quality as well as quantity which counts. And yet how honourable a mission and how glorious a risk! If mortal men could bring it, then the corn should come from Minsk. I said so, and spoke a few burning words about a brave man's duty until the Marshal was so moved that he rose and, taking me affectionately by the shoulders, pushed me out of the waggon.

It was clear to me that in order to succeed in my enterprise I should take a small force and depend rather upon surprise than upon numbers. A large body could not conceal itself, would have great difficulty in getting food, and would cause all the Russians around us to concentrate for its certain destruction. On the other hand, if a small body of cavalry could get past the Cossacks unseen it was probable that they would find no troops to oppose them, for we knew that the main Russian army was several days' march behind us. This corn was meant, no doubt, for their consumption. A squadron of Hussars and thirty Polish Lancers were all whom I chose for the venture. That very night we rode out of the camp, and struck south in the direction of Minsk.

Fortunately there was but a half moon, and we were able to pass without being attacked by the enemy. Twice we saw great fires burning amid the snow, and around them a thick bristle of long poles. These were the lances of Cossacks, which they had stood upright while they slept. It would have been a great joy to us to have charged in amongst them, for we had much to revenge, and the eyes of my comrades looked longingly from me to those red flickering patches in the darkness. My faith, I was sorely tempted to do it, for it would have been a good lesson to teach them that they must keep a few miles between themselves and a French army. It is the essence of good generalship, however, to keep one thing before one at a time, and so we rode silently on through the snow, leaving these Cossack bivouacs to right and left. Behind us the black sky was all mottled with a line of flame which showed where our own poor wretches were trying to keep themselves alive for another day of misery and starvation.

All night we rode slowly onwards, keeping our horses' tails to the Pole Star. There were many tracks in the snow, and we kept to the line of these, that no one might remark that a body of cavalry had passed that way. These are the little precautions which mark the experienced officer. Besides, by keeping to the tracks we were most likely to find the villages, and only in the villages could we hope to get food. The dawn of day found us in a thick fir-wood, the trees so loaded with snow that the light could hardly reach us. When we had found our way out of it it was full daylight, the rim of the rising sun peeping over the edge of the great snow-plain and turning it crimson from end to end. I halted my Hussars and Lancers under the shadow of the wood, and I studied the country. Close to us there was a small farmhouse. Beyond, at the distance of several miles, was a village. Far away on the sky-line rose a considerable town all bristling with church towers. This must be Minsk. In no direction could I see any signs of troops. It was evident that we had passed through the Cossacks and that there was nothing between us and our goal. A joyous shout burst from my men when I told them our position, and we advanced rapidly towards the village.

I have said, however, that there was a small farmhouse immediately in front of us. As we rode up to it I observed that a fine grey horse with a military saddle was tethered by the door. Instantly I galloped forwards, but before I could reach it a man dashed out of the door, flung himself on to the horse, and rode furiously away, the crisp, dry snow flying up in a cloud behind him. The sunlight gleamed upon his gold epaulettes, and I knew that he was a Russian officer. He would raise the whole countryside if we did not catch him. I put spurs to Violette and flew after him. My troopers followed; but there was no horse among them to compare with Violette, and I knew well that if I could not catch the Russian I need expect no help from them.

But it is a swift horse indeed and a skilful rider who can hope to escape from Violette with Etienne Gerard in the saddle. He rode well, this young Russian, and his mount was a good one, but gradually we wore him down. His face glanced continually over his shoulder—a dark, handsome face, with eyes like an eagle—and I saw as I closed with him that he was measuring the distance between us. Suddenly he half turned; there were a flash and a crack as his pistol bullet hummed past my ear. Before he could draw his sword I was upon him; but he still spurred his horse, and the two galloped together over the plain, I with my leg against the Russian's and my left hand upon his right shoulder. I saw his hand fly up to his mouth. Instantly I dragged him across my pommel and seized him by the throat, so that he could not swallow. His horse shot from under him, but I held him fast and Violette came to a stand. Sergeant Oudin of the Hussars was the first to join us. He was an old soldier, and he saw at a glance what I was after.

"Hold tight, Colonel," said he, "I'll do the rest."

He slipped out his knife, thrust the blade between the clenched teeth of the Russian, and turned it so as to force his mouth open. There, on his tongue, was the little wad of wet paper which he had been so anxious to swallow. Oudin picked it out and I let go of the man's throat. From the way in which, half strangled as he was, he glanced at the paper I was sure that it was a message of extreme importance. His hands twitched as if he longed to snatch it from me. He shrugged his shoulders, however, and smiled good-humouredly when I apologized for my roughness.

"And now to business," said I, when he had done coughing and hawking. "What is your name?"

"Alexis Barakoff."

"Your rank and regiment?"

"Captain of the Dragoons of Grodno."

"What is this note which you were carrying?"

"It is a line which I had written to my sweetheart."

"Whose name," said I, examining the address, "is the Hetman Platoff. Come, come, sir, this is an important military document, which you are carrying from one general to another. Tell me this instant what it is."

"Read it and then you will know." He spoke perfect French, as do most of the educated Russians. But he knew well that there is not one French officer in a thousand who knows a word of Russian. The inside of the note contained one single line, which ran like this: —

"Pustj Franzuzy pridutt v Minsk. Min gotovy."

I stared at it, and I had to shake my head. Then I showed it to my Hussars, but they could make nothing of it. The Poles were all rough fellows who could not read or write, save only the sergeant, who came from Memel, in East Prussia, and knew no Russian. It was maddening, for I felt that I had possession of some important secret upon which the safety of the army might depend, and yet I could make no sense of it. Again I entreated our prisoner to translate it, and offered him his freedom if he would do so. He only smiled at my request. I could not but admire him, for it was the very smile which I should have myself smiled had I been in his position.

"At least," said I, "tell us the name of this village."

"It is Dobrova."

"And that is Minsk over yonder, I suppose?"

"Yes, that is Minsk."

"Then we shall go to the village and we shall very soon find someone who will translate this despatch."

So we rode onward together, a trooper with his carbine unslung on either side of our prisoner. The village was but a little place, and I set a guard at the ends of the single street, so that no one could escape from it. It was necessary to call a halt and to find some food for the men and horses, since they had travelled all night and had a long journey still before them.

There was one large stone house in the centre of the village, and to this I rode. It was the house of the priest—a snuffy and ill-favoured old man who had not a civil answer to any of our questions. An uglier fellow I never met, but, my faith, it was very different with his only daughter, who kept house for him. She was a brunette, a rare thing in Russia, with creamy skin, raven hair, and a pair of the most glorious dark eyes that ever kindled at the sight of a Hussar. From the first glance I saw that she was mine. It was no time for love-making when a soldier's duty had to be done, but still, as I took the simple meal which they laid before me, I chatted lightly with the lady, and we were the best of friends before an hour had passed. Sophie was her first name, her second I never knew. I taught her to call me Etienne, and I tried to cheer her up, for her sweet face was sad and there were tears in her beautiful dark eyes. I pressed her to tell me what it was which was grieving her.

"How can I be otherwise," said she, speaking French with a most adorable lisp, "when one of my poor countrymen is a prisoner in your hands? I saw him between two of your Hussars as you rode into the village."

"It is the fortune of war," said I. "His turn to-day; mine, perhaps, to-morrow."

"But consider, Monsieur—" said she.

"Etienne," said I.

"Oh, Monsieur—"

"Etienne," said I.

"Well, then," she cried, beautifully flushed and desperate, "consider, Etienne, that this young officer will be taken back to your army and will be starved or frozen, for if, as I hear, your own soldiers have a hard march, what will be the lot of a prisoner?"

I shrugged my shoulders.

"You have a kind face, Etienne," said she; "you would not condemn this poor man to certain death. I entreat you to let him go."

Her delicate hand rested upon my sleeve, her dark eyes looked imploringly into mine.

A sudden thought passed through my mind. I would grant her request, but I would demand a favour in return. At my order the prisoner was brought up into the room.

"Captain Barakoff," said I, "this young lady has begged me to release you, and I am inclined to do so. I would ask you to give your parole that you will remain in this dwelling for twenty-four hours, and take no steps to inform anyone of our movements."

"I will do so," said he.

"Then I trust in your honour. One man more or less can make no difference in a struggle between great armies, and to take you back as a prisoner would be to condemn you to death. Depart, sir, and show your gratitude not to me, but to the first French officer who falls into your hands."

When he was gone I drew my paper from my pocket.

"Now, Sophie," said I, "I have done what you asked me, and all that I ask in return is that you will give me a lesson in Russian."

"With all my heart," said she.

"Let us begin on this," said I, spreading out the paper before her. "Let us take it word for word and see what it means."

She looked at the writing with some surprise. "It means," said she, "if the French come to Minsk all is lost." Suddenly a look of consternation passed over her beautiful face. "Great heavens!" she cried, "what is it that I have done? I have betrayed my country! Oh, Etienne, your eyes are the last for whom this message is meant. How could you be so cunning as to make a poor, simple-minded, and unsuspecting girl betray the cause of her country?"

I consoled my poor Sophie as best I might, and I assured her that it was no reproach to her that she should be outwitted by so old a campaigner and so shrewd a man as myself. But it was no time now for talk. This message made it clear that the corn was indeed at Minsk, and that there were no troops there to defend it. I gave a hurried order from the window, the trumpeter blew the assembly, and in ten minutes we had left the village behind us and were riding hard for the city, the gilded domes and minarets of which glimmered above the snow of the horizon. Higher they rose and higher, until at last, as the sun sank towards the west, we were in the broad main street, and galloped up it amid the shouts of the moujiks and the cries of frightened women until we found ourselves in front of the great town hall. My cavalry I drew up in the square, and I, with my two sergeants, Oudin and Papilette, rushed into the building.

Heavens! shall I ever forget the sight which greeted us? Right in front of us was drawn up a triple line of Russian Grenadiers. Their muskets rose as we entered, and a crashing volley burst into our very faces. Oudin and Papilette dropped upon the floor, riddled with bullets. For myself, my busby was shot away and I had two holes through my dolman. The Grenadiers ran at me with their bayonets. "Treason!" I cried. "We are betrayed! Stand to your horses!" I rushed out of the hall, but the whole square was swarming with troops. From every side street Dragoons and Cossacks were riding down upon us, and such a rolling fire had burst from the surrounding houses that half my men and horses were on the ground. "Follow me!" I yelled, and sprang upon Violette, but a giant of a Russian Dragoon officer threw his arms round me and we rolled on the ground together. He shortened his sword to kill me, but, changing his mind, he seized me by the throat and banged my head against the stones until I was unconscious. So it was that I became the prisoner of the Russians.

When I came to myself my only regret was that my captor had not beaten out my brains. There in the grand square of Minsk lay half my troopers dead or wounded, with exultant crowds of Russians gathered round them. The rest in a melancholy group were herded into the porch of the town-hall, a sotnia of Cossacks keeping guard over them. Alas! what could I say, what could I do? It was evident that I had led my men into a carefully-baited trap. They had heard of our mission and they had prepared for us. And yet there was that despatch which had caused me to neglect all precautions and to ride straight into the town. How was I to account for that? The tears ran down my cheeks as I surveyed the ruin of my squadron, and as I thought of the plight of my comrades of the Grand Army who awaited the food which I was to have brought them. Ney had trusted me and I had failed him. How often he would strain his eyes over the snowfields for that convoy of grain which should never gladden his sight! My own fate was hard enough. An exile in Siberia was the best which the future could bring me. But you will believe me, my friends, that it was not for his own sake, but for that of his starving comrades, that Etienne Gerard's cheeks were lined by his tears, frozen even as they were shed.

"What's this?" said a gruff voice at my elbow; and I turned to face the huge, black-bearded Dragoon who had dragged me from my saddle. "Look at the Frenchman crying! I thought that the Corsican was followed by brave men and not by children."

"If you and I were face to face and alone, I should let you see which is the better man," said I.

For answer the brute struck me across the face with his open hand. I seized him by the throat, but a dozen of his soldiers tore me away from him, and he struck me again while they held my hands.

"You base hound," I cried, "is this the way to treat an officer and a gentleman?"

"We never asked you to come to Russia," said he. "If you do you must take such treatment as you can get. I would shoot you off hand if I had my way."

"You will answer for this some day," I cried, as I wiped the blood from my moustache.

"If the Hetman Platoff is of my way of thinking you will not be alive this time to-morrow," he answered, with a ferocious scowl. He added some words in Russian to his troops, and instantly they all sprang to their saddles. Poor Violette, looking as miserable as her master, was led round and I was told to mount her. My left arm was tied with a thong which was fastened to the stirrup-iron of a sergeant of Dragoons. So in most sorry plight I and the remnant of my men set forth from Minsk.

Never have I met such a brute as this man Sergine, who commanded the escort. The Russian army contains the best and the worst in the world, but a worse than Major Sergine of the Dragoons of Kieff I have never seen in any force outside of the guerillas of the Peninsula. He was a man of great stature, with a fierce, hard face and a bristling black beard, which fell over his cuirass. I have been told since that he was noted for his strength and his bravery, and I could answer for it that he had the grip of a bear, for I had felt it when he tore me from my saddle. He was a wit, too, in his way, and made continual remarks in Russian at our expense which set all his Dragoons and Cossacks laughing. Twice he beat my comrades with his riding-whip, and once he approached me with the lash swung over his shoulder, but there was something in my eyes which prevented it from falling. So in misery and humiliation, cold and starving, we rode in a disconsolate column across the vast snowplain. The sun had sunk, but still in the long northern twilight we pursued our weary journey. Numbed and frozen, with my head aching from the blows it had received, I was borne onwards by Violette, hardly conscious of where I was or whither I was going. The little mare walked with a sunken head, only raising it to snort her contempt for the mangy Cossack ponies who were round her.

But suddenly the escort stopped, and I found that we had halted in the single street of a small Russian village. There was a church on one side, and on the other was a large stone house, the outline of which seemed to me to be familiar. I looked around me in the twilight, and then I saw that we had been led back to Dobrova, and that this house at the door of which we were waiting was the same house of the priest at which we had stopped in the morning. Here it was that my charming Sophie in her innocence had translated the unlucky message which had in some strange way led us to our ruin. To think that only a few hours before we had left this very spot with such high hopes and all fair prospects for our mission, and now the remnants of us waited as beaten and humiliated men for whatever lot a brutal enemy might ordain! But such is the fate of the soldier, my friends—kisses to-day, blows to-morrow, Tokay in a palace, ditch-water in a hovel, furs or rags, a full purse or an empty pocket, ever swaying from the best to the worst, with only his courage and his honour unchanging.

The Russian horsemen dismounted, and my poor fellows were ordered to do the same. It was already late, and it was clearly their intention to spend the night in this village. There were great cheering and joy amongst the peasants when they understood that we had all been taken, and they flocked out of their houses with flaming torches, the women carrying out tea and brandy for the Cossacks. Amongst others the old priest came forth—the same whom we had seen in the morning. He was all smiles now, and he bore with him some hot punch on a salver, the reek of which I can remember still. Behind her father was Sophie. With horror I saw her clasp Major Sergine's hand as she congratulated him upon the victory he had won and the prisoners he had made. The old priest, her father, looked at me with an insolent face and made insulting remarks at my expense, pointing at me with his lean and grimy hand. His fair daughter Sophie looked at me also, but she said nothing, and I could read her tender pity in her dark eyes. At last she turned to Major Sergine and said something to him in Russian, on which he frowned and shook his head impatiently. She appeared to plead with him, standing there in the flood of light which shone from the open door of her father's house. My eyes were fixed upon the two faces, that of the beautiful girl and of the dark, fierce man, for my instinct told me that it was my own fate which was under debate. For a long time the soldier shook his head, and then, at last softening before her pleadings, he appeared to give way. He turned to where I stood with my guardian sergeant beside me.

"These good people offer you the shelter of their roof for the night," said he to me, looking me up and down with vindictive eyes. "I find it hard to refuse them, but I tell you straight that for my part I had rather see you on the snow. It would cool your hot blood, you rascal of a Frenchman!"

I looked at him with the contempt that I felt.

"You were born a savage and you will die one," said I.

My words stung him, for he broke into an oath, raising his whip as if he would strike me.

"Silence, you crop-eared dog!" he cried. "Had I my way some of the insolence would be frozen out of you before morning." Mastering his passion, he turned upon Sophie with what he meant to be a gallant manner. "If you have a cellar with a good lock," said he, "the fellow may lie in it for the night, since you have done him the honour to take an interest in his comfort. I must have his parole that he will not attempt to play us any tricks, as I am answerable for him until I hand him over to the Hetman Platoff to-morrow."

His supercilious manner was more than I could endure. He had evidently spoken French to the lady in order that I might understand the humiliating way in which he referred to me.

"I will take no favour from you," said I. "You may do what you like, but I will never give you my parole."

The Russian shrugged his great shoulders, and turned away as if the matter were ended.

"Very well, my fine fellow, so much the worse for your fingers and toes. We shall see how you are in the morning after a night in the snow."

"One moment, Major Sergine," cried Sophie. "You must not be so hard upon this prisoner. There are some special reasons why he has a claim upon our kindness and mercy."

The Russian looked with suspicion upon his face from her to me.

"What are the special reasons? You certainly seem to take a remarkable interest in this Frenchman," said he.

"The chief reason is that he has this very morning of his own accord released Captain Alexis Barakoff, of the Dragoons of Grodno."

"It is true," said Barakoff, who had come out of the house. "He captured me this morning, and he released me upon parole rather than take me back to the French army, where I should have been starved."

"Since Colonel Gerard has acted so generously you will surely, now that fortune has changed, allow us to offer him the poor shelter of our cellar upon this bitter night," said Sophie. "It is a small return for his generosity."

But the Dragoon was still in the sulks.

"Let him give me his parole first that he will not attempt to escape," said he. "Do you hear, sir? Do you give me your parole?"

"I give you nothing," said I.

"Colonel Gerard," cried Sophie, turning to me with a coaxing smile, "you will give *me* your parole, will you not?"

"To you, mademoiselle, I can refuse nothing. I will give you my parole, with pleasure."

"There, Major Sergine," cried Sophie, in triumph, "that is surely sufficient. You have heard him say that he gives me his parole. I will be answerable for his safety."

In an ungracious fashion my Russian bear grunted his consent, and so I was led into the house, followed by the scowling father and by the big, black-bearded Dragoon. In the basement there was a large and roomy chamber; where the winter logs were stored. Thither it was that I was led, and I was given to understand that this was to be my lodging for the night. One side of this bleak apartment was heaped up to the ceiling with fagots of firewood. The rest of the room was stone-flagged and bare-walled, with a single, deep-set window upon one side, which was safely guarded with iron bars. For light I had a large stable lantern, which swung from a beam of the low ceiling. Major Sergine smiled as he took this down, and swung it round so as to throw its light into every corner of that dreary chamber.

"How do you like our Russian hotels, monsieur?" he asked, with his hateful sneer. "They are not very grand, but they are the best that we can give you. Perhaps the next time that you Frenchmen take a fancy to travel you will choose some other country where they will make you more comfortable." He stood laughing at me, his white teeth gleaming through his beard. Then he left me, and I heard the great key creak in the lock.

For an hour of utter misery, chilled in body and soul, I sat upon a pile of fagots, my face sunk upon my hands and my mind full of the saddest thoughts. It was cold enough within those four walls, but I thought of the sufferings of my poor troopers outside, and I sorrowed with their sorrow. Then I paced up and down, and I clapped my hands together and kicked my feet against the walls to keep them from being frozen. The lamp gave out some warmth, but still it was bitterly cold, and I had had no food since morning. It seemed to me that everyone had forgotten me, but at last I heard the key turn in the lock, and who should enter but my prisoner of the morning, Captain Alexis Barakoff. A bottle of wine projected from under his arm, and he carried a great plate of hot stew in front of him.

"Hush!" said he; "not a word! Keep up your heart! I cannot stop to explain, for Sergine is still with us. Keep awake and ready!" With these hurried words he laid down the welcome food and ran out of the room.

"Keep awake and ready!" The words rang in my ears. I ate my food and I drank my wine, but it was neither food nor wine which had warmed the heart within me. What could those words of Barakoff mean? Why was I to remain awake? For what was I to be ready? Was it possible that there was a chance yet of escape? I have never respected the man who neglects his prayers at all other times and yet prays when he is in peril. It is like a bad soldier who pays no respect to the colonel save when he would demand a favour of him. And yet when I thought of the salt-mines of Siberia on the one side and of my mother in France upon the other, I could not help a prayer rising, not from my lips, but from my heart, that the words of Barakoff might mean all that I hoped. But hour after hour struck upon the village-clock, and still I heard nothing save the call of the Russian sentries in the street outside.

Then at last my heart leaped within me for I heard a light step in the passage. An instant later the key turned, the door opened and Sophie was in the room.

"Monsieur—" she cried.

"Etienne," said I.

"Nothing will change you," said she. "But is it possible that you do not hate me? Have you forgiven me the trick which I played you?"

"What trick?" I asked.

"Good heavens! is it possible that even now you have not understood it? You have asked me to translate the despatch. I have told you that it meant, 'If the French come to Minsk all is lost.'"

"What did it mean, then?"

"It means, 'Let the French come to Minsk. We are awaiting them.'"

I sprang back from her.

"You betrayed me!" I cried. "You lured me into this trap. It is to you that I owe the death and capture of my men. Fool that I was to trust a woman!"

"Do not be unjust, Colonel Gerard. I am a Russian woman, and my first duty is to my country. Would you not wish a French girl to have acted as I have done? Had I translated the message correctly you would not have gone to Minsk and your squadron would have escaped. Tell me that you forgive me!"

She looked bewitching as she stood pleading her cause in front of me. And yet, as I thought of my dead men, I could not take the hand which she held out to me.

"Very good," said she, as she dropped it by her side. "You feel for your own people and I feel for mine, and so we are equal. But you have said one wise and kindly thing within these walls, Colonel Gerard. You have said, 'One man more or less can make no difference in a struggle between two great armies.' Your lesson of nobility is not wasted. Behind those fagots is an unguarded door. Here is the key to it. Go forth, Colonel Gerard, and I trust that we may never look upon each other's faces again."

I stood for an instant with the key in my hand and my head in a whirl. Then I handed it back to her.

"I cannot do it," I said.

"Why not?"

"I have given my parole."

"To whom?" she asked.

"Why, to you!"

"And I release you from it."

My heart bounded with joy. Of course, it was true what she said. I had refused to give my parole to Sergine. I owed him no duty. If she relieved me from my promise my honour was clear. I took the key from her hand.

"You will find Captain Barakoff at the end of the village street," said she. "We of the North never forget either an injury or a kindness. He has your mare and your sword waiting for you. Do not delay an instant, for in two hours it will be dawn."

So I passed out into the starlit Russian night, and had that last glimpse of Sophie as she peered after me through the open door. She looked wistfully at me as if she expected something more than the cold thanks which I gave her, but even the humblest man has his pride, and I will not deny that mine was hurt by the deception which she had played upon me. I could not have brought myself to kiss her hand, far less her lips. The door led into a narrow alley, and at the end of it stood a muffled figure who held Violette by the bridle.

"You told me to be kind to the next French officer whom I found in distress," said he. "Good luck! Bon voyage!" he whispered, as I bounded into the saddle. "Remember, 'Poltava' is the watchword."

It was well that he had given it to me, for twice I had to pass Cossack pickets before I was clear of the lines. I had just ridden past the last vedettes and hoped that I was a free man again when there was a soft thudding in the snow behind me, and a heavy man upon a great black horse came swiftly after me. My first impulse was to put spurs to Violette. My second, as I saw a long black beard against a steel cuirass, was to halt and await him.

"I thought that it was you, you dog of a Frenchman," he cried, shaking his drawn sword at me. "So you have broken your parole, you rascal!"

"I gave no parole."

"You lie, you hound!"

I looked around and no one was coming. The vedettes were motionless and distant. We were all alone, with the moon above and the snow beneath. Fortune has ever been my friend.

"I gave you no parole."

"You gave it to the lady."

"Then I will answer for it to the lady."

"That would suit you better, no doubt. But, unfortunately, you will have to answer for it to me."

"I am ready."

"Your sword, too! There is treason in this! Ah, I see it all! The woman has helped you. She shall see Siberia for this night's work."

The words were his death-warrant. For Sophie's sake I could not let him go back alive. Our blades crossed, and an instant later mine was through his black beard and deep in his throat. I was on the ground almost as soon as he, but the one thrust was enough. He died, snapping his teeth at my ankles like a savage wolf.

Two days later I had rejoined the army at Smolensk, and was a part once more of that dreary procession which tramped onwards through the snow, leaving a long weal of blood to show the path which it had taken.

Enough, my friends; I would not re-awaken the memory of those days of misery and death. They still come to haunt me in my dreams. When we halted at last in Warsaw we had left behind us our guns, our transport, three-fourths of our comrades. But we did not leave behind us the honour of Etienne Gerard. They have said that I broke my parole. Let them beware how they say it to my face, for the story is as I tell it, and old as I am my forefinger is not too weak to press a trigger when my honour is in question.

BRIGADIER GERARD AT WATERLOO

I. THE ADVENTURE OF THE FOREST INN

OF all the great battles in which I had the honour of drawing my sword for the Emperor and for France there was not one which was lost. At Waterloo, although, in a sense, I was present, I was unable to fight, and the enemy was victorious. It is not for me to say that there is a connection between these two things. You know me too well, my friends, to imagine that I would make such a claim. But it gives matter for thought, and some have drawn flattering conclusions from it. After all, it was only a matter of breaking a few English squares and the day would have been our own. If the Hussars of Conflans, with Etienne Gerard to lead them, could not do this, then the best judges are mistaken. But let that pass. The Fates had ordained that I should hold my hand and that the Empire should fall. But they had also ordained that this day of gloom and sorrow should bring such honour to me as had never come when I swept on the wings of victory from Boulogne to Vienna. Never had I burned so brilliantly as at that supreme moment when the darkness fell upon all around me. You are aware that I was faithful to the Emperor in his adversity, and that I refused to sell my sword and my honour to the Bourbons. Never again was I to feel my war horse between my knees, never again to hear the kettledrums and silver trumpets behind me as I rode in front of my little rascals. But it comforts my heart, my friends, and it brings the tears to my eyes, to think how great I was upon that last day of my soldier life, and to remember that of all the remarkable exploits which have won me the love of so many beautiful women, and the respect of so many noble men, there was none which, in splendour, in audacity, and in the great end which was attained, could compare with my famous ride upon the night of June 18th, 1815. I am aware that the story is often told at mess-tables and in barrack-rooms, so that there are few in the army who have not heard it, but modesty has sealed my lips, until now, my friends, in the privacy of these intimate gatherings, I am inclined to lay the true facts before you.

In the first place, there is one thing which I can assure you. In all his career Napoleon never had so splendid an army as that with which he took the field for that campaign. In 1813 France was exhausted. For every veteran there were five children — Marie Louises as we called them, for the Empress had busied herself in raising levies while the Emperor took the field. But it was very different in 1815. The prisoners had all come back — the men from the snows of Russia, the men from the dungeons of Spain, the men from the hulks in England. These were the dangerous men, veterans of twenty battles, longing for their old trade, and with hearts filled with hatred and revenge. The ranks were full of soldiers who wore two and three chevrons, every chevron meaning five years' service. And the spirit of these men was terrible. They were raging, furious, fanatical, adoring the Emperor as a Mameluke does his prophet, ready to fall upon their own bayonets if their blood could serve him. If you had seen these fierce old veterans going into battle, with their flushed faces, their savage eyes, their furious yells, you would wonder that anything could stand against them. So high was the spirit of France at that time that every other spirit would have quailed before it; but these people, these English, had neither spirit nor soul, but only solid, immovable beef, against which we broke ourselves in vain. That was it, my friends! On the one side, poetry, gallantry, self-sacrifice — all that is beautiful and heroic. On the other side, beef. Our hopes, our ideals, our dreams — all were shattered on that terrible beef of Old England.

You have read how the Emperor gathered his forces, and then how he and I, with a hundred and thirty thousand veterans, hurried to the northern frontier and fell upon the Prussians and the English. On the 16th of June Ney held the English in play at Quatre Bras while we beat the Prussians at Ligny. It is not for me to say how far I contributed to that victory, but it is well known that the Hussars of Conflans covered themselves with glory. They fought well, these Prussians, and eight thousand of them were left upon the field. The Emperor thought that he had done with them, as he sent Marshal Grouchy with thirty-two thousand men to follow them up and to prevent their interfering with his plans. Then, with nearly eighty thousand men, he turned upon these "Goddam" Englishmen. How much we had to avenge upon them, we Frenchmen — the guineas of Pitt, the hulks of Portsmouth, the invasion of Wellington, the perfidious victories of Nelson! At last the day of punishment seemed to have arisen.

Wellington had with him sixty-seven thousand men, but many of them were known to be Dutch and Belgian, who had no great desire to fight against us. Of good troops he had not fifty thousand. Finding himself in the presence of the Emperor in person with eighty thousand men, this Englishman was so paralyzed with fear that he could neither move himself nor his army. You have seen the rabbit when the snake approaches. So stood the English upon the ridge of Waterloo. The night before, the Emperor, who had lost an aide-de-camp at Ligny, ordered me to join his staff, and I had left my Hussars to the charge of Major Victor. I know not which of us was the most grieved, they or I, that I should be called away upon the eve of battle, but an order is an order, and a good soldier can but shrug his shoulders and obey. With the Emperor I rode across the front of the enemy's position on the morning of the 18th, he looking at them through his glass and planning which was the shortest way to destroy them. Soult was at his elbow, and Ney and Foy and others who had fought the English in Portugal and Spain. "Have a care, Sire," said Soult. "The English infantry is very solid."

"You think them good soldiers because they have beaten you," said the Emperor, and we younger men turned away our faces and smiled. But Ney and Foy were grave and serious. All the time the English line, chequered with red and blue and dotted with batteries, was drawn up silent and watchful within a long musket-shot of us. On the other side of the shallow valley our own people, having finished their soup, were assembling for the battle. It had rained very heavily, but at this moment the sun shone out and beat upon the French army, turning our brigades of cavalry into so many dazzling rivers of steel, and twinkling and sparkling on the innumerable bayonets of the infantry. At the sight of that splendid army, and the beauty and majesty of its appearance, I could contain myself no longer, but, rising in my stirrups, I waved my busby and cried, "Vive l'Empereur!" a shout which growled and roared and clattered from one end of the line to the other, while the horsemen waved their swords and the footmen held up their shakos upon their bayonets. The English remained petrified upon their ridge. They knew that their hour had come.

And so it would have come if at that moment the word had been given and the whole army had been permitted to advance. We had but to fall upon them and to sweep them from the face of the earth. To put aside all question of courage, we were the more numerous, the older soldiers, and the better led. But the Emperor desired to do all things in order, and he waited until the ground should be drier and harder, so that his artillery could manœuvre. So three hours were wasted, and it was eleven o'clock before we saw Jerome Buonaparte's columns advance upon our left and heard the crash of the guns which told that the battle had begun. The loss of those three hours was our destruction. The attack upon the left was directed upon a farmhouse which was held by the English Guards, and we heard the three loud shouts of apprehension which the defenders were compelled to utter. They were still holding out, and D'Erlon's corps was advancing upon the right to engage another portion of the English line, when our attention was called away from the battle beneath our noses to a distant portion of the field of action.

The Emperor had been looking through his glass to the extreme left of the English line, and now he turned suddenly to the Duke of Dalmatia, or Soult, as we soldiers preferred to call him.

"What is it, Marshal?" said he.

We all followed the direction of his gaze, some raising our glasses, some shading our eyes. There was a thick wood over yonder, then a long, bare slope, and another wood beyond. Over this bare strip between the two woods there lay something dark, like the shadow of a moving cloud.

"I think that they are cattle, Sire," said Soult.

At that instant there came a quick twinkle from amid the dark shadow.

"It is Grouchy," said the Emperor, and he lowered his glass. "They are doubly lost, these English. I hold them in the hollow of my hand. They cannot escape me."

He looked round, and his eyes fell upon me.

"Ah! here is the prince of messengers," said he. "Are you well mounted, Colonel Gerard?"

I was riding my little Violette, the pride of the brigade. I said so.

"Then ride hard to Marshal Grouchy, whose troops you see over yonder. Tell him that he is to fall upon the left flank and rear of the English while I attack them in front. Together we should crush them and not a man escape."

I saluted and rode off without a word, my heart dancing with joy that such a mission should be mine. I looked at that long, solid line of red and blue looming through the smoke of the guns, and I shook my fist at it as I went. "We shall crush them and not a man escape." They were the Emperor's words, and it was I, Etienne Gerard, who was to turn them into deeds. I burned to reach the Marshal, and for an instant I thought of riding through the English left wing, as being the shortest cut. I have done bolder deeds and come out safely, but I reflected that if things went badly with me and I was taken or shot the message would be lost and the plans of the Emperor miscarry. I passed in front of the cavalry therefore, past the Chasseurs, the Lancers of the Guard, the

Carabineers, the Horse Grenadiers, and, lastly, my own little rascals, who followed me wistfully with their eyes. Beyond the cavalry the Old Guard was standing, twelve regiments of them, all veterans of many battles, sombre and severe, in long blue overcoats and high bearskins from which the plumes had been removed. Each bore within the goatskin knapsack upon his back the blue and white parade uniform which they would use for their entry into Brussels next day. As I rode past them I reflected that these men had never been beaten, and, as I looked at their weather-beaten faces, and their stern and silent bearing, I said to myself that they never would be beaten. Great heavens, how little could I foresee what a few more hours would bring!

On the right of the Old Guard were the Young Guard and the 6th Corps of Lobau, and then I passed Jacquinot's Lancers and Marbot's Hussars, who held the extreme flank of the line. All these troops knew nothing of the corps which was coming towards them through the wood, and their attention was taken up in watching the battle which raged upon their left. More than a hundred guns were thundering from each side, and the din was so great that of all the battles which I have fought I cannot recall more than half-a-dozen which were as noisy. I looked back over my shoulder, and there were two brigades of Cuirassiers, English and French, pouring down the hill together, with the sword-blades playing over them like summer lightning. How I longed to turn Violette, and to lead my Hussars into the thick of it! What a picture! Etienne Gerard with his back to the battle, and a fine cavalry action raging behind him. But duty is duty, so I rode past Marbot's vedettes and on in the direction of the wood, passing the village of Frishermont upon my left.

In front of me lay the great wood, called the Wood of Paris, consisting mostly of oak trees, with a few narrow paths leading through it. I halted and listened when I reached it, but out of its gloomy depths there came no blare of trumpet, no murmur of wheels, no tramp of horses to mark the advance of that great column which with my own eyes I had seen streaming towards it. The battle roared behind me, but in front all was as silent as that grave in which so many brave men would shortly sleep. The sunlight was cut off by the arches of leaves above my head, and a heavy damp smell rose from the sodden ground. For several miles I galloped at such a pace as few riders would care to go with roots below and branches above. Then, at last, for the first time I caught a glimpse of Grouchy's advance guard. Scattered parties of Hussars passed me on either side, but some distance off, among the trees. I heard the beating of a drum far away, and the low, dull murmur which an army makes upon the march. Any moment I might come upon the staff and deliver my message to Grouchy in person, for I knew well that on such a march a Marshal of France would certainly ride with the van of his army.

Suddenly the trees thinned in front of me, and I understood with delight that I was coming to the end of the wood, whence I could see the army and find the Marshal. Where the track comes out from amid the trees there is a small cabaret, where woodcutters and waggoners drink their wine. Outside the door of this I reined up my horse for an instant while I took in the scene which was before me. Some few miles away I saw a second great forest, that of St Lambert, out of which the Emperor had seen the troops advancing. It was easy to see, however, why there had been so long a delay in their leaving one wood and reaching the other, because between the two ran the deep defile of the Lasnes, which had to be crossed. Sure enough, a long column of troops—horse, foot, and guns—was streaming down one side of it and swarming up the other, while the advance guard was already among the trees on either side of me. A battery of Horse Artillery was coming along the road, and I was about to gallop up to it and ask the officer in command if he could tell me where I should find the Marshal, when suddenly I observed that, though the gunners were dressed in blue, they had not the dolman trimmed with red brandenburgs as our own horse-gunners wear it. Amazed at the sight, I was looking at these soldiers to left and right when a hand touched my thigh, and there was the landlord, who had rushed from his inn.

"Madman!" he cried, "why are you here? What are you doing?"

"I am seeking Marshal Grouchy."

"You are in the heart of the Prussian army. Turn and fly!"

"Impossible; this is Grouchy's corps."

"How do you know?"

"Because the Emperor has said it."

"Then the Emperor has made a terrible mistake! I tell you that a patrol of Silesian Hussars has this instant left me. Did you not see them in the wood?"

"I saw Hussars."

"They are the enemy."

"Where is Grouchy?"

"He is behind. They have passed him."

"Then how can I go back? If I go forward I may see him yet. I must obey my orders and find him wherever he is."

The man reflected for an instant.

"Quick! quick!" he cried, seizing my bridle. "Do what I say and you may yet escape. They have not observed you yet. Come with me and I will hide you until they pass."

Behind his house there was a low stable, and into this he thrust Violette. Then he half led and half dragged me into the kitchen of the inn. It was a bare, brick-floored room. A stout, red-faced woman was cooking cutlets at the fire.

"What's the matter now?" she asked, looking with a frown from me to the innkeeper. "Who is this you have brought in?"

"It is a French officer, Marie. We cannot let the Prussians take him."

"Why not?"

"Why not? Sacred name of a dog, was I not myself a soldier of Napoleon? Did I not win a musket of honour among the Vélites of the Guard? Shall I see a comrade taken before my eyes? Marie, we must save him."

But the lady looked at me with most unfriendly eyes.

"Pierre Charras," she said, "you will not rest until you have your house burned over your head. Do you not understand, you block-head, that if you fought for Napoleon it was because Napoleon ruled Belgium? He does so no longer. The Prussians are our allies and this is our enemy. I will have no Frenchman in this house. Give him up!"

The innkeeper scratched his head and looked at me in despair, but it was very evident to me that it was neither for France nor for Belgium that this woman cared, but that it was the safety of her own house that was nearest her heart.

"Madame," said I, with all the dignity and assurance I could command, "the Emperor is defeating the English and the French army will be here before evening. If you have used me well you will be rewarded, and if you have denounced me you will be punished and your house will certainly be burned by the provost-marshal."

She was shaken by this, and I hastened to complete my victory by other methods.

"Surely," said I, "it is impossible that anyone so beautiful can also be hard-hearted? You will not refuse me the refuge which I need."

She looked at my whiskers and I saw that she was softened. I took her hand, and in two minutes we were on such terms that her husband swore roundly that he would give me up himself if I pressed the matter farther.

"Besides, the road is full of Prussians," he cried. "Quick! quick! into the loft!"

"Quick! quick! into the loft!" echoed his wife, and together they hurried me towards a ladder which led to a trap-door in the ceiling. There was loud knocking at the door, so you can think that it was not long before my spurs went twinkling through the hole and the board was dropped behind me. An instant later I heard the voices of the Germans in the rooms below me.

The place in which I found myself was a single long attic, the ceiling of which was formed by the roof of the house. It ran over the whole of one side of the inn, and through the cracks in the flooring I could look down either upon the kitchen, the sitting-room, or the bar at my pleasure. There were no windows, but the place was in the last stage of disrepair, and several missing slates upon the roof gave me light and the means of observation. The place was heaped with lumber—fodder at one end and a huge pile of empty bottles at the other. There was no door or window save the hole through which I had come up.

I sat upon the heap of hay for a few minutes to steady myself and to think out my plans. It was very serious that the Prussians should arrive upon the field of battle earlier than our reserves, but there appeared to be only one corps of them, and a corps more or less makes little difference to such a man as the Emperor. He could afford to give the English all this and beat them still. The best way in which I could serve him, since Grouchy was behind, was to wait here until they were past, and then to resume my journey, to see the Marshal, and to give him his orders. If he advanced upon the rear of the English instead of following the Prussians all would be well. The fate of France depended upon my judgment and my nerve. It was not the first time, my friends, as you are well aware, and you know the reasons that I had to trust that neither nerve nor judgement would ever fail me. Certainly, the Emperor had chosen the right man for his mission. "The prince of messengers" he had called me. I would earn my title.

It was clear that I could do nothing until the Prussians had passed, so I spent my time in observing them. I have no love for these people, but I am compelled to say that they kept excellent discipline, for not a man of them entered the inn, though their lips were caked with dust and they were ready to drop with fatigue. Those who had knocked at the door were bearing an insensible comrade, and having left him they returned at once to the ranks. Several others were carried in in the same fashion and laid in the kitchen, while a young surgeon, little more than a boy, remained behind in charge of them. Having observed them through the cracks in the floor, I next turned my attention to the holes in the roof, from which I had an excellent view of all that was passing outside. The Prussian corps was still streaming past. It was easy to see that they had made a terrible march and had little food, for the faces of the men were ghastly, and they were plastered from head to foot with mud from their falls upon the foul and slippery roads. Yet, spent as they were, their spirit was excellent, and they pushed and hauled at the gun-carriages when the wheels sank up to the axles in the mire, and the weary horses were floundering knee-deep unable to draw them through. The officers rode up and down the column encouraging the more active with words of praise, and the laggards with blows from the flat of their swords. All the time from over the wood in front of them there came the tremendous roar of the battle, as if all the rivers on earth had united in one gigantic cataract, booming and crashing in a mighty fall. Like the spray of the cataract was the long veil of smoke which rose high over the trees. The officers pointed to it with their swords, and with hoarse cries from their parched lips the mud-stained men pushed onwards to the battle. For an hour I watched them pass, and I reflected that their vanguard must have come into touch with Marbot's vedettes and that the Emperor knew already of their coming. "You are going very fast up the road, my friends, but you will come down it a great deal faster," said I to myself, and I consoled myself with the thought.

But an adventure came to break the monotony of this long wait. I was seated beside my loophole and congratulating myself that the corps was nearly past, and that the road would soon be clear for my journey, when suddenly I heard a loud altercation break out in French in the kitchen.

"You shall not go!" cried a woman's voice.

"I tell you that I will!" said a man's, and there was a sound of scuffling.

In an instant I had my eye to the crack in the floor. There was my stout lady, like a faithful watch-dog, at the bottom of the ladder, while the young German surgeon, white with anger, was endeavouring to come up it. Several of the German soldiers who had recovered from their prostration were sitting about on the kitchen floor and watching the quarrel with stolid, but attentive, faces. The landlord was nowhere to be seen.

"There is no liquor there," said the woman.

"I do not want liquor; I want hay or straw for these men to lie upon. Why should they lie on the bricks when there is straw overhead?"

"There is no straw."

"What is up there?"

"Empty bottles."

"Nothing else?"

"No."

For a moment it looked as if the surgeon would abandon his intention, but one of the soldiers pointed up to the ceiling. I gathered from what I could understand of his words that he could see the straw sticking out between the planks. In vain the woman protested. Two of the soldiers were able to get upon their feet and to drag her aside, while the young surgeon ran up the ladder, pushed open the trap-door, and climbed into the loft. As he swung the door back I slipped behind it, but as luck would have it he shut it again behind him, and there we were left standing face to face.

Never have I seen a more astonished young man.

"A French officer!" he gasped.

"Hush!" said I, "hush! Not a word above a whisper." I had drawn my sword.

"I am not a combatant," he said; "I am a doctor. Why do you threaten me with your sword? I am not armed."

"I do not wish to hurt you, but I must protect myself. I am in hiding here."

"A spy!"

"A spy does not wear such a uniform as this, nor do you find spies on the staff of an army. I rode by mistake into the heart of this Prussian corps, and I concealed myself here in the hope of escaping when they are past. I will not hurt you if you do not hurt me, but if you do not swear that you will be silent as to my presence you will never go down alive from this attic."

"You can put up your sword, sir," said the surgeon, and I saw a friendly twinkle in his eyes. "I am a Pole by birth, and I have no ill-feeling to you or your people. I will do my best for my patients, but

I will do no more. Capturing Hussars is not one of the duties of a surgeon. With your permission I will now descend with this truss of hay to make a couch for these poor fellows below."

I had intended to exact an oath from him, but it is my experience that if a man will not speak the truth he will not swear the truth, so I said no more. The surgeon opened the trap-door, threw out enough hay for his purpose, and then descended the ladder, letting down the door behind him. I watched him anxiously when he rejoined his patients, and so did my good friend the landlady, but he said nothing and busied himself with the needs of his soldiers.

By this time I was sure that the last of the army corps was past, and I went to my loop-hole confident that I should find the coast clear, save, perhaps, for a few stragglers, whom I could disregard. The first corps was indeed past, and I could see the last files of the infantry disappearing into the wood; but you can imagine my disappointment when out of the Forest of St Lambert I saw a second corps emerging, as numerous as the first. There could be no doubt that the whole Prussian army, which we thought we had destroyed at Ligny, was about to throw itself upon our right wing while Marshal Grouchy had been coaxed away upon some fool's errand. The roar of guns, much nearer than before, told me that the Prussian batteries which had passed me were already in action. Imagine my terrible position! Hour after hour was passing; the sun was sinking towards the west. And yet this cursed inn, in which I lay hid, was like a little island amid a rushing stream of furious Prussians. It was all-important that I should reach Marshal Grouchy, and yet I could not show my nose without being made prisoner. You can think how I cursed and tore my hair. How little do we know what is in store for us! Even while I raged against my ill-fortune, that same fortune was reserving me for a far higher task than to carry a message to Grouchy — a task which could not have been mine had I not been held tight in that little inn on the edge of the Forest of Paris.

Two Prussian corps had passed and a third was coming up, when I heard a great fuss and the sound of several voices in the sitting-room. By altering my position I was able to look down and see what was going on.

Two Prussian generals were beneath me, their heads bent over a map which lay upon the table. Several aides-de-camp and staff officers stood round in silence. Of the two generals one was a fierce old man, white-haired and wrinkled, with a ragged, grizzled moustache and a voice like the bark of a hound. The other was younger, but longfaced and solemn. He measured distances upon the map with the air of a student, while his companion stamped and fumed and cursed like a corporal of Hussars. It was strange to see the old man so fiery and the young one so reserved. I could not understand all that they said, but I was very sure about their general meaning.

"I tell you we must push on and ever on!" cried the old fellow, with a furious German oath. "I promised Wellington that I would be there with the whole army even if I had to be strapped to my horse. Billow's corps is in action, and Ziethen's shall support it with every man and gun. Forwards, Gneisenau forwards!"

The other shook his head.

"You must remember, your Excellency, that if the English are beaten they will make for the coast. What will your position be then, with Grouchy between you and the Rhine?"

"We shall beat them, Gneisenau; the Duke and I will grind them to powder between us. Push on, I say! The whole war will be ended in one blow. Bring Pirsch up, and we can throw sixty thousand men into the scale while Thielmann holds Grouchy beyond Wavre."

Gneisenau shrugged his shoulders, but at that instant an orderly appeared at the door.

"An aide-de-camp from the Duke of Wellington," said he.

"Ha, ha!" cried the old man; "let us hear what he has to say!"

An English officer, with mud and blood all over his scarlet jacket, staggered into the room. A crimson-stained handkerchief was knotted round his arm, and he held the table to keep himself from falling.

"My message is to Marshal Blücher," said he.

"I am Marshal Blücher. Go on! go on!" cried the impatient old man.

"The Duke bade me to tell you, sir, that the British Army can hold its own and that he has no fears for the result. The French cavalry has been destroyed, two of their divisions of infantry have ceased to exist, and only the Guard is in reserve. If you give us a vigorous support the defeat will be changed to absolute rout and—" His knees gave way under him and he fell in a heap upon the floor.

"Enough! enough!" cried Blucher. "Gneisenau, send an aide-de-camp to Wellington and tell him to rely upon me to the full. Come on, gentlemen, we have our work to do!" He bustled eagerly out of the room with all his staff clanking behind him, while two orderlies carried the English messenger to the care of the surgeon.

Gneisenau, the Chief of the Staff, had lingered behind for an instant, and he laid his hand upon one of the aides-de-camp. The fellow had attracted my attention, for I have always a quick eye for a fine man. He was tall and slender, the very model of a horseman; indeed, there was something in his appearance which made it not unlike my own. His face was dark and as keen as that of a hawk, with fierce black eyes under thick, shaggy brows, and a moustache which would have put him in the crack squadron of my Hussars. He wore a green coat with white facings, and a horsehair helmet—a Dragoon, as I conjectured, and as dashing a cavalier as one would wish to have at the end of one's sword-point.

"A word with you, Count Stein," said Gneisenau. "If the enemy are routed, but if the Emperor escapes, he will rally another army, and all will have to be done again. But if we can get the Emperor, then the war is indeed ended. It is worth a great effort and a great risk for such an object as that."

The young Dragoon said nothing, but he listened attentively.

"Suppose the Duke of Wellington's words should prove to be correct, and the French army should be driven in utter rout from the field, the Emperor will certainly take the road back through Genappe and Charleroi as being the shortest to the frontier. We can imagine that his horses will be fleet, and that the fugitives will make way for him. Our cavalry will follow the rear of the beaten army, but the Emperor will be far away at the front of the throng."

The young Dragoon inclined his head.

"To you, Count Stein, I commit the Emperor. If you take him your name will live in history. You have the reputation of being the hardest rider in our army. Do you choose such comrades as you may select—ten or a dozen should be enough. You are not to engage in the battle, nor are you to follow the general pursuit, but you are to ride clear of the crowd, reserving your energies for a nobler end. Do you understand me?"

Again the Dragoon inclined his head. This silence impressed me. I felt that he was indeed a dangerous man.

"Then I leave the details in your own hands. Strike at no one except the highest. You cannot mistake the Imperial carriage, nor can you fail to recognise the figure of the Emperor. Now I must follow the Marshal. Adieu! If ever I see you again I trust that it will be to congratulate you upon a deed which will ring through Europe."

The Dragoon saluted and Gneisenau hurried from the room. The young officer stood in deep thought for a few moments. Then he followed the Chief of the Staff. I looked with curiosity from my loophole to see what his next proceeding would be. His horse, a fine, strong chestnut with two white stockings, was fastened to the rail of the inn. He sprang into the saddle, and, riding to intercept a column of cavalry which was passing, he spoke to an officer at the head of the leading regiment. Presently after some talk I saw two Hussars—it was a Hussar regiment—drop out of the ranks and take up their position beside Count Stein. The next regiment was also stopped, and two Lancers were added to his escort. The next furnished him with two Dragoons and the next with two Cuirassiers. Then he drew his little group of horsemen aside and he gathered them round him, explaining to them what they had to do. Finally the nine soldiers rode off together and disappeared into the Wood of Paris.

I need not tell you, my friends, what all this portended. Indeed, he had acted exactly as I should have done in his place. From each colonel he had demanded the two best horsemen in the regiment, and so he had assembled a band who might expect to catch whatever they should follow. Heaven help the Emperor if, without an escort, he should find them on his track!

And I, dear friends—imagine the fever, the ferment, the madness of my mind! All thought of Grouchy had passed away. No guns were to be heard to the east. He could not be near. If he should come up he would not now be in time to alter the event of the day. The sun was already low in the sky and there could not be more than two or three hours of daylight. My mission might be dismissed as useless. But here was another mission, more pressing, more immediate, a mission which meant the safety, and perhaps the life, of the Emperor. At all costs, through every danger, I must get back to his side. But how was I to do it? The whole Prussian army was now between me and the French lines. They blocked every road, but they could not block the path of duty when Etienne Gerard sees it lie before him. I could not wait longer. I must be gone.

There was but the one opening to the loft, and so it was only down the ladder that I could descend. I looked into the kitchen and I found that the young surgeon was still there. In a chair sat the wounded English aide-de-camp, and on the straw lay two Prussian soldiers in the last stage of exhaustion. The others had all recovered and been sent on. These were my enemies, and I must pass through them in order to gain my horse. From the surgeon I had nothing to fear; the Englishman was wounded, and his sword stood with his cloak in a corner; the two Germans were half insensible, and their muskets were not beside them. What could be simpler? I opened the trap-door, slipped down the ladder, and appeared in the midst of them, my sword drawn in my hand.

What a picture of surprise! The surgeon, of course, knew all, but to the Englishman and the two Germans it must have seemed that the god of war in person had descended from the skies. With my appearance, with my figure, with my silver and grey uniform, and with that gleaming sword in my hand, I must indeed have been a sight worth seeing. The two Germans lay petrified with staring eyes. The English officer half rose, but sat down again from weakness, his mouth open and his hand on the back of his chair.

"What the deuce!" he kept on repeating, "what the deuce!"

"Pray do not move," said I; "I will hurt no one, but woe to the man who lays hands upon me to stop me. You have nothing to fear if you leave me alone, and nothing to hope if you try to hinder me. I am Colonel Etienne Gerard, of the Hussars of Conflans."

"The deuce!" said the Englishman. "You are the man that killed the fox." A terrible scowl had darkened his face. The jealousy of sportsmen is a base passion. He hated me, this Englishman, because I had been before him in transfixing the animal. How different are our natures! Had I seen him do such a deed I would have embraced him with cries of joy. But there was no time for argument.

"I regret it, sir," said I; "but you have a cloak here and I must take it."

He tried to rise from his chair and reach his sword, but I got between him and the corner where it lay.

"If there is anything in the pockets—"

"A case," said he.

"I would not rob you," said I; and raising the coat I took from the pockets a silver flask, a square wooden case, and a field-glass. All these I handed to him. The wretch opened the case, took out a pistol, and pointed it straight at my head.

"Now, my fine fellow," said he, "put down your sword and give yourself up."

I was so astounded at this infamous action that I stood petrified before him. I tried to speak to him of honour and gratitude, but I saw his eyes fix and harden over the pistol.

"Enough talk!" said he. "Drop it!"

Could I endure such a humiliation? Death were better than to be disarmed in such a fashion. The word "Fire!" was on my lips when in an instant the Englishman vanished from before my face, and in his place was a great pile of hay, with a red-coated arm and two Hessian boots waving and kicking in the heart of it. Oh, the gallant landlady! It was my whiskers that had saved me.

"Fly, soldier, fly!" she cried, and she heaped fresh trusses of hay from the floor on to the struggling Englishman. In an instant I was out in the courtyard, had led Violette from her stable, and was on her back. A pistol bullet whizzed past my shoulder from the window, and I saw a furious face looking out at me. I smiled my contempt and spurred out into the road. The last of the Prussians had passed, and both my road and my duty lay clear before me. If France won, all was well. If France lost, then on me and on my little mare depended that which was more than victory or defeat— the safety and the life of the Emperor. "On, Etienne, on!" I cried. "Of all your noble exploits, the greatest, even if it be the last, lies now before you!"

BRIGADIER GERARD AT WATERLOO

II. THE ADVENTURE OF THE NINE PRUSSIAN HORSEMEN

I told you when last we met, my friends, of the important mission from the Emperor to Marshal Grouchy, which failed through no fault of my own, and I described to you how during a long afternoon I was shut up in the attic of a country inn, and was prevented from coming out because the Prussians were all around me. You will remember also how I overheard the Chief of the Prussian Staff give his instructions to Count Stein, and so learned the dangerous plan which was on foot to kill or capture the Emperor in the event of a French defeat. At first I could not have believed in such a thing, but since the guns had thundered all day, and since the sound had made no advance in my direction, it was evident that the English had at least held their own and beaten off all our attacks.

I have said that it was a fight that day between the soul of France and the beef of England, but it must be confessed that we found the beef was very tough. It was clear that if the Emperor could not defeat the English when alone, then it might, indeed, go hard with him now that sixty thousand of these cursed Prussians were swarming on his flank. In any case, with this secret in my possession, my place was by his side.

I had made my way out of the inn in the dashing manner which I have described to you when last we met, and I left the English aide-de-camp shaking his foolish fist out of the window. I could not but laugh as I looked back at him, for his angry red face was framed and frilled with hay. Once out on the road I stood erect in my stirrups, and I put on the handsome black riding-coat, lined with red, which had belonged to him. It fell to the top of my high boots, and covered my telltale uniform completely. As to my busby, there are many such in the German service, and there was no reason why it should attract attention. So long as no one spoke to me there was no reason why I should not ride through the whole of the Prussian army; but though I understood German, for I had many friends among the German ladies during the pleasant years that I fought all over that country, still I spoke it with a pretty Parisian accent which could not be confounded with their rough, unmusical speech. I knew that this quality of my accent would attract attention, but I could only hope and pray that I would be permitted to go my way in silence.

The Forest of Paris was so large that it was useless to think of going round it, and so I took my courage in both hands and galloped on down the road in the track of the Prussian army. It was not hard to trace it, for it was rutted two feet deep by the gun-wheels and the caissons. Soon I found a fringe of wounded men, Prussians and French, on each side of it, where Billow's advance had come into touch with Marbot's Hussars. One old man with a long white beard, a surgeon, I suppose, shouted at me, and ran after me still shouting, but I never turned my head and took no notice of him save to spur on faster. I heard his shouts long after I had lost sight of him among the trees.

Presently I came up with the Prussian reserves. The infantry were leaning on their muskets or lying exhausted on the wet ground, and the officers stood in groups listening to the mighty roar of the battle and discussing the reports which came from the front. I hurried past at the top of my speed, but one of them rushed out and stood in my path with his hand up as a signal to me to stop. Five thousand Prussian eyes were turned upon me. There was a moment! You turn pale, my friends, at the thought of it. Think how every hair upon me stood on end. But never for one instant did my wits or my courage desert me. "General Blücher!" I cried. Was it not my guardian angel who whispered the words in my ear? The Prussian sprang from my path, saluted, and pointed forwards. They are well disciplined, these Prussians, and who was he that he should dare to stop the officer who bore a message to the general? It was a talisman that would pass me out of every danger, and my heart sang within me at the thought. So elated was I that I no longer waited to be asked, but as I rode through the army I shouted to right and left, "General Blücher! General Blücher!" and every man pointed me onwards and cleared a path to let me pass. There are times when the most supreme impudence is the highest wisdom. But discretion must also be used, and I must admit that I became indiscreet. For as I rode upon my way, ever nearer to the fighting line, a Prussian officer of Uhlans gripped my bridle and pointed to a group of men who stood near a burning farm. "There is Marshal Blücher. Deliver your message!" said he, and sure enough my terrible old grey-whiskered veteran was there within a pistol shot, his eyes turned in my direction.

But the good guardian angel did not desert me. Quick as a flash there came into my memory the name of the general who commanded the advance of the Prussians. "General Bülow!" I cried. The Uhlan let go my bridle. "General Bülow!" "General Bülow!" I shouted, as every stride of the dear little mare took me nearer my own people. Through the burning village of Plancenoit I galloped, spurred my way between two columns of Prussian infantry, sprang over a hedge, cut down a Silesian Hussar who flung himself before me, and an instant afterwards, with my coat flying open to show the uniform below, I passed through the open files of the tenth of the line, and was back in the heart of Lobau's corps once more. Outnumbered and outflanked, they were being slowly driven in by the pressure of the Prussian advance. I galloped onwards, anxious only to find myself by the Emperor's side.

But a sight lay before me which held me fast as though I had been turned into some noble equestrian statue. I could not move, I could scarce breathe, as I gazed upon it. There was a mound over which my path lay, and as I came out on the top of it I looked down the long, shallow valley of Waterloo I had left it with two great armies on either side and a clear field between them. Now there were but long, ragged fringes of broken and exhausted regiments upon the two ridges, but a real army of dead and wounded lay between. For two miles in length and half a mile across the ground was strewed and heaped with them. But slaughter was no new sight to me, and it was not that which held me spellbound. It was that up the long slope of the British position was moving a walking forest—black, tossing, waving, unbroken. Did I not know the bearskins of the Guard? And did I not also know, did not my soldier's instinct tell me, that it was the last reserve of France; that the Emperor, like a desperate gamester, was staking all upon his last card? Up they went and up—grand, solid, unbreakable, scourged with musketry, riddled with grape, flowing onwards in a black, heavy tide, which lapped over the British batteries. With my glass I could see the English gunners throw themselves under their pieces or run to the rear. On rolled the crest of the bearskins, and then, with a crash which was swept across to my ears, they met the British infantry. A minute passed, and another, and another. My heart was in my mouth. They swayed back and forwards; they no longer advanced; they were held. Great Heaven! was it possible that they were breaking? One black dot ran down the hill, then two, then four, then ten, then a great, scattered, struggling mass, halting, breaking, halting, and at last shredding out and rushing madly downwards. "The Guard is beaten! The Guard is beaten!" From all around me I heard the cry. Along the whole line the infantry turned their faces and the gunners flinched from their guns.

"The Old Guard is beaten! The Guard retreats!" An officer with a livid face passed me yelling out these words of woe. "Save yourselves! Save yourselves! You are betrayed!" cried another. "Save yourselves! Save yourselves!" Men were rushing madly to the rear, blundering and jumping like frightened sheep. Cries and screams rose from all around me. And at that moment, as I looked at the British position, I saw what I can never forget. A single horseman stood out black and clear upon the ridge against the last red angry glow of the setting sun. So dark, so motionless against that grim light, he might have been the very spirit of Battle brooding over that terrible valley. As I gazed he raised his hat high in the air, and at the signal, with a low, deep roar like a breaking wave, the whole British Army flooded over their ridge and came rolling down into the valley. Long steel-fringed lines of red and blue, sweeping waves of cavalry, horse batteries rattling and bounding — down they came on to our crumbling ranks. It was over. A yell of agony, the agony of brave men who see no hope, rose from one flank to the other, and in an instant the whole of that noble army was swept in a wild, terror-stricken crowd from the field. Even now, dear friends, I cannot, as you see, speak of that dreadful moment with a dry eye or with a steady voice.

At first I was carried away in that wild rush, whirled off like a straw in a flooded gutter. But, suddenly, what should I see amongst the mixed regiments in front of me but a group of stern horsemen, in silver and grey, with a broken and tattered standard held aloft in the heart of them! Not all the might of England and of Prussia could break the Hussars of Conflans. But when I joined them it made my heart bleed to see them. The major, seven captains, and five hundred men were left upon the field. Young, Captain Sabbatier was in command, and when I asked him where were the five missing squadrons he pointed back and answered: "You will find them round one of those British squares." Men and horses were at their last gasp, caked with sweat and dirt, their black tongues hanging out from their lips; but it made me thrill with pride to see how that shattered remnant still rode knee to knee, with every man, from the boy trumpeter to the farrier-sergeant, in his own proper place. Would that I could have brought them on with me as an escort for the Emperor! In the heart of the Hussars of Conflans he would be safe indeed. But the horses were too spent to trot. I left them behind me with orders to rally upon the farmhouse of St Aunay, where we had camped two nights before. For my own part I forced my horse through the throng in search of the Emperor.

There were things which I saw then, as I pressed through that dreadful crowd, which can never be banished from my mind. In evil dreams there comes back to me the memory of that flowing stream of livid, staring, screaming faces upon which I looked down. It was a nightmare. In victory one does not understand the horror of war. It is only in the cold chill of defeat that it is brought home to you. I remember an old Grenadier of the Guard lying at the side of the road with his broken leg doubled at a right angle. "Comrades, comrades, keep off my leg!" he cried, but they tripped and stumbled over him all the same. In front of me rode a Lancer officer without his coat. His arm had just been taken off in the ambulance. The bandages had fallen. It was horrible. Two gunners tried to drive through with their gun. A Chasseur raised his musket and shot one of them through the head. I saw a major of Cuirassiers draw his two holster pistols and shoot first his horse and then himself. Beside the road a man in a blue coat was raging and raving like a madman. His face was black with powder, his clothes were torn, one epaulette was gone, the other hung dangling over his breast. Only when I came close to him did I recognise that it was Marshal Ney. He howled at the flying troops and his voice was hardly human. Then he raised the stump of his sword—it was broken three inches from the hilt. "Come and see how a Marshal of France can die!" he cried. Gladly would I have gone with him, but my duty lay elsewhere. He did not, as you know, find the death he sought, but he met it a few weeks later in cold blood at the hands of his enemies.

There is an old proverb that in attack the French are more than men, in defeat they are less than women. I knew that it was true that day. But even in that rout I saw things which I can tell with pride. Through the fields which skirt the road moved Cambronne's three reserve battalions of the Guard, the cream of our army. They walked slowly in square, their colours waving over the sombre line of the bearskins. All round them raged the English cavalry and the black Lancers of Brunswick, wave after wave thundering up, breaking with a crash, and recoiling in ruin.

When last I saw them the English guns, six at a time, were smashing grape-shot through their ranks and the English infantry were closing in upon three sides and pouring volleys into them; but still, like a noble lion with fierce hounds clinging to its flanks, the glorious remnant of the Guard, marching slowly, halting, closing up, dressing, moved majestically from their last battle. Behind them the Guard's battery of twelve-pounders was drawn up upon the ridge. Every gunner was in his place, but no gun fired. "Why do you not fire?" I asked the colonel as I passed. "Our powder is finished." "Then why not retire?" "Our appearance may hold them back for a little. We must give the Emperor time to escape." Such were the soldiers of France.

Behind this screen of brave men the others took their breath, and then went on in less desperate fashion. They had broken away from the road, and all over the countryside in the twilight I could see the timid, scattered, frightened crowd who ten hours before had formed the finest army that ever went down to battle. I with my splendid mare was soon able to get clear of the throng, and just after I passed Genappe I overtook the Emperor with the remains of his Staff. Soult was with him still, and so were Drouot, Lobau, and Bertrand, with five Chasseurs of the Guard, their horses hardly able to move. The night was falling, and the Emperor's haggard face gleamed white through the gloom as he turned it towards me.

"Who is that? "he asked.

"It is Colonel Gerard," said Soult.

"Have you seen Marshal Grouchy?"

"No, Sire. The Prussians were between."

"It does not matter. Nothing matters now. Soult, I will go back."

He tried to turn his horse, but Bertrand seized his bridle. "Ah, Sire," said Soult, "the enemy has had good fortune enough already." They forced him on among them. He rode in silence with his chin upon his breast, the greatest and the saddest of men. Far away behind us those remorseless guns were still roaring. Sometimes out of the darkness would come shrieks and screams and the low thunder of galloping hoofs. At the sound we would spur our horses and hasten onwards through the scattered troops. At last, after riding all night in the clear moonlight, we found that we had left both pursued and pursuers behind. By the time we passed over the bridge at Charleroi the dawn was breaking. What a company of spectres we looked in that cold, clear, searching light, the Emperor with his face of wax, Soult blotched with powder, Lobau dabbled with blood! But we rode more easily now and had ceased to glance over our shoulders, for Waterloo was more than thirty miles behind us. One of the Emperor's carriages had been picked up at Charleroi, and we halted now on the other side of the Sambre, and dismounted from our horses.

You will ask me why it was that during all this time I had said nothing of that which was nearest my heart, the need for guarding the Emperor. As a fact, I had tried to speak of it both to Soult and to Lobau, but their minds were so overwhelmed with the disaster and so distracted by the pressing needs of the moment that it was impossible to make them understand how urgent was my message. Besides, during this long flight we had always had numbers of French fugitives beside us on the road, and, however demoralized they might be, we had nothing to fear from the attack of nine men. But now, as we stood round the Emperor's carriage in the early morning, I observed with anxiety that not a single French soldier was to be seen upon the long, white road behind us. We had outstripped the army. I looked round to see what means of defence were left to us. The horses of the Chasseurs of the Guard had broken down, and only one of them, a grey-whiskered sergeant, remained. There were Soult, Lobau, and Bertrand; but, for all their talents, I had rather, when it came to hard knocks, have a single quarter-master-sergeant of Hussars at my side than the three of them put together. There remained the Emperor himself, the coachman, and a valet of the household who had joined us at Charleroi—eight all told; but of the eight only two, the Chasseur and I, were fighting soldiers who could be depended upon at a pinch. A chill came over me as

I reflected how utterly helpless we were. At that moment I raised my eyes, and there were the nine Prussian horsemen coming over the hill.

On either side of the road at this point are long stretches of rolling plain, part of it yellow with corn and part of it rich grass land watered by the Sambre. To the south of us was a low ridge, over which was the road to France. Along this road the little group of cavalry was riding. So well had Count Stein obeyed his instructions that he had struck far to the south of us in his determination to get ahead of the Emperor. Now he was riding from the direction in which we were going—the last in which we could expect an enemy. When I caught that first glimpse of them they were still half a mile away.

"Sire!" I cried, "the Prussians!"

They all started and stared. It was the Emperor who broke the silence.

"Who says they are Prussians?"

"I do, Sire—I, Etienne Gerard!"

Unpleasant news always made the Emperor furious against the man who broke it. He railed at me now in the rasping, croaking, Corsican voice which only made itself heard when he had lost his self-control.

"You are always a buffoon," he cried. "What do you mean, you numskull, by saying that they are Prussians? How could Prussians be coming from the direction of France? You have lost any wits that you ever possessed."

His words cut me like a whip, and yet we all felt towards the Emperor as an old dog does to its master. His kick is soon forgotten and forgiven. I would not argue or justify myself. At the first glance I had seen the two white stockings on the forelegs of the leading horse, and I knew well that Count Stein was on its back. For an instant the nine horsemen had halted and surveyed us. Now they put spurs to their horses, and with a yell of triumph they galloped down the road. They had recognised that their prey was in their power.

At that swift advance all doubt had vanished. "By heavens, Sire, it is indeed the Prussians!" cried Soult. Lobau and Bertrand ran about the road like two frightened hens. The sergeant of Chasseurs drew his sabre with a volley of curses. The coachman and the valet cried and wrung their hands. Napoleon stood with a frozen face, one foot on the step of the carriage. And I—ah, my friends, I was magnificent! What words can I use to do justice to my own bearing at that supreme instant of my life? So coldly alert, so deadly cool, so clear in brain and ready in hand. He had called me a numskull and a buffoon. How quick and how noble was my revenge! When his own wits failed him, it was Etienne Gerard who supplied the want.

To fight was absurd; to fly was ridiculous. The Emperor was stout, and weary to death. At the best he was never a good rider. How could he fly from these, the picked men of an army? The best horseman in Prussia was among them. But I was the best horseman in France. I, and only I, could hold my own with them. If they were on *my* track instead of the Emperor's, all might still be well. These were the thoughts which flashed so swiftly through my mind that in an instant I had sprung from the first idea to the final conclusion. Another instant carried me from the final conclusion to prompt and vigorous action. I rushed to the side of the Emperor, who stood petrified, with the carriage between him and our enemies. "Your coat, Sire! your hat!" I cried. I dragged them off him. Never had he been so hustled in his life. In an instant I had them on and had thrust him into the carriage. The next I had sprung on to his famous white Arab and had ridden clear of the group upon the road.

You have already divined my plan; but you may well ask how could I hope to pass myself off as the Emperor. My figure is as you still see it, and his was never beautiful, for he was both short and stout. But a man's height is not remarked when he is in the saddle, and for the rest one had but to sit forward on the horse and round one's back and carry oneself like a sack of flour. I wore the little cocked hat and the loose grey coat with the silver star which was known to every child from one end of Europe to the other. Beneath me was the Emperor's own famous white charger. It was complete.

Already as I rode clear the Prussians were within two hundred yards of us. I made a gesture of terror and despair with my hands, and I sprang my horse over the bank which lined the road. It was enough. A yell of exultation and of furious hatred broke from the Prussians. It was the howl of starving wolves who scent their prey. I spurred my horse over the meadow-land and looked back under my arm as I rode. Oh, the glorious moment when one after the other I saw eight horsemen come over the bank at my heels! Only one had stayed behind, and I heard shouting and the sounds of a struggle. I remembered my old sergeant of Chasseurs, and I was sure that number nine would trouble us no more. The road was clear and the Emperor free to continue his journey.

But now I had to think of myself. If I were overtaken the Prussians would certainly make short work of me in their disappointment. If it were so — if I lost my life — I should still have sold it at a glorious price. But I had hopes that I might shake them off. With ordinary horsemen upon ordinary horses I should have had no difficulty in doing so, but here both steeds and riders were of the best. It was a grand creature that I rode, but it was weary with its long night's work, and the Emperor was one of those riders who do not know how to manage a horse. He had little thought for them and a heavy hand upon their mouths. On the other hand, Stein and his men had come both far and fast. The race was a fair one.

So quick had been my impulse, and so rapidly had I acted upon it, that I had not thought enough of my own safety. Had I done so in the first instance I should, of course, have ridden straight back the way we had come, for so I should have met our own people. But I was off the road and had galloped a mile over the plain before this occurred to me. Then when I looked back I saw that the Prussians had spread out into a long line, so as to head me off from the Charleroi road. I could not turn back, but at least I could edge towards the north. I knew that the whole face of the country was covered with our flying troops, and that sooner or later I must come upon some of them.

But one thing I had forgotten — the Sambre. In my excitement I never gave it a thought until I saw it, deep and broad, gleaming in the morning sunlight. It barred my path, and the Prussians howled behind me. I galloped to the brink, but the horse refused the plunge. I spurred him, but the bank was high and the stream deep. He shrank back trembling and snorting. The yells of triumph were louder every instant. I turned and rode for my life down the river bank. It formed a loop at this part, and I must get across somehow, for my retreat was blocked. Suddenly a thrill of hope ran through me, for I saw a house on my side of the stream and another on the farther bank. Where there are two such houses it usually means that there is a ford between them. A sloping path led to the brink and I urged my horse down it. On he went, the water up to the saddle, the foam flying right and left. He blundered once and I thought we were lost, but he recovered and an instant later was clattering up the farther slope. As we came out I heard the splash behind me as the first Prussian took the water. There was just the breadth of the Sambre between us.

I rode with my head sunk between my shoulders in Napoleon's fashion, and I did not dare to look back for fear they should see my moustache. I had turned up the collar of the grey coat so as partly to hide it. Even now if they found out their mistake they might turn and overtake the carriage. But when once we were on the road I could tell by the drumming of their hoofs how far distant they were, and it seemed to me that the sound grew perceptibly louder, as if they were slowly gaining upon me. We were riding now up the stony and rutted lane which led from the ford. I peeped back very cautiously from under my arm and I perceived that my danger came from a single rider, who was far ahead of his comrades. He was a Hussar, a very tiny fellow, upon a big black horse, and it was his light weight which had brought him into the foremost place. It is a place of honour; but it is also a place of danger, as he was soon to learn. I felt the holsters, but, to my horror, there were no pistols. There was a field-glass in one and the other was stuffed with papers. My sword had been left behind with Violette. Had I only my own weapons and my own little mare I could have played with these rascals. But I was not entirely unarmed. The Emperor's own sword hung to the saddle. It was curved and short, the hilt all crusted with gold—a thing more fitted to glitter at a review than to serve a soldier in his deadly need. I drew it, such as it was, and I waited my chance. Every instant the clink and clatter of the hoofs grew nearer. I heard the panting of the horse, and the fellow shouted some threat at me. There was a turn in the lane, and as I rounded it I drew up my white Arab on his haunches. As we spun round I met the Prussian Hussar face to face. He was going too fast to stop, and his only chance was to ride me down. Had he done so he might have met his own death, but he would have injured me or my horse past all hope of escape. But the fool flinched as he saw me waiting and flew past me on my right. I lunged over my Arab's neck and buried my toy sword in his side. It must have been the finest steel and as sharp as a razor, for I hardly felt it enter, and yet his blood was within three inches of the hilt. His horse galloped on and he kept his saddle for a hundred yards before he sank down with his face on the mane and then dived over the side of the neck on to the road. For my own part I was already at his horse's heels. A few seconds had sufficed for all that I have told.

I heard the cry of rage and vengeance which rose from the Prussians as they passed their dead comrade, and I could not but smile as I wondered what they could think of the Emperor as a horseman and a swordsman. I glanced back cautiously as before, and I saw that none of the seven men stopped. The fate of their comrade was nothing compared to the carrying out of their mission. They were as untiring and as remorseless as bloodhounds. But I had a good lead and the brave Arab was still going well. I thought that I was safe. And yet it was at that very instant that the most terrible danger befell me. The lane divided, and I took the smaller of the two divisions because it was the more grassy and the easier for the horse's hoofs. Imagine my horror when, riding through a gate, I found myself in a square of stables and farm-buildings, with no way out save that by which I had come! Ah, my friends, if my hair is snowy white, have I not had enough to make it so?

To retreat was impossible. I could hear the thunder of the Prussians' hoofs in the lane. I looked round me, and Nature has blessed me with that quick eye which is the first of gifts to any soldier, but most of all to a leader of cavalry. Between a long, low line of stables and the farmhouse there was a pig-sty. Its front was made of bars of wood four feet high; the back was of stone, higher than the front. What was beyond I could not tell. The space between the front and the back was not more than a few yards. It was a desperate venture, and yet I must take it. Every instant the beating of those hurrying hoofs was louder and louder. I put my Arab at the pig-sty. She cleared the front beautifully and came down with her forefeet upon the sleeping pig within, slipping forward upon her knees. I was thrown over the wall beyond, and fell upon my hands and face in a soft flower-bed. My horse was upon one side of the wall, I upon the other, and the Prussians were pouring into the yard. But I was up in an instant and had seized the bridle of the plunging horse over the top of the wall. It was built of loose stones, and I dragged down a few of them to make a gap. As I tugged at the bridle and shouted the gallant creature rose to the leap, and an instant afterwards she was by my side and I with my foot on the stirrup.

An heroic idea had entered my mind as I mounted into the saddle. These Prussians, if they came over the pig-sty, could only come one at once, and their attack would not be formidable when they had not had time to recover from such a leap. Why should I not wait and kill them one by one as they came over? It was a glorious thought. They would learn that Etienne Gerard was not a safe man to hunt. My hand felt for my sword, but you can imagine my feelings, my friends, when I came upon an empty scabbard. It had been shaken out when the horse had tripped over that infernal pig. On what absurd trifles do our destinies hang—a pig on one side, Etienne Gerard on the other! Could I spring over the wall and get the sword? Impossible! The Prussians were already in the yard. I turned my Arab and resumed my flight.

But for a moment it seemed to me that I was in a far worse trap than before. I found myself in the garden of the farmhouse, an orchard in the centre and flower-beds all round. A high wall surrounded the whole place. I reflected, however, that there must be some point of entrance, since every visitor could not be expected to spring over the pig-sty. I rode round the wall. As I expected, I came upon a door with a key upon the inner side. I dismounted, unlocked it, opened it, and there was a Prussian Lancer sitting his horse within six feet of me.

For a moment we each stared at the other. Then I shut the door and locked it again. A crash and a cry came from the other end of the garden. I understood that one of my enemies had come to grief in trying to get over the pig-sty. How could I ever get out of this *cul-de-sac*? It was evident that some of the party had galloped round, while some had followed straight upon my tracks. Had I my sword I might have beaten off the Lancer at the door, but to come out now was to be butchered. And yet if I waited some of them would certainly follow me on foot over the pig-sty, and what could I do then? I must act at once or I was lost. But it is at such moments that my wits are most active and my actions most prompt. Still leading my horse, I ran for a hundred yards by the side of the wall away from the spot where the Lancer was watching. There I stopped, and with an effort I tumbled down several of the loose stones from the top of the wall. The instant I had done so I hurried back to the door. As I had expected, he thought I was making a gap for my escape at that point, and I heard the thud of his horse's hoofs as he galloped to cut me off. As I reached the gate I looked back, and I saw a green-coated horseman, whom I knew to be Count Stein, clear the pig-sty and gallop furiously with a shout of triumph across the garden. "Surrender, your Majesty, surrender!" he yelled; "we will give you quarter!" I slipped through the gate, but had no time to lock it on the other side. Stein was at my very heels, and the Lancer had already turned his horse. Springing upon my Arab's back, I was off once more with a clear stretch of grass land before me. Stein had to dismount to open the gate, to lead his horse through, and to mount again before he could follow. It was he that I feared rather than the Lancer, whose horse was coarse-bred and weary. I galloped hard for a mile before I ventured to look back, and then Stein was a musket-shot from me, and the Lancer as much again, while only three of the others were in sight. My nine Prussians were coming down to more manageable numbers, and yet one was too much for an unarmed man.

It had surprised me that during this long chase I had seen no fugitives from the army, but I reflected that I was considerably to the west of their line of flight, and that I must edge more towards the east if I wished to join them. Unless I did so it was probable that my pursuers, even if they could not overtake me themselves, would keep me in view until I was headed off by some of their comrades coming from the north. As I looked to the eastward I saw afar off a line of dust which stretched for miles across the country. This was certainly the main road along which our unhappy army was flying. But I soon had proof that some of our stragglers had wandered into these side tracks, for I came suddenly upon a horse grazing at the corner of a field, and beside him, with his back against the bank, his master, a French Cuirassier, terribly wounded and evidently on the point of death. I sprang down, seized his long, heavy sword, and rode on with it. Never shall I forget the poor man's face as he looked at me with his failing sight. He was an old, grey-moustached soldier, one of the real fanatics, and to him this last vision of his Emperor was like a revelation from on high. Astonishment, love, pride—all shone in his pallid face. He said something—I fear they were his last words—but I had no time to listen, and I galloped on my way.

All this time I had been on the meadowland, which was intersected in this part by broad ditches. Some of them could not have been less than from fourteen to fifteen feet, and my heart was in my mouth as I went at each of them, for a slip would have been my ruin. But whoever selected the Emperor's horses had done his work well. The creature, save when it balked on the bank of the Sambre, never failed me for an instant. We cleared everything in one stride. And yet we could not shake off those infernal Prussians. As I left each watercourse behind me I looked back with renewed hope, but it was only to see Stein on his white-legged chestnut flying over it as lightly as I had done myself. He was my enemy, but I honoured him for the way in which he carried himself that day.

Again and again I measured the distance which separated him from the next horseman. I had the idea that I might turn and cut him down, as I had the Hussar, before his comrade could come to his help. But the others had closed up and were not far behind. I reflected that this Stein was probably as fine a swordsman as he was a rider, and that it might take me some little time to get the better of him. In that case the others would come to his aid and I should be lost. Or the whole, it was wiser to continue my flight.

A road with poplars on either side ran across the plain from east to west. It would lead me towards that long line of dust which marked the French retreat. I wheeled my horse, therefore, and galloped down it. As I rode I saw a single house in front of me upon the right, with a great bush hung over the door to mark it as an inn. Outside there were several peasants, but for them I cared nothing. What frightened me was to see the gleam of a red coat, which showed that there were British in the place. However, I could not turn and I could not stop, so there was nothing for it but to gallop on and to take my chance. There were no troops in sight, so these men must be stragglers or marauders, from whom I had little to fear. As I approached I saw that there were two of them sitting drinking on a bench outside the inn door. I saw them stagger to their feet, and it was evident that they were both very drunk. One stood swaying in the middle of the road. "It's Boney! So help me, it's Boney!" he yelled. He ran with his hands out to catch me, but luckily for himself his drunken feet stumbled and he fell on his face on the road. The other was more dangerous. He had rushed into the inn, and just as I passed I saw him run out with his musket in his hand. He dropped upon one knee, and I stooped forward over my horse's neck. A single shot from a Prussian or an Austrian is a small matter, but the British were at that time the best shots in Europe, and my drunkard seemed steady enough when he had a gun at his shoulder. I heard the crack, and my horse gave a convulsive spring which would have unseated many a rider. For an instant I thought he was killed, but when I turned in my saddle I saw a stream of blood running down the off hind-quarter. I looked back at the Englishman, and the brute had bitten the end off another cartridge and was ramming it into his musket, but before he had it primed we were beyond his range. These men were foot-soldiers and could not join in the chase, but I heard them whooping and tally-hoing behind me as if I had been a fox. The peasants also shouted and ran through the fields flourishing their sticks. From all sides I heard cries, and everywhere were the rushing, waving figures of my pursuers. To think of the great Emperor being chivvied over the countryside in this fashion! It made me long to have these rascals within the sweep of my sword.

But now I felt that I was nearing the end of my course. I had done all that a man could be expected to do—some would say more—but at last I had come to a point from which I could see no escape. The horses of my pursuers were exhausted, but mine was exhausted and wounded also. It was losing blood fast, and we left a red trail upon the white, dusty road. Already his pace was slackening, and sooner or later he must drop under me. I looked back, and there were the five inevitable Prussians—Stein a hundred yards in front, then a Lancer, and then three others riding together. Stein had drawn his sword, and he waved it at me. For my own part I was determined not to give myself up. I would try how many of these Prussians I could take with me into the other world. At this supreme moment all the great deeds of my life rose in a vision before me, and I felt that this, my last exploit, was indeed a worthy close to such a career. My death would be a fatal blow to those who loved me, to my dear mother, to my Hussars, to others who shall be nameless. But all of them had my honour and my fame at heart, and I felt that their grief would be tinged with pride when they learned how I had ridden and how I had fought upon this last day. Therefore I hardened my heart and, as my Arab limped more and more upon his wounded leg, I drew the great sword which I had taken from the Cuirassier, and I set my teeth for my supreme struggle. My hand was in the very act of tightening the bridle, for I feared that if I delayed longer I might find myself on foot fighting against five mounted men. At that instant my eye fell upon something which brought hope to my heart and a shout of joy to my lips.

From a grove of trees in front of me there projected the steeple of a village church. But there could not be two steeples like that, for the corner of it had crumbled away or been struck by lightning, so that it was of a most fantastic shape. I had seen it only two days before, and it was the church of the village of Gosselies. It was not the hope of reaching the village which set my heart singing with joy, but it was that I knew my ground now, and that farmhouse not half a mile ahead, with its gable end sticking out from amid the trees, must be that very farm of St Aunay where we had bivouacked, and which I had named to Captain Sabbatier as the rendezvous of the Hussars of Conflans. There they were, my little rascals, if I could but reach them. With every bound my horse grew weaker. Each instant the sound of the pursuit grew louder. I heard a gust of crackling German oaths at my very heels. A pistol bullet sighed in my ears. Spurring frantically and beating my poor Arab with the flat of my sword I kept him at the top of his speed. The open gate of the farmyard lay before me. I saw the twinkle of steel within. Stein's horse's head was within ten yards of me as I thundered through. "To me, comrades! To me!" I yelled. I heard a buzz as when the angry bees swarm from their nest. Then my splendid white Arab fell dead under me and I was hurled on to the cobble-stones of the yard, where I can remember no more.

Such was my last and most famous exploit, my dear friends, a story which rang through Europe and has made the name of Etienne Gerard famous in history. Alas! that all my efforts could only give the Emperor a few weeks more liberty, since he surrendered upon the 15th of July to the English. But it was not my fault that he was not able to collect the forces still waiting for him in France, and to fight another Waterloo with a happier ending. Had others been as loyal as I was the history of the world might have been changed, the Emperor would have preserved his throne, and such a soldier as I would not have been left to spend his life in planting cabbages or to while away his old age telling stories in a *café*. You ask me about the fate of Stein and the Prussian horseman! Of the three who dropped upon the way I know nothing. One you will remember that I killed. There remained five, three of whom were cut down by my Hussars, who, for the instant, were under the impression that it was indeed the Emperor whom they were defending. Stein was taken, slightly wounded, and so was one of the Uhlans. The truth was not told to them, for we thought it best that no news, or false news, should get about as to where the Emperor was, so that Count Stein still believed that he was within a few yards of making that tremendous capture. "You may well love and honour your Emperor," said he, "for such a horseman and such a swordsman I have never seen." He could not understand why the young colonel of Hussars laughed so heartily at his words — but he has learned since.

THE BRIGADIER IN ENGLAND

I have told you, my friends, how I triumphed over the English at the fox-hunt when I pursued the animal so fiercely that even the herd of trained dogs was unable to keep up, and alone with my own hand I put him to the sword. Perhaps I have said too much of the matter, but there is a thrill in the triumphs of sport which even warfare cannot give, for in warfare you share your successes with your regiment and your army, but in sport it is you yourself unaided who have won the laurels. It is an advantage which the English have over us that in all classes they take great interest in every form of sport. It may be that they are richer than we, or it may be that they are more idle; but I was surprised when I was a prisoner in that country to observe how widespread was this feeling, and how much it filled the minds and the lives of the people. A horse that will run, a cock that will fight, a dog that will kill rats, a man that will box—they would turn away from the Emperor in all his glory in order to look upon any of these.

I could tell you many stories of English sport, for I saw much of it during the time that I was the guest of Lord Rufton, after the order for my exchange had come to England. There were months before I could be sent back to France, and during that time I stayed with this good Lord Rufton at his beautiful house of High Combe, which is at the northern end of Dartmoor. He had ridden with the police when they had pursued me from Princetown, and he had felt towards me when I was overtaken as I would myself have felt had I, in my own country, seen a brave and debonair soldier without a friend to help him. In a word he took me to his house, clad me, fed me, and treated me as if he had been my brother. I will say this of the English, that they were always generous enemies, and very good people with whom to fight. In the Peninsula the Spanish outposts would present their muskets at ours, but the British their brandy flasks. And of all these generous men there was none who was the equal of this admirable milord, who held out so warm a hand to an enemy in distress.

Ah! what thoughts of sport it brings back to me, the very name of High Combe! I can see it now, the long, low brick house, warm and ruddy, with white plaster pillars before the door. He was a great sportsman this Lord Rufton, and all who were about him were of the same sort. But you will be pleased to hear that there were few things in which I could not hold my own, and in some I excelled. Behind the house was a wood in which pheasants were reared, and it was Lord Rufton's joy to kill these birds, which was done by sending in men to drive them out while he and his friends stood outside and shot them as they passed. For my part I was more crafty, for I studied the habits of the bird, and stealing out in the evening I was able to kill a number of them as they roosted in the trees. Hardly a single shot was wasted, but the keeper was attracted by the sound of the firing, and he implored me in his rough English fashion to spare those that were left. That night I was able to place twelve birds as a surprise upon Lord Rufton's supper table, and he laughed until he cried, so overjoyed was he to see them. "Gad, Gerard, you'll be the death of me yet!" he cried. Often he said the same thing, for at every turn I amazed him by the way in which I entered into the sports of the English.

There is a game called cricket which they play in the summer, and this also I learned. Rudd, the head gardener, was a famous player of cricket, and so was Lord Rufton himself. Before the house was a lawn, and here it was that Rudd taught me the game. It is a brave pastime, a game for soldiers, for each tries to strike the other with the ball, and it is but a small stick with which you may ward it off. Three sticks behind show the spot beyond which you may not retreat. I can tell you that it is no game for children, and I will confess that, in spite of my nine campaigns, I felt myself turn pale when first the ball flashed past me. So swift was it that I had not time to raise my stick to ward it off, but by good fortune it missed me and knocked down the wooden pins which marked the boundary. It was for Rudd then to defend himself and for me to attack. When I was a boy in Gascony I learned to throw both far and straight, so that I made sure that I could hit this gallant Englishman. With a shout I rushed forward and hurled the ball at him. It flew as swift as a bullet towards his ribs, but without a word he swung his staff and the ball rose a surprising distance in the air. Lord Rufton clapped his hands and cheered. Again the ball was brought to me, and again it was for me to throw. This time it flew past his head, and it seemed to me that it was his turn to look pale. But he was a brave man this gardener, and again he faced me. Ah, my friends, the hour of my triumph had come! It was a red waistcoat that he wore, and at this I hurled the ball. You would have said that I was a gunner, not a hussar, for never was so straight an aim. With a despairing cry—the cry of the brave man who is beaten—he fell upon the wooden pegs behind him, and they all rolled upon the ground together. He was cruel, this English milord, and he laughed so that he could not come to the aid of his servant. It was for me, the victor, to rush forwards to embrace this intrepid player, and to raise him to his feet with words of praise, and encouragement, and hope. He was in pain and could not stand erect, yet the honest fellow confessed that there was no accident in my victory. "He did it a-purpose! He did it a-purpose!" Again and again he said it. Yes, it is a great game this cricket, and I would gladly have ventured upon it again but Lord Rufton and Rudd said that it was late in the season, and so they would play no more.

How foolish of me, the old broken man, to dwell upon these successes, and yet I will confess that my age has been very much soothed and comforted by the memory of the women who have loved me and the men whom I have overcome. It is pleasant to

think that five years afterwards, when Lord Rufton came to Paris
after the peace, he was able to assure me that my name was still a
famous one in the North of Devonshire for the fine exploits that I
had performed. Especially, he said, that they still talked over my
boxing match with the Honourable Baldock. It came about in this
way. Of an evening many sportsmen would assemble at the house
of Lord Rufton, where they would drink much wine, make wild
bets, and talk of their horses and their foxes. How well I remember those strange creatures. Sir Barrington, Jack Lupton of
Barnstaple, Colonel Addison, Johnny Miller, Lord Sadler, and my
enemy the Honourable Baldock. They were of the same stamp all
of them, drinkers, madcaps, fighters, gamblers, full of strange
caprices and extraordinary whims. Yet they were kindly fellows in
their rough fashion, save only this Baldock, a fat man who prided
himself on his skill at the box-fight. It was he who, by his laughter
against the French because they were ignorant of sport, caused me
to challenge him in the very sport at which he excelled. You will
say that it was foolish, my friends, but the decanter had passed
many times, and the blood of youth ran hot in my veins. I would
fight him, this boaster; I would show him that if we had not skill at
least we had courage. Lord Rufton would not allow it. I insisted.
The others cheered me on and slapped me on the back. "No, dash
it, Baldock, he's our guest," said Rufton. "It's his own doing," the
other answered. "Look here, Rufton, they can't hurt each other if
they wear the mawleys," cried Lord Sadler. And so it was agreed.

What the mawleys were I did not know, but presently they
brought out four great puddings of leather, not unlike a fencing
glove, but larger. With these our hands were covered after we had
stripped ourselves of our coats and our waistcoats. Then the table,
with the glasses and decanters, was pushed into the corner of the
room, and behold us, face to face! Lord Sadler sat in the arm-chair
with a watch in his open hand. "Time!" said he.

I will confess to you, my friends, that I felt at that moment a
tremor such as none of my many duels have ever given me. With
sword or pistol I am at home, but here I only understood that I

must struggle with this fat Englishman and do what I could, in spite of these great puddings upon my hands, to overcome him. And at the very outset I was disarmed of the best weapon that was left to me. "Mind, Gerard, no kicking!" said Lord Rufton in my ear. I had only a pair of thin dancing slippers, and yet the man was fat, and a few well-directed kicks might have left me the victor. But there is an etiquette just as there is in fencing, and I refrained. I looked at this Englishman and I wondered how I should attack him. His ears were large and prominent. Could I seize them I might drag him to the ground. I rushed in, but I was betrayed by this flabby glove, and twice I lost my hold. He struck me, but I cared little for his blows, and again I seized him by the ear. He fell, and I rolled upon him and thumped his head upon the ground. How they cheered and laughed, these gallant Englishmen, and how they clapped me on the back!

"Even money on the Frenchman," cried Lord Sadler.

"He fights foul," cried my enemy, rubbing his crimson ears. "He savaged me on the ground."

"You must take your chance of that," said Lord Rufton, coldly.

"Time," cried Lord Sadler, and once again we advanced to the assault.

He was flushed, and his small eyes were as vicious as those of a bulldog. There was hatred on his face. For my part I carried myself lightly and gaily. A French gentleman fights but he does not hate. I drew myself up before him, and I bowed as I have done in the duello. There can be grace and courtesy as well as defiance in a bow; I put all three into this one, with a touch of ridicule in the shrug which accompanied it. It was at this moment that he struck me. The room spun round me. I fell upon my back. But in an instant I was on my feet again and had rushed to a close combat. His ear, his hair, his nose, I seized them each in turn. Once again the mad joy of the battle was in my veins. The old cry of triumph rose to my lips. "Vive l'Empereur!" I yelled as I drove my head into his stomach. He threw his arm round my neck, and holding me with one hand he struck me with the other. I buried my teeth in his arm, and he shouted with pain. "Call him off, Rufton!" he screamed. "Call him off, man! He's worrying me!" They dragged me away from him. Can I ever forget it? — the laughter, the cheering, the congratulations! Even my enemy bore me no ill will, for he shook me by the hand. For my part I embraced him on each cheek. Five years afterwards I learned from Lord Rufton that my noble bearing upon that evening was still fresh in the memory of my English friends.

It is not, however, of my own exploits in sport that I wish to speak to you to-night, but it is of the Lady Jane Dacre and the strange adventure of which she was the cause. Lady Jane Dacre was Lord Rufton's sister and the lady of his household. I fear that until I came it was lonely for her, since she was a beautiful and refined woman with nothing in common with those who were about her. Indeed, this might be said of many women in the England of those days, for the men were rude and rough and coarse, with boorish habits and few accomplishments, while the women were the most lovely and tender that I have ever known. We became great friends, the Lady Jane and I, for it was not possible for me to drink three bottles of port after dinner like those Devonshire gentlemen, and so I would seek refuge in her drawing-room, where evening after evening she would play the harpsichord and I would sing the songs of my own land. In those peaceful moments I would find a refuge from the misery which filled me, when I reflected that my regiment was left in the front of the enemy without the chief whom they had learned to love and to follow. Indeed, I could have torn my hair when I read in the English papers of the fine fighting which was going on in Portugal and on the frontiers of Spain, all of which I had missed through my misfortune in falling into the hands of Milord Wellington.

From what I have told you of the Lady Jane you will have guessed what occurred, my friends. Etienne Gerard is thrown into the company of a young and beautiful woman. What must it mean for him? What must it mean for her? It was not for me, the guest, the captive, to make love to the sister of my host. But I was reserved. I was discreet. I tried to curb my own emotions and to discourage hers. For my own part I fear that I betrayed myself, for the eye becomes more eloquent when the tongue is silent. Every quiver of my fingers as I turned over her music-sheets told her my secret. But she — she was admirable. It is in these matters that women have a genius for deception. If I had not penetrated her secret I should often have thought she forgot even that I was in the house. For hours she would sit lost in a sweet melancholy, while I admired her pale face and her curls in the lamp-light, and thrilled within me to think that I had moved her so deeply. Then at last I would speak, and she would start in her chair and stare at me with the most admirable pretence of being surprised to find me in the room. Ah! how I longed to hurl myself suddenly at her feet, to kiss her white hand, to assure her that I had surprised her secret and that I would not abuse her confidence. But, no, I was not her equal, and I was under her roof as a castaway enemy. My lips were sealed. I endeavoured to imitate her own wonderful affectation of indifference, but, as you may think, I was eagerly alert for any opportunity of serving her.

One morning Lady Jane had driven in her phaeton to Okehampton, and I strolled along the road which led to that place in the hope that I might meet her on her return. It was the early winter, and banks of fading fern sloped down to the winding road. It is a bleak place this Dartmoor, wild and rocky — a country of wind and mist. I felt as I walked that it is no wonder Englishmen should suffer from the spleen. My own heart was heavy within me, and I sat upon a rock by the wayside looking out on the dreary view with my thoughts full of trouble and foreboding. Suddenly, however, as I glanced down the road I saw a sight which drove everything else from my mind, and caused me to leap to my feet with a cry of astonishment and anger.

Down the curve of the road a phaeton was coming, the pony tearing along at full gallop. Within was the very lady whom I had come to meet. She lashed at the pony like one who endeavours to escape from some pressing danger, glancing ever backwards over her shoulder. The bend of the road concealed from me what it was that had alarmed her, and I ran forward not knowing what to expect. The next instant I saw the pursuer, and my amazement was increased at the sight. It was a gentleman in the red coat of an English fox-hunter, mounted on a great grey horse. He was galloping as if in a race, and the long stride of the splendid creature beneath him soon brought him up to the lady's flying carriage. I saw him stoop and seize the reins of the pony, so as to bring it to a halt. The next instant he was deep in talk with the lady, he bending forward in his saddle and speaking eagerly, she shrinking away from him as if she feared and loathed him.

You may think, my dear friends, that this was not a sight at which I could calmly gaze. How my heart thrilled within me to think that a chance should have been given to me to serve the Lady Jane! I ran—oh, good Lord, how I ran! At last, breathless, speechless, I reached the phaeton. The man glanced up at me with his blue English eyes, but so deep was he in his talk that he paid no heed to me, nor did the lady say a word. She still leaned back, her beautiful pale face gazing up at him. He was a good-looking fellow—tall, and strong, and brown; a pang of jealousy seized me as I looked at him. He was talking low and fast, as the English do when they are in earnest.

"I tell you, Jinny, it's you and only you that I love," said he. "Don't bear malice, Jinny. Let bygones be bygones. Come now, say it's all over."

"No, never, George, never!" she cried.

A dusky red suffused his handsome face. The man was furious.

"Why can't you forgive me, Jinny?"

"I can't forget the past."

"By George, you must! I've asked enough. It's time to order now. I'll have my rights. D'ye hear?" His hand closed upon her wrist.

At last my breath had returned to me.

"Madame," I said, as I raised my hat, "do I intrude, or is there any possible way in which I can be of service to you?"

But neither of them minded me any more than if I had been a fly who buzzed between them. Their eyes were locked together.

"I'll have my rights, I tell you. I've waited long enough."

"There's no use bullying, George."

"Do you give in?"

"No, never!"

"Is that your final answer?"

"Yes, it is."

He gave a bitter curse and threw down her hand.

"All right, my lady, we'll see about this."

"Excuse me, sir," said I, with dignity.

"Oh, go to blazes!" he cried, turning on me with his furious face. The next instant he had spurred his horse and was galloping down the road once more.

Lady Jane gazed after him until he was out of sight, and I was surprised to see that her face wore a smile and not a frown. Then she turned to me and held out her hand.

"You are very kind, Colonel Gerard. You meant well, I am sure."

"Madame," said I, "if you can oblige me with the gentleman's name and address I will arrange that he shall never trouble you again."

"No scandal, I beg of you," she cried.

"Madame, I could not so far forget myself. Rest assured that no lady's name would ever be mentioned by me in the course of such an incident. In bidding me to go to blazes this gentleman has relieved me from the embarrassment of having to invent a cause of quarrel."

"Colonel Gerard," said the lady, earnestly, "you must give me your word as a soldier and a gentleman that this matter goes no farther, and also that you will say nothing to my brother about what you have seen. Promise me!"

"If I must."

"I hold you to your word. Now drive with me to High Combe, and I will explain as we go."

The first words of her explanation went into me like a sabre-point.

"That gentleman," said she, "is my husband."

"Your husband!"

"You must have known that I was married." She seemed surprised at my agitation.

"I did not know."

"This is Lord George Dacre. We have been married two years. There is no need to tell you how he wronged me. I left him and sought a refuge under my brother's roof. Up till to-day he has left me there unmolested. What I must above all things avoid is the chance of a duel betwixt my husband and my brother. It is horrible to think of. For this reason Lord Rufton must know nothing of this chance meeting of to-day."

"If my pistol could free you from this annoyance—"

"No, no, it is not to be thought of. Remember your promise, Colonel Gerard. And not a word at High Combe of what you have seen!"

Her husband! I had pictured in my mind that she was a young widow. This brown-faced brute with his "go to blazes" was the husband of this tender dove of a woman. Oh, if she would but allow me to free her from so odious an encumbrance! There is no divorce so quick and certain as that which I could give her. But a promise is a promise, and I kept it to the letter. My mouth was sealed. In a week I was to be sent back from Plymouth to St Malo, and it seemed to me that I might never hear the sequel of the story. And yet it was destined that it should have a sequel and that I should play a very pleasing and honourable part in it.

It was only three days after the event which I have described when Lord Rufton burst hurriedly into my room. His face was pale and his manner that of a man in extreme agitation.

"Gerard," he cried, "have you seen Lady Jane Dacre?"

I had seen her after breakfast and it was now midday.

"By Heaven, there's villainy here!" cried my poor friend, rushing about like a madman. "The bailiff has been up to say that a chaise and pair were seen driving full split down the Tavistock Road. The blacksmith heard a woman scream as it passed his forge. Jane has disappeared. By the Lord, I believe that she has been kidnapped by this villain Dacre." He rang the bell furiously. "Two horses this instant!" he cried. "Colonel Gerard, your pistols! Jane comes back with me this night from Gravel Hanger or there will be a new master in High Combe Hall."

Behold us then within half an hour, like two knight-errants of old, riding forth to the rescue of this lady in distress. It was near Tavistock that Lord Dacre lived, and at every house and toll-gate along the road we heard the news of the flying post-chaise in front of us, so there could be no doubt whither they were bound. As we rode Lord Rufton told me of the man whom we were pursuing. His name, it seems, was a household word throughout all England for every sort of mischief. Wine, women, dice, cards, racing—in all forms of debauchery he had earned for himself a terrible name. He was of an old and noble family, and it had been hoped that he had sowed his wild oats when he married the beautiful Lady Jane Rufton. For some months he had indeed behaved well, and then he had wounded her feelings in their most tender part by some unworthy liaison. She had fled from his house and taken refuge with her brother, from whose care she had now been dragged once more, against her will. I ask you if two men could have had a fairer errand than that upon which Lord Rufton and myself were riding?

"That's Gravel Hanger," he cried at last, pointing with his crop, and there on the green side of a hill was an old brick and timber building as beautiful as only an English country house can be. "There's an inn by the park-gate, and there we shall leave our horses," he added.

For my own part it seemed to me that with so just a cause we should have done best to ride boldly up to his door and summon him to surrender the lady. But there I was wrong. For the one thing which every Englishman fears is the law. He makes it himself, and when he has once made it it becomes a terrible tyrant before whom the bravest quails. He will smile at breaking his neck, but he will turn pale at breaking the law. It seems, then, from what Lord Rufton told me as we walked through the park, that we were on the wrong side of the law in this matter. Lord Dacre was in the right in carrying off his wife, since she did indeed belong to him, and our own position now was nothing better than that of burglars and trespassers. It was not for burglars to openly approach the front door. We could take the lady by force or by craft, but we could not take her by right, for the law was against us. This was what my friend explained to me as we crept up towards the shelter of a shrubbery which was close to the windows of the house. Thence we could examine this fortress, see whether we could effect a lodgment in it, and, above all, try to establish some communication with the beautiful prisoner inside.

There we were, then, in the shrubbery, Lord Rufton and I, each with a pistol in the pockets of our riding coats, and with the most resolute determination in our hearts that we should not return without the lady. Eagerly we scanned every window of the wide-spread house. Not a sign could we see of the prisoner or of anyone else; but on the gravel drive outside the door were the deep-sunk marks of the wheels of the chaise. There was no doubt that they had arrived. Crouching among the laurel bushes we held a whispered council of war, but a singular interruption brought it to an end.

Out of the door of the house there stepped a tall, flaxen-haired man, such a figure as one would choose for the flank of a Grenadier company. As he turned his brown face and his blue eyes towards us I recognised Lord Dacre. With long strides he came down the gravel path straight for the spot where we lay.

"Come out, Ned!" he shouted; "you'll have the game-keeper putting a charge of shot into you. Come out, man, and don't skulk behind the bushes."

It was not a very heroic situation for us. My poor friend rose with a crimson face. I sprang to my feet also and bowed with such dignity as I could muster.

"Halloa! it's the Frenchman, is it?" said he, without returning my bow. "I've got a crow to pluck with him already. As to you, Ned, I knew you would be hot on our scent, and so I was looking out for you. I saw you cross the park and go to ground in the shrubbery. Come in, man, and let us have all the cards on the table."

He seemed master of the situation, this handsome giant of a man, standing at his ease on his own ground while we slunk out of our hiding-place. Lord Rufton had said not a word, but I saw by his darkened brow and his sombre eyes that the storm was gathering. Lord Dacre led the way into the house, and we followed close at his heels. He ushered us himself into an oak-panelled sitting-room, closing the door behind us. Then he looked me up and down with insolent eyes.

"Look here, Ned," said he, "time was when an English family could settle their own affairs in their own way. What has this foreign fellow got to do with your sister and my wife?"

"Sir," said I, "permit me to point out to you that this is not a case merely of a sister or a wife, but that I am the friend of the lady in question, and that I have the privilege which every gentleman possesses of protecting a woman against brutality. It is only by a gesture that I can show you what I think of you." I had my riding glove in my hand, and I flicked him across the face with it. He drew back with a bitter smile and his eyes were as hard as flint.

"So you've brought your bully with you, Ned?" said he. "You might at least have done your fighting yourself, if it must come to a fight."

"So I will," cried Lord Rufton. "Here and now."

"When I've killed this swaggering Frenchman," said Lord Dacre. He stepped to a side table and opened a brass-bound case. "By Gad," said he, "either that man or I go out of this room feet foremost. I meant well by you, Ned; I did, by George, but I'll shoot this led-captain of yours as sure as my name's George Dacre. Take your choice of pistols, sir, and shoot across this table. The barkers are loaded. Aim straight and kill me if you can, for by the Lord, if you don't, you're done."

In vain Lord Rufton tried to take the quarrel upon himself. Two things were clear in my mind—one that the Lady Jane had feared above all things that her husband and brother should fight, the other that if I could but kill this big milord, then the whole question would be settled for ever in the best way. Lord Rufton did not want him. Lady Jane did not want him. Therefore, I, Etienne Gerard, their friend, would pay the debt of gratitude which I owed them by freeing them of this encumbrance. But, indeed, there was no choice in the matter, for Lord Dacre was as eager to put a bullet into me as I could be to do the same service to him. In vain Lord Rufton argued and scolded. The affair must continue.

"Well, if you must fight my guest instead of myself, let it be to-morrow morning with two witnesses," he cried, at last; "this is sheer murder across the table."

"But it suits my humour, Ned," said Lord Dacre.

"And mine, sir," said I.

"Then I'll have nothing to do with it," cried Lord Rufton. "I tell you, George, if you shoot Colonel Gerard under these circumstances you'll find yourself in the dock instead of on the bench. I won't act as second, and that's flat."

"Sir," said I, "I am perfectly prepared to proceed without a second."

"That won't do. It's against the law," cried Lord Dacre. "Come, Ned, don't be a fool. You see we mean to fight. Hang it, man, all I want you to do is to drop a handkerchief."

"I'll take no part in it."

"Then I must find someone who will," said Lord Dacre. He threw a cloth over the pistols, which lay upon the table, and he rang the bell. A footman entered. "Ask Colonel Berkeley if he will step this way. You will find him in the billiard-room."

A moment later there entered a tall thin Englishman with a great moustache, which was a rare thing amid that cleanshaven race. I have heard since that they were worn only by the Guards and the Hussars. This Colonel Berkeley was a guardsman. He seemed a strange, tired, languid, drawling creature with a long black cigar thrusting out, like a pole from a bush, amidst that immense moustache. He looked from one to the other of us with true English phlegm, and he betrayed not the slightest surprise when he was told our intention.

"Quite so," said he; "quite so."

"I refuse to act, Colonel Berkeley," cried Lord Rufton.

"Remember, this duel cannot proceed without you, and I hold you personally responsible for anything that happens."

This Colonel Berkeley appeared to be an authority upon the question, for he removed the cigar from his mouth and he laid down the law in his strange, drawling voice.

"The circumstances are unusual but not irregular, Lord Rufton," said he. "This gentleman has given a blow and this other gentleman has received it. That is a clear issue. Time and conditions depend upon the person who demands satisfaction. Very good. He claims it here and now, across the table. He is acting within his rights. I am prepared to accept the responsibility."

There was nothing more to be said. Lord Rufton sat moodily in the corner with his brows drawn down and his hands thrust deep into the pockets of his riding breeches. Colonel Berkeley examined the two pistols and laid them both in the centre of the table. Lord Dacre was at one end and I at the other, with eight feet of shining mahogany between us. On the hearth-rug, with his back to the fire, stood the tall colonel, his handkerchief in his left hand, his cigar between two fingers of his right.

"When I drop the handkerchief," said he, "you will pick up your pistols and you will fire at your own convenience. Are you ready?"

"Yes," we cried.

His hand opened and the handkerchief fell. I bent swiftly forward and seized a pistol, but the table, as I have said, was eight feet across, and it was easier for this long-armed milord to reach the pistols than it was for me. I had not yet drawn myself straight before he fired, and to this it was that I owe my life. His bullet would have blown out my brains had I been erect. As it was it whistled through my curls. At the same instant, just as I threw up my own pistol to fire, the door flew open and a pair of arms were thrown round me. It was the beautiful, flushed, frantic face of Lady Jane which looked up into mine.

"You sha'n't fire! Colonel Gerard, for my sake don't fire," she cried. "It is a mistake, I tell you, a mistake, a mistake! He is the best and dearest of husbands. Never again shall I leave his side." Her hands slid down my arm and closed upon my pistol.

"Jane, Jane," cried Lord Rufton; "come with me. You should not be here. Come away."

"It is all confoundedly irregular," said Colonel Berkeley.

"Colonel Gerard, you won't fire, will you? My heart would break if he were hurt."

"Hang it all, Jinny, give the fellow fair play," cried Lord Dacre. "He stood my fire like a man, and I won't see him interfered with. Whatever happens I can't get worse than I deserve."

But already there had passed between me and the lady a quick glance of the eyes which told her everything. Her hands slipped from my arm. "I leave my husband's life and my own happiness to Colonel Gerard," said she.

How well she knew me, this admirable woman! I stood for an instant irresolute, with the pistol cocked in my hand. My antagonist faced me bravely, with no blenching of his sunburnt face and no flinching of his bold, blue eyes.

"Come, come, sir, take your shot!" cried the colonel from the mat.

"Let us have it, then," said Lord Dacre.

I would, at least, show them how completely his life was at the mercy of my skill. So much I owed to my own self-respect. I glanced round for a mark. The colonel was looking towards my antagonist, expecting to see him drop. His face was sideways to me, his long cigar projecting from his lips with an inch of ash at the end of it. Quick as a flash I raised my pistol and fired.

"Permit me to trim your ash, sir," said I, and I bowed with a grace which is unknown among these islanders.

I am convinced that the fault lay with the pistol and not with my aim. I could hardly believe my own eyes when I saw that I had snapped off the cigar within half an inch of his lips. He stood staring at me with the ragged stub of the cigar-end sticking out from his singed moustache. I can see him now with his foolish, angry eyes and his long, thin, puzzled face. Then he began to talk. I have always said that the English are not really a phlegmatic or a taciturn nation if you stir them out of their groove. No one could have talked in a more animated way than this colonel. Lady Jane put her hands over her ears.

"Come, come, Colonel Berkeley," said Lord Dacre, sternly, "you forget yourself. There is a lady in the room."

The colonel gave a stiff bow.

"If Lady Dacre will kindly leave the room," said he, "I will be able to tell this infernal little Frenchman what I think of him and his monkey tricks."

I was splendid at that moment, for I ignored the words that he had said and remembered only the extreme provocation.

"Sir," said I, "I freely offer you my apologies for this unhappy incident. I felt that if I did not discharge my pistol Lord Dacre's honour might feel hurt, and yet it was quite impossible for me, after hearing what this lady had said, to aim it at her husband. I looked round for a mark, therefore, and I had the extreme misfortune to blow your cigar out of your mouth when my intention had merely been to snuff the ash. I was betrayed by my pistol. This is my explanation, sir, and if after listening to my apologies you still feel that I owe you satisfaction, I need not say that it is a request which I am unable to refuse."

It was certainly a charming attitude which I had assumed, and it won the hearts of all of them. Lord Dacre stepped forward and wrung me by the hand. "By George, sir," said he, "I never thought to feel towards a Frenchman as I do to you. You're a man and a gentleman, and I can't say more." Lord Rufton said nothing, but his hand-grip told me all that he thought. Even Colonel Berkeley paid me a compliment, and declared that he would think no more about the unfortunate cigar. And she—ah, if you could have seen the look she gave me, the flushed cheek, the moist eye, the tremulous lip! When I think of my beautiful Lady Jane it is at that moment that I recall her. They would have had me stay to dinner, but you will understand, my friends, that this was no time for either Lord Rufton or myself to remain at Gravel Hanger. This reconciled couple desired only to be alone. In the chaise he had persuaded her of his sincere repentance, and once again they were a loving husband and wife. If they were to remain so it was best perhaps that I should go. Why should I unsettle this domestic peace? Even against my own will my mere presence and appearance might have their effect upon the lady. No, no, I must tear myself away—even her persuasions were unable to make me stop. Years afterwards I heard that the household of the Dacres was among the happiest in the whole country, and that no cloud had ever come again to darken their lives. Yet I dare say if he could have seen into his wife's mind—but there, I say no more! A lady's secret is her own, and I fear that she and it are buried long years ago in some Devonshire churchyard. Perhaps all that gay circle are gone and the Lady Jane only lives now in the memory of an old half-pay French brigadier. He at least can never forget.

HOW THE BRIGADIER JOINED
THE HUSSARS OF CONFLANS

HAVE I ever told you, my friends, the circumstances connected with my joining the Hussars of Conflans at the time of the siege of Saragossa and the very remarkable exploit which I performed in connection with the taking of that city? No? Then you have indeed something still to learn. I will tell it to you exactly as it occurred. Save for two or three men and a score or two of women, you are the first who have ever heard the story.

You must know, then, that it was in the 2nd Hussars—called the Hussars of Chamberan—that I had served as a lieutenant and as a junior captain. At the time I speak of I was only twenty-five years of age, as reckless and desperate a man as any in that great army. It chanced that the war had come to a halt in Germany, while it was still raging in Spain, so the Emperor, wishing to reinforce the Spanish army, transferred me as senior captain to the Hussars of Conflans, which were at that time in the 5th Army Corps under Marshal Lannes.

It was a long journey from Berlin to the Pyrenees. My new regiment formed part of the force which, under Marshal Lannes, was then besieging the Spanish town of Saragossa. I turned my horse's head in that direction, therefore, and behold me a week or so later at the French head-quarters, whence I was directed to the camp of the Hussars of Conflans.

You have read, no doubt, of this famous siege of Saragossa, and I will only say that no general could have had a harder task than that with which Marshal Lannes was confronted. The immense city was crowded with a horde of Spaniards—soldiers, peasants, priests—all filled with the most furious hatred of the French, and the most savage determination to perish before they would surrender. There were eighty thousand men in the town and only thirty thousand to besiege them. Yet we had a powerful artillery, and our Engineers were of the best. There was never such a siege, for it is usual that when the fortifications are taken the city falls, but here it was not until the fortifications were taken that the real fighting began. Every house was a fort and every street a battlefield, so that slowly, day by day, we had to work our way inwards, blowing up the houses with their garrisons until more than half the city had disappeared. Yet the other half was as determined as ever and in a better position for defence, since it consisted of enormous convents and monasteries with walls like the Bastille, which could not be so easily brushed out of our way. This was the state of things at the time that I joined the army.

I will confess to you that cavalry are not of much use in a siege, although there was a time when I would not have permitted anyone to have made such an observation. The Hussars of Conflans were encamped to the south of the town, and it was their duty to throw out patrols and to make sure that no Spanish force was advancing from that quarter. The colonel of the regiment was not a good soldier, and the regiment was at that time very far from being in the high condition which it afterwards attained. Even in that one evening I saw several things which shocked me, for I had a high standard, and it went to my heart to see an ill-arranged camp, an ill-groomed horse, or a slovenly trooper. That night I supped with twenty-six of my new brother-officers, and I fear that in my zeal I showed them only too plainly that I found things very different to what I was accustomed in the army of Germany. There was silence in the mess after my remarks, and I felt that I had been indiscreet when I saw the glances that were cast at me. The colonel especially was furious, and a great major named Olivier, who was the fire-eater of the regiment, sat opposite to me curling his huge black moustaches, and staring at me as if he would eat me.

However, I did not resent his attitude, for I felt that I had indeed been indiscreet, and that it would give a bad impression if upon this my first evening I quarrelled with my superior officer.

So far I admit that I was wrong, but now I come to the sequel. Supper over, the colonel and some other officers left the room, for it was in a farmhouse that the mess was held. There remained a dozen or so, and a goat-skin of Spanish wine having been brought in we all made merry. Presently this Major Olivier asked me some questions concerning the army of Germany and as to the part which I had myself played in the campaign. Flushed with the wine, I was drawn on from story to story. It was not unnatural, my friends. You will sympathize with me. Up there I had been the model for every officer of my years in the army. I was the first swordsman, the most dashing rider, the hero of a hundred adventures. Here I found myself not only unknown, but even disliked. Was it not natural that I should wish to tell these brave comrades what sort of man it was that had come among them? Was it not natural that I should wish to say, "Rejoice, my friends, rejoice! It is no ordinary man who has joined you to-night, but it is I, *the* Gerard, the hero of Ratisbon, the victor of Jena, the man who broke the square at Austerlitz"? I could not say all this. But I could at least tell them some incidents which would enable them to say it for themselves. I did so. They listened unmoved. I told them more. At last, after my tale of how I had guided the army across the Danube, one universal shout of laughter broke from them all. I sprang to my feet, flushed with shame and anger. They had drawn me on. They were making game of me. They were convinced that they had to do with a braggart and a liar. Was this my reception in the Hussars of Conflans? I dashed the tears of mortification from my eyes, and they laughed the more at the sight.

"Do you know, Captain Pelletan, whether Marshal Lannes is still with the army?" asked the major.

"I believe that he is, sir," said the other.

"Really, I should have thought that his presence was hardly necessary now that Captain Gerard has arrived."

Again there was a roar of laughter. I can see the ring of faces, the mocking eyes, the open mouths—Olivier with his great black bristles, Pelletan thin and sneering, even the young sub-lieutenants convulsed with merriment. Heavens, the indignity of it! But my rage had dried my tears. I was myself again, cold, quiet, self-contained, ice without and fire within.

"May I ask, sir," said I to the major, "at what hour the regiment is paraded?"

"I trust, Captain Gerard, that you do not mean to alter our hours," said he, and again there was a burst of laughter, which died away as I looked slowly round the circle.

"What hour is the assembly?" I asked, sharply, of Captain Pelletan. Some mocking answer was on his tongue, but my glance kept it there. "The assembly is at six," he answered.

"I thank you," said I. I then counted the company and found that I had to do with fourteen officers, two of whom appeared to be boys fresh from St Cyr. I could not condescend to take any notice of their indiscretion. There remained the major, four captains, and seven lieutenants.

"Gentlemen," I continued, looking from one to the other of them, "I should feel myself unworthy of this famous regiment if I did not ask you for satisfaction for the rudeness with which you have greeted me, and I should hold you to be unworthy of it if on any pretext you refused to grant it."

"You will have no difficulty upon that score," said the major. "I am prepared to waive my rank and to give you every satisfaction in the name of the Hussars of Conflans."

"I thank you," I answered. "I feel, however, that I have some claim upon these other gentlemen who laughed at my expense."

"Whom would you fight, then?" asked Captain Pelletan.

"All of you," I answered.

They looked in surprise from one to the other. Then they drew off to the other end of the room, and I heard the buzz of their whispers. They were laughing. Evidently they still thought that they had to do with some empty braggart. Then they returned.

"Your request is unusual," said Major Olivier, "but it will be granted. How do you propose to conduct such a duel? The terms lie with you."

"Sabres," said I. "And I will take you in order of seniority, beginning with you, Major Olivier, at five o'clock. I will thus be able to devote five minutes to each before the assembly is blown. I must, however, beg you to have the courtesy to name the place of meeting, since I am still ignorant of the locality."

They were impressed by my cold and practical manner. Already the smile had died away from their lips. Olivier's face was no longer mocking, but it was dark and stern.

"There is a small open space behind the horse lines," said he. "We have held a few affairs of honour there and it has done very well. We shall be there, Captain Gerard, at the hour you name."

I was in the act of bowing to thank them for their acceptance when the door of the mess-room was flung open and the colonel hurried into the room, with an agitated face.

"Gentlemen," said he, "I have been asked to call for a volunteer from among you for a service which involves the greatest possible danger. I will not disguise from you that the matter is serious in the last degree, and that Marshal Lannes has chosen a cavalry officer because he can be better spared than an officer of infantry or of Engineers. Married men are not eligible. Of the others, who will volunteer?"

I need not say that all the unmarried officers stepped to the front. The colonel looked round in some embarrassment. I could see his dilemma. It was the best man who should go, and yet it was the best man whom he could least spare.

"Sir," said I, "may I be permitted to make a suggestion?"

He looked at me with a hard eye. He had not forgotten my observations at supper. "Speak!" said he.

"I would point out, sir," said I, "that this mission is mine both by right and by convenience."

"Why so, Captain Gerard?"

"By right because I am the senior captain. By convenience because I shall not be missed in the regiment, since the men have not yet learned to know me."

The colonel's features relaxed.

"There is certainly truth in what you say, Captain Gerard," said he. "I think that you are indeed best fitted to go upon this mission. If you will come with me I will give you your instructions."

I wished my new comrades good-night as I left the room, and I repeated that I should hold myself at their disposal at five o'clock next morning. They bowed in silence, and I thought that I could see from the expression of their faces that they had already begun to take a more just view of my character.

I had expected that the colonel would at once inform me what it was that I had been chosen to do, but instead of that he walked on in silence, I following behind him. We passed through the camp and made our way across the trenches and over the ruined heaps of stones which marked the old wall of the town. Within there was a labyrinth of passages formed among the *débris* of the houses which had been destroyed by the mines of the Engineers. Acres and acres were covered with splintered walls and piles of brick which had once been a populous suburb. Lanes had been driven through it and lanterns placed at the corners with inscriptions to direct the wayfarer. The colonel hurried onwards until at last, after a long walk, we found our way barred by a high grey wall which stretched right across our path. Here behind a barricade lay our advanced guard. The colonel led me into a roofless house, and there I found two general officers, a map stretched over a drum in front of them, they kneeling beside it and examining it carefully by the light of a lantern. The one with the clean-shaven face and the twisted neck was Marshal Lannes, the other was General Razout, the head of the Engineers.

"Captain Gerard has volunteered to go," said the colonel.

Marshal Lannes rose from his knees and shook me by the hand.

"You are a brave man, sir," said he. "I have a present to make to you," he added, handing me a very tiny glass tube. "It has been specially prepared by Dr Fardet. At the supreme moment you have but to put it to your lips and you will be dead in an instant."

This was a cheerful beginning. I will confess to you, my friends, that a cold chill passed up my back and my hair rose upon my head.

"Excuse me, sir," said I, as I saluted, "I am aware that I have volunteered for a service of great danger, but the exact details have not yet been given to me."

"Colonel Perrin," said Lannes, severely, "it is unfair to allow this brave officer to volunteer before he has learned what the perils are to which he will be exposed."

But already I was myself once more.

"Sir," said I, "permit me to remark that the greater the danger the greater the glory, and that I could only repent of volunteering if I found that there were no risks to be run."

It was a noble speech, and my appearance gave force to my words. For the moment I was a heroic figure. As I saw Lannes's eyes fixed in admiration upon my face it thrilled me to think how splendid was the *début* which I was making in the army of Spain. If I died that night my name would not be forgotten. My new comrades and my old, divided in all else, would still have a point of union in their love and admiration of Etienne Gerard.

"General Razout, explain the situation!" said Lannes, briefly.

The Engineer officer rose, his compasses in his hand. He led me to the door and pointed to the high grey wall which towered up amongst the *débris* of the shattered houses.

"That is the enemy's present line of defence," said he. "It is the wall of the great Convent of the Madonna. If we can carry it the city must fall, but they have run countermines all round it, and the walls are so enormously thick that it would be an immense labour to breach it with artillery. We happen to know, however, that the enemy have a considerable store of powder in one of the lower chambers. If that could be exploded the way would be clear for us."

"How can it be reached?" I asked.

"I will explain. We have a French agent within the town named Hubert. This brave man has been in constant communication with us, and he had promised to explode the magazine. It was to be done in the early morning, and for two days running we have had a storming party of a thousand Grenadiers waiting for the breach to be formed. But there has been no explosion, and for these two days we have had no communication from Hubert. The question is, what has become of him?"

"You wish me to go and see?"

"Precisely. Is he ill, or wounded, or dead? Shall we still wait for him, or shall we attempt the attack elsewhere? We cannot determine this until we have heard from him. This is a map of the town, Captain Gerard. You perceive that within this ring of convents and monasteries are a number of streets which branch off from a central square. If you come so far as this square you will find the cathedral at one corner. In that corner is the Street of Toledo. Hubert lives in a small house between a cobbler's and a wine-shop, on the right-hand side as you go from the cathedral. Do you follow me?"

"Clearly."

"You are to reach that house, to see him, and to find out if his plan is still feasible or if we must abandon it." He produced what appeared to be a roll of dirty brown flannel. "This is the dress of a Franciscan friar," said he. "You will find it the most useful disguise."

I shrank away from it.

"It turns me into a spy," I cried. "Surely I can go in my uniform?"

"Impossible! How could you hope to pass through the streets of the city? Remember, also, that the Spaniards take no prisoners, and that your fate will be the same in whatever dress you are taken."

It was true, and I had been long enough in Spain to know that that fate was likely to be something more serious than mere death. All the way from the frontier I had heard grim tales of torture and mutilation. I enveloped myself in the Franciscan gown.

"Now I am ready."

"Are you armed?"

"My sabre."

"They will hear it clank. Take this knife and leave your sword. Tell Hubert that at four o'clock before dawn the storming party will again be ready. There is a sergeant outside who will show you how to get into the city. Good-night and good luck!"

Before I had left the room the two generals had their cocked hats touching each other over the map. At the door an under-officer of Engineers was waiting for me. I tied the girdle of my gown, and taking off my busby I drew the cowl over my head. My spurs I removed. Then in silence I followed my guide.

It was necessary to move with caution, for the walls above were lined by the Spanish sentries, who fired down continually at our advance posts. Slinking along under the very shadow of the great convent, we picked our way slowly and carefully among the piles of ruins until we came to a large chestnut tree. Here the sergeant stopped.

"It is an easy tree to climb," said he. "A scaling ladder would not be simpler. Go up it, and you will find that the top branch will enable you to step upon the roof of that house. After that it is your guardian angel who must be your guide, for I can help you no more."

Girding up the heavy brown gown I ascended the tree as directed. A half moon was shining brightly, and the line of roof stood out dark and hard against the purple, starry sky. The tree was in the shadow of the house. Slowly I crept from branch to branch until I was near the top. I had but to climb along a stout limb in order to reach the wall. But suddenly my ears caught the patter of feet, and I cowered against the trunk and tried to blend myself with its shadow. A man was coming towards me on the roof. I saw his dark figure creeping along, his body crouching, his head advanced, the barrel of his gun protruding. His whole bearing was full of caution and suspicion. Once or twice he paused, and then came on again until he had reached the edge of the parapet within a few yards of me. Then he knelt down, levelled his musket, and fired.

I was so astonished at this sudden crash at my very elbow that I nearly fell out of the tree. For an instant I could not be sure that he had not hit me. But when I heard a deep groan from below, and the Spaniard leaned over the parapet and laughed aloud, I understood what had occurred. It was my poor, faithful sergeant who had waited to see the last of me. The Spaniard had seen him standing under the tree and had shot him. You will think that it was good shooting in the dark, but these people used trebucos, or blunderbusses, which were filled up with all sorts of stones and scraps of metal, so that they would hit you as certainly as I have hit a pheasant on a branch. The Spaniard stood peering down through the darkness, while an occasional groan from below showed that the sergeant was still living. The sentry looked round and everything was still and safe. Perhaps he thought that he would like to finish off this accursed Frenchman, or perhaps he had a desire to see what was in his pockets; but whatever his motive he laid down his gun, leaned forward, and swung himself into the tree. The same instant I buried my knife in his body, and he fell with a loud crashing through the branches and came with a thud to the ground. I heard a short struggle below and an oath or two in French. The wounded sergeant had not waited long for his vengeance.

For some minutes I did not dare to move, for it seemed certain that someone would be attracted by the noise. However, all was silent save for the chimes striking midnight in the city. I crept along the branch and lifted myself on to the roof. The Spaniard's gun was lying there, but it was of no service to me, since he had the powder-horn at his belt. At the same time, if it were found it would warn the enemy that something had happened, so I thought it best to drop it over the wall. Then I looked round for the means of getting off the roof and down into the city.

It was very evident that the simplest way by which I could get down was that by which the sentinel had got up, and what this was soon became evident. A voice along the roof called "Manuelo! Manuelo!" several times, and, crouching in the shadow, I saw in the moonlight a bearded head, which protruded from a trap-door. Receiving no answer to his summons the man climbed through, followed by three other fellows, all armed to the teeth. You will see here how important it is not to neglect small precautions, for had I left the man's gun where I found it a search must have followed and I should certainly have been discovered. As it was, the patrol saw no sign of their sentry and thought, no doubt, that he had moved along the line of the roofs. They hurried on, therefore, in that direction, and I, the instant that their backs were turned, rushed to the open trap-door and descended the flight of steps which led from it. The house appeared to be an empty one, for I passed through the heart of it and out, by an open door, into the street beyond.

It was a narrow and deserted lane, but it opened into a broader road, which was dotted with fires, round which a great number of soldiers and peasants were sleeping. The smell within the city was so horrible that one wondered how people could live in it, for during the months that the siege had lasted there had been no attempt to cleanse the streets or to bury the dead. Many people were moving up and down from fire to fire, and among them I observed several monks. Seeing that they came and went unquestioned, I took heart and hurried on my way in the direction of the great square. Once a man rose from beside one of the fires and stopped me by seizing my sleeve. He pointed to a woman who lay motionless on the road, and I took him to mean that she was dying, and that he desired me to administer the last offices of the Church. I sought refuge, however, in the very little Latin that was left to me. "Ora pro nobis," said I, from the depths of my cowl. "Te Deum laudamus. Ora pro nobis." I raised my hand as I spoke and pointed forwards. The fellow released my sleeve and shrank back in silence, while I, with a solemn gesture, hurried upon my way.

As I had imagined, this broad boulevard led out into the central square, which was full of troops and blazing with fires. I walked swiftly onwards, disregarding one or two people who addressed remarks to me. I passed the cathedral and followed the street which had been described to me. Being upon the side of the city which was farthest from our attack, there were no troops encamped in it, and it lay in darkness, save for an occasional glimmer in a window. It was not difficult to find the house to which I had been directed, between the wine-shop and the cobbler's. There was no light within and the door was shut. Cautiously I pressed the latch and I felt that it had yielded. Who was within I could not tell, and yet I must take the risk. I pushed the door open and entered.

It was pitch-dark within—the more so as I had closed the door behind me. I felt round and came upon the edge of a table. Then I stood still and wondered what I should do next and how I could gain some news of this Hubert, in whose house I found myself. Any mistake would cost me not only my life but the failure of my mission. Perhaps he did not live alone. Perhaps he was only a lodger in a Spanish family, and my visit might bring ruin to him as well as to myself. Seldom in my life have I been more perplexed. And then, suddenly, something turned my blood cold in my veins. It was a voice, a whispering voice, in my very ear. "Mon Dieu!" cried the voice in a tone of agony. "Oh, mon Dieu! mon Dieu!" Then there was a dry sob in the darkness and all was still once more.

It thrilled me with horror, that terrible voice, but it thrilled me also with hope, for it was the voice of a Frenchman.

"Who is there?" I asked.

There was a groaning, but no reply.

"Is that you, Monsieur Hubert?"

"Yes, yes," sighed the voice, so low that I could hardly hear it. "Water, water, for Heaven's sake, water!"

I advanced in the direction of the sound, but only to come in contact with the wall. Again I heard a groan, but this time there could be no doubt that it was above my head. I put up my hands, but they felt only empty air.

"Where are you?" I cried.

"Here! Here!" whispered the strange, tremulous voice. I stretched my hand along the wall and I came upon a man's naked foot. It was as high as my face and yet, so far as I could feel, it had nothing to support it. I staggered back in amazement. Then I took a tinder-box from my pocket and struck a light. At the first flash a man seemed, to be floating in the air in front of me, and I dropped the box in my amazement. Again with tremulous fingers I struck the flint against the steel, and this time I lit not only the tinder but the wax taper. I held it up, and if my amazement was lessened my horror was increased by that which it revealed.

The man had been nailed to the wall as a weasel is nailed to the door of a barn. Huge spikes had been driven through his hands and his feet. The poor wretch was in his last agony, his head sunk upon his shoulder and his blackened tongue protruding from his lips. He was dying as much from thirst as from his wounds, and these inhuman wretches had placed a beaker of wine upon the table in front of him to add a fresh pang to his tortures. I raised it to his lips. He had still strength enough to swallow, and the light came back a little to his dim eyes.

"Are you a Frenchman?" he whispered.

"Yes. They have sent me to learn what had befallen you."

"They discovered me. They have killed me for it. But before I die let me tell you what I know. A little more of that wine, please! Quick! Quick! I am very near the end. My strength is going. Listen to me! The powder is stored in the Mother Superior's room. The wall is pierced, and the end of the train is in Sister Angela's cell next the chapel. All was ready two days ago. But they discovered a letter and they tortured me."

"Good heavens! have you been hanging here for two days?"

"It seems like two years. Comrade, I have served France, have I not? Then do one little service for me. Stab me to the heart, dear friend! I implore you, I entreat you to put an end to my sufferings."

The man was indeed in a hopeless plight, and the kindest action would have been that for which he begged. And yet I could not in cold blood drive my knife into his body, although I knew how I should have prayed for such a mercy had I been in his place. But a sudden thought crossed my mind. In my pocket I held that which would give an instant and a painless death. It was my own safeguard against torture, and yet this poor soul was in very pressing need of it, and he had deserved well of France. I took out my phial and emptied it into the cup of wine. I was in the act of handing it to him when I heard a sudden clash of arms outside the door. In an instant I put out my light and slipped behind the window-curtains. Next moment the door was flung open and two Spaniards strode into the room, fierce, swarthy men in the dress of citizens, but with muskets slung over their shoulders. I looked through the chink in the curtains in an agony of fear lest they had come upon my traces, but it was evident that their visit was simply in order to feast their eyes upon my unfortunate compatriot. One of them held the lantern which he carried up in front of the dying man, and both of them burst into a shout of mocking laughter. Then the eyes of the man with the lantern fell upon the flagon of wine upon the table. He picked it up, held it with a devilish grin to the lips of Hubert, and then, as the poor wretch involuntarily inclined his head forward to reach it, he snatched it back and took a long gulp himself. At the same instant he uttered a loud cry, clutched wildly at his own throat, and fell stone-dead upon the floor. His comrade stared at him in horror and amazement. Then, overcome by his own superstitious fears, he gave a yell of terror and rushed madly from the room. I heard his feet clattering wildly on the cobble-stones until the sound died away in the distance.

The lantern had been left burning upon the table, and by its light I saw, as I came out from behind my curtain, that the unfortunate Hubert's head had fallen forward upon his chest and that he also was dead. That motion to reach the wine with his lips had been his last. A clock ticked loudly in the house, but otherwise all was absolutely still. On the wall hung the twisted form of the Frenchman, on the floor lay the motionless body of the Spaniard, all dimly lit by the horn lantern. For the first time in my life a frantic spasm of terror came over me. I had seen ten thousand men in every conceivable degree of mutilation stretched upon the ground, but the sight had never affected me like those two silent figures who were my companions in that shadowy room. I rushed into the street as the Spaniard had done, eager only to leave that house of gloom behind me, and I had run as far as the cathedral before my wits came back to me. There I stopped panting in the shadow, and, my hand pressed to my side, I tried to collect my scattered senses and to plan out what I should do. As I stood there, breathless, the great brass bells roared twice above my head. It was two o'clock. Four was the hour when the storming party would be in its place. I had still two hours in which to act.

The cathedral was brilliantly lit within, and a number of people were passing in and out; so I entered, thinking that I was less likely to be accosted there and that I might have quiet to form my plans. It was certainly a singular sight, for the place had been turned into an hospital, a refuge, and a storehouse. One aisle was crammed with provisions, another was littered with sick and wounded, while in the centre a great number of helpless people had taken up their abode and had even lit their cooking fires upon the mosaic floors. There were many at prayer, so I knelt in the shadow of a pillar and I prayed with all my heart that I might have the good luck to get out of this scrape alive, and that I might do such a deed that night as would make my name as famous in Spain as it had already become in Germany. I waited until the clock struck three and then I left the cathedral and made my way towards the Convent of the Madonna, where the assault was to be delivered. You will understand, you who know me so well, that I was not the man to return tamely to the French camp with the report that our agent was dead and that other means must be found of entering the city. Either I should find some means to finish his uncompleted task or there would be a vacancy for a senior captain in the Hussars of Conflans.

I passed unquestioned down the broad boulevard, which I have already described, until I came to the great stone convent which formed the outwork of the defence. It was built in a square with a garden in the centre. In this garden some hundreds of men were assembled, all armed and ready, for it was known, of course, within the town that this was the point against which the French attack was likely to be made. Up to this time our fighting all over Europe had always been done between one army and another. It was only here in Spain that we learned how terrible a thing it is to fight against a people. On the one hand there is no glory, for what glory could be gained by defeating this rabble of elderly shopkeepers, ignorant peasants, fanatical priests, excited women, and all the other creatures who made up the garrison? On the other hand there were extreme discomfort and danger, for these people would give you no rest, would observe no rules of war, and were desperately earnest in their desire by hook or by crook to do you an injury. I began to realize how odious was our task as I looked upon the motley but ferocious groups who were gathered round the watch-fires in the garden of the Convent of the Madonna. It was not for us soldiers to think about politics, but from the beginning there always seemed to be a curse upon this war in Spain.

However, at the moment I had no time to brood over such matters as these. There was, as I have said, no difficulty in getting as far as the convent garden, but to pass inside the convent unquestioned was not so easy. The first thing which I did was to walk round the garden, and I was soon able to pick out one large stained-glass window which must belong to the chapel. I had understood from Hubert that the Mother Superior's room in which the powder was stored was near to this, and that the train had been laid through a hole in the wall from some neighbouring cell. I must at all costs get into the convent. There was a guard at the door, and how could I get in without explanations? But a sudden inspiration showed me how the thing might be done. In the garden was a well, and beside the well were a number of empty buckets. I filled two of these and approached the door. The errand of a man who carries a bucket of water in each hand does not need to be explained. The guard opened to let me through. I found myself in a long, stone-flagged corridor lit with lanterns, with the cells of the nuns leading out from one side of it. Now at last I was on the high road to success. I walked on without hesitation, for I knew by my observations in the garden which way to go for the chapel.

A number of Spanish soldiers were lounging and smoking in the corridor, several of whom addressed me as I passed. I fancy it was for my blessing that they asked, and my "Ora pro nobis" seemed to entirely satisfy them. Soon I had got as far as the chapel, and it was easy enough to see that the cell next door was used as a magazine, for the floor was all black with powder in front of it. The door was shut, and two fierce-looking fellows stood on guard outside it, one of them with a key stuck in his belt. Had we been alone it would not have been long before it would have been in my hand, but with his comrade there it was impossible for me to hope to take it by force. The cell next door to the magazine on the far side from the chapel must be the one which belonged to Sister Angela. It was half open. I took my courage in both hands and, leaving my buckets in the corridor, I walked unchallenged into the room.

I was prepared to find half-a-dozen fierce Spanish desperadoes within, but what actually met my eyes was even more embarrassing. The room had apparently been set aside for the use of some of the nuns, who for some reason had refused to quit their home. Three of them were within, one an elderly, stern-faced dame who was evidently the Mother Superior, the others young ladies of charming appearance. They were seated together at the far side of the room, but they all rose at my entrance, and I saw with some amazement, by their manner and expressions, that my coming was both welcome and expected. In a moment my presence of mind had returned, and I saw exactly how the matter lay. Naturally, since an attack was about to be made upon the convent, these sisters had been expecting to be directed to some place of safety. Probably they were under vow not to quit the walls and they had been told to remain in this cell until they received further orders. In any case I adapted my conduct to this supposition, since it was clear that I must get them out of the room, and this would give me a ready excuse to do so. I first cast a glance at the door and observed that the key was within. I then made a gesture to the nuns to follow me. The Mother Superior asked me some question, but I shook my head impatiently and beckoned to her again. She hesitated, but I stamped my foot and called them forth in so imperious a manner that they came at once. They would be safer in the chapel, and thither I led them, placing them at the end which was farthest from the magazine. As the three nuns took their places before the altar my heart bounded with joy and pride within me, for I felt that the last obstacle had been lifted from my path.

And yet how often have I not found that that is the very moment of danger? I took a last glance at the Mother Superior, and to my dismay I saw that her piercing dark eyes were fixed, with an expression in which surprise was deepening into suspicion, upon my right hand. There were two points which might well have attracted her attention. One was that it was red with the blood of the sentinel whom I had stabbed in the tree. That alone might count for little, as the knife was as familiar as the breviary to the monks of Saragossa. But on my forefinger I wore a heavy gold ring—the gift of a certain German baroness whose name I may not mention. It shone brightly in the light of the altar lamp. Now, a ring upon a friar's hand is an impossibility, since they are vowed to absolute poverty. I turned quickly and made for the door of the chapel, but the mischief was done. As I glanced back I saw that the Mother Superior was already hurrying after me. I ran though the chapel door and along the corridor, but she called out some shrill warning to the two guards in front. Fortunately I had the presence of mind to call out also, and to point down the passage as if we were both pursuing the same object. Next instant I had dashed past them, sprang into the cell, slammed the heavy door, and fastened it upon the inside. With a bolt above and below and a huge lock in the centre it was a piece of timber that would take some forcing.

Even now if they had had the wit to put a barrel of powder against the door I should have been ruined. It was their only chance, for I had come to the final stage of my adventure. Here at last, after such a string of dangers as few men have ever lived to talk of, I was at one end of the powder train, with the Saragossa magazine at the other. They were howling like wolves out in the passage, and muskets were crashing against the door. I paid no heed to their clamour, but I looked eagerly around for that train of which Hubert had spoken. Of course, it must be at the side of the room next to the magazine. I crawled along it on my hands and knees, looking into every crevice, but no sign could I see. Two bullets flew through the door and flattened themselves against the wall. The thudding and smashing grew ever louder. I saw a grey pile in a corner, flew to it with a cry of joy, and found that it was only dust. Then I got back to the side of the door where no bullets could ever reach me—they were streaming freely into the room—and I tried to forget this fiendish howling in my ear and to think out where this train could be. It must have been carefully laid by Hubert lest these nuns should see it. I tried to imagine how I should myself have arranged it had I been in his place. My eye was attracted by a statue of St Joseph which stood in the corner. There was a wreath of leaves along the edge of the pedestal, with a lamp burning amidst them. I rushed across to it and tore the leaves aside. Yes, yes, there was a thin black line, which disappeared through a small hole in the wall. I tilted over the lamp and threw myself on the ground. Next instant came a roar like thunder, the walls wavered and tottered around me, the ceiling clattered down from above, and over the yell of the terrified Spaniards was heard the terrific shout of the storming column of Grenadiers. As in a dream—a happy dream—I heard it, and then I heard no more.

When I came to my senses two French soldiers were propping me up, and my head was singing like a kettle. I staggered to my feet and looked around me. The plaster had fallen, the furniture was scattered, and there were rents in the bricks, but no signs of a breach. In fact, the walls of the convent had been so solid that the explosion of the magazine had been insufficient to throw them down. On the other hand, it had caused such a panic among the defenders that our stormers had been able to carry the windows and throw open the doors almost without assistance. As I ran out into the corridor I found it full of troops, and I met Marshal Lannes himself, who was entering with his staff. He stopped and listened eagerly to my story.

"Splendid, Captain Gerard, splendid!" he cried. "These facts will certainly be reported to the Emperor."

"I would suggest to your Excellency," said I, "that I have only finished the work that was planned and carried out by Monsieur Hubert, who gave his life for the cause."

"His services will not be forgotten," said the Marshal. "Meanwhile, Captain Gerard, it is half-past four and you must be starving after such a night of exertion. My staff and I will breakfast inside the city. I assure you that you will be an honoured guest."

"I will follow your Excellency," said I. "There is a small engagement which detains me."

He opened his eyes.

"At this hour?"

"Yes, sir," I answered. "My fellow-officers, whom I never saw until last night, will not be content unless they catch another glimpse of me the first thing this morning."

"Au revoir, then," said Marshal Lannes, as he passed upon his way.

I hurried through the shattered door of the convent. When I reached the roofless house in which we had held the consultation the night before, I threw off my gown and I put on the busby and sabre which I had left there. Then, a Hussar once more, I hurried onwards to the grove which was our rendezvous. My brain was still reeling from the concussion of the powder, and I was exhausted by the many emotions which had shaken me during that terrible night. It is like a dream, all that walk in the first dim grey light of dawn, with the smouldering camp-fires around me and the buzz of the waking army. Bugles and drums in every direction were mustering the infantry, for the explosion and the shouting had told their own tale. I strode onwards until, as I entered the little clump of cork oaks behind the horse lines, I saw my twelve comrades waiting in a group, their sabres at their sides. They looked at me curiously as I approached. Perhaps with my powder-blackened face and my bloodstained hands I seemed a different Gerard to the young captain whom they had made game of the night before.

"Good morning, gentlemen," said I. "I regret exceedingly if I have kept you waiting, but I have not been master of my own time."

They said nothing, but they still scanned me with curious eyes. I can see them now, standing in a line before me, tall men and short men, stout men and thin men: Olivier, with his warlike moustache; the thin, eager face of Pelletan; young Oudin, flushed by his first duel; Mortier, with the sword-cut across his wrinkled brow. I laid aside my busby and drew my sword.

"I have one favour to ask you, gentlemen," said I. "Marshal Lannes has invited me to breakfast and I cannot keep him waiting."

"What do you suggest?" asked Major Olivier.

"That you release me from my promise to give you five minutes each, and that you will permit me to attack you all together." I stood upon my guard as I spoke.

But their answer was truly beautiful and truly French. With one impulse the twelve swords flew from their scabbards and were raised in salute. There they stood, the twelve of them, motionless, their heels together, each with his sword upright before his face.

I staggered back from them. I looked from one to the other. For an instant I could not believe my own eyes. They were paying me homage, these, the men who had jeered me! Then I understood it all. I saw the effect that I had made upon them and their desire to make reparation. When a man is weak he can steel himself against danger, but not against emotion. "Comrades," I cried, "comrades—!" but I could say no more. Something seemed to take me by the throat and choke me. And then in an instant Olivier's arms were round me, Pelletan had seized me by the right hand, Mortier by the left, some were patting me on the shoulder, some were clapping me on the back, on every side smiling faces were looking into mine; and so it was that I knew that I had won my footing in the Hussars of Conflans.

HOW ETIENNE GERARD SAID
GOOD-BYE TO HIS MASTER

5 MAY 1821

I will tell you no more stories, my dear friends. It is said that man is like the hare, which runs in a circle and comes back to die at the point from which it started. Gascony has been calling to me of late. I see the blue Garonne winding among the vineyards and the bluer ocean towards which its waters sweep. I see the old town also, and the bristle of masts from the side of the long stone quay. My heart hungers for the breath of my native air and the warm glow of my native sun. Here in Paris are my friends, my occupations, my pleasures. There all who have known me are in their grave. And yet the south-west wind as it rattles on my windows seems always to be the strong voice of the motherland calling her child back to that bosom into which I am ready to sink. I have played my part in my time. The time has passed. I must pass also. Nay, dear friends, do not look sad, for what can be happier than a life completed in honour and made beautiful with friendship and love? And yet it is solemn also when a man approaches the end of the long road and sees the turning which leads him into the unknown. But the Emperor and all his Marshals have ridden round that dark turning and passed into the beyond. My Hussars, too — there are not fifty men who are not waiting yonder. I must go. But on this the last night I will tell you that which is more than a tale — it is a great historical secret. My lips have been sealed, but I see no reason why I should not leave behind me some account of this remarkable adventure, which must otherwise be entirely lost, since I, and only I of all living men, have a knowledge of the facts.

I will ask you to go back with me to the year 1821. In that year our great Emperor had been absent from us for six years, and only now and then from over the seas we heard some whisper which showed that he was still alive. You cannot think what a weight it was upon our hearts for us who loved him to think of him in captivity eating his giant soul out upon that lonely island. From the moment we rose until we closed our eyes in sleep the thought was always with us, and we felt dishonoured that he, our chief and master, should be so humiliated without our being able to move a hand to help him. There were many who would most willingly have laid down the remainder of their lives to bring him a little ease, and yet all that we could do was to sit and grumble in our *cafés* and stare at the map, counting up the leagues of water which lay between us. It seemed that he might have been in the moon for all that we could do to help him. But that was only because we were all soldiers and knew nothing of the sea.

Of course, we had our own little troubles to make us bitter, as well as the wrongs of our Emperor. There were many of us who had held high rank and would hold it again if he came back to his own. We had not found it possible to take service under the white flag of the Bourbons, or to take an oath which might turn our sabres against the man whom we loved. So we found ourselves with neither work nor money. What could we do save gather together and gossip and grumble, while those who had a little paid the score and those who had nothing shared the bottle? Now and then, if we were lucky, we managed to pick a quarrel with one of the Garde du Corps, and if we left him on his back in the Bois we felt that we had struck a blow for Napoleon once again. They came to know our haunts in time, and they avoided them as if they had been hornets' nests.

There was one of these—the Sign of the Great Man—in the Rue Varennes, which was frequented by several of the more distinguished and younger Napoleonic officers. Nearly all of us had been colonels or aides-de-camp, and when any man of less distinction came among us we generally made him feel that he had taken a liberty. There were Captain Lepine, who had won the medal of honour at Leipzig; Colonel Bonnet, aide-de-camp to Macdonald; Colonel Jourdan, whose fame in the army was hardly second to my own; Sabbatier of my own Hussars, Meunier of the Red Lancers, Le Breton of the Guards, and a dozen others. Every night we met and talked, played dominoes, drank a glass or two, and wondered how long it would be before the Emperor would be back and we at the head of our regiments once more. The Bourbons had already lost any hold they ever had upon the country, as was shown a few years afterwards, when Paris rose against them and they were hunted for the third time out of France. Napoleon had but to show himself on the coast, and he would have marched without firing a musket to the capital, exactly as he had done when he came back from Elba.

Well, when affairs were in this state there arrived one night in February, in our *café*, a most singular little man. He was short but exceedingly broad, with huge shoulders, and a head which was a deformity, so large was it. His heavy brown face was scarred with white streaks in a most extraordinary manner, and he had grizzled whiskers such as seamen wear. Two gold earrings in his ears, and plentiful tattooing upon his hands and arms, told us also that he was of the sea before he introduced himself to us as Captain Fourneau, of the Emperor's navy. He had letters of introduction to two of our number, and there could be no doubt that he was devoted to the cause. He won our respect, too, for he had seen as much fighting as any of us, and the burns upon his face were caused by his standing to his post upon the *Orient*, at the Battle of the Nile, until the vessel blew up underneath him. Yet he would say little about himself, but he sat in the corner of the *café* watching us all with a wonderfully sharp pair of eyes and listening intently to our talk.

One night I was leaving the *café* when Captain Fourneau followed me, and touching me on the arm he led me without saying a word for some distance until we reached his lodgings. "I wish to have a chat with you," said he, and so conducted me up the stair to his room.

There he lit a lamp and handed me a sheet of paper which he took from an envelope in his bureau. It was dated a few months before from the Palace of Schönbrunn at Vienna. "Captain Fourneau is acting in the highest interests of the Emperor Napoleon. Those who love the Emperor should obey him without question.—Marie Louise." That is what I read. I was familiar with the signature of the Empress, and I could not doubt that this was genuine.

"Well," said he, "are you satisfied as to my credentials?"

"Entirely."

"Are you prepared to take your orders from me?" "This document leaves me no choice."

"Good! In the first place, I understand from something you said in the *café* that you can speak English?"

"Yes, I can."

"Let me hear you do so."

I said in English, "Whenever the Emperor needs the help of Etienne Gerard, I am ready night and day to give my life in his service." Captain Fourneau smiled.

"It is funny English," said he, "but still it is better than no English. For my own part I speak English like an Englishman. It is all that I have to show for six years spent in an English prison. Now I will tell you why I have come to Paris. I have come in order to choose an agent who will help me in a matter which affects the interests of the Emperor. I was told that it was at the *café* of the Great Man that I would find the pick of his old officers, and that I could rely upon every man there being devoted to his interests. I studied you all, therefore, and I have come to the conclusion that you are the one who is most suited for my purpose."

I acknowledged the compliment. "What is it that you wish me to do?" I asked.

"Merely to keep me company for a few months," said he. "You must know that after my release in England I settled down there, married an English wife, and rose to command a small English merchant ship, in which I have made several voyages from Southampton to the Guinea coast. They look on me there as an Englishman. You can understand, however, that with my feelings about the Emperor I am lonely sometimes, and that it would be an advantage to me to have a companion who would sympathize with my thoughts. One gets very bored on these long voyages, and I would make it worth your while to share my cabin."

He looked hard at me with his shrewd grey eyes all the time that he was uttering this rigmarole, and I gave him a glance in return which showed him that he was not dealing with a fool. He took out a canvas bag full of money.

"There are a hundred pounds in gold in this bag," said he. "You will be able to buy some comforts for your voyage. I should recommend you to get them in Southampton, whence we will start in ten days. The name of the vessel is the *Black Swan*. I return to Southampton to-morrow, and I shall hope to see you in the course of the next week."

"Come now," said I. "Tell me frankly what is the destination of our voyage?"

"Oh, didn't I tell you?" he answered. "We are bound for the Guinea coast of Africa."

"Then how can that be in the highest interests of the Emperor?" I asked.

"It is in his highest interests that you ask no indiscreet questions and I give no indiscreet replies," he answered, sharply. So he brought the interview to an end, and I found myself back in my lodgings with nothing save this bag of gold to show that this singular interview had indeed taken place.

There was every reason why I should see the adventure to a conclusion, and so within a week I was on my way to England. I passed from St Malo to Southampton, and on inquiry at the docks I had no difficulty in finding the *Black Swan,* a neat little vessel of a shape which is called, as I learned afterwards, a brig. There was Captain Fourneau himself upon the deck, and seven or eight rough fellows hard at work grooming her and making her ready for sea. He greeted me and led me down to his cabin.

"You are plain Mr Gerard now," said he, "and a Channel Islander. I would be obliged to you if you would kindly forget your military ways and drop your cavalry swagger when you walk up and down my deck. A beard, too, would seem more sailor-like than those moustaches."

I was horrified by his words, but, after all, there are no ladies on the high seas, and what did it matter? He rang for the steward.

"Gustav," said he, "you will pay every attention to my friend, Monsieur Etienne Gerard, who makes this voyage with us. This is Gustav Kerouan, my Breton steward," he explained, "and you are very safe in his hands."

This steward, with his harsh face and stern eyes, looked a very warlike person for so peaceful an employment. I said nothing, however, though you may guess that I kept my eyes open. A berth had been prepared for me next the cabin, which would have seemed comfortable enough had it not contrasted with the extraordinary splendour of Fourneau's quarters. He was certainly a most luxurious person, for his room was new-fitted with velvet and silver in a way which would have suited the yacht of a noble better than a little West African trader. So thought the mate, Mr Burns, who could not hide his amusement and contempt whenever he looked at it. This fellow, a big, solid, red-headed Englishman, had the other berth connected with the cabin. There was a second mate named Turner, who lodged in the middle of the ship, and there were nine men and one boy in the crew, three of whom, as I was informed by Mr Burns, were Channel Islanders like myself. This Burns, the first mate, was much interested to know why I was coming with them.

"I come for pleasure," said I.

He stared at me.

"Ever been to the West Coast?" he asked.

I said that I had not.

"I thought not," said he. "You'll never come again for that reason, anyhow."

Some three days after my arrival we untied the ropes by which the ship was tethered and we set off upon our journey. I was never a good sailor, and I may confess that we were far out of sight of any land before I was able to venture upon deck. At last, however, upon the fifth day I drank the soup which the good Kerouan brought me, and I was able to crawl from my bunk and up the stair. The fresh air revived me, and from that time onwards I accommodated myself to the motion of the vessel. My beard had begun to grow also, and I have no doubt that I should have made as fine a sailor as I have a soldier had I chanced to be born to that branch of the service. I learned to pull the ropes which hoisted the sails, and also to haul round the long sticks to which they are attached. For the most part, however, my duties were to play écarté with Captain Fourneau, and to act as his companion. It was not strange that he should need one, for neither of his mates could read or write, though each of them was an excellent seaman. If our captain had died suddenly I cannot imagine how we should have found our way in that waste of waters, for it was only he who had the knowledge which enabled him to mark our place upon the chart. He had this fixed upon the cabin wall, and every day he put our course upon it so that we could see at a glance how far we were from our destination. It was wonderful how well he could calculate it, for one morning he said that we should see the Cape Verd light that very night, and there it was, sure enough, upon our left front the moment that darkness came. Next day, however, the land was out of sight, and Burns, the mate, explained to me that we should see no more until we came to our port in the Gulf of Biafra. Every day we flew south with a favouring wind, and always at noon the pin upon the chart was moved nearer and nearer to the African coast. I may explain that palm oil was the cargo which we were in search of, and that our own lading consisted of coloured cloths, old muskets, and such other trifles as the English sell to the savages.

At last the wind which had followed us so long died away, and for several days we drifted about on a calm and oily sea under a sun which brought the pitch bubbling out between the planks upon the deck. We turned and turned our sails to catch every wandering puff, until at last we came out of this belt of calm and ran south again with a brisk breeze, the sea all round us being alive with flying fishes. For some days Burns appeared to be uneasy, and I observed him continually shading his eyes with his hand and staring at the horizon as if he were looking for land. Twice I caught him with his red head against the chart in the cabin, gazing at that pin, which was always approaching and yet never reaching the African coast. At last one evening, as Captain Fourneau and I were playing écarté in the cabin, the mate entered with an angry look upon his sunburned face.

"I beg your pardon, Captain Fourneau," said he. "But do you know what course the man at the wheel is steering?"

"Due south," the captain answered, with his eyes fixed upon his cards.

"And he should be steering due east."

"How do you make that out?"

The mate gave an angry growl.

"I may not have much education," said he, "but let me tell you this, Captain Fourneau, I've sailed these waters since I was a little nipper of ten, and I know the line when I'm on it, and I know the doldrums, and I know how to find my way to the oil rivers. We are south of the line now, and we should be steering due east instead of due south if your port is the port that the owners sent you to."

"Excuse me, Mr Gerard. Just remember that it is my lead," said the captain, laying down his cards. "Come to the map here, Mr Burns, and I will give you a lesson in practical navigation. Here is the trade wind from the south-west and here is the line, and here is the port that we want to make, and here is a man who will have his own way aboard his own ship." As he spoke he seized the unfortunate mate by the throat and squeezed him until he was nearly senseless. Kerouan, the steward, had rushed in with a rope, and between them they gagged and trussed the man, so that he was utterly helpless.

"There is one of our Frenchmen at the wheel. We had best put the mate overboard," said the steward.

"That is safest," said Captain Fourneau.

But that was more than I could stand. Nothing would persuade me to agree to the death of a helpless man. With a bad grace Captain Fourneau consented to spare him, and we carried him to the after-hold, which lay under the cabin. There he was laid among the bales of Manchester cloth.

"It is not worth while to put down the hatch," said Captain Fourneau. "Gustav, go to Mr Turner and tell him that I would like to have a word with him."

The unsuspecting second mate entered the cabin, and was instantly gagged and secured as Burns had been. He was carried down and laid beside his comrade. The hatch was then replaced.

"Our hands have been forced by that red-headed dolt," said the captain, "and I have had to explode my mine before I wished. However, there is no great harm done, and it will not seriously disarrange my plans. Kerouan, you will take a keg of rum forward to the crew and tell them that the captain gives it to them to drink his health on the occasion of crossing the line. They will know no better. As to our own fellows, bring them down to your pantry so that we may be sure that they are ready for business. Now, Colonel Gerard, with your permission we will resume our game of écarté."

It is one of those occasions which one does not forget. This captain, who was a man of iron, shuffled and cut, dealt and played, as if he were in his *café*. From below we heard the inarticulate murmurings of the two mates, half smothered by the handkerchiefs which gagged them. Outside the timbers creaked and the sails hummed under the brisk breeze which was sweeping us upon our way. Amid the splash of the waves and the whistle of the wind we heard the wild cheers and shoutings of the English sailors as they broached the keg of rum. We played half-a-dozen games and then the captain rose. "I think they are ready for us now," said he. He took a brace of pistols from a locker, and he handed one of them to me.

But we had no need to fear resistance, for there was no one to resist. The Englishman of those days, whether soldier or sailor, was an incorrigible drunkard. Without drink he was a brave and good man. But if drink were laid before him it was a perfect madness—nothing could induce him to take it with moderation. In the dim light of the den which they inhabited, five senseless figures and two shouting, swearing, singing madmen represented the crew of the *Black Swan*. Coils of rope were brought forward by the steward, and with the help of two French seamen (the third was at the wheel) we secured the drunkards and tied them up, so that it was impossible for them to speak or move. They were placed under the fore-hatch as their officers had been under the after one, and Kerouan was directed twice a day to give them food and drink. So at last we found that the *Black Swan* was entirely our own.

Had there been bad weather I do not know what we should have done, but we still went gaily upon our way with a wind which was strong enough to drive us swiftly south, but not strong enough to cause us alarm. On the evening of the third day I found Captain Fourneau gazing eagerly out from the platform in the front of the vessel. "Look, Gerard, look!" he cried, and pointed over the pole which stuck out in front.

A light blue sky rose from a dark blue sea, and far away, at the point where they met, was a shadowy something like a cloud, but more definite in shape.

"What is it?" I cried.

"It is land."

"And what land?"

I strained my ears for the answer, and yet I knew already what the answer would be.

"It is St Helena."

Here, then, was the island of my dreams! Here was the cage where our great Eagle of France was confined! All those thousands of leagues of water had not sufficed to keep Gerard from the master whom he loved. There he was, there on that cloud-bank yonder over the dark blue sea. How my eyes devoured it! How my soul flew in front of the vessel—flew on and on to tell him that he was not forgotten, that after many days one faithful servant was coming to his side! Every instant the dark blur upon the water grew harder and clearer. Soon I could see plainly enough that it was indeed a mountainous island. The night fell, but still I knelt upon the deck, with my eyes fixed upon the darkness which covered the spot where I knew that the great Emperor was. An hour passed and another one, and then suddenly a little golden twinkling light shone out exactly ahead of us. It was the light of the window of some house — perhaps of his house. It could not be more than a mile or two away. Oh, how I held out my hands to it! — they were the hands of Etienne Gerard, but it was for all France that they were held out.

Every light had been extinguished aboard our ship, and presently, at the direction of Captain Fourneau, we all pulled upon one of the ropes, which had the effect of swinging round one of the sticks above us, and so stopping the vessel. Then he asked me to step down to the cabin.

"You understand everything now, Colonel Gerard," said he, "and you will forgive me if I did not take you into my complete confidence before. In a matter of such importance I make no man my confidant. I have long planned the rescue of the Emperor, and my remaining in England and joining their merchant service was entirely with that design. All has worked out exactly as I expected. I have made several successful voyages to the West Coast of Africa, so that there was no difficulty in my obtaining the command of this one. One by one I got these old French man-of-war's-men among the hands. As to you, I was anxious to have one tried fighting man in case of resistance, and I also desired to have a fitting companion for the Emperor during his long homeward voyage. My cabin is already fitted up for his use. I trust that before to-morrow morning he will be inside it, and we out of sight of this accursed island."

You can think of my emotion, my friends, as I listened to these words. I embraced the brave Fourneau, and implored him to tell me how I could assist him.

"I must leave it all in your hands," said he. "Would that I could have been the first to pay him homage, but it would not be wise for me to go. The glass is falling, there is a storm brewing, and we have the land under our lee. Besides, there are three English cruisers near the island which may be upon us at any moment. It is for me, therefore, to guard the ship and for you to bring off the Emperor."

I thrilled at the words.

"Give me your instructions!" I cried.

"I can only spare you one man, for already I can hardly pull round the yards," said he. "One of the boats has been lowered, and this man will row you ashore and await your return. The light which you see is indeed the light of Longwood. All who are in the house are your friends, and all may be depended upon to aid the Emperor's escape. There is a cordon of English sentries, but they are not very near to the house. Once you have got as far as that you will convey our plans to the Emperor, guide him down to the boat, and bring him on board."

The Emperor himself could not have given his instructions more shortly and clearly. There was not a moment to be lost. The boat with the seaman was waiting alongside. I stepped into it, and an instant afterwards we had pushed off. Our little boat danced over the dark waters, but always shining before my eyes was the light of Longwood, the light of the Emperor, the star of hope. Presently the bottom of the boat grated upon the pebbles of the beach. It was a deserted cove, and no challenge from a sentry came to disturb us. I left the seaman by the boat and began to climb the hillside.

There was a goat-track winding in and out among the rocks, so I had no difficulty in finding my way. It stands to reason that all paths in St Helena would lead to the Emperor. I came to a gate. No sentry—and I passed through. Another gate—still no sentry! I wondered what had become of this cordon of which Fourneau had spoken. I had come now to the top of my climb, for there was the light burning steadily right in front of me. I concealed myself and took a good look round, but still I could see no sign of the enemy. As I approached I saw the house, a long, low building with a veranda. A man was walking up and down upon the path in front. I crept nearer and had a look at him. Perhaps it was this cursed Hudson Lowe. What a triumph if I could not only rescue the Emperor, but also avenge him! But it was more likely that this man was an English sentry. I crept nearer still, and the man stopped in front of the lighted window, so that I could see him. No; it was no soldier, but a priest. I wondered what such a man could be doing there at two in the morning. Was he French or English? If he were one of the household I might take him into my confidence. If he were English he might ruin all my plans. I crept a little nearer still, and at that moment he entered the house, a flood of light pouring out through the open door. All was clear for me now, and I understood that not an instant was to be lost. Bending myself double I ran swiftly forward to the lighted window. Raising my head I peeped through, and there was the Emperor lying dead before me!

My friends, I fell down upon the gravel walk as senseless as if a bullet had passed through my brain. So great was the shock that I wonder that I survived it. And yet in half an hour I had staggered to my feet again, shivering in every limb, my teeth chattering, and there I stood staring with the eyes of a maniac into that room of death.

He lay upon a bier in the centre of the chamber, calm, composed, majestic, his face full of that reserve power which lightened our hearts upon the day of battle. A half-smile was fixed upon his pale lips, and his eyes, half-opened, seemed to be turned on mine. He was stouter than when I had seen him at Waterloo, and there was a gentleness of expression which I had never seen in life. On either side of him burned rows of candles, and this was the beacon which had welcomed us at sea, which had guided me over the water, and which I had hailed as my star of hope. Dimly I became conscious that many people were kneeling in the room; the little Court, men and women, who had shared his fortunes, Bertrand, his wife, the priest, Montholon — all were there. I would have prayed too, but my heart was too heavy and bitter for prayer. And yet I must leave, and I could not leave him without a sign. Regardless of whether I was seen or not, I drew myself erect before my dead leader, brought my heels together, and raised my hand in a last salute. Then I turned and hurried off through the darkness, with the picture of the wan, smiling lips and the steady grey eyes dancing always before me.

It had seemed to me but a little time that I had been away, and yet the boatman told me that it was hours. Only when he spoke of it did I observe that the wind was blowing half a gale from the sea and that the waves were roaring in upon the beach. Twice we tried to push out our little boat, and twice it was thrown back by the sea. The third time a great wave filled it and stove the bottom. Helplessly we waited beside it until the dawn broke, to show a raging sea and a flying scud above it. There was no sign of the *Black Swan*. Climbing the hill we looked down, but on all the great torn expanse of the ocean there was no gleam of a sail. She was gone. Whether she had sunk, or whether she was recaptured by her English crew, or what strange fate may have been in store for her, I do not know. Never again in this life did I see Captain Fourneau to tell him the result of my mission. For my own part I gave myself up to the English, my boatman and I pretending that we were the only survivors of a lost vessel—though, indeed, there was no pretence in the matter. At the hands of their officers I received that generous hospitality which I have always encountered, but it was many a long month before I could get a passage back to the dear land outside of which there can be no happiness for so true a Frenchman as myself.

And so I tell you in one evening how I bade good-bye to my master, and I take my leave also of you, my kind friends, who have listened so patiently to the long-winded stories of an old broken soldier. Russia, Italy, Germany, Spain, Portugal, and England, you have gone with me to all these countries, and you have seen through my dim eyes something of the sparkle and splendour of those great days, and I have brought back to you some shadow of those men whose tread shook the earth. Treasure it in your minds and pass it on to your children, for the memory of a great age is the most precious treasure that a nation can possess. As the tree is nurtured by its own cast leaves, so it is these dead men and vanished days which may bring out another blossoming of heroes, of rulers, and of sages. I go to Gascony, but my words stay here in your memory, and long after Etienne Gerard is forgotten a heart may be warmed or a spirit braced by some faint echo of the words that he has spoken. Gentlemen, an old soldier salutes you and bids you farewell.

APPENDIX:
THE MARRIAGE OF THE BRIGADIER

I am speaking, my friends, of days which are long gone by, when I had scarcely begun to build up that fame which has made my name so familiar. Among the thirty officers of the Hussars of Conflans there was nothing to indicate that I was superior in any way to the others. I can well imagine how surprised they would all have been had they realized that young Lieutenant Etienne Gerard was destined for so glorious a career, and would live to command a brigade and to receive from the Emperor's own hand that cross which I can show you any time that you do me the honour to visit me in my little cottage—you know, do you not, the little whitewashed cottage with the vine in front, in the field beside the Garonne?

People have said of me that I have never known what fear was. No doubt you have heard them say it. For many years out of a foolish pride I have let the saying pass. And yet now, in my old age, I can afford to be honest. The brave man dares to be frank. It is only the coward who is afraid to make admissions. So I tell you now that I also am human, that I also have felt my skin grow cold and my hair rise, that I have even known what it was to run until my limbs could scarce support me. It shocks you to hear it? Well, some day it may comfort you, when your own courage has reached its limit, to know that even Etienne Gerard has known what it was to be afraid. I will tell you now how this experience befell me, and also how it brought me a wife.

For the moment France was at peace, and we, the Hussars of Conflans, were in camp all that summer a few miles from the town of Les Andelys, in Normandy. It is not a very gay place by itself, but we of the Light Cavalry make all places gay which we visit, and so we passed our time very pleasantly. Many years and many scenes have dulled my remembrance, but still the name Les Andelys brings back to me a huge ruined castle, great orchards of apple trees, and, above all, a vision of the lovely maidens of Normandy. They were the very finest of their sex, as we may be said to have been of ours, and so we were well met in that sweet sunlit summer. Ah, the youth, the beauty, the valour, and then the dull, dead years that blur them all! There are times when the glorious past weighs on my heart like lead. No, sir; no wine can wash away such thoughts, for they are of the spirit and the soul. It is only the gross body which responds to wine; but if you offer it for that, then I will not refuse it.

Now, of all the maidens who dwelt in those parts there was one who was so superior in beauty and in charm that she seemed to be very specially marked out for me. Her name was Marie Ravon, and her people, the Ravons, were of yeoman stock who had farmed their own land in those parts since the days when Duke William went to England. If I close my eyes now I see her as she then was, her cheeks like dusky moss-roses, her hazel eyes so gentle and yet so full of spirit, her hair of that deepest black which goes most fitly with poetry and with passion, her figure as supple as a young birch tree in the wind. Ah! how she swayed away from me when first I laid my arm round it, for she was full of fire and pride, ever evading, ever resisting, fighting to the last that her surrender might be the more sweet. Out of a hundred and forty women—but who can compare where all are so near perfection?

You will wonder why it should be, if this maiden was so beautiful, that I should be left without a rival. There was a very good reason, my friends, for I so arranged it that my rivals were in the hospital. There was Hippolyte Lesœur—he visited them for two Sundays; but if he lives I dare swear that he still limps from the bullet which lodged in his knee. Poor Victor also—up to his death at Austerlitz he wore my mark. Soon it was understood that if I could not win Marie I should at least have a fair field in which to try. It was said in our camp that it was safer to charge a square of unbroken infantry than to be seen too often at the farm-house of the Ravons.

Now let me be precise for a moment. Did I wish to marry Marie? Ah, my friends, marriage is not for a Hussar. To-day he is in Normandy; to-morrow he is in the hills of Spain or in the bogs of Poland. What shall he do with a wife? Would it be fair to either of them? Can it be right that his courage should be blunted by the thought of the despair which his death would bring, or is it reasonable that she should be left fearing lest every post should bring her the news of irreparable misfortune? A Hussar can but warm himself at the fire and then hurry onwards, too happy if he can but pass another fire from which some comfort may come. And Marie, did she wish to marry me? She knew well that when our silver trumpets blew the march it would be over the grave of our married life. Better far to hold fast to her own people and her own soil, where she and her husband could dwell for ever amid the rich orchards and within sight of the great Castle of Le Galliard. Let her remember her Hussar in her dreams, but let her waking days be spent in the world as she finds it.

Meanwhile we pushed such thoughts from our mind and gave ourselves up to a sweet companionship, each day complete in itself, with never a thought of the morrow. It is true that there were times when her father, a stout old gentleman, with a face like one of his own apples, and her mother, a thin, anxious woman of the country, gave me hints that they would wish to be clearer as to my intentions, but in their hearts they each knew well that Etienne Gerard was a man of honour, and that their daughter was very safe, as well as very happy, in his keeping. So the matter stood until the night of which I speak.

It was the Sunday evening, and I had ridden over from the camp. There were several of our fellows who were visiting the village, and we all left our horses at the inn. Thence I had to walk to the Ravons', which was only separated by a single very large field which extended to the very door. I was about to start when the landlord ran after me.

"Excuse me, lieutenant," said he, "it is farther by the road, and yet I should advise you to take it."

"It is a mile or more out of my way."

"I know it. But I think that it would be wiser," and he smiled as he spoke.

"And why?" I asked.

"Because," said he, "the English bull is loose in the field."

If it were not for that odious smile, I might have considered it. But to hold a danger over me and then to smile in such a fashion was more than my proud temper could bear. I indicated by a gesture what I thought of the English bull.

"I will go by the shortest way," said I.

I had no sooner set foot in the field than I felt that my spirit had betrayed me into rashness. It was a very large square field, and as I came farther out into it I felt like the cockleshell which ventures out from land, and sees no port save that from which it has issued. There was wall on every side of the field save that from which I had come. In front of me was the farm-house of the Ravons, with wall extending to right and left. A back door opened upon the field, and there were several windows, but all were barred, as is usual in the Norman farms. I pushed on rapidly to the door, as being the only harbour of safety, walking with dignity as befits the soldier, and yet with such speed as I could summon. From the waist upwards I was unconcerned and even debonair. Below, I was swift and alert.

I had nearly reached the middle of the field when I perceived the creature. He was rooting about with his fore-feet under a large beech tree which lay upon my right hand. I did not turn my head, nor would the bystander have detected that I took notice of him, but my eye was watching him with anxiety. It may have been that he was in a contented mood, or it may have been that he was arrested by the nonchalance of my bearing; but he made no movement in my direction. Reassured, I fixed my eyes upon the open window of Marie's bedchamber, which was immediately over the back door, in the hope that those dear, tender, dark eyes were surveying me from behind the curtains. I flourished my little cane, loitered to pick a primrose, and sang one of our devil-may-care choruses, in order to insult this English beast, and to show my love how little I cared for danger when it stood between her and me. The creature was abashed by my fearlessness, and so, pushing open the back door, I was able to enter the farm-house in safety and in honour.

And was it not worth the danger? Had all the bulls of Castile guarded the entrance, would it not still have been worth it? Ah, the hours—the sunny hours—which can never come back, when our youthful feet seemed scarce to touch the ground, and we lived in a sweet dreamland of our own creation! She honoured my courage, and she loved me for it. As she lay with her flushed cheek pillowed against the silk of my dolman, looking up at me with her wondering eyes, shining with love and admiration, she marvelled at the stories in which I gave her some picture of the true character of her lover!

"Has your heart never failed you? Have you never known the feeling of fear?" she asked.

I laughed at such a thought. What place could fear have in the mind of a Hussar? Young as I was, I had given my proofs. I told her how I had led my squadron into a square of Hungarian Grenadiers. She shuddered as she embraced me. I told her also how I had swum my horse over the Danube at night with a message for Davoust. To be frank, it was not the Danube, nor was it so deep that I was compelled to swim; but when one is twenty and in love one tells a story as best one can. Many such stories I told her while her dear eyes grew more and more amazed.

"Never in my dreams, Etienne," said she, "did I believe that so brave a man existed. Lucky France that has such a soldier; lucky Marie that has such a lover!"

You can think how I flung myself at her feet as I murmured that I was the luckiest of all—I who had found someone who could appreciate and understand.

It was a charming relationship, too infinitely sweet and delicate for the interference of coarser minds. But you can understand that the parents imagined that they also had their duty to do. I played dominoes with the old man and I wound wool for his wife, and yet they could not be led to believe that it was from love of them that I came thrice a week to their farm. For some time an explanation was inevitable, and that night it came. Marie, in delightful mutiny, was packed off to her room, and I faced the old people in the parlour as they plied me with questions upon my prospects and my intentions.

"One way or the other," they said, in their blunt country fashion. "Let us hear that you are betrothed to Marie, or let us never see your face again."

I spoke of my honour, my hopes, and my future, but they remained immovable upon the present. I pleaded my career, but they in their selfish way would think of nothing but their daughter. It was indeed a difficult position in which I found myself. On the one hand, I could not forsake my Marie. On the other, what would a young Hussar do with marriage? At last, hard-pressed, I begged them to leave the matter, if it were only for a day.

"I will see Marie," said I; "I will see her without delay. It is her heart and her happiness which come before all else."

They were not satisfied, these grumbling old people, but they could say no more. They bade me a short good night and I departed, full of perplexity, for the inn. I came out by the same door which I had entered, and I heard them lock and bar it behind me.

I walked across the field lost in thought, with my mind entirely filled with the arguments of the old people, and the skillful replies which I had made to them. What should I do? I had promised to see Marie without delay. What should I say to her when I did see her? Would I surrender to her beauty and turn my back upon my profession? If Etienne Gerard's sword were turned to a scythe, then, indeed, it was a bad day for the Emperor and France. Or should I harden my heart and turn away from Marie? Or was it not possible that all might be reconciled, that I might be a happy husband in Normandy but a brave soldier elsewhere? All these thoughts were buzzing in my head, when a sudden noise made me look up. The moon had come from behind a cloud, and there was the bull before me.

He had seemed a large animal beneath the beech tree, but now he appeared enormous. He was black in colour. His head was held down, and the moon shone upon two menacing and bloodshot eyes. His tail switched swiftly from side to side, and his fore-feet dug into the earth. A more horrible-looking monster was never seen in a nightmare. He was moving slowly and stealthily in my direction.

I glanced behind me, and I found that in my distraction I had come a very long way from the edge of the field. I was more than half-way across it. My nearest refuge was the inn, but the bull was between me and it. Perhaps if the creature understood how little I feared him he would make way for me. I shrugged my shoulders and made a gesture of contempt. I even whistled. The creature thought I called it, for he approached with alacrity. I kept my face boldly towards him, but I walked swiftly backwards. When one is young and active one can almost run backwards and yet keep a brave and smiling face to the enemy. As I ran I menaced the animal with my cane. Perhaps it would have been wiser had I restrained my spirit. He regarded it as a challenge—which, indeed, was the last thing in my mind. It was a misunderstanding, but a fatal one. With a snort he raised his tail and charged.

Have you ever seen a bull charge, my friends? It is a strange sight. You think, perhaps, that he trots, or even that he gallops. No; it is worse than this. It is a succession of bounds by which he advances, each more menacing than the last. I have no fear of anything which man can do. When I deal with man I feel that the nobility of my own attitude, the gallant ease with which I face him, will in itself go far to disarm him. What he can do, I can do, so why should I fear him? But when it is a ton of enraged beef with which you contend, it is another matter. You cannot hope to argue, to soften, to conciliate. There is no resistance possible. My proud assurance was all wasted upon the creature. In an instant my ready wit had weighed every possible course, and had determined that no one, not the Emperor himself, could hold his ground. There was but one course—to fly.

But one may fly in many ways. One may fly with dignity or one may fly in panic. I fled, I trust, like a soldier. My bearing was superb, through my legs moved rapidly. My whole appearance was a protest against the position in which I was placed. I smiled as I ran—the bitter smile of the brave man who mocks his own fate. Had all my comrades surrounded the field they could not have thought the less of me when they saw the disdain with which I avoided the bull.

But here it is that I must make my confession. When once flight commences, though it be ever so soldierly, panic follows hard upon it. Was it not so with the Guard at Waterloo? So it was that night with Etienne Gerard. After all, there was no one to note my bearing—no one save this accursed bull. If for a minute I forgot my dignity, who would be the wiser? Every moment the thunder of the hoofs and the horrible snorts of the monster drew nearer to my heels. Horror filled me at the thought of so ignoble a death. The brutal rage of the creature sent a chill to my heart. In an instant everything was forgotten. There were in all the world but two creatures, the bull and I— he trying to kill me, I striving to escape. I put down my head and I ran—I ran for my life.

It was for the house of the Ravons that I raced. But even as I reached it, it flashed into my mind that there was no refuge for me there. The door was locked; the lower windows were barred; the wall was high upon either side; and the bull was nearer me with every stride. But, oh, my friends, it is at that supreme moment of danger that Etienne Gerard has ever risen to his height. There was but one path to safety, and in an instant I had chosen it.

I have said that the window of Marie's bedroom was above the door. The curtains were closed, but the folding sides were thrown open, and a lamp burned in the room. Young and active, I felt that I could spring high enough to reach the edge of the window-sill and to draw myself out of danger. The monster was within touch of me as I sprang. Had I been unaided I should have done what I had planned. But even as in a superb effort I rose from the earth, he butted me into the air. I shot through the curtains as if I had been fired from a gun, and I dropped upon my hands and knees in the centre of the room.

There was, as it appears, a bed in the window, but I had passed over it in safety. As I staggered to my feet I turned towards it in consternation, but it was empty. My Marie sat in a low chair in the corner of the room, and her flushed cheeks showed that she had been weeping. No doubt her parents had given her some account of what had passed between us. She was too amazed to move, and could only sit looking at me with her mouth open.

"Etienne!" she gasped. "Etienne!"

In an instant I was as full of resource as ever. There was but one course for a gentleman, and I took it.

"Marie," I cried, "forgive, oh, forgive the abruptness of my return! Marie, I have seen your parents to-night. I could not return to the camp without asking you whether you will make me for ever happy by promising to be my wife."

It was long before she could speak, so great was her amazement. Then every emotion was swept away in the one great flood of her admiration.

"Oh, Etienne, my wonderful Etienne!" she cried, her arms round my neck. "Was ever such love? Was ever such a man? As you stand there, white and trembling with passion, you seem to me the very hero of my dreams. How hard you breathe, my love; and what a spring it must have been which brought you to my arms! At the instant that you came I had heard the tramp of your war-horse without."

There was nothing more to explain, and when one is newly betrothed one finds other uses for one's lips. But there was a scurry in the passage and a pounding at the panels. At the crash of my arrival the old folk had rushed to the cellar to see if the great cider-cask had toppled off the trestles, but now they were back and eager for admittance. I flung open the door and stood with Marie's hand in mine.

"Behold your son!" I said.

Ah, the joy which I had brought to that humble household! It warms my heart still when I think of it. It did not seem too strange to them that I should fly in through the window, for who should be a hot-headed suitor if it is not a gallant Hussar? And if the door be locked, then what way is there but the window? Once more we assembled all four in the parlour, while the cobwebbed bottle was brought up and the ancient glories of the House of Ravon were unrolled before me. Once more I see the heavy-raftered room, the two old smiling faces, the golden circle of the lamp-light, and she, my Marie, the bride of my youth, won so strangely, and kept for so short a time.

It was late when we parted. The old man came with me into the hall.

"You can go by the front door or the back," said he. "The back way is the shorter."

"I think that I will take the front way," I answered. "It may be a little longer, but it will give me the more time to think of Marie."

ENDNOTES

HOW THE BRIGADIER HELD THE KING

[1] December, 1894.

SUGGESTED READING

BOOTH, MARTIN. *The Doctor, The Detective and Arthur Conan Doyle.* London: Hodder and Stoughton, 1997.

CARR, JOHN DICKSON. *The Life of Sir Arthur Conan Doyle: The Man Who Was Sherlock Holmes.* New York: Vintage Books, 1949.

COIGNET, CAPTAIN JEAN ROCH. *The Notebooks of Captain Coignet: Soldier of the Empire.* Trans. M. Cary. Ed. Lorédan Larchey. London: Chatto & Windus, 1897.

DOYLE, ARTHUR CONAN. *The Great Shadow.* New York: Harper Bros, 1893.

---. *Uncle Bernac.* New York: Appleton, 1897.

---. *Waterloo, A Play.* New York and London: Samuel French & Co., 1907 (acting copy).

---. *Rodney Stone.* New York: Appleton, 1896.

---. *Through the Magic Door.* London: Smith, Elder, 1907.

DOYLE, GEORGINA. *Out of the Shadows: The Untold Story of Arthur Conan Doyle's First Family.* Ashcroft, B.C.: Calabash Press, 2004.

DUMAS, ALEXANDRE. *The Count of Monte Cristo.* New York: Barnes & Noble Books, 2004.

EDWARDS, OWEN DUDLEY. *The Quest for Sherlock Holmes: A Biographical Study of Arthur Conan Doyle.* Edinburgh: Mainstream Publishing Co., 1983.

GOLDFARB, CLIFFORD S. *The Great Shadow: Arthur Conan Doyle, Brigadier Gerard and Napoleon.* Ashcroft, B.C.: Calabash Press, 1997.

HUGO, VICTOR. *Les Misérables.* New York: Barnes & Noble Books, 2003.

KING, W. DAVIES. *Henry Irving's Waterloo: Theatrical Engagements with Arthur Conan Doyle, George Bernard Shaw, Ellen Terry, Edward Gordon Craig: Late Victorian Culture: Assorted Ghosts, Old Men, War and History.* Berkeley: University of California Press, 1993.

LELLENBERG, JON, ED. *The Quest for Sir Arthur Conan Doyle: Thirteen Biographers in Search of a Life.* Carbondale: Southern Illinois University Press, 1987.

MARBOT, JEAN-BAPTISTE-ANTOINE-MARCELIN, BARON DE. *The Memoirs of Baron de Marbot,* 2 Vols. Trans. Arthur John Butler. London: Longmans, Green, and Co., 1892, 1897.

OREL, HAROLD, ED. *Sir Arthur Conan Doyle: Interviews and Recollections.* New York: St. Martin's Press, 1991.

STASHOWER, DANIEL. *Teller of Tales: The Life of Arthur Conan Doyle.* New York: Henry Holt & Co., 1999.

STENDHAL [HENRI MARIE BEYLE]. *The Charterhouse of Parma.* London: Penguin Books, 1958.